"I'M TRYING TO KEEP AN OPEN MIND," JANEWAY SAID.

rt of the job, right?" said Chakotay.

way shrugged. "I suppose. But if we'd made this contact
ve were out here the first time, we'd already have resumed
urse for home by now."

ou think so?"

resider Cin is a lovely person. I think she genuinely cares
r people. But I have a feeling that the differences between
a lot deeper than economics or technology."

he same can be said of many Federation members and
"

rue," Janeway said. "They control more space than any
in the Delta Quadrant we've encountered aside from the
They're civilized, technologically advanced, have a stable,
entative government; in theory they're an ideal ally for us."

Command pushing you to form this alliance?"

ey could use some good news. It would also ensure the
osition. But I won't make a deal with the devil."

akotay smiled at a memory. "I thought those were sort of
ecialty."

STAR TREK
VOYAGER®

ACTS OF CONTRITION

KIRSTEN BEYER

Based on *Star Trek*®
created by Gene Roddenberry
and
Star Trek: Voyager
created by Rick Berman & Michael Piller
& Jeri Taylor

POCKET BOOKS

New York   London   Toronto   Sydney   New Delhi

Pocket Books
A Division of Simon & Schuster, Inc.
1230 Avenue of the Americas
New York, NY 10020

This book is a work of fiction. Any references to historical events, real people, or real places are used fictitiously. Other names, characters, places, and events are products of the author's imagination, and any resemblance to actual events or places or persons, living or dead, is entirely coincidental.

First Pocket Books paperback edition October 2014

POCKET and colophon are registered trademarks of Simon & Schuster, Inc.

For information about special discounts for bulk purchases, please contact Simon & Schuster Special Sales at 1-866-506-1949 or business@simonandschuster.com.

The Simon & Schuster Speakers Bureau can bring authors to your live event. For more information or to book an event, contact the Simon & Schuster Speakers Bureau at 1-866-248-3049 or visit our website at www.simonspeakers.com.

Cover design by Alan Dingman
Cover art by Michael Stetson

Manufactured in the United States of America

10   9   8   7   6   5   4   3   2   1

ISBN 978-1-4767-6551-8
ISBN 978-1-4767-6555-6 (ebook)

For my Jack

HISTORIAN'S NOTE

Billions killed by the Borg, hundreds of starships destroyed, a new threat in the rising power of the Typhon Pact, but the United Federation of Planets will not let this define who they are and what they will do. Starfleet Command will continue the mission of the Full Circle Fleet (*Star Trek: Typhon Pact—Rough Beasts of Empire*).

The *Starship Vesta*, the test bed of the new slipstream drive, has been tasked to the Full Circle Fleet. The new fleet commander is an officer known for succeeding with limited resources: Vice Admiral Kathryn Janeway.

The still rising death tolls from an insidious new illness leads Starfleet Medical to believe that a possible catomic plague threatens the lives of every Federation citizen. Seven and Doctor Sharak, along with Commander Tom Paris, travel back to Earth to try to help.

In the Delta Quadrant, the Confederacy of the Worlds of the First Quadrant warmly welcomes *Voyager*, *Galen*, and *Demeter*. Captain Chakotay is grateful for the reception, but he knows the horrors that were committed to create the Confederacy. He does not completely trust them (*Star Trek: Voyager: Protectors*).

The story begins at the end of January and continues through February 2382 (ACE).

"The spirits of our foolish deeds haunt us, with or without repentance."

—GILBERT PARKER

Prologue

"*I'm sorry, Reg, but I just don't see it,*" Vice Admiral Kathryn Janeway said.

Lieutenant Reginald Barclay barely refrained from taking the companel before him in both hands and shaking it in frustration. The *Galen*'s captain, Commander Clarissa Glenn, often reminded her crew to breathe during moments of extreme stress. Barclay took her advice before responding to the new commander of the Full Circle Fleet, an officer he had known and respected for years.

"Sector JLX-16 of SB-11989 was initially scanned by *Voyager*'s astrometrics sensors during your first visit to New Talax," Barclay began.

"*Reg, that was more than four years ago,*" Janeway said. "*The sensor resolution of the sector you reference was barely adequate to display basic topography. We weren't interested in details.*"

"Still," Barclay continued, "the surface of the asteroid in question was undisturbed at the time of those scans."

"*As were thousands of others,*" Janeway interjected. "*But since then, Nacona and the Talaxians have mined hundreds of local asteroids and radically altered their surfaces.*"

Barclay refused to be deterred. "Six discreet holes, their depth less than five meters and less than half a meter in diameter, are visible now at Sector JLX-16. That is not consistent with mining operations."

"*They barely register as holes, Reg. I agree that if that's what we're seeing, they didn't occur naturally. But we're not well-versed in Nacona's mining protocols, or the specs of his vessels."*

"I could ask Neelix for those specs," Barclay suggested. "He's been trading with Nacona's people for years now. I'm sure he has current information."

"No," Janeway said, her tone leaving no room for argument. *"We're less than an hour from rendezvous with the* Demeter *in Confederacy space. We're out of communications range with New Talax, and will be for the next several weeks. We already have intelligence that puts individual Voth near enough to Neelix's people to make me very nervous. If you ask Neelix for anything, he's going to want to know the reason why. I can no longer order him not to, and because his curiosity will always trump his sense of self-preservation, he's going to go out to that asteroid and take a look for himself. We cannot risk instigating a confrontation Neelix could not possibly hope to survive while we're too far away to answer a distress call."*

"*Galen* could go back, just for a few hours, to confirm these results," Barclay suggested, going all in. "If Meegan was there, and if she buried six of the original Neyser canisters on that asteroid, there might still be one or more left behind. If we got to them before she returns . . ."

"That's three big ifs, *Reg,"* Janeway said patiently. *"I understand how important this is to you. I've already told you that I intend to make finding Meegan a priority. Our orders are to focus our efforts on opening diplomatic relations with an interstellar confederacy that could prove to be a valuable ally to the Federation in the Delta Quadrant. Once we ascertain the potential viability of that alliance, I will have the latitude to spare resources to confirm your hypothesis. Until then, the matter is closed."*

Barclay bowed his head, hoping to hide his disappointment.

"If you find anything else, notify me at once," Janeway said. *"And try not to worry, Reg. We're going to find her eventually. I promise."*

"Of course," Barclay said. "Thank you, Admiral."

Once his commanding officer signed off, Barclay rose from the desk in his quarters and paced his small cabin fitfully. It was possible that Admiral Janeway was right. He could be seeing six holes at Sector JLX-16 because that's what he *needed* to see to provide evidence of Meegan's actions since she had departed *Voyager* aboard a stolen shuttle. With her, she had taken seven containers containing the consciousness of individuals the Neyser had deemed worthy of permanent incarceration. Should those canisters have been opened and the inhabitants allowed to possess others the way they had taken control of Meegan, the most advanced hologram Barclay and Lewis Zimmerman had ever created, the damage they might do was unthinkable.

And no matter what Admiral Janeway said, that damage would be his fault.

Chapter One

Commander Liam O'Donnell had never served on a ship the size of the *Vesta*. He estimated it could hold twenty *Demeter*s, the special mission ship attached to the Full Circle Fleet that was his responsibility. He lost his way three times between the shuttlebay and Admiral Kathryn Janeway's quarters.

It was possible he wasn't lost, so much as dreading making his request of the fleet's new commanding officer. He paused for almost a full minute once he reached her door before activating the chime and announcing himself.

"Enter," the admiral said.

No turning back now.

"Commander O'Donnell," Janeway greeted him as he stepped over the threshold to her private office and residence aboard the *Vesta*. He had seen her once before, at the memorial service on New Talax, and they hadn't spoken that evening. She was shorter than he remembered—diminutive, in fact—but her stature was the only small thing about her. A genuine smile of welcome radiated over her fair face as she moved toward him, extending her right hand and grasping his firmly. Her presence easily filled the room, giving the space a warm, homey feel. She even made the incredibly restrictive full-dress uniform she wore look comfortable.

"Your reputation precedes you, Commander," Janeway said as she shook his hand. "I'm so pleased to finally meet you, and eager to hear more from you about the last few weeks you've spent with the Confederacy. It goes without saying that your work thus far with the fleet, your efforts to communicate with the Children of the Storm and to aid the wave forms recently discovered, has been exemplary. I trust I can count on more of the same from you."

O'Donnell sighed as he released her hand. No one who knew him had ever been this happy to see him.

"Thank you, Admiral," he responded uneasily. He noted her smile falter and added *keen awareness* to the list of attributes he was in the process of applying to Janeway.

"Obviously there won't be time now to hear your full report," Janeway began.

"No," O'Donnell agreed.

"The Ceremony of Welcoming begins in less than an hour."

"Yes—about that," O'Donnell interrupted.

Janeway stepped back, analyzing him without making her attention feel intrusive.

Quite the diplomat, O'Donnell added to his list.

"Is there a problem?" Janeway finally asked.

"Depends," O'Donnell replied.

"On what?"

"Your definition of the term, Admiral," O'Donnell clarified.

"Go on."

"Request permission not to attend the ceremony tonight, Admiral," O'Donnell said.

He read more curious amusement than anger at his request, which was a good start.

"Why?" she asked.

"I'm really not good at parties," O'Donnell replied.

The admiral crossed her arms at her chest, her eyes shining mischievously.

"This isn't just a party, Commander," Janeway said. "It's a diplomatic mission."

"All the more reason you don't want me there," O'Donnell insisted.

"You've been the Federation's chief representative among the Confederacy for almost two weeks," Janeway said. "Was it a mistake to ask you to assume that role?" she asked.

"No, Admiral," he assured her. "One-on-one, small groups, I'm fine. When there's a specific problem in front of me to solve, I'll gladly talk your ear off. But large groups like this; I never know what to do with myself."

"So *small talk* is the issue?"

"I would have skipped my own wedding reception had my wife allowed it."

Janeway chuckled. She seemed to consider taking mercy on him, but the amusement fled quickly from her face.

"Request denied, Commander," she said with finality.

"Admiral," O'Donnell began.

"You are one of a handful of officers already acquainted with many of the diplomats who will be present tonight," Janeway said. "They'll be expecting you to make casual introductions. And they will most certainly note your absence and might take it as an insult."

"Aren't they more likely to take my genuine discomfort and displeasure at attending the function as an insult?" O'Donnell asked.

"If you allowed yourself to betray any of those emotions, I'm sure they would," Janeway replied. "So you will be your best, most personable self tonight. Do I need to make that a direct order?" she asked.

"It wouldn't help, Admiral," O'Donnell said. "I did not make this request lightly. I'm not here simply because I believe there are a thousand things I could do with the next few hours that would be more constructive than attending this ceremony, although there are. I cannot pretend to be something I am not. It's a valuable skill but one I never took the time to acquire. My feelings will be read clearly on my face, whether I wish them to or not. I would spare all of us the accompanying embarrassment. Commander Fife is prepared to take my place and will much better serve our interests."

Janeway looked away for a moment, clearly reflecting on his words. Finally, she said, "A few months ago, your ship was captured by the Children of the Storm. There were no telepaths aboard your vessel, so you could not communicate directly with them. Based solely on their behavior, you decided that their primary interest in *Demeter* was observing the growth cycles of the botanical life-forms aboard. You were willing to risk your ship, your crew, and your life on this intuitive leap. To gain their trust, you departed your vessel in an environmental suit and used an untested tool to inject a hybrid life-form you had created into one of the Children, hoping that it would grow."

Janeway's clear blue eyes locked with O'Donnell's. "Did I misread or misremember that report?"

"No, Admiral."

"You risked *death* for that first contact, Commander. Why are you unwilling to risk considerably less for this one?"

O'Donnell's eyes remained fixed on Janeway's. "The Children had earned my respect and my compassion. For all our apparent differences, we were kindred spirits. I cannot say the same for the Confederacy."

"Why not?"

O'Donnell shrugged. "They're rich. They're powerful. They believe they are the center of the civilized universe," he replied. "Their charms and social graces could induce insulin resistance. The only species they've ever encountered that was immune to their hospitality or unimpressed by their technological accomplishments was the Borg. That's about to change, and while part of me is curious to see that realization take hold, the rest of me already knows how this story has to end."

"And how is that, Commander?" Janeway asked.

"With disappointment," O'Donnell replied.

Janeway considered his words, then said, "That's always a possibility. But those of us tasked with making first contact must always remember that where there is common ground, the opportunity to move beyond disappointment toward mutual understanding and acceptance also exists."

"Of course, Admiral," O'Donnell agreed.

"I'll see you in the shuttlebay at 1800," Janeway said, dismissing him.

"Aye, Admiral."

VOYAGER

As Commander B'Elanna Torres's fingers slipped and failed to close her full-dress jacket for the fifteenth time, she cursed under her breath. Her daughter Miral was watching her closely, and she took great delight in repeating every word that fell from her mother's lips at the most inopportune moments possible.

Come on, Torres thought, gritting her teeth, wiping her sweaty fingers on her pants and redoubling her efforts.

"There's still time to replicate a new one," suggested Lieutenant Nancy Conlon, *Voyager*'s chief engineer and one of B'Elanna's closest friends. Conlon wasn't attending the ceremony and had offered to play with Miral until her bedtime. Both were sprawled on the floor of Torres's quarters amidst magnetic building blocks, but neither had eyes for anything at the moment beyond B'Elanna's attempt to force herself into her dress uniform.

"I don't need a new one," Torres insisted. "This is already a full size larger than my normal one." Releasing all of the air in her lungs and pulling her abdomen into its flattest orientation, she refused to take another breath. Finally, the jacket relented.

"See?" Torres said, raising her hands to pose for them.

Conlon bit both of her lips to hide a smile.

"What?" Torres demanded.

"The point was for your pregnancy not to show, right?"

"Yes," Torres replied.

"Mirror," Conlon suggested.

Dropping her arms, B'Elanna ducked into her bedroom and examined her reflection in the full-length mirror affixed to the wall beside the threshold. There was no arguing that the jacket was now closed, but it was already pulling apart and the fabric stretched unflatteringly across her stomach. More important, the short waist of the jacket emphasized her rounding lower abdomen rather than drawing attention away from it.

"Damn it," Torres said without thinking.

"Damn it," Miral instantly repeated from the living room.

"Miral Paris," Torres said, the warning clear in her voice as she returned to the living area and crossed to the replicator.

"Sorry, Mommy," Miral said instantly.

As Torres hastily ordered a new dress uniform jacket a size and a half larger than normal and extra long, she wondered if whoever had designed these torture devices had ever considered the possibility that a pregnant officer might need to wear one. Miral came to her mother's side and, looking up, asked, "Is the baby still a secret, Mommy?"

Draping a hand over her daughter's shoulder and pulling her close, Torres replied, "No, honey. Not anymore."

Miral turned back to Conlon and said, "I'm going to have a baby brother."

Conlon laughed in genuine delight. "I know. It's exciting, isn't it?"

"And I am going to teach him everything I know."

"I bet you are," Conlon said.

"And I will be the mommy and he will be the baby."

"Whoa there, kiddo," Torres said, pulling on her new jacket and relieved by how much better it felt than the first. "I'm always the mommy."

"But when you and Daddy aren't here, I get to be the mommy," Miral insisted.

"You get to be the big sister," Torres corrected her gently.

"That's a lot of responsibility," Conlon said. "I was a big sister, you know."

"You had a baby brother?"

"I had a baby sister."

"Where is she?"

"She's home."

"My daddy went home," Miral said, her face suddenly clouding over.

Fully dressed and able to breathe, Torres bent to one knee to meet Miral at her eye level. "That's right, honey. But he's going to be back before you know it."

"Before the baby comes?"

"Definitely," Torres assured her.

Miral sighed. She was doing her three-and-a-half-year-old best to accept the sudden departure of her beloved daddy. It had been more than a week since he left, and her fits of sudden sadness were most intense near bedtime and first thing in the morning. "I want my daddy," she finally admitted softly.

"I know," Torres said, pulling her into a tight hug.

"I was thinking that instead of playing here tonight, I might take you to one of my favorite ice cream shops on the holodeck," Conlon said, rising and crossing to Miral.

"Ice cream?" Miral asked.

"Do you like hot fudge?"

Miral's eyes widened as she nodded.

"Me too," Conlon said with a wink. "You ready?"

"Yes," Miral said.

Torres mouthed a sincere "thank you" to Conlon as she led her daughter toward the door. *Voyager*'s chief engineer nodded knowingly, then bent to whisper something in Miral's ear.

Turning back, Miral said, "You look beautiful, Mommy."

The compliment nearly undid Torres. "Thank you, honey. I love you."

"Love you," Miral replied as she tugged Conlon out the door.

Ten days before, it would have been Tom complimenting her appearance. Torres would have reveled in his words, knowing that her swelling belly truly was a thing of beauty to him. By now he was back on Earth, preparing to meet his mother in a series of court-ordered mediation sessions meant to determine their fitness as parents and the ultimate custody of Miral and her unborn brother.

They had argued right before he left. The memory of it still stung, the only sign of life in an otherwise suddenly lonely heart. Not long before, Torres's life was near perfect. She hadn't seen it, of course. You never did until it was gone.

Nothing fit anymore.

With a Herculean force of will, Torres set these dispiriting thoughts aside, squared her shoulders, and departed for the shuttlebay.

Counselor Hugh Cambridge was due in *Voyager*'s shuttlebay for transfer to the First World of the Confederacy of the Worlds of the First Quadrant. To arrive late was to court the displeasure of his commanding officer, Captain Chakotay, and the new fleet commander, Admiral Janeway.

He didn't care.

The computer had alerted him to the Doctor's arrival on *Voyager,* and for the next few minutes, his duties could wait.

Cambridge had learned days earlier that Seven was lost to him forever. It was possible he was transferring his understandable anger and disappointment with Seven onto the Doctor.

But Cambridge didn't think so. The Doctor had been the prime mover in the series of events that had ended with Seven's departure from the fleet. The counselor did not make a habit of sharing personal matters with the rest of the crew. His position required a well-honed detachment. In this case, however, he had decided to make an exception. He owed the Doctor pain, and once he had fulfilled this obligation, his own was sure to diminish.

He found the Doctor standing in his small office, conferring with a nurse. Though assigned to the *Galen* for the fleet's mission, the Doctor had been temporarily transferred to *Voyager* when Seven's CMO, Doctor Sharak, had been ordered to accompany her to Earth. Cambridge had not seen nor spoken to the Doctor in almost two months.

As soon as the Doctor saw him, he immediately dismissed the nurse. The door had barely slid shut behind her before Cambridge said, "You just couldn't help yourself, could you?"

The Doctor sighed dramatically. "I missed you too, Counselor."

"Seven explicitly requested that you keep all of your research into her catoms private. She told me about your little breakthrough before the *Galen* left to ferry Admiral Janeway back to Earth. She was astonished that you had successfully visualized a catom. But that brilliant discovery did not release you from your ethical duty to her as your patient and your friend."

"Counselor—" the Doctor began.

"You had no right to share that breakthrough without her permission. But you *had* to, didn't you? You couldn't bear for your genius to remain hidden. You knew what they'd do to her when they learned of her potential usefulness. But you didn't care."

For a moment, the Doctor appeared stricken. Then, ever so briefly, a strange serenity descended over his features. He crossed to stand directly in front of Cambridge and raised a medical tricorder between them, directing it at the counselor.

"What are you doing?" Cambridge demanded.

"You are clearly unwell, Counselor," the Doctor replied. "I would suggest you forgo the ceremony this evening and remain here for a thorough medical evaluation."

Cambridge stepped back, stunned. "What the hell is wrong with you?"

"With me? Nothing," the Doctor replied. "Seven did ask that I keep my research private, but shortly after I reached the Beta Quadrant and began treating the former Borg drone known as Axum, I was ordered by my superiors at Starfleet Medical to brief them on all of my work related to Seven and her catoms. Naturally, I found the orders ethically troubling, but Admiral Janeway assured me that it would be a violation of my duties as a Starfleet officer to refuse the direct order. Moreover, once I realized the nature of the medical threat now facing several Federation worlds, this new 'catomic plague,' I was certain that were she free to do so, Seven would agree to the disclosure. Perhaps you do not know her as well as I do, Counselor," the Doctor said.

Not for the first time, Cambridge wished he could punch the hologram in the face.

"And the experimental therapy you decided to use on Axum?" he demanded. "You shared Seven's catoms with him?"

"Axum was dying. His catoms had become dormant. Without the infusion he *would have* died. He nearly did, as it was."

"Did it occur to you that mingling those catoms would have the unintended effect of forcing Seven to share his thoughts?"

"It did not," the Doctor admitted. "When Seven advised me

of that development, I was surprised. But Doctor Sharak was able to relieve that symptom for the most part."

"She suffered a great deal before that relief came, Doctor," Cambridge said.

"Seven also learned a great deal, and what she learned will undoubtedly help her as she begins her work with Starfleet Medical."

"So you're sleeping just fine these days," Cambridge said.

"I don't sleep, Counselor," the Doctor corrected him. "But if I did, my actions in this case would not disturb it."

Cambridge considered him carefully. Were he human, as he appeared to be, a diagnosis would be easy enough to reach. But he wasn't. He was a sophisticated holographic program that, according to the "experts," had transcended its basic directives and attained sentience. He was more like a new life-form, one that, until this moment, Cambridge thought he'd understood.

"You realize that because you did this, Seven will never again return to this fleet?" Cambridge asked.

The Doctor's ire flared unexpectedly. "I did what I had to do," he said. "I was not responsible for the plague that set this entire chain of events in motion. I do not blame Seven, nor should you, for wishing to help those now working to aid its victims. Tens of thousands of people are already dead, and hundreds of thousands more will be, unless a treatment regimen is devised. *I* know that the thought of standing idly by while so many suffer would pain Seven deeply. I would never interfere with a choice that was hers. And because I care more . . ."

Cambridge waited as the Doctor halted himself midthought. Confusion replaced his anger, followed almost immediately by that odd, flat, eerie calm.

"Doctor?" Cambridge finally asked.

"Seven will return to the fleet when her services at Starfleet Medical are no longer required. I will hasten that return by working without cease until I have cured the plague myself," the Doctor said calmly, almost as if the idea had just occurred to him.

"The best minds in Starfleet have already worked without success toward that goal for how long?" Cambridge asked.

"Over a year," the Doctor replied. "But they are not Seven. They are not *me*. Had we been advised earlier, this plague would already be nothing more than a painful memory."

"Unbelievable," Cambridge said.

"Only for those of limited imagination," the Doctor said.

"Axum was her first love. You know as well as I do the power of primacy. Whether the plague is cured or not, she won't abandon him again," Cambridge said.

"Should that be her choice, I would understand," the Doctor said. "I would be happy for her. Wouldn't you?"

Cambridge was at a complete loss. He knew the Doctor had once loved Seven. He knew the Doctor was appalled by her choice to enter into an intimate relationship with the counselor a few months earlier. He suspected that if the Doctor could not have her, he would have done anything, including forcing her into Axum's arms, to make sure that what she had begun with Cambridge would never have a chance to develop. But to hear him now, the Doctor could have been talking about any member of the crew. The shift between vehement protestation and clinical reserve was astonishing.

It made no sense.

"Chakotay to Counselor Cambridge."

Cambridge tapped his combadge. "Go ahead, Captain."

"We're waiting, Counselor."

"On my way."

Cambridge considered the Doctor for a moment longer, then turned on his heel and directed his hurried steps toward the shuttlebay, wondering if the Doctor had ever truly been the *man* so many believed him to be.

THE FIRST WORLD

The room into which Captain Chakotay and his crew were ushered to wait for their fellow officers attending the ceremony was clearly not often used for this purpose. A small metallic desk had been shoved into a corner with a plant, its large flowing lavender leaves trailing over an indiscernible vase, clearly meant to camouflage the workstation. Chairs were set along three of the four walls, and a small table placed in the center held a carafe of water with several cups stacked beside it.

Chakotay suspected they wouldn't be here long. Neither he nor any of his crew—Fleet Chief B'Elanna Torres, Lieutenant Harry Kim, Lieutenant Kenth Lasren, or Counselor Hugh Cambridge—chose to sit.

"What do you think they normally use this room for?" Kim asked of Torres. She seemed annoyed by the question and merely shrugged. Chakotay appreciated the attempt by his acting first officer to make this situation feel normal, but he understood that the tension flaring from most of them was going to be difficult to overcome.

Ten days earlier, Torres had been separated from her husband, *Voyager's* first officer, Commander Tom Paris, under the most painful of circumstances. Lieutenant Lasren, *Voyager's* only full Betazoid, had been selected to attend the ceremony in hopes that his empathic abilities would be useful to Admiral Janeway as she formally opened diplomatic relations with the Confederacy. Lasren did not use his special abilities on a routine basis, and the anticipated stress of doing so was clear on the young man's face. Counselor Cambridge could usually be counted on to lighten the atmosphere, but his mood had been excessively dark since he'd learned of Seven's departure. Chakotay knew he needed to make time to speak with Cambridge, but there simply hadn't been any since *Voyager* had returned to Confederacy space, bringing the *Galen* and the *Vesta* with them.

Not to mention the fact that Chakotay had only spoken a few times with Kathryn since she had taken command of the Full Circle Fleet, and none of those conversations had been what he'd hoped for from the woman with whom he intended to spend the rest of his life. He was eager to see her tonight, though he knew the evening would be all-business. Anticipation of her imminent arrival, however, was accompanied by a fair amount of trepidation.

"B'Elanna, Harry, Kenth, Hugh," Chakotay said, immediately drawing the attention of all present to him, "I know things have been happening pretty fast the last week or so. There has been a great deal of change to absorb, much of it difficult. But for the next several hours, we need to set all that aside. Tonight we are honored guests of the leadership of a confederacy of planets that, as best I can tell, is the first we have ever encountered in the Delta Quadrant that rivals our Federation. Commander O'Donnell's early reports indicate, among other things, that they are incredibly excited to meet with us and explore the possibility of an alliance with our people. I don't have to tell you what an asset such an alliance would be for our fleet, and the Federation.

"Our galaxy seems to have grown a little smaller since the development of our slipstream capabilities. The 'streams' the Confederacy uses to traverse the space they claim, subspace corridors that bridge vast distances, have had a similar effect here. Even a few years ago, the thought of entering into relations with a civilization as far distant as this one would have been unlikely to hold the potential for much meaningful exchange of information or resources. That is no longer the case. Starfleet's most important role is as an ambassador to all warp-capable cultures in the galaxy. Tonight we embody that role. Opinions of the Federation will be shaped by the way in which we conduct ourselves.

"I'm not going to bother ordering you all to be at your best. I'm simply going to ask you to consider all that is at stake here, and to remember that opportunities such as this have been too few and far between. All of the challenges we are facing will still be with us tomorrow morning. Tonight, let's enjoy ourselves, shall we?"

"Well said, Captain," a familiar voice noted.

Turning, Chakotay saw that Admiral Janeway had entered during his remarks. Always at her right hand was a slightly built Vulcan male, Lieutenant Decan, Kathryn's personal aide. The *Galen*'s captain, Commander Clarissa Glenn, the *Vesta*'s CMO, Doctor El'nor Sal, and her captain, Regina Farkas, followed behind Janeway, along with *Demeter*'s Commander Liam O'Donnell, who looked as if he had come to attend a funeral, but he nodded in Chakotay's direction as soon as their eyes met.

"Admiral on deck," Kim said crisply.

The admiral bit back her amusement as she quickly ordered, "At ease." Crossing to Kim she said softly, "I appreciate the courtesy, Lieutenant Kim, but let's go easy on the formalities when it's just us."

"Of course, Admiral," Kim said.

Turning to Chakotay, her smile widened. "Captain," she greeted him. Her eyes held his for a brief moment, and much of the worry he'd felt prior to her arrival dissipated.

"Admiral," he said warmly. Bending to her ear, he whispered, "You look stunning."

Janeway nodded, accepting the compliment before moving among *Voyager*'s officers and greeting each of them personally. She briefly pulled Torres aside, and a firm hug between them suggested that the admiral had just availed herself of her first opportunity to congratulate Torres on her pregnancy. Soft conversations erupted all around as old friends and acquaintances greeted one another. Doctor Sal, a tall woman in her eighties, moved quickly to Chakotay's side and, without warning, threaded an arm through his.

"I hope you don't mind, Captain," she offered with a sly smile.

"Not at all," he said.

"I always like to enter a room on the arm of the best-looking man around," Sal teased.

"I guess you'll just have to make do with me tonight," Chakotay teased back.

"Is my CMO bothering you, Captain?" Farkas asked, moving to stand before them.

"No," Chakotay assured her.

"I've ordered her to behave herself," Farkas said. "If she steps out of line, you have my permission to shoot her."

"I'm sure it won't come to that, Captain," Chakotay said.

"Don't be," Sal suggested.

"It seems we are all present and accounted for," Admiral Janeway said, raising her voice above the low din. Immediately all other conversation in the room ceased.

Gazing at those around her, her eyes bright and her face flush with anticipation, Janeway said, "I'm truly looking forward to this evening. If our schedule is any indication, our hosts have gone to great lengths to impress us tonight. Let's allow them to do that. I know from experience that large gatherings like this can feel impersonal and become tedious. Just remember, we are the first Federation citizens to set foot on this world. Our presence here is a gift to us from those who came before; those who first braved unexplored space with a desire to expand their knowledge of the universe. I don't pretend to know right now what may or may not come of our eventual negotiations. That's not important now. Take this moment for what it is and make the most of it. It is a once-in-a-lifetime experience. Savor it."

Nods all around seemed to satisfy the admiral as the door slid open and a tall humanoid in a long tunic that might have been spun from pure gold entered. As he moved, the fabric rippled, more like a liquid than a solid. A wide, long, dark metallic chain draped over his shoulders enhanced the effect by appearing to float on the fabric's surface. Chakotay knew him to be Leodt, one of the two primary species that had founded the Confederacy. The other was the Djinari. The Leodt's skin was a deep brown, his eyes black as pitch, and his most striking facial feature was the circle of pointed teeth his thin lips did little to conceal. Janeway immediately moved to stand before him.

"Federation representatives," he greeted them with sincere warmth, "I am First Consul Lant Dreeg. It is my honor to welcome you to the First World."

"It is our honor to be so welcomed," Janeway said, clearly a rehearsed response, likely settled upon in the negotiations leading up to this moment.

"If you will follow me?" Dreeg asked.

Chakotay and Sal fell in line directly behind Janeway as the others assumed their preappointed positions for their entrance into the ceremony.

Here we go, Chakotay thought.

Chapter Two

Seven had arrived at the main entrance to Starfleet Medical at 0600 hours as requested. She was hurried down hallways, through laboratories and past offices at what felt like a breakneck pace. Doctor Sharak practically had to jog to keep up with her and the silent security officer who had appeared from behind a hidden door in the atrium the moment Seven had identified herself to the duty officer.

Two separate turbolifts and several more nondescript hallways later, Seven and Sharak were ushered into a spacious lab in which eight individuals were hard at work. Only one looked up from her data terminal when they entered. She immediately tapped her combadge, saying, "Doctor Frist, they have arrived."

"Is everyone at work on this project so rude?" Sharak murmured to Seven.

"From what I've heard," Seven said softly.

Seconds later, a Trill female, with short brown hair pulled back to reveal characteristic dark spots beginning at her forehead and trailing down her neck, emerged from a door at the far end of the room. She wore the standard blue sciences uniform under a short, bright yellow smock.

"Seven of Nine," she said, extending her hand. "I am Doctor Pauline Frist. Thank you so much for joining us here."

"I prefer 'Seven,'" she corrected Frist. "The rest of my former designation has not been applicable for many years."

"Or 'Miss Seven,'" Sharak suggested.

"Also accurate." Seven nodded.

"And you are?" Frist asked, addressing Sharak.

"I am Doctor Sharak, chief medical officer of the Federation *Starship Voyager*, and Child of Tama."

"I've heard of you," Frist said, nodding slightly. "The first Tamarian to serve in Starfleet, yes?"

"Yes."

"Welcome," Frist said, offering her hand.

When Sharak released it, Frist focused her attention on Seven. "I assume you know why you are here?"

"Admiral Janeway briefed me on your efforts to cure a new illness first detected on Coridan almost a year ago. She indicated you believe it to be catomic in nature," Seven said.

"We *know* it to be catomic in nature," Frist said.

Seven nodded, though she would assume nothing until she had been granted access to all of the facility's current research.

"When the plague first appeared, we had no idea what we were looking at. It took months to make the potential connection between catomic matter and the illness. That deduction was made by the Commander now in charge of our efforts here. Once that determination was made, it became essential for us to expand our understanding of catoms. We sincerely hoped that pulling you from your current work with the Full Circle Fleet would not be necessary. As it stands, however . . ." Frist opened her hands before her.

"I wish you had asked for my input sooner," Seven said.

"You are here now," Frist said. "That's what matters."

"I would appreciate it if you would escort me at once to the patient you have been evaluating for the last several months," Seven said. "It was my understanding that I would be permitted to see him before my work here began."

"Patient C-1, yes," Frist said, nodding.

"Axum," Seven insisted.

"We need to run a complete physical analysis of you prior to entering the lab," Frist said.

Seven looked around in dismay. "This is not the lab?"

"No," Frist replied. "I am working with teams from Starfleet Medical and the Federation Institute of Health to analyze the dispersal of the plague, the rates of infection, and to administer our containment efforts. Those tasked with curing it do so within a special classified lab several floors above us. Most of them took up residence there months ago. They do not enter or leave casually. Every effort has been made to ensure that their work with this highly hazardous substance is safe and contained. C-1—pardon me—*Axum* is there."

"He is your prisoner?" Seven asked.

"Hardly," Frist said, offended at the thought. "He is a former enemy combatant who has agreed to assist us by allowing us to study the catoms present in his body. I assure you, no harm has come to him since he was brought here."

Seven's mental connection with Axum over the last several months belied that, but she held her peace for now.

"How long will this physical evaluation take?" Seven asked.

"Not long. The sooner we get started, the sooner you may see Axum," Frist replied.

Seven nodded. "Very well."

"I will observe this examination," Sharak said.

"Of course," Frist said, smiling.

The analysis was the most thorough Doctor Sharak had ever seen. It went well beyond a baseline physical, standard for a new, noncritical patient or crew evaluation. In addition to the customary scans, Seven was required to give multiple tissue and catomic samples. A full genetic analysis was run, along with a subatomic scan. Seven commented during the exam that the *Galen*'s CMO, known as the Doctor, had performed a similar scan of her several months earlier. Frist replied that his work had been essential for the Commander's team to visualize individual catoms. "We are all very much in his debt," Frist noted. Seven did not seem to believe her, but given the reported indifference with which the Doctor had been treated by Frist and her associates, that was not surprising to the Tamarian.

Sharak had spoken briefly with the Doctor before departing the Delta Quadrant with Seven. While he was aware of the EMH's many concerns, Sharak had determined to keep an open mind about these people and their procedures. It would not help Seven for Sharak to jump to any conclusions. The Doctor's experiences were his own. But Sharak would not fail to step in should anything inappropriate be suggested.

Several hours later, a light lunch was replicated for all of the staff members, and Seven and Sharak were invited to partake. They did so, though Seven did not seem to have much of an appetite.

As they were finishing, a stocky woman with pale blue skin and hairless scalp suggesting Bolian heritage entered the lab and moved directly toward them. Frist was quick to introduce her.

"Seven, Doctor Sharak, permit me to introduce you to Ensign J'Ohans," Frist said. "She is a member of the Commander's team and will take Seven into the classified section of our lab, where she will remain until her work with us has concluded."

"The ensign will take both of us to that lab," Sharak corrected Frist.

"I'm sorry, Doctor Sharak," J'Ohans said. "Access to the classified division is restricted to those assigned to the Commander's team. Our resources are limited and we cannot accommodate any who are not essential to our work."

"Doctor Sharak has come to observe and assist me where necessary," Seven said. "He is *essential* to me."

"I understand," J'Ohans said. "And I truly wish I could accede to this request. However, our protocols are not flexible on this point."

"Doctor Sharak could certainly assist us here for the duration of your stay," Frist interjected. "Although we are not working directly with the live virus, our work on the epidemiology of the plague is also essential. I am sure his expertise would be very valuable to us."

"I trust I will be able to communicate with Doctor Sharak whenever I desire to do so?" Seven asked.

"Of course," J'Ohans replied.

"That is unacceptable," Sharak said firmly.

J'Ohans looked plaintively at Frist.

Seven seemed to consider the matter briefly before asking Frist and J'Ohans to direct her to a place where she and Sharak could speak alone.

Frist found a small office for them and departed.

"You must not agree to their request to separate us," Doctor Sharak insisted.

"I do not believe either of us has the authority to insist that they alter their protocols," Seven said.

"I was sent here to observe their interactions with you," Sharak continued. "I cannot do that if you are locked in a classified lab where I cannot reach you."

"Unless I enter that lab I cannot see Axum," Seven argued.

"Until they agree to allow me to accompany you, you should not enter that lab," Sharak said.

"I can take care of myself," Seven said. "I have willingly entered many situations more dangerous than this one."

"You haven't seen that lab," Sharak countered. "You have no idea how dangerous it might be. Did you not advise the Doctor and Counselor Cambridge that you believe they were torturing Axum?"

"Yes," Seven replied. "And if they are still doing so, I cannot help him from out here."

"You have continued to wear the neural inhibitor I gave you for the last several weeks. Remain outside the lab tonight. I will observe as you disengage the inhibitor. You may find yourself able to connect with Axum again and better ascertain any current threats to him."

"Doctor, I appreciate your concern," Seven said, "but I made the choice to come here in large part to satisfy myself of Axum's well-being. I will not wait another night to determine his present status."

"Has it not occurred to you that there might be a reason they wish to separate us?" Sharak asked.

"Of course it has," Seven replied. "But there is no alternative."

"You have been patient this long," Sharak counseled. "It is clear that they require your presence here. Make that dependent upon agreeing to my demand to join you. Indicate your willingness to refuse them by leaving here now, and perhaps they will reconsider come morning. If they do not, you will at least have explored every alternative."

"The scans they just performed have already provided them with all of the data they require about me and my catoms," Seven argued. "Should I make myself difficult at this juncture, they may simply decide they don't need me. In that case, I will have lost the opportunity to see Axum."

"That does not change the risk."

"I am willing to accept it."

Malra at Bethaom.

He could tell her the story. He could use the clumsy words of Federation Standard to warn her of the dangers of heeding her heart when her mind knew better. A Child of Tama would have understood instantly the danger of following in Malra's footsteps. They would have grasped the intensity of Sharak's fear in a single image: a girl, only just become a woman, thrusting a dagger into her own heart to stop the burning pain of regret. Her body lying limp over Jescha, the boy/man she had trusted and hoped to save.

There was wisdom in the Federation, to be sure. They chronicled their past in minute detail but the staggering volume of extant material made it difficult to cull from that past its simplest and most essential truths. The Children of Tama had no word for "research." They passed their truths to future generations in bold images that impressed themselves on the heart before the mind. All one needed to know, one learned as they learned to speak. The most potent examples of every mistake an individual could make were woven into the fabric of their daily lives.

How to share this with Miss Seven? *How to make her see?*

Impatient, Seven said, "I will speak with you as soon as I have confirmed Axum's status. I will apprise you of any concerns, and should I fear for myself, I will respond with whatever force is necessary."

"If you already anticipate that such measures might be necessary, you would do well to consider once more."

"I have made my decision, Doctor," Seven said.

"And I am unable to persuade you of its hazards?"

"Your concern is noted," Seven said. "But it cannot change my present course."

"Some lessons we must learn for ourselves," Sharak said sadly.

"Some information we can only gather firsthand," Seven said. *"Kiteo. His eyes closed."*

"Doctor?"

"You speak of data. I speak of truth."

Seven sighed in frustration.

Sharak bowed his head.

"Please advise me of your safety at the first possible moment," Sharak said.

"You have my word."

Too many of them, Sharak agreed silently.

The Commander waited impatiently for the secondary airlock's release. When it finally did so with a loud *whoosh* that barely registered through the biohazard suit's receiver, he stepped gingerly over the base of the doorframe, taking each side in hand to steady himself.

One would think that after working in these conditions for so many months, he would have become more comfortable with the inconveniences, but that was not the case. Each step was precious and filled with potentially deadly pitfalls.

Naria sat upright on the biobed within the small chamber. Her legs hung over the long side, the paper-thin gown she wore ending just at her knees. Her back was ramrod-straight. Her posture had never failed to impress him.

Long, straight black hair fell almost to her waist. Her flesh had a deep lavender hue to it this afternoon. The color indicated curious calm. When she was agitated, dark black lines would appear, running from her neck over her face and down her torso, arms, and legs, cascading into whorls that to an untrained eye appeared calligraphic. When she was angry, the lavender transmuted into a vivid purple the Commander dreaded. Despite the trust she had given him for so long, he had rarely seen her flesh take the color of tranquil pink, betraying unreserved peace.

He couldn't blame her.

"Good afternoon, Naria," the Commander said.

"Hello, Jefferson."

The Commander checked her bioscans, visible on the room's single display panel mounted on a small shelf embedded in the wall to his left. Once he confirmed that they were optimal, he asked Naria to lie down.

"This won't hurt, will it?" she asked.

"No more than usual," he replied honestly.

Naria did as she had been asked and, when she was settled, nodded to him.

The Commander carried with him a hard plastic container slung over his shoulder like a satchel. He placed it into a depression on the shelf meant to secure it before he released the containment seals and removed a hypospray.

He moved to the head of the biobed, offering a smile to Naria. Most likely she could not see it through the cumbersome helmet he wore. Placing the end of the hypospray on her upper arm, he depressed the trigger.

The effect was instantaneous.

Alarms began to blare from the diagnostic console before the Commander could raise his medical tricorder. Naria's eyes widened before slamming shut, as if she could avoid the pain by refusing to look at it.

He immediately activated the bed's restraints to hold her steady.

The Commander then moved back to his case and retrieved a second hypospray. Her heart rate was already in dangerous territory; her blood pressure indicated the onset of a massive vascular disruption. Glancing back, he noted that areas of her flesh near the injection site and the restraints had turned pitch black and begun to transmute from a solid state.

For the next several minutes, the Commander worked frantically to undo the damage he had just done.

WATERFRONT, SAN FRANCISCO

Lieutenant Commander Thomas Eugene Paris was running late. The waterfront café was crowded with lunch patrons, many of them in uniform. His representative for the upcoming mediation, Lieutenant Garvin Shaw, had left a message for him to meet here at noon. Paris had first seen that message when he was settling into his temporary quarters upon arriving in orbit in the middle of San Francisco's night. Nine hours' advance warning had not been sufficient for him to adjust to the time difference. The sun had risen before he fell into an uneasy sleep that the computer's automated alarm had failed to pull him from before eleven-thirty. He scanned the patrons, looking for a human male with dark brown hair, despairing of identifying Shaw until the restaurant's host asked his name and directed him to a small table on a deck overlooking the bay.

Shaw rose as Paris approached.

"Commander Paris," he said, extending his hand.

Paris took it, the firm handshake immediately conveying confidence. If Shaw had appeared to be more than fifteen years old, Paris might have decided instantly that the JAG corps had chosen well.

"Lieutenant Shaw," Paris said. *Is your dad joining us and is he by any chance the Lieutenant Shaw assigned to my case?* Paris took the only empty seat at the table and was immediately accosted by a server.

"Just water, for now," Paris insisted.

"You should eat," Shaw suggested.

"I will, just as soon as I have an appetite," Paris said.

"They do extraordinary things here with shrimp," Shaw assured him, "things that probably shouldn't be legal."

"Tell me your legal expertise extends beyond shellfish," Paris said.

Shaw sat back, his dark brown eyes narrowing. "Is there a problem, Commander?"

"When did you graduate, Lieutenant?" Paris asked.

"I've served in the JAG corps for sixteen years," Shaw replied.

Paris was taken aback. "Were you accepted into law school the moment you graduated from kindergarten?"

Shaw chuckled. "Good genes," he replied. "And I try to stay out of the sun. My duties help a lot with that."

"Are you an expert in family law?"

"Yes."

"How often do cases like mine come across your desk?"

"More often than you might think, Commander." Shaw paused, leaning forward across the table. "When Starfleet first began to allow families to serve together aboard some of our bigger ships, they hoped the number of custody issues between civilians and officers would diminish."

"They didn't?"

"Living on starships is hard for those who choose to be there. It's harder for those who don't, even when they're trying to create something like a normal life for their children. The number of custody cases increased because the divorce rate did."

Paris's empty stomach turned. He'd been telling himself and B'Elanna for months that theirs was a well-worn path. Many officers raised families while in service. He'd never let himself think about how many families that service might have torn apart.

"Your mother has a tough road to hoe, however," Shaw continued. "Your daughter has two living, healthy parents stationed aboard the same ship. While your records are not what I would call pristine, both you and Commander Torres have distinguished yourselves on numerous occasions since turning from your respective lives of crime and joining *Voyager*. It is clear to me that every choice you have made regarding your daughter's well-being since her birth, but one, were in her best interest and demanded self-sacrifice by you and your wife."

"But one?" Paris asked.

"Commander Torres abandoned Miral when she was only a few weeks old to stay on Boreth."

"She left Miral with *me*," Paris said, feeling his cheeks flush.

"Her mother, Miral Torres, was reported dead. The mediator's going to wonder why claiming her mother's remains couldn't have waited until her daughter was a little older, or why she didn't take the baby with her."

"B'Elanna's mother wasn't dead. Because she made the choice to go to Boreth when she did, B'Elanna was able to see her mother again. It was important to both of them. And do you have any idea what's involved in the Klingon Challenge of the Spirit? You can't take infants."

"Commander Torres didn't know that her mother was still alive when she made that choice," Shaw said.

"There was a note from her mother, and a map," Paris insisted. "There was a good chance . . ."

"A note and a map that were more than two years old? How confident could any sane person have been that Miral Torres was still alive on Boreth?"

Paris didn't have a good answer for that one.

"*Your* mother is going to argue that, from the beginning, your wife demonstrated neglect. She put her own needs before Miral's."

"That's a lie," Paris said.

"I never said it wasn't," Shaw said. "And if you can't handle hearing this from me, we're in trouble."

Paris took a deep breath.

Shaw's eyes remained glued to his. "By the way, next time you feel inclined to accuse anyone of *lying*, you're going to want to count to ten in your head and let the words die on your lips."

Paris nodded.

"Better," Shaw said.

"We haven't even gotten to the recent past and you make it sound like my mother has already won," Paris said.

"She's nowhere near winning. *You* can lose, but unless you do, she won't win."

"I don't understand."

"Your mother is the one bringing the complaint. The onus is on her to prove two things: that you and your wife are unfit parents, *and* that she is fit to raise Miral."

"Setting the first part aside for a minute," Paris said, "she already raised three kids. My sisters are both at the top of their respective fields, and despite some early setbacks, I've turned out all right. I don't think my mom will have a hard time proving to anyone that she's a good mother."

Shaw smiled faintly. "She's admitting she failed with you by bringing the case at all."

"I made my own choices," Paris said. "She did her best by me. I won't ever say otherwise." After a moment he went on: "I just need to talk to her. This whole thing is about lousy timing and her grief. If my dad were still alive, she wouldn't be doing this."

"Are you sure?"

Paris nodded. "She doesn't think I'm an unfit parent. She's just mad that I lied to her."

Shaw said nothing for a very long time. Finally, he said, "A couple of ground rules. You will not under any circumstances contact your mother outside our scheduled mediation sessions. You will not speak about her to anyone other than me. You will not speak to any old friends or other family members about this case unless I direct you to do so, and should that time come, you will say only what I tell you to say."

"I really think—" Paris began.

"You will not *think* anything without first running it past me."

"Look—" Paris said.

"No, you look," Shaw interrupted. "You're here because you told your mother, your family, and your closest friends that your wife and daughter were dead when you knew for a fact that they were alive. *That* is where *thinking* got you. There were other choices you could have made, but apparently none of them occurred to you at the time. You don't get to *think* anymore. You don't get to decide that you know better. Not unless you're ready to hand Miral over tomorrow to your mother's care."

Paris's cheeks had begun to burn again. His stomach was a nauseous tangle and his shoulders felt hard as rocks.

"Okay," he finally said.

"You're going to win, Tom," Shaw said. "But it's going to be hard and you're going to have to trust me."

"Okay."

"Tell me more about your mother," Shaw said.

For reasons he could not name, Paris hesitated.

He thought of his mother, waking alone in her bed, preparing breakfast for one, and rambling around that huge house alone all day. He thought of the way she'd held him when he was a boy who had just awakened from a nightmare. He thought of the pride in her eyes the first time he'd seen her when he returned from *Voyager*'s maiden journey.

He thought of B'Elanna.

He thought of Miral.

He thought of his unborn son.

He began to speak of Julia Paris.

Chapter Three

Admiral Kathryn Janeway had always thought that Starfleet's dress uniform was classic, if a bit understated. Compared to the uniforms of the officers of the Confederacy Interstellar Fleet—tailored jackets that fell to the knee in vivid hues that denoted rank and position, belted by sashes of a satinlike fabric and adorned copiously with metallic insignia, ribbons, knots, and epaulettes fringed with braid that extended to the elbow—Starfleet's were positively austere.

An honor guard flanked a pattern of silver-blue tiles inlaid into the floor of the entrance hall in a way that suggested a flowing river. Looking down, it was hard to shake the immediate sensation that one was walking on water.

The tiles ended at an open arched doorway separating the hall from the rooftop garden that had been created for the Ceremony of Welcoming. Trellises of flowering plants in varied riotous colors ran along the low walls that edged the space as far as the eye could see. Trees taller than some buildings Janeway had seen were spaced evenly, and millions of pinpoints of light suspended by no visible means rose from the tops of the trees over the assembly, creating the breathtaking illusion that the stars above were almost close enough to touch.

Janeway already knew that hundreds of the Confederacy's elite citizens had been invited to the ceremony, but at first glance it looked more like thousands. The vast majority were either Leodt or Djinari, but occasionally Janeway caught sight of an alien species she could not name from the briefing materials she had received. To a person, however, they were garbed in finery that was spectacular without simultaneously appearing garish.

The admiral couldn't help but feel underdressed.

Metallic fabrics flowed like mercury over bodies of every shape and size. Several females wore gowns made of small beads that changed colors as they moved and exposed varying parts of their anatomy. Many of the skirts kept one several paces from the man or woman wearing it, as they extended more than a meter out from the wearer's waist in solid cones of shimmering light. Most ensembles were accented with jeweled accessories that ran the gamut from exotic animals perched on shoulders to gossamer cloaks that rose like wings above the wearer's shoulders. Even the silent servers moving among the throng holding trays of delicacies wore uniforms of midnight blue that, despite the depth of color, still emitted a glorious, rich light.

"Now *this* is a party," Sal said softly behind Janeway. A soft groan might have come from O'Donnell, but it was immediately lost in waves of tinkling that sounded like glass being broken. As the sound grew in intensity its source remained unclear but its purpose was not. This was obviously the assembly's version of applause at the appearance of their honored guests.

The throngs formed a corridor of bodies through which Janeway and her officers were led to a central raised platform on which several round tables had been set. Two or three of her officers would eventually sit at each, while the other chairs were reserved for Confederacy leadership and their guests.

Although none of the attendees were close enough to touch Janeway or her officers, the feeling of being examined was tangible. Janeway smiled, made eye contact with those nearby, and immediately discerned curiosity and pleasure along with the occasional look of disappointment. *Scorn* was probably too strong a word, but a fair amount of disdain was clearly visible on a few scattered faces.

Before being seated, Janeway and her officers had formed a

line before the tables, as requested, to await the arrival of the presider of the Confederacy, an office Janeway understood to be the rough equivalent of the Federation president.

"I don't even know where to look," Chakotay whispered to Janeway as he took his place beside her.

"It's a feast for all of the senses, isn't it?" she agreed.

"It's a bloody bacchanal," Cambridge noted from her other side.

"Did those include ritual sacrifice?" Farkas asked.

"Not usually, but the night is young," Cambridge quipped.

Almost immediately, the question of where to look was resolved as a hush fell over the crowd and all eyes turned upward. From a distance, it appeared that one of the brightest stars was descending from above. By the time it had moved through the artificial starscape, it was clear that the yellow-white light emanated from an intricate gown worn by a tall female figure.

"The presider?" Chakotay asked.

Janeway nodded.

"I wasn't aware that the Djinari could fly."

"They can't. They use protectors as crude transporters," Janeway advised him softly.

The female finally touched the ground several meters before the line of Federation officers. Cosmetically, the Djinari shared no physical attributes with the Leodts. The woman's skin was golden. Her scalp was covered by fine layers of flesh that looked like small, diamond-shaped scales. They extended just below batlike ears and to the tip of a sharply pointed nose. Vivid green eyes were accentuated by the scales above, and the remainder of her face resembled a human's, with high cheekbones and a delicate, tight-lipped mouth. Numerous thin, whiplike tendrils extended from the base of her skull, ending just above the floor. They moved freely but gracefully behind her, almost like a head of living hair that had been pulled into a low ponytail.

Her gown ended any debate for the title of "best-dressed." A fitted, strapless bodice was set above a long flowing skirt that seemed to be made of stars. The light coming from them should have been blinding, but some trick of the fabric muted it just enough to make it hard to tear your eyes away from it.

Janeway had to remind herself that the presider was now in her ninth decade of life. Though that was considered middle aged among the Djinari, to the untrained eye she appeared to be quite young.

The presider approached Janeway, a genuine smile playing over her lips as someone behind the admiral announced, "The presider of the Confederacy of the Worlds of the First Quadrant, Isorla Cin."

More tinkling crashed over the assembly until Cin came within a meter of Janeway and bowed her head ever so slightly. The admiral responded with a bow of her own before extending her hand. Well prepared, Cin accepted it and shook it gamely, though the gesture was obviously unfamiliar to her.

"Admiral Kathryn Janeway, honored Federation representatives, on behalf of the fifty-three worlds and six aligned planets that form the Confederacy of the Worlds of the First Quadrant, I bid you welcome. Our ancient protectors called you friends. We do not question their wisdom. The Source of our lives, our worlds, our confederacy, is ever mindful of our needs. We believe you have been brought to us to begin a brilliant new chapter in our illustrious history. That which is ours to give, we offer freely. May the Source guide your path as it has always guided ours."

More crashing glass followed this short speech. Janeway stepped aside as the presider moved to stand beside her on the platform.

"Presider Cin," Janeway began. "The United Federation of Planets we call home is countless light-years from this Confederacy. It was born of a desire between like-minded species to expand our knowledge of the universe and all who share it with us. Our first hope in making contact with the Confederacy is that an open exchange of ideas will foster mutual regard that will bridge the vast distances between us. We come in peace, seeking only to add to our understanding of our fellow citizens of the universe, and we are most grateful for your generosity and hospitality."

Applause followed, though decidedly less enthusiastic than that which had followed Cin's remarks.

"I have welcomed you on behalf of my people," Cin said. "With your permission, they wish to welcome you personally."

"Of course," the admiral replied, curious. Her understanding of the evening's itinerary was that, following their formal greeting, gifts would be exchanged between the admiral and the presider, followed by dinner. That the presider was going off-script this soon was disconcerting, but Janeway read nothing beyond excitement and a little mischief from her counterpart. Decan immediately stepped to her side and began to whisper something apologetic in her ear but Janeway cut him off, saying softly, "When in Rome, Lieutenant."

Decan was clearly puzzled, a rare event that pleased Janeway enormously.

Further conversation was made impossible as a deep, rhythmic pounding began somewhere below the roof of the building, rising in intensity until the air surrounding the admiral thrummed with the sound. Immediately, everyone assembled moved to the edges of the roof and peered over the sides. Transparent guardrails edged the building to ensure the guests' safety as they strained to look down.

The streets a hundred meters below that surrounded the building were filled by citizens of the First World, all garbed in luminescent clothing of varying colors. High-pitched, sustained sounds began to rise from them in time with the drumbeats, and soon the sounds of other notes obviously made from native musical instruments were added to the song.

Janeway was about to follow her officers to the nearest vantage point from which to view the celebration, when Cin gently touched her arm.

"Would you care to join me for the best view of the plaza?" she asked.

"I would be delighted, Presider," Janeway replied.

Cin nodded to someone in the retinue behind her and stepped close enough to Janeway for the folds of her gown to brush the admiral's uniform pants. "The sensation of transport will be unfamiliar to you, Admiral, but do not be alarmed. It is quite safe."

Janeway smiled and nodded as a faint, almost electric hum coursed over her skin, causing the hair that covered it to rise. The sounds were muted, but not silenced, as she and Cin began to rise above the assembly. *Another protector*, Janeway realized, and she was glad that her people's own experience with this advanced technology could already assure her of its efficacy and security.

Her officers immediately turned to look as she departed the platform, and she raised a hand to wave off their concern. Only Chakotay shook his head, a good-natured chastisement. She could not resist a slight shrug and smile in return, communicating silently that she intended to enjoy this particular privilege of her rank.

The protector did not take them far above the assembly, but high enough to be able to see all four of the plaza streets below in one glance. Only now could Janeway truly appreciate the choreography on display. The crowds were singing and dancing, their wardrobes shifting colors in lines that suggested dozens of independent streams ultimately joining into one large moving river.

Janeway's breath caught in her throat. She had been treated to her fair share of alien entertainment spectacles in her career, but she could honestly say that none of them had compared to this. It put most Federation Day displays to shame. She estimated that more than ten thousand individuals had assembled below to create this amazing moment.

"This is extraordinary," Janeway said, pleased that, even with the din, she and the presider could converse comfortably while carried by the protector's energy field.

"I am glad it pleases you, Admiral Janeway," Cin said.

"You have put yourselves to too much trouble on our account," Janeway said.

"It has been more than a hundred years since outsiders were deemed worthy by the protectors to pass through the Gateway," Cin reminded her. "This is not a routine occurrence for our people. Their enthusiasm mirrors that felt by the Confederacy's leadership."

"It is most impressive," Janeway assured her.

"As are your people, Admiral," Cin said.

Janeway did not reply immediately, unsure as to what, exactly, Cin might mean. She'd adopted few rules for herself as she had expanded her diplomatic duties, but the first was: *If you don't know what to say, keep your mouth shut.*

Off her silence, Cin went on: "The Djinari-odt dialect is difficult to master. That your people took the time to make it their own before contacting us speaks volumes of your commitment to the open exchange of ideas between our cultures."

Janeway bowed her head briefly to hide her disappointment. None of the reports she had read thus far made mention of comments such as this. Clearly all of the representatives her people had met with thus far had made the same mistake as the presider.

Janeway gently unclipped the combadge affixed to the front of her uniform and held it up for the presider to see. "I wish I could say that my people had learned your language," she began, "but I would hate for us to begin our friendship in misunderstanding. This piece of technology is called a combadge. My people use it for routine conversation between us, but embedded within is something we call a universal translator. I am not speaking to you now in your native language. This device is translating what I say into words you understand and simultaneously rendering your words into Federation Standard for me."

For the first time, Janeway saw sincere surprise on Cin's face, replaced almost immediately by awe.

"Do you mean to suggest that this technology allows you to speak without confusion with every single alien race your people encounter?" Cin asked.

"It has limits," Janeway admitted. "We have come across languages it is unable to parse. In those cases, establishing communication is more difficult, but it always remains our priority when making first contact with a new species."

"My people have nothing that compares to this simple yet

incredibly powerful device," Cin said, deflated. "In the dark days before we discovered the Great River and the First World, we happened upon an alien species that was very skilled with translation. We pressed some of them into our service, and their descendants perform this vital function when we contact new species, even to this day," Cin said. "Every world that seeks to join our Confederacy must implement an educational program to teach its people Djinari-odt. It is the only language of our civilization."

"Every culture that willingly seeks out new ones must grapple with this issue," Janeway said kindly. "You found one solution. My people found another."

"I wonder what other *solutions* your Federation has devised that so clearly show the limits of our creativity," Cin said. "It would never have occurred to me that such a thing would be possible."

"In the days and weeks to come, we will both learn about each other. We will both have the opportunity to expand our understanding. That is the great gift peace brings among people."

The display had ended with blinding explosions of light below, and the protector began to descend again to the rooftop. As it did, Cin watched as Janeway refastened her combadge, a mixture of sadness and shock still plain on her face. Finally she asked, "Is this technology something you would consider sharing with us?"

"It is," Janeway replied. "But before you decide to embrace it, you must consider how it would change the lives of your citizens. Is it something you genuinely require? Or does your current communication system work well enough and better reflect the needs of your Confederacy? Speaking the same language can create a sense of cohesion among your people, a unique identity they may cherish. A universal translator might rob them of that."

"But it also limits our ability to speak directly with those who have no interest in joining our Confederacy," Cin noted. "You are right, of course. It is a complicated decision. A more limited initial application might be more appropriate than widespread dissemination."

"I am sure that will be true of many things we are about to learn of one another," Janeway said.

Finally their feet again touched solid ground and Janeway struggled for a moment with a brief bout of dizziness. Cin took her arm, a gesture of genuine concern. "Are you well, Admiral?"

"Yes," Janeway assured her. "I'm simply not accustomed to your method of transport."

"Perhaps something we might share with you," Cin said, clearly jockeying for a way to resume surer footing with her guest.

Janeway smiled but said nothing. Chakotay's first instinct when encountering the Confederacy had been to hide their transporter capabilities. The admiral would have made the same call and was pleased he had taken this precaution. If the universal translator had so impressed Cin, Federation transport capabilities were going to look like magic, and she had no desire to overwhelm her hosts. She made a mental note to continue this restriction, among others, as she climbed the steps back up to the platform and took her seat beside Cin for dinner.

As the demonstration below ended and the sound of a few clapping hands was overwhelmed by the odd, shattering sound of Confederacy applause, Captain Chakotay felt a firm hand grasp his shoulder. Turning, he saw a familiar alien face.

"General Mattings," Chakotay said, smiling widely. "It's good to see you again."

"I lost you in the crowd as soon as the spectacle started. For a few minutes there, I thought I was going to have to send out a search party if I wanted to speak with you before the feast."

"What's on your mind, General?" Chakotay asked as they both began to make their way slowly back to the platform and their assigned seats at different tables.

Mattings was the first Confederacy officer Chakotay had met when *Voyager* encountered the Worlds of the First Quadrant. Though predisposed otherwise, he found himself genuinely liking the Leodt, in no small part because his ship, the *Twelfth Lamont,* and its accompanying fleet had saved *Voyager* from certain destruction at the hands of a hostile alien force. The general's ancestors had been responsible for one of the most egregious ethical lapses Chakotay had ever witnessed, the use of the wave forms they called "protectors" to destroy several terrestrial planets. The captain had chosen to meet Mattings and his people on their own terms and give them an opportunity to demonstrate who they had become, hundreds of years later.

Chakotay and Mattings had spent several pleasant hours together on the *Twelfth Lamont*. It was an unusually informal first-contact situation. Although Chakotay had withheld information about his ship and its capabilities of necessity, he had formed a positive initial impression of Mattings and looked forward to seeing how their relationship progressed.

"Come now, Captain. You're an educated man, as am I," the general said. "Did you really think you'd be able to keep your secret from me for long?"

The list of *secrets* Chakotay had kept from Mattings was too extensive to risk guessing. Immediately, Chakotay raised his game face, along with his personal shields.

"Your fleet began scanning our vessels the moment we made contact," Chakotay said. "You monitored all of our ship-to-ship communications while we were within range of the Confederacy. I told you then that we had nothing to hide."

"*Voyager* left Confederacy space under the power of a propulsion system my best engineers tell me is a theoretical impossibility, Captain," Mattings said more seriously. "You told me you didn't need to use the Gateway to regroup with the rest of your fleet on the other side. I figured at maximum warp you were looking at a journey of several weeks at least. Just how far away was that fleet?"

"Far," Chakotay said. "But we did leave your territory at maximum warp. I can't imagine that our warp capabilities outpace yours."

"We utilize the streams for most of our travels of any considerable distance. The Great River makes our Confederacy feel smaller than it actually is. But my people tell me your ship can likely achieve speeds that surpass entering the flow."

"Upon what do they base this assessment?" Chakotay asked.

The general's face hardened visibly. "We followed you as far as we could, Captain. Just watching your back, of course."

Chakotay had not engaged *Voyager*'s slipstream drive until they were well clear of what he understood to be the outermost limits of Confederacy space. *Voyager, Vesta,* and *Galen* had rendezvoused at a similar distance before reentering the Confederacy's territory at high warp. He had believed the general would recon their departure. Starfleet would likely have done the same were their positions reversed. But sensors hadn't detected any contacts for several hours before Chakotay had brought the slipstream drive online.

"From hidden vessels?" Chakotay asked. He feigned insult at the apparent betrayal.

"We use the protectors for many things beyond transportation and reinforcing the streams, Captain. They can hide our ships when we need them to," Mattings admitted. "So," he went on, "now that my slip's showing, perhaps you'd consider raising your skirt a bit? It embarrasses a man when his advances aren't reciprocated."

Chakotay knew he had to tread carefully. The information the general was requesting was classified and would remain so until Admiral Janeway determined otherwise. But it would also be unwise to crush the fragile trust that existed between the two men, or their respective peoples.

"Your reliance on the streams has likely made it unnecessary for the Confederacy to develop propulsion systems that surpass warp capabilities," Chakotay said. "My people haven't had that luxury. As I told you when we met, *Voyager*'s first trip to the Delta Quadrant—"

"The First Quadrant," Mattings interjected, obviously teasing.

"Or the First Quadrant," Chakotay said, smiling, "was at the hands of an alien species that brought us here using technology we had never seen. The ship was pulled seventy thousand light-years in a matter of minutes."

"So you reverse-engineered that tech?" Mattings asked.

"We never had the chance," Chakotay replied. "It was destroyed before we could scratch the surface. But with so far to travel if we ever wanted to see our homes again, enhancing our propulsion capabilities became a priority. We came across lots of promising possibilities. One of them was seized on by Starfleet once we made contact with them again, but before we were home, and it has been installed on an experimental basis on the few ships we have that are meant to travel great distances."

"Congratulations, Captain," Mattings said. "You do vague like few men I've had the pleasure to meet."

"Many of our technological capabilities have been developed of necessity, General," Chakotay said. "Once formal negotiations begin between our diplomats, Admiral Janeway will make the determination as to which ones are most appropriate to consider sharing. I'm not at liberty to tell you more, but should the time come that I am in a position to do so, I will gladly show you what you want to see."

"Fair enough," Mattings replied. "I didn't honestly expect you'd hand over the specs, but it was worth a shot."

"We're at the beginning of what I hope will be a long road, General. There's no reason to rush things now."

"As you say," Mattings agreed. "But I do have another proposal for you."

"What is it?"

"As soon as this ceremony is over, our delegation is going to submit a list of joint ventures between our people to hurry along the 'getting-to-know-you' portion of our negotiations. I've already asked that *Voyager* accompany the *Lamont* to one of our centers of technological development. It's a trip of a couple of days, but if you're willing, I'd be interested in exchanging a few officers for the duration. We'll show you how we work, and you could return the favor."

Starfleet rarely agreed to such exchanges, and almost never

with species as relatively unknown as those of the Confederacy. But Chakotay could not deny the value of an opportunity for intelligence gathering that Mattings was suggesting. Still, his gut told him it was much too soon to consider such a thing.

"As you know, *Voyager* took quite a beating when we engaged the forces at the Gateway. We've managed to make some repairs since then, but we have many more to make before I'd be ready to show her off, General," Chakotay said. "I really do want you to see her at her best. Of course, if you're willing to permit me to send one of my officers to the *Lamont*, I wouldn't hesitate to agree."

Mattings's eyes narrowed but his smile remained in place. At least Chakotay hoped that the protrusion of sharp teeth characteristic of the Leodts was a smile. He'd been reading it as such thus far. "I guess it's a start, Captain," Mattings agreed.

"Great."

"Reports indicate that those bastards who attacked you are re-forming at the Gateway," Mattings went on. "They've always come. But lately there are more and more."

"What do they want?" Chakotay asked.

"The Gateway, of course."

"But they must know that the majority of your forces are on this side of it," Chakotay said. "Even if they successfully breached it, they wouldn't get farther than the outskirts of this system, would they?"

"It would depend on their tactics," Mattings said. "I'd like to think not, but you never know. It worries me, Captain. Our way of life has come under attack before, and we survived. We built something from its ashes of which all of us are rightly proud. I just wonder when it ends. When will they leave us in peace?"

"If I knew the answer to that, General . . ." Chakotay began.

"You'd be leading this fleet?"

"I'd retire," Chakotay replied.

Lieutenant Harry Kim was enjoying his dinner. There were dozens of options when it came to the food. He'd sampled three different appetizers before the first of four entrees was served. Most of the fare was more generously seasoned than he was accustomed to, but with the exception of a particularly bitter root that overwhelmed what seemed to be some sort of soup, everything he tasted was edible, if not delicious.

The food was improved tremendously by the company. To his left was a garrulous young Leodt whose father was a member of the Market Consortium and who apparently intended his son to follow in his footsteps. His name was Shrell, and he seemed inordinately amused by everything Kim said. He might have just been being polite, but Kim didn't think so. Shrell seemed truly happy with his lot in life, and Kim paused to reflect on how rare that had been among many of his friends in recent years.

To the lieutenant's right, a woman old enough to be his grandmother but who looked like his youngest cousin—had that cousin possessed the golden skin and striking scales of a Djinari—soon eclipsed Shrell as a conversationalist. Ligah was vague about her occupation, assuming she even had one, but she had captured Kim's attention by discussing openly her faith in the Source.

"Would you define the Source as that which created the streams of the Great River?" Kim asked.

Ligah's smile held trace amounts of condescension, but she replied congenially. "It is more than that. It *is* the river. It has carried us through trials and tragedies. It is the lifeblood of our Confederacy. It revealed itself to us at our moment of greatest need, and because we were wise enough to accept it, the Source has rewarded us with several generations of peace and prosperity."

"Has anyone ever seen it?" Kim asked.

"Are all of your people so literal?" Ligah asked. "Anyone who has traveled through the streams has known the Source."

Kim had traveled through several types of subspace corridors in his years of service without any such revelation.

"I'm curious about the wave forms, what you call the 'protectors,' some of which are contained in those streams," Kim admitted. "You use them to maintain the stability of the streams.

Without them the streams would collapse. But they were created beyond the streams, were they not?"

"They are, but by their nature they are of the Source," Ligah replied. "There is harmony between the streams and the protectors. They need each other."

"Has that always been the case?" Kim asked.

"Yes," Ligah replied, unfazed. "Without the protectors, the streams become difficult to travel. The Source created them to make continuous use possible, among other things."

Kim had assumed that the technology that created the protectors was of alien origin. Whether or not the Djinari or Leodt had created them remained an open question. That they used them was undeniable. But how had they been folded into the religious mythology of the Confederacy?

"Are there consequences for displeasing the Source?" Kim asked.

Before Ligah could respond, the face of another Djinari thrust itself between them.

"Federation representative," the man began, "have you truly come to the Confederacy seeking peace, or are you here to conquer?"

"I beg your pardon," Kim said. "Who are you?"

"Leave our guest alone," Ligah said, warning clear in her tone. She placed protective arms around Kim, one over his shoulder and the other resting on his chest. "The press has been allowed limited access to this ceremony. You are meant to wait in the designated area for official statements."

"Our citizens have a right to know whom the presider has invited to our space," the man insisted defiantly.

Ligah rose. "Please excuse me, Lieutenant Kim. I must contact security to see that this man is expelled from the gathering. Permit me to apologize for his rudeness."

Kim had only a second to look down as Ligah released him and began to shoo away the intruder. Kim quickly came to his feet and placed one hand around Ligah's nearest wrist.

"Why don't you allow me to escort him to security," Kim said.

"That won't be necessary," Ligah assured him.

"I'm afraid I must insist," Kim said.

Ligah's eyes met the man's, and unmistakable frustration passed between them.

"Very well," Ligah said. "You will find several security officers positioned at the rear of the platform." She raised her free hand to point them out, but Kim held on to the other tightly.

"Lieutenant Kim," Ligah said, the condescension back in full force. "Please release my hand."

"I'll be happy to, just as soon as you return my combadge to me."

Frustration turned to anger.

"Your what?" she demanded.

"The small metallic object that was affixed to my uniform until a few seconds ago," Kim replied.

Shrell had observed the exchange, and he chuckled into his napkin. Ligah favored him with a withering glare.

"I don't know what you are talking about," Ligah insisted gamely.

"Then allow me," Kim said. Gently he pried her fingers open, and as he did so, the unmistakable sound of metal hitting a solid surface met his ears.

Kim bent automatically to retrieve his combadge from the spot where Ligah had just dropped it. By the time he had raised himself upright again, she had vanished into the crowd, along with her compatriot.

"Damn," Kim said, resuming his seat.

"You're security on your ship, aren't you?" Shrell asked.

"I am." Kim nodded.

"She should have known better," Shrell observed.

"Who was she?" Kim asked.

Shrell shrugged. "Who knows? But she sure read you wrong."

"I get that a lot," Kim said.

"It's your face," Shrell said. "Too soft. Too squishy."

"What did she want with my combadge?" Kim wondered aloud.

"Same thing everybody wants," Shrell replied. "Any advantage it might have given her."

Kim didn't touch another thing that was served to him, nor did he manage to find Ligah again in the crowd as the evening continued.

B'Elanna Torres needed to excuse herself after the third appetizer course had been served to relieve her bladder, one of pregnancy's many nuisances. Lieutenant Lasren, *Voyager's* ops officer who was also seated at her table, had seemed contemplative when the meal began, but after only a few courses he had a decidedly nauseated look on his face. Perhaps dinner was disagreeing with him. Torres had made polite conversation with her nearer companions, a science officer with the Confederacy Fleet and an administrator on the presider's staff. The administrator, a Leodt female, was kind enough to quietly direct her toward the facilities when she rose.

En route, Torres got her first really close look at many of the other guests, both seated and mingling near stations for beverages. An alarming number of the women, or so it seemed to Torres, were obviously with child. More stunning, however, was the way their pregnancies were exposed for all to see. She'd had her fair share of difficulties dressing herself this evening. She could only imagine what these women had endured.

Even the smallest abdominal bump was displayed by the gowns worn. The fabric usually divided just below the sternum and was held draped open to the top of the pelvis. Some were adorned with body paint in colorful designs. Others were encrusted with stones that either glowed or caught the light brilliantly. Whatever the accessories chosen, what was clear was the announcement each woman was making of her condition. Less amazing, but worth noting, was the way the other guests, male and female, doted on these women. Chairs were vacated as they approached to offer them room. Plates and glasses were filled to order by hands anxious to assist them. Arms were offered for strolls through the garden. And everywhere, men and women alike were touching the exposed areas gently and offering the women praise and encouragement.

Some of these things were common to the Federation as well. It seemed to be a natural law rather than one specific to any species that pregnant women were an object of scrutiny. The Klingons were never so delicate about it. Female warriors were expected to fight right up until the moment their babies fell from their bodies. Less aggressive species—her human family, for instance—were also fascinated by swelling bellies. Strangers suddenly felt they had a right to reach out and touch one if they were certain a new life was growing within it.

There was nothing prudish about Torres. She was both proud and fiercely protective of the son in her womb. But she could not imagine walking comfortably through a room of strangers and announcing her condition in the way the Confederacy women did.

When she finally reached the facilities, she found a short line. Two of the women directly in front of her were pregnant. Apparently many things were universal to their shared condition, including the frequency with which they needed to relieve themselves. The nearest one turned to look at Torres and smiled broadly.

"Good evening, Federation citizen," she said, extending her hand. "Welcome to the Confederacy of the Worlds of the First Quadrant."

"Thank you," Torres replied. "I am Lieutenant Commander B'Elanna Torres."

"Orla," the woman said. "And this is Wentin," she added, gesturing to the woman on her left.

At a loss but truly curious, Torres finally ventured, "Don't you get a little cold in that dress?"

Orla looked as if a light had just gone off above her head. "Of course," she said. "Our species must have different comfort levels when it comes to temperature."

"We must," Torres agreed congenially, unsure if Orla had really understood the question. The light fabric woven over her body left almost nothing, including her due date, to the imagination. Even in long sleeves and pants, Torres was still a little chilled by the night air.

"Is that why you hide your child?" Wentin asked agreeably.

Torres immediately placed a hand over her belly. "I'm not hiding him," she said. "This is our dress uniform."

"I told you," Wentin said conspiratorially to Orla.

"Told her what?" Torres asked, determined not to take immediate offense but open to the possibility, depending upon Wentin's answer.

"Orla thought you refused to display your child because the Federation must have some cultural taboo. She suggested your people do not take pride in your obvious accomplishment. I told her that was silly. No right-thinking people would want to hide such a thing. It is natural. It is beautiful. And it is every woman's first duty to her civilization."

The first thought to strike Torres was discomfort with the fact that she and her pregnancy had been a source of conversation among these total strangers. All of her fellow officers were on display tonight, but not for the shape of their bodies; more for the content of their character, or so Torres hoped. The second was the judgment coming from these women with very little in the way of real data upon which to base that judgment.

"I am actually of mixed heritage," Torres explained. "Each race from which I was descended, the humans and the Klingons, have different customs when it comes to bearing children. Neither is ashamed of it. But I guess neither feels the need to emphasize it either. It is a simple bodily function of the females of both species. When a child is born, there is great happiness for its family and community. Until then, the mothers tend to go about their daily lives as usual, unless their physical condition makes that difficult for some medical reason."

Both Orla's and Wentin's faces shared the same puzzled expression. "Your bearing women are not revered and appropriately rewarded by your people?" Orla finally asked.

"Not for simply *bearing*," Torres replied.

Orla placed a gentle hand on Torres's arm. "I'm so sorry to hear that," she said.

Torres didn't know why she should feel embarrassed by this, but she did. "How exactly are your *bearing* women rewarded?" she asked.

Orla shrugged. "There are so many ways. Once we mature to the point that bearing is possible, our obligations as citizens are reduced to finding an appropriate mate. We receive considerable support from our mates and the Confederacy during the years we produce our children. Nonbearing females assist with their rearing and education. But unlike us, the career paths open to them once they are no longer fertile are extremely limited. I've chosen to study medicine once my children are grown. When I have completed my indoctrination I will enjoy as many years as I wish of service to my people and absolute financial security."

"Are you saying that as long as you are capable of bearing children, you are expected to do nothing else?" Torres asked.

"What else could we possibly do that any civilized society would regard more highly?" Wentin asked.

Any hopes for an alliance between the Federation and the Confederacy might have ended right then had two stalls not opened up, into which Orla and Wentin swiftly disappeared.

It had come as no surprise that the Confederacy's overseer of agriculture, a Leodt named Racha Bralt, was at the table Commander O'Donnell shared with Captain Farkas and Doctor Sal. He and O'Donnell had spoken several times when *Demeter* was the lone ship in Confederacy territory, and Bralt had learned of the ship's unique capabilities and function within the Federation fleet.

Bralt had already gone on at great length and with considerable pride in his people's developments on several worlds to ensure large harvests of a variety of edible plant life. He was particularly effulgent when the conversation turned to some unique weather maintenance systems that had enhanced their grain yields.

O'Donnell didn't need a crystal ball to look a few decades into the future and see what these choices were doing to the soil of those worlds. The Confederacy was not the first to make this particular mistake, and O'Donnell knew that among sentient life-forms they would not be the last. But one day they were going to wake up and find that, for all their control mechanisms, the soil would refuse to grow what it once had. Regular crop rotation and nutrient replacement was vital for the health of most soil, and yet under Bralt's direction, and that of his predecessors, Confederacy farmers were reaping vast financial gain in the short run and courting disaster in the long run.

Because Captain Farkas didn't know soil from fertilizer, she was permitted to be impressed. But as Bralt droned on, O'Donnell found himself lapsing into silence that only Farkas and Sal seemed to note. It wasn't that he didn't have anything to say. It was simply that to speak his mind on the subject at hand would do nothing to forward the Federation's diplomatic objectives.

"In the last decade, these worlds have gone from feeding ten billion annually to almost twice that number," Bralt said.

"That's wonderful," Farkas said.

"With statistics like that, I'm assuming very few of your citizens go hungry," Sal noted.

O'Donnell placed his fist firmly over his mouth to repress any potential sound. He already knew the answer.

"The Source knows that all civilized cultures, even those with the most advanced technology, are forced to struggle with the realities of poverty," Bralt said.

No, they're not, O'Donnell didn't say.

"The Confederacy was founded on the diligent labor of thousands who became hundreds of thousands, then millions. Every individual who fled our homeworlds was required to offer whatever service they could to sustain the whole. Those lessons, however, seem to have been lost on some once we achieved a certain degree of prosperity. And to be honest, communicating our value of hard work has been difficult with some of our member worlds. Painful choices must always be made. Our people reward those who strive daily to care for themselves and their brothers. Those who are less willing may find themselves in more challenging straits."

You mean "hungry"? O'Donnell didn't ask.

"But surely, when resources are so plentiful, the excess may be used to relieve their suffering?" Farkas asked.

You'd think, wouldn't you, O'Donnell did not say.

"To deny the less fortunate or less industrious among us the pain that would teach them to apply themselves more diligently would dishonor the efforts of those who are willing to work," Bralt replied. "We would do them a disservice by making their lives too comfortable. There is only one way for them to learn the error of their ways."

At this, Farkas put her utensils down and kept her gaze fixed a little too long on her plate.

"What about those who fall on hard times through no fault of their own?" Sal asked. "Maybe their skills are no longer needed and they require time to learn new ones."

"Every member of our society who contributes to its betterment on a daily basis enjoys a very comfortable standard of living," Bralt said. "Those who refuse to do so must get by as best they can. When they demonstrate their ability to contribute, they are permitted, once again, to assume the dignities and benefits of citizenship."

"Do you mean to say that it's possible for a Confederacy resident to lose their rights as a citizen and the protection of your government?" Farkas asked.

Yep, O'Donnell refrained from adding.

"Citizenship is a privilege, reserved for those willing to earn it every day of their lives," Bralt replied. "That privilege may be lost, but it may also be restored depending upon an individual's personal choices."

"Who decides who is contributing enough to earn their citizenship?" Sal asked.

"Our standards are high," Bralt conceded. "But what you see all around you is the result of those standards. There are minimums that have been in place for centuries, administered by our Market Consortium, and all new worlds are presented with their own baselines upon entrance into the Confederacy. Those who fail to meet them always have the opportunity to change their ways. But we will not tolerate laziness. Without these goals to strive for, what else would ever motivate anyone to work hard?"

"Curiosity, passion, intelligence, creativity, the biological imperative all sentient species are born with to learn and grow," O'Donnell said, surprised that sound had unintentionally escaped his lips.

Every set of eyes at the table was suddenly upon him.

"Not all individuals within our society possess those attributes, Commander. They may be learned, of course, and must be, to share in our civilization's bounty."

"In my experience, every sentient being is born with them to one degree or another," O'Donnell said. "What they may lack is the opportunity to apply them because they are forced to busy themselves conforming to a system they had no hand in creating, and in which their particular gifts are not considered worth rewarding."

"Commander O'Donnell," Captain Farkas said, rising from the table. "Would you accompany me to the bar?"

"One of the servers will be by momentarily," Bralt tried to assure her.

"I don't wish to trouble them," Farkas said. "They've got their hands full tonight and are doing a wonderful job. We won't be long."

O'Donnell rose and followed Farkas from the table. As soon as they were lost in the crowd, he said, "I'm sorry. I shouldn't have said that."

"El'nor is usually the one I worry about keeping on a short leash at these things," Farkas admitted. "I had no idea you and she have so much in common."

O'Donnell shrugged. "These people aren't ready for Federation membership," he said softly. "You know it and I know it. Their ancestors destroyed countless planets and stole their resources to build all of this. Their descendants live under a virtual caste system. Their market-based economy rewards the fortunate and ignores the rest. Don't let the clothing fool you. They're barbarians."

"They're a work in progress, Commander," Farkas corrected him coldly, "just as we are. Let's not judge them too harshly for only knowing what they've had time to learn. We're not looking for a new Federation member here. We're just looking for an ally."

O'Donnell was about to reply when Sal found them and asked, "Did you really have to pull him away when the conversation was finally getting interesting, Regina?"

For the first time all evening, O'Donnell smiled. "And I was worried I wouldn't find any friends at this party."

Counselor Cambridge was seated at the table next to Lieutenant Lasren's, and he'd kept the young man in his line of sight all evening. It was the counselor's job to read the guests he spoke with, but his would be a psychological analysis. Lasren had drawn the much shorter straw. For him to use his empathic abilities to "read" the guests required him to lower his mental discipline and actually *feel* what the other guests did. Cambridge did not envy him the task, as he had a pretty good idea of what Lasren would encounter.

Before the second appetizer course had been served, Lasren was looking a little pale. He politely moved the food around on his plate for the next two courses, but he did not eat a bite. Shortly after Commander Torres had excused herself from their table, Lasren rose and did the same. At first Cambridge thought he might be searching for the exit, and the counselor rose to follow. As it happened, Lasren simply sought the most secluded corner of the garden and, once he believed himself to be beyond notice, turned away from the crowd and took several deep breaths.

"Are you all right, Lieutenant?" Cambridge asked once he had reached the young man.

"Yes, sir," Lasren replied, turning back, tugging at his uniform jacket and squaring his shoulders.

"It doesn't take an empath, or even a trained counselor, to see that you're struggling, Lieutenant. I'm sure you've already picked up enough impressions for one evening. Clear your mind. Put up whatever mental barriers you customarily use to block the feelings of those around you, and keep them firmly in place for the rest of the night. You may consider that a direct order if it makes you feel better."

Lasren looked at Cambridge with wide black eyes.

"I don't know if I can, sir," he said.

"Why not?"

"It's so big."

Cambridge looked around the rooftop, noting the size of the crowd, and thought he understood.

"Too many people?" he asked.

"No, sir," Lasren replied, "too much of the same emotion. You could drown in it, it's so thick."

To the untrained eye, the only visible emotional state of the vast majority of guests was pleasure, with a healthy dose of self-satisfaction and a fair amount of condescension. But for any society founded on competition, driven by insatiable appetites for more and valuing success above all, their true emotional state was easy to guess.

"Fear?" Cambridge asked.

"Terror," Lasren replied.

Chapter Four

It should have been such a happy reunion. When Tom Paris had said good-bye to his mother just before the Full Circle Fleet had launched, he'd never expected to see her again. Had everything gone according to plan, once he and B'Elanna were reunited in the Delta Quadrant, he would have resigned his commission, departed *Voyager,* and begun a new life with his wife and daughter aboard the *Home Free,* the shuttle B'Elanna had designed for that purpose.

That hadn't happened. As Paris entered the mediation chamber behind Lieutenant Shaw and caught his first glimpse of his mother seated beside her lawyer, it occurred to him that had he and B'Elanna stuck to that plan, he might not be here now.

Since the day Miral had been released by the *qawHaq'hoch* over two years ago, every choice Tom Paris had made had been designed to do one thing: protect his daughter. While he'd almost lost his closest friends as a result, he'd never doubted himself or his chosen course. He didn't believe any parent in his place would have doubted him either.

He'd obviously been wrong.

The last time he'd been reunited with his mother, she'd thrown herself into his arms, weeping with joy, gratitude, and pride. Now she refused to meet his eyes, keeping hers glued on the bony hands clasped before her on the table that would divide them during the mediation.

He wanted so badly to go to her, to take her in his arms, and to whisper over and over that he was so very sorry. He wanted to sit beside her watching holos of Miral over the past few years, sharing the million unexpected things she had done during that time. He wanted to tell her what an extraordinary person her granddaughter was.

Instead, Paris moved to the chair opposite her and looked to Shaw, who nodded in his direction and gestured to the chair.

Moments later, an aide called the session to order. Everyone at the table rose as an ancient Tellarite appeared from an antechamber and took his place at the head of the table. He cleared his throat loudly, though the room was already silent as any grave.

"Good afternoon. I am Ozimat, and I have been assigned to mediate the issue now before us. Before we begin, I will make my role here clear for all of the participants.

"It is customary when questions of custody are brought before the Federation Family Court that mediation between the parties is offered as an alternative to trial. The claimant—Julia Paris—and the defendants—Lieutenant Commander Thomas Eugene Paris and Lieutenant Commander B'Elanna Torres—have agreed independently to this mediation regarding the matter of the dispensation of the natural-born issue of Commanders Paris and Torres, Miral Paris. Once both parties have entered into discussion, it is hoped that they will, with our assistance, reach a mutually satisfactory resolution. Should they fail to do so, I will weigh the testimony of both parties, the respective merits of their claims, and render a final decision, which will then be filed with the Family Court.

"By agreeing to this mediation, both parties waive their claim to any further action by the court. The final decision made here will not be subject to appeal.

"Do both parties understand everything I have just said?" Ozimat asked.

Shaw looked to Paris, who immediately said, "Yes, sir."

Julia followed briskly with, "I do, Your Honor."

Paris wondered if he had managed to err with his first words.

Shaw had told him that the mediator was a retired Starfleet admiral. His mother's address suggested he was also a retired judge. He wondered which title Ozimat preferred.

"Your Honor," Paris said, hedging his bets.

"Please be seated," Ozimat said, unimpressed.

Another long silence followed as everyone took their seats and Ozimat busied himself with the padd he'd carried with him into the chamber. "Before I invite Mrs. Paris to begin what I hope will be a productive conversation between herself and her son, I have a question for Commander Paris," Ozimat finally said.

Paris didn't know why this unnerved him immediately.

"Yes, Your Honor?" Shaw asked in Paris's stead.

"Good to see you again, Mister Shaw," Ozimat said, nodding in Shaw's direction but keeping his gaze fixed on Paris. "Commander Paris, where is your wife?"

Had the circumstances been less fraught, the congenial manner in which Ozimat inquired would have made Paris feel more at ease. Despite Ozimat's tone, Paris felt he was being invited to step into a trap.

Before Paris could respond, Shaw jumped in. "Your Honor, Commander Torres advised the court in writing of her decision to waive her right to appear at this session. You should have it in the preliminary filings. Both Commanders Paris and Torres are stationed with the Full Circle Fleet in the Delta Quadrant. It was determined that to deny the fleet two of its senior officers at this juncture would compromise its safety. Commander Torres has agreed to allow Commander Paris to speak in her place, and his testimony will be accepted as hers for the purposes of this proceeding."

For the first time, Julia's eyes met her son's and searched for the truth of Shaw's words. Paris knew she saw it on his face. B'Elanna was furious with Julia and determined that, no matter what outcome this mediation should reach, Miral would never be taken from her. This didn't seem to surprise Julia. If anything, it seemed to strengthen her resolve.

"I read the filing, Mister Shaw," Ozimat replied. "I was addressing Commander Paris."

Paris knew the absolute truth would not serve him well. He settled for the most acceptable version of it he could muster. "B'Elanna and I spoke at length about whether or not both of us should attend this session. We concluded that Miral has been subjected to more change in her short life than either of us believe to be ideal. For the last several months, she has thrived as her life has become more routine aboard *Voyager*. We didn't want to disrupt that again so soon."

This seemed to satisfy Ozimat. Paris breathed an internal sigh of relief.

"Very well. Your wife understands that her failure to appear does not give her the right to contest these proceedings?"

"She does, Your Honor."

"Mrs. Paris," Ozimat continued. "Were this a trial, you would address yourself to the judge or jury. It's not. The point of this mediation is for you and your son to attempt to resolve your differences. With that in mind, I ask you to open a dialogue now with your son toward that end."

"Thank you, Your Honor," Julia said stiffly. Shifting her gaze to Paris, she said, "I hope you know how seriously it grieves me to have been forced to make this claim."

Paris nodded automatically. Every instinct in his body cried out to make this as easy for his mother as possible.

"I was, as you know, devastated when you brought me word that B'Elanna and Miral had been killed during the Borg Invasion. My only thought was how to comfort you. During those dark days, I had never loved you more. I wanted to take your pain from you. Even given all I had lost, I was ready to assume your burden as well. It's what a mother does.

"When you wrote to me a few months ago to tell me that you had intentionally lied about this, I was beyond devastated. I realized that for you to be capable of such a betrayal, I must have long ago stopped understanding who you were. Many of the choices you have made in your life have been difficult to accept. Over the course of several years, you seemed to put your former indiscretions behind you, but due to circumstances beyond my control, I was unable to witness that transformation. When you returned from the Delta Quadrant as a Starfleet officer, a husband, and a father, and according to your captain having given exemplary service to your ship while it was lost, I hoped for the best. I believed that the experiences you had endured had allowed you to finally grow into the man I always knew you could be. I let my heart blind me to the truth."

"What truth?" Paris interjected.

"That you never changed," Julia said sadly. "As a young man, you sought to avoid the consequences of your choices by lying. You chose to abandon the principles your father and I tried to instill in you, the character we tried to help you build. You turned away from your Starfleet oath. The man I thought you had become could never have lied about his daughter's death; at least not to me. That you could, with such ease, tells me everything I never wished to know. I don't believe you would intentionally raise Miral to follow the path you have walked. But your choices clearly indicate that you are incapable of doing otherwise. You can only teach her what you know. Her character, her future, her safety is threatened by your presence in her life.

"Granted, I do not know B'Elanna as well as I would like. There has not been time for us to become acquainted. You both lied to your father and me when you told us your marriage had ended and you were separated. Your letter indicated that it was her decision to stage her death and Miral's, but that you agreed with it. As best I can tell, she is no more suited to raise Miral than you are.

"That's why I have made this request, and I ask you to not make this more difficult on us than it has to be. You know I love Miral, as I love you and your sisters. You know I want only the best for her. There's nothing you can say now that will change my feelings. If you cannot agree to my request, I'm afraid we will have to leave it to His Honor to decide what will best serve Miral's interests."

Paris couldn't say for sure at what point during this recitation his compassion for his mother had vanished, but by the time she had finished, it was gone.

"Wow," he began.

"Commander Paris?" Ozimat asked.

"I'm sorry, Your Honor," Paris replied. "It's just hard to know where to begin."

"Tom," Shaw said softly.

"Before I was a parent, I never understood why you stood by me when everyone else in my life had decided I wasn't worth it," Paris said. "I didn't know the depth of love that existed between a father and his child; possibly because my own father was incredibly good at hiding that love from me."

Julia blanched. Paris didn't care. She'd had her say. Now it was his turn.

"The mistake I made as a cadet was lying about my actions. I lied because I thought that, by doing so, I could spare myself some of the pain I had caused. It's true that I have lied since then. But *lying* is not the issue. The question is *why*. I lied about my separation from B'Elanna and about their deaths to save Miral's life. In doing so, I took unimagined pain onto myself. I saw it in you and Dad. I *lived* it every day I was separated from my wife and daughter. But I did it because it was the only way I could be sure that Miral would survive.

"I came here today to tell you that I'm sorry, Mom. I'm sorry for the pain I had to put you through. But the choices I made are not evidence that I am an unfit parent. They are evidence of the lengths I am willing to go to protect my child."

"You make it sound like you had no other choice, Tom," Julia said.

"I didn't," Paris insisted.

"Of course you did. You serve among men and women who are tasked with protecting every Federation citizen from harm. Had you told them, had you told *us*, the nature of the threat you perceived to Miral's life, we would have taken all of you in and willingly died to protect Miral, should it have come to that, just as your crew did when you finally were forced to reveal your deception," Julia said. "You lied to us because it was the path of least resistance. You ran toward that path, just as you always have. That is a path Miral must never learn to be comfortable walking."

"The Warriors of *Gre'thor* have dedicated their lives for thousands of years to a single task: They were going to find Miral and kill her. They escaped from the chancellor of the Klingon Empire. You think *you* were a threat to them?" Paris said. "Yes, I wanted Miral safe, but I didn't want to purchase her safety with the deaths of my family and friends. My concern, *our concern*, as B'Elanna and I executed this plan, was to protect those we hold dear, especially you, Mom."

"But you didn't protect us," Julia said. "You simply substituted one potential pain for another definite one."

"How did you feel when you learned Miral was still alive?" Paris asked.

Julia paused to consider the question.

"Were you even a little bit happy?"

"Of course I was."

"Then what are we doing here?"

"That Miral has survived this long with you and B'Elanna as parents is the only blessing the universe has bestowed on any of us thus far," Julia replied. "The time has come, however, to secure her future."

"What do you think B'Elanna and I are trying to do?"

"I haven't had a clue since I received that letter."

Paris sat back in his chair. His mother had begun by saying she no longer knew who he was. He could now say the same.

"Hello, Annika."

Seven turned from the view she had been studying: a large, furnished patio teeming with botanical life accessible to several other adjoining quarters.

Standing before her, at long last in the flesh, was a man she had only ever known in dreams.

"Axum," she said softly.

He hesitated to bridge the distance between them too quickly. For both, this was as much a first meeting as a reunion. In two separate incarnations they had shared every aspect of their physical selves with one another. But they had never touched in the real world.

Seven's recent dreams and the Doctor's reports of Axum's injuries had prepared her for the worst. For almost four years, Axum had lived as a Borg drone while still retaining his memories of his identity before he had been assimilated. That had been the mixed blessing granted by the destruction of Unimatrix Zero. Axum had escaped the Collective only to endure months of torment by the Borg queen. Driven to madness, he had tried to remove his Borg implants with what remained of his hands. The Caeliar transformation had saved what survived that process. It had been Seven's catoms, provided by the Doctor as a therapy of last resort, that had brought him back to the world of the living.

The scars were still visible. But they were considerably less striking than she had expected. Some of the worst were now all but hidden by newly grown, sandy brown hair. A deep gash where he had removed an auditory implant ran in front of his left ear and down the side of his neck. To her surprise, Seven saw two hands lifted to take hers as he stepped closer. The Doctor had indicated that Axum had lost all but the thumb of his left hand. Obviously it had been replaced by a prosthetic in the last few months.

The only scars that really troubled Seven were those his mind and spirit had suffered. Though his eyes spoke of unrestrained joy in seeing her, the pain Axum had endured to find her lurked behind them.

Seven did not bother taking his hands in hers. She simply opened her arms as he half fell into her. Her strength held both of them upright as his gentle embrace became more intent. It might have been hours that they stood like that before they finally parted to look again into each other's eyes.

"Where are we?" Seven asked, to break the tension.

Axum stood on his own feet, but he still held Seven by both arms. "I live here now," he replied.

Seven pulled back, allowing him to retain their physical connection by holding her hand as she examined his quarters. The room was spacious and equipped as any standard Starfleet apartment. The large patio was a pleasant surprise, but, given how many officers working in this classified division must call it home, it seemed an appropriate luxury. The light outside was dimming, but Seven imagined that the access to open space was a welcome respite from the duties of the officers' days. Three recessed doorways were spaced almost evenly along the walls. A replicator was tucked into a corner and likely was restricted in its uses.

"I expected to find you in a holding cell," Seven said honestly.

Axum nodded his understanding. "I expected the same when they transferred me from Starbase 185."

Seven turned back to Axum and searched his eyes. "I don't understand," she said. "The last time I saw through your eyes, you were suffering horrible torments. I assumed you were in distress."

"Just because it's comfortable doesn't make it any less a cell," Axum said. "But as to suffering, I'm afraid I don't understand. Ever since your catoms were joined with mine, I have been treated with care and respect. No one has hurt me, physically."

"Mentally?" Seven asked.

"I did not know until today that you were coming. My only fear, my only torment, has been wondering if I would ever see you again."

Seven released his hand and moved toward the patio. What Axum had said appeared to be true, but her memories of his torture remained fresh.

"For several weeks, after the infusion of my catoms, I dreamed of you," Seven said. "We shared those dreams, did we not?"

"We did," Axum replied, smiling faintly at the pleasant memory.

"But I saw you at the mercy of a group of people who were studying you, or subjecting you to some sort of painful treatment. There was a tub of ice-cold water." It still chilled her to remember it.

Axum was baffled. "I'm sorry, Annika. I don't know what that was. Maybe a nightmare I don't remember. But I promise you, ever since I arrived here, I have been provided with everything I need to live . . . except you."

"I had to terminate our contact," Seven admitted, feeling a strange new shame. "My fear for you made it impossible for me to function."

"I know," Axum said. "It was difficult at first. I could still sense you. But there was a wall between us."

"A neural inhibitor," she explained.

"I tried many times to breach that wall, but I never succeeded. I was forced to wait and hope that you would come to me. I knew Starfleet Medical would never release me to search for you."

"Have they told you of the plague they are fighting?" Seven asked.

"They have," Axum replied. "They took samples of my catoms when I arrived. I attempted to resist, but when they explained the nature of the threat, I agreed."

"As did I," Seven said.

"I don't really understand what happened between your people, the Borg and the Caeliar. I have read the reports they provided, and Doctor Glenn tried to explain, but none of them have told me what I need to know."

"What is that?"

"Are we, *am I*, because I was once Borg, still considered a Federation enemy?"

Seven sighed. It was a complicated question.

"The Borg invaded the Alpha Quadrant. They killed sixty-three billion people before the Caeliar intervened. It was believed at that time that all Borg, other than me, had become part of the Caeliar gestalt and departed our galaxy."

"I've always known you were special, Annika," Axum teased. "But the *only* one?"

Seven felt heat rise to her cheeks. "The fleet I now serve was dispatched to the Delta Quadrant to confirm that theory. Since then, we have learned that very few former Borg chose to remain outside the gestalt."

"How many others?"

"I know of thirty-four. They had been severed from the hive mind for many years and formed their own unique cooperative. During that time, they procreated. Thirteen children were born. Their parents did not accept the Caeliar's invitation because it could not be extended to their offspring."

"Thirty-five now, including me," Axum noted.

"Yes," Seven said, nodding. "And given how many once inhabited Unimatrix Zero, I suppose there could be more like you."

"I doubt it," Axum said.

"Why?"

"Perhaps the desire to join the Caeliar was not as strong for you. But even in my condition at the time, I could barely refuse. It was an end to so much suffering. But I couldn't find you there. I didn't want to be there without you."

Seven smiled sadly. She could not say the same. Her sense of self, her cherished individuality, had kept her outside the gestalt. A million things had run through her mind at that moment, but Axum had not been one of them.

"I believe that had this plague never arisen, you would have been treated differently when you were found. Obviously, you would have been questioned and perhaps studied, as I was after the transformation. But once that was done, you would have been allowed to live here on Earth, or perhaps returned to your homeworld in the Delta Quadrant."

"Mysstren no longer exists," Axum said. "It was completely assimilated. There is no home for me to return to now."

"You would have been an object of some curiosity, as I am," Seven continued. "But you would not have been held against your will, as you have been. That is the result of the plague. I have come to assist those trying to cure it and, by doing so, secure your freedom as well."

Axum considered her thoughtfully.

"And when you have done so, will you still be part of my freedom?" he asked.

"Always," Seven replied. "But I do not wish to speculate about a future that is not yet realized."

Axum appeared disconcerted by her response, but he said nothing.

"I've been told this research group has a commanding officer. I need to speak with him at once. My first priority was to see you, but now that I am assured of your well-being, I must direct my efforts where they are needed most."

A sad smile returned to Axum's lips. "One does not demand to see the Commander," he said. "Should your presence be required, he will ask to see you, and only when he is good and ready."

"That is unacceptable," Seven said, moving toward the door she believed was the room's exit.

"That's the 'fresher," Axum cautioned her.

"Oh," Seven said.

"Before you go, there's something I'd like to show you," Axum continued.

"What?"

Axum moved to the door situated between the replicator and the sofa and motioned for her to follow. Beyond it was another large room, this one filled with long tables, data panels, and diagnostic tools. It was, to all intents and purposes, a fully equipped science lab.

"They provided this to you for your personal use?" Seven asked, genuinely surprised.

"I have been given everything I have requested," Axum assured her. "It didn't take long for me to grow restless here. There was always the chance that you would not be able to rescue me this time. What I need to know, the Commander and his team could not tell me. It also happens that what I need to know, *they need to know.*"

"What is that?" Seven asked.

"We are now rare hybrid life-forms, Annika. We retain the organic components of our respective species, but those components are now sustained by catoms. Do you know what catoms are?"

"Programmable matter," Seven replied. "Down to the subatomic level, they mimic organic matter and integrate seamlessly with it to perform vital functions once maintained by our Borg implants."

"Do you believe that these catoms could have caused this plague you seek to cure?"

"I have my doubts," Seven replied. "I need to see samples of the mutation. The Doctor, *Voyager*'s former emergency medical hologram, has seen some of the applicable research and is convinced that catoms could not have caused illness in other humanoids. He was also able to visualize individual catoms. He discovered a unique synthetic tag. I believe I can build on his work to hasten that of this *Commander*."

"I honestly don't care if catoms caused the plague or not," Axum said. "You'll forgive my lack of interest. I know you think of these people as your family. I know how dear they are to you. But they have yet to earn my regard.

"However, I want to understand exactly what the Caeliar did to us. What are catoms? What can they do? What are they meant to do? What am I, now that I can no longer live without them?"

"Have you made any progress?" Seven asked.

"Yes," Axum replied. "I'd like to show you what I've learned."

"Proceed," Seven said.

Several times a day, the Commander left his private sanctuary to walk the halls. His visible presence comforted and reassured his team. Few addressed him unless they had a new development to share. But his *presence* was essential. It reminded each of them that they were one, and dedicated to the same purpose.

These short breaks also cleared the Commander's mind. He found himself visualizing new possibilities as he walked, breakthroughs that often eluded him at his data terminal.

Thus far he had found seventy-six access nodes on the catoms he had extracted from Patient C-1. To call them conduits or programming interfaces was going too far. They were more like semipermeable cell walls. They were capable of allowing certain information to pass through barriers that were otherwise solid. The Commander believed that they were the key to unlocking a catom; that if he could learn the programming language, or write a new one the catoms would accept, he could begin to direct their activities.

He had failed seventy-six times. But that did not mean that the next time would be the same. He had only just begun his studies of the newly extracted catoms from Seven of Nine.

The Commander paused before a large data panel. Behind that wall, muffled but mortifying cries could be heard. In a normal lab, the therapy room beyond would have possessed a window through which consulting physicians could view the activities within. The object of his team's inquiry made that a security hazard.

Not caring to see, but sensate that he *should,* the Commander activated the data panel, and immediately the room's interior became visible through high-resolution data imaging. Six of his officers, all dressed in biohazard suits, attended their patient. He had arrived from Ardana that morning and his treatment had begun immediately.

Several long tubes snaked over his body, some distributing life-sustaining fluids, others draining away those that were already tainted. The patient's screams were silenced on the playback, but the Commander could hear muffled versions of them anyway.

A subscreen on the panel indicated current vital signs. A glance told him what the next course of action would be.

The Commander deactivated the screen and continued his walk. He tried not to think about the "tank." It was medicine at its crudest. But it might be the only thing that would buy the poor man a little more time.

The Commander's pace quickened. With each day that passed, his certainty grew stronger.

I am running out of time.

Ensign J'Ohans had been invited to join the Commander's team nine months earlier. It was an honor she had never dared dream would come to pass. Like a few other team members, she had been "Ensign" while on duty. She could claim several different areas of relevant scientific expertise, but none of them had been noteworthy enough among her illustrious peers to demand a more specific designation.

Today, that had changed. At the morning's briefing, the Commander had addressed her as "Liaison." Her feet had barely touched the ground since then.

Her assignment had been challenging but certainly not beyond her abilities. It had not occurred to her to question the research. If the Commander deemed it necessary, it was.

Liaison keyed her authorization commands into the terminal and, as expected, the new files she required were present. She opened the first and listened intently as Seven of Nine began to address her Academy students. The recording was several years out of date. Her more recent, and certainly more relevant, personal logs were also present and would be accessed soon enough.

Doctor Sharak sat at his new workstation. The screen before him displayed the history, in statistical form, of the catomic plague.

It made for disheartening reading. Sharak had held out hope that the severity of the threat might have been exaggerated. That was clearly not the case.

Since Miss Seven had departed, he had applied himself diligently to his new studies. So concentrated were his efforts that he jumped when a light hand came to rest on his shoulder.

"I'm sorry, Doctor Sharak," Frist said. "I did not mean to startle you."

"No apology is necessary," he assured her.

"Do you need anything?" she asked.

"No."

Frist appeared ready to move on but, after a second thought, said, "You know, all of us have dedicated most of our waking hours to this project for the last several months. I admire your diligence, but you aren't going to solve this alone tonight."

"*Tonight?*" Sharak asked. Looking beyond Frist, he realized that most of the stations around him were empty and dimmed.

"It's been almost nine hours since you began," Frist said with a faint smile of understanding.

Sharak sighed. He had lost track of the time.

More important, Miss Seven had not made contact with him for nine hours.

Frist seemed to read his mind. "It is my understanding that Seven and Axum shared a deep personal bond with one another. Their story is rather tragic, but at least now, a new chapter might begin for them. Should our efforts here succeed, there is no telling what the future might hold for them. There is a lot to discuss. I would not take her lack of responsiveness to heart."

"Miss Seven will . . ." Sharak began, and as he did so, a flashing light on his terminal indicated an incoming transmission.

"I'll leave you to it," Frist said, her smile widening. "But afterwards, go home. Get some rest. We'll still be here tomorrow."

As soon as Sharak was certain Frist had departed, he opened the terminal's comm channel. Seven's face filled the screen.

"Miss Seven, are you well?" he asked immediately.

"*I am. Thank you, Doctor,*" Seven replied.

"You have seen Axum?"

"*Yes. He is unharmed.*"

Sharak paused as the screen distorted for a few seconds. When it settled he said, "I take it your worst fears have not been confirmed?"

Seven shook her head and looked away. When their eyes met again she said, "*Fear is irrelevant. I have a great deal of work to do. I have already begun.*"

"Good," Sharak said, unable to adequately express his relief. "I waited to hear from you."

"*That will not be necessary in the future,*" she assured him. "*I will contact you again when I have information worth reporting.*"

Sharak was taken aback.

"I would prefer to hear from you daily," he said.

The faintest of smiles crossed Seven's lips. *"I will comply,"* she said.

Her image distorted again. When it returned to normal Sharak asked, "Are you experiencing a technical malfunction at your end?"

"I have been advised that the internal power systems of the secured area have been difficult to regulate. I will ask one of the technicians to address it in the morning."

"I will speak with you again tomorrow," Sharak said, his tone indicating that he would brook no refusal.

"Good night, Doctor," Seven said.

The channel closed, Sharak rested his back against the chair. It had been a long day for both of them. Clearly, she was exhausted and perhaps concerned about discussing anything in detail over what was likely a monitored comm line. Nothing could be done about that for now.

Still, he was pleased his patience had been rewarded; as had hers, apparently.

Certain liberties were granted to Academy cadets in their final year of studies. Icheb was grateful that one of them was to remain off-campus for extended periods of time, as long as a cadet could justify the absence. Icheb suspected that his academic advisor, Commander Treadon, would appreciate his desire to overachieve in his new internship posting with Starfleet Medical. She would see it as part of a positive pattern of behavior in her advisee.

But if Icheb remained outside the building much longer, even Treadon was going to question his actions.

He had paced the hedge that lined the main entrance's south side for over two hours. Most of the time he assumed he had gone unnoticed, as many of the officers assigned there were leaving while others arrived for the next duty shift. An hour before, traffic had slowed to a trickle. Icheb had found a quiet spot to sit that kept the entrance in his line of sight. He had studied a padd he brought for just such a necessity. But he had been unable to apply himself to anything other than watching the entrance. The pacing resumed.

Finally, the man he sought exited the building. He moved slowly, as if wearied by the day.

Icheb immediately moved to block his path. "Doctor Sharak?" he said.

Sharak halted. "Yes, Cadet?" he finally said.

"Perhaps you do not remember me. We met briefly a few months ago. I am Icheb, Seven's friend."

Sharak nodded solemnly. "I do, Cadet. It is unexpected to see you here."

"I knew you and Seven were arriving today. She sent me a message while you were still en route. I hoped to see her."

"I'm afraid that will not be possible," Sharak said. "Miss Seven has entered a quarantine area within the complex and will remain there until her work is complete."

"A quarantine area?" Icheb asked.

"Yes. I just spoke with her. She is fine."

"Is she ill?" Icheb asked.

"No. She is working to help the other doctors there cure an illness."

Icheb nodded. "Admiral Janeway told me that she had recommended that I be assigned to Starfleet Medical for my internship. I believe she intended for me to be near should Seven need me."

Sharak might have smiled. His Tamarian visage made it hard for Icheb to tell. "While we are here, I am responsible for Miss Seven's well-being. You should pursue your work here diligently, but do not trouble yourself on her behalf. She is fine, and should that situation change, I will inform those in a position to best assist her."

Icheb wanted to feel relief. He couldn't. Seven was one of the few people in the universe he thought of as family. Admiral Janeway obviously believed Icheb's presence here was warranted. Doctor Sharak seemed confident but he could not know Seven very well.

"Can you ask her to contact me?" Icheb requested.

"I can, and I will. I cannot promise you that she will comply. It is apparently going to be challenging for her to report to me daily. But I will make the effort. In the meantime, I will tell you what I am sure she would tell you if she were here."

"Yes, sir?"

"Attend to your studies. They should be your only concern."

"Understood, sir," Icheb said. "Good night."

Sharak nodded.

Icheb made haste to the nearest transporter station. He had hoped seeing Sharak would assuage his fears. Now he knew that the only relief he would feel would come from seeing Seven for himself.

Chapter Five

The Doctor stared at the four largest system storage blocks resourced to *Voyager*'s sickbay by the main computer. It was not his area of expertise, but his time spent assisting Lieutenant Reg Barclay and Doctor Zimmerman with the design of the *Galen* had not been entirely wasted.

There were over two thousand diagnostic subroutines he had created specifically for the *Galen*. Most of them were unique to his sickbay. Looking around *Voyager*'s, which had been refitted prior to the fleet's launch and certainly improved in many ways since his time there, he could only see all that it lacked.

Given the necessity of Doctor Sharak's departure, the Doctor had not resisted temporary reassignment to *Voyager*. He had already grown accustomed to the *Galen,* and he certainly preferred it, but he had hoped to discover a familiar and comforting sense of reunion with his former sickbay.

Instead, he found its lack of suitability for the project he now intended to pursue most frustrating. When he considered that *he*, rather than Sharak, should have accompanied Seven back to Starfleet Medical, his frustration briefly reached levels near seething. Once this had passed, he reminded himself that as little as Doctors Frist and Everett seemed to respect him, this feeling was multiplied several times over when he considered them. Should he have been forced to work by their side for an extended period of time, he doubted this opinion would have improved. Admiral Janeway had managed to secure copies of their latest research.

It would be out of date by now, but not unmanageably so. He actually preferred to follow his own original line of inquiry, rather than be unduly influenced by the many useless paths the "best minds in the Federation" were pursuing.

He would be well under way, were *Voyager*'s databanks free to hold all of the programs he required.

Barclay had provided him with copies of many of the essential programs. The Doctor had selected the destination for them and was ready to install them when the computer automatically began to sound warnings.

He silenced it and requested that ops open a channel for him to the *Galen*.

Barclay looked weary when his face appeared on the Doctor's private data screen. But that had been the case for several months. Given that Commander Glenn was likely still on the planet's surface—*Voyager*'s officers had yet to return from the ceremony—he doubted Barclay would have gone to sleep yet.

"*What time is it?*" Barclay asked.

"Late," the Doctor replied. "Am I disturbing you?"

"*No,*" Barclay said, then sighed. Clearly his mind was elsewhere.

"Would it be possible for you to transport over for a few minutes?" the Doctor asked. "I'm having difficulty installing some of the programs you sent."

"*Has the restriction on transporter use been lifted?*" Barclay asked.

"No," the Doctor said, remembering the unusual prohibition as soon as Barclay mentioned it.

Barclay stared at him intently for a moment.

"*Give me a minute,*" Barclay said, and he terminated the transmission. When he returned he said, "*I can't. No shuttle traffic is permitted in orbit until our officers return from the surface.*"

"According to whom?"

"*Lieutenant Patel, who has your bridge right now.*"

"Did you tell her it is an emergency?"

"*No.*"

"Why not?"

"*Because it isn't.*"

"Reg, until the programs I require are integrated into this sickbay, it is impossible for me to begin my work."

Barclay sighed again. "*I've already put in a request to come over as soon as it is permitted. Our officers are scheduled to return shortly.*"

"And what am I supposed to do until then?"

"*Run a self-diagnostic,*" Barclay replied.

"Why would I do that?" the Doctor asked.

"*Because it will save me the time of running it when I get there. I don't know how long we'll have. There are already rumors that our ships will be separating as early as tomorrow.*"

"You performed a level-ten diagnostic a few months ago. You said I was functioning within normal parameters," the Doctor insisted.

"*You just forgot that we are not permitted to use our transporters. That order has been in effect since we arrived in Confederacy space.*"

"I have a lot on my mind," the Doctor said.

"*You don't 'forget' orders, Doctor,*" Barclay said. "*You can't. Except just now, you did.*"

"I misspoke."

"*You can't do that either.*"

"Obviously, I can."

"*Doctor?*"

"I'm sorry," the Doctor said. "I'll run the diagnostic."

"*I'll be there as soon as I can.*"

"Thank you, Reg."

When Barclay's face vanished from the screen, the Doctor initiated the diagnostic. To his relief, it showed no loss of function or program corruption.

Satisfied with the results, he began to prioritize the *real work* to be done when Barclay arrived.

VESTA

Lieutenant Julian Psilakis, *Vesta*'s third officer and bridge commander for gamma shift, intended only to step briefly into the captain's ready room to collect a few reports Roach had left for him at shift change. All had been quiet at the start of gamma shift, and he assumed it would remain so now that his captain and the admiral had returned from the celebration.

Psilakis was surprised to find Captain Farkas sitting at her desk when he entered. He knew her shuttle had docked a few minutes before, but he assumed she would go straight to her quarters. She had to be exhausted.

The look on her face confirmed that suspicion.

"Captain," he greeted her immediately.

"Anything to report, Lieutenant?" she asked.

"All systems are nominal. Gamma shift is under way."

"You could just say, 'no,' Psilakis," Farkas reproached him gently.

"Yes, Captain," Psilakis said. "I'll return to the bridge. Unless there's anything you need?"

"A time machine?" Farkas teased. "No. Scratch that. Never a good idea."

"Was the celebration not what you had hoped for?" Psilakis ventured.

"It was a good party," she allowed. "Lost my appetite early in the evening, but they'd already served us three meals worth of calories so I'm still stuffed."

"Was the food not to your liking?"

"Most of it was delicious," she replied.

"Why did you lose your appetite?"

"The company, mostly."

"You were not impressed?"

"Oh, I was," she corrected him, "just not in a good way."

"Captain?"

"They put on a great show, and a lovely dinner. Whoever designs their clothing made out like a bandit tonight. But scratch a little beneath that glittering surface and there are a lot of troubling realities that disturb digestion."

"Do you believe the admiral will continue to pursue diplomatic relations?"

"I do. I would if I were her. We don't have to love every single thing about another civilization to make diplomatic overtures. There's a case to be made that *especially* when there are so many differences between two cultures, diplomacy is essential to avoiding pointless conflicts."

"Agreed," Psilakis said.

Farkas motioned Psilakis closer and turned her viewer so that he could see the image she had been studying: an alien armada grouped around the Gateway that led to the Confederacy.

"They seem to have a lot of enemies, don't they?" Farkas observed.

"So does the Federation."

"*Touché*," Farkas said. "And in this case, against some pretty staggering odds, it appears that some of the Confederacy's enemies were once ours as well: the Turei, the Vaadwaur, and the Devore," Farkas said, sighing. "On paper, the Turei and Vaadwaur don't bury centuries of enmity in a few years, nor do they make new friends with the Devore—a vast Imperium, to be sure, but one located tens of thousands of light-years from Turei space. Yet here they are, sitting at the front door to a Gateway leading directly to the Confederacy's First World, and right now, the only thing preventing them from entering is superior firepower on the Confederacy's part."

"Do you believe that will change?"

"Given enough time, it usually does."

"You don't want to see the Federation make an alliance if it means that, as a result, we'll soon find ourselves in the middle of someone else's war?"

"That's part of it," Farkas agreed.

"What's the rest?"

"I don't know if our fleet is ready to take on an allied force comprised largely of alien races predisposed to hate us. I didn't want that time machine so I could go back and get out of attending tonight's dinner. I wanted it so I could spend some time with *Voyager* during their first mission out here," Farkas said.

"As her captain?" Psilakis asked.

"No, thank you," Farkas replied. "As a fly on the wall."

"Why?"

"The logs indicate a number of successful diplomatic exchanges, but it sure seems like they managed to piss off more species than they befriended."

"Given the circumstances . . ." Psilakis began.

"I'm not judging them, Lieutenant," Farkas interjected. "I wouldn't wish their fate on an enemy, let alone a fellow officer, and by all rights they should never have made it home in one piece. But their choices have resulted in massive alterations to this quadrant. The Voth originated tens of thousands of light-years from our communications relays, but clearly, upon learning the Federation was back in the Delta Quadrant, they decided it was worth the trip to try and hamstring our efforts. The Vaadwaur should still be asleep beneath their planet's surface, but thanks to *Voyager* they are now alive and well. *Voyager* barely escaped destruction at the hands of the none-too-pleasant Turei when Admiral Janeway successfully pitted them against the Vaadwaur. The Devore are my favorite, though. Have you read the admiral's reports of that encounter?"

"No," Psilakis admitted.

"*Voyager* was granted safe passage—if you call being boarded and searched every five minutes 'safe'—through Devore space, so long as they offered no assistance to any telepathic individuals they encountered on the way. Apparently the Devore really don't like telepaths."

"Why not?"

"How should I know? My PS-scale readings don't even register," Farkas said, smiling. "Obviously Janeway's telepathic crew members are an exception. She had to hide them. But she also intentionally took on telepathic refugees, at their risk and hers, and engaged in a long game of cat and mouse with the Devore's chief inspector to save them. It was the right thing to do. We don't ignore distress calls, like the one *Voyager* received from those telepaths. But we also keep our word. I can't decide if Janeway didn't care, or cared too much."

"Either way, I'm guessing she didn't make a friend of the Devore," Psilakis said.

"Nope," Farkas agreed. "And they're one of the bigger guns out there on the Confederacy's front porch. But here's my question: Have they come to the Gateway for their own reasons, or did they somehow follow *Voyager*'s trail when she came out here to investigate the wave forms a few months ago? And how much of this would be happening if Admiral Janeway had made different choices the first time around?"

"Would you like me to take a closer look at those logs?" Psilakis asked.

"I would," Farkas replied. "I'm going to do the same."

"Tonight? Due respect, Captain, you need your rest."

"Your concern is noted, Lieutenant. Now get back to the bridge before my chair gets cold," she added, dismissing him.

Captain Chakotay had made his way to the admiral's quarters at her request as discreetly as possible. It wasn't a violation of duty or protocol for him to meet with the fleet's commander, even this late in the evening. No one he passed in the halls en route would have given his presence a second thought. But Starfleet Command had ordered Kathryn to keep quarters aboard the *Vesta* when she was reinstated, and Chakotay hoped that most of *Vesta*'s junior officers didn't know the reason why.

He didn't bother with the chime. He had left the admiral in the shuttlebay and knew she would be along momentarily. He was shocked when he entered, however, to find Counselor Hugh Cambridge waiting, nightcap in hand, in a chair before the admiral's desk.

"Captain," Cambridge greeted him, lifting his glass.

"Does the admiral know you are here?" Chakotay asked. He was accustomed to Cambridge's routine flouting of propriety, but Kathryn would never allow it.

"The admiral asked me to let myself in and wait here for her," Cambridge replied. "I didn't ask about using the replicator, though. Do you think she'll mind?"

"No," Chakotay replied. "How did the evening go for you, Counselor?" he asked, taking the seat next to him.

"Do you think there is even a word in Djinari-odt for *subtle*?" Cambridge asked.

"It was quite a spectacle," Chakotay agreed.

"The admiral said the formal debriefing could wait until the morning," Cambridge said. "But here you are."

"I know you don't have a problem with that," Chakotay said, wondering at the faint contempt he was reading from the counselor.

"Of course not. You're grown-ups. You're entitled to do what you like with your off hours."

Chakotay stared at the counselor. He could have used some wise counsel regarding the challenges he and Kathryn were facing communicating with one another right now. But something in Hugh's demeanor silenced those questions.

"How are you adjusting to Seven's departure?" Chakotay asked instead.

"Better than I'd expected," Cambridge replied.

Chakotay found this hard to believe. "As soon as she's given Starfleet Medical what help she can, she'll be back."

"Please don't lie to me or, worse, yourself," Cambridge retorted. "She's never coming back."

"Of course she is," Chakotay said, stunned.

"You sent her off alone to become guinea pig two of two," Cambridge said.

"Doctor Sharak is with her and Tom Paris is near at hand."

"How is it possible you are still that naive?"

"Gentlemen," the admiral's voice cut through the tension. Chakotay and Cambridge both rose to face her.

"Admiral," Chakotay greeted her.

"What did you wish to speak with me about, Counselor?" Janeway asked.

"I wanted to make sure you were aware that Lieutenant Lasren barely survived the party tonight," Cambridge replied. "I'm sure you're going to want him by your side as you begin negotiations, but you need to know how hard it is on him to use his empathic abilities with the Leodt and Djinari."

"Thank you, Counselor," Janeway said. "Did the lieutenant say why?"

"There is a tangible terror that lives just beneath the surface of the Confederacy's elite," Cambridge said.

"Fear of those on the outside and what might happen if they breach the Gateway?" Janeway asked.

"Fear that everyone around them is doing better than they are. Fear that they'll never accumulate enough to keep the wolf from their door," Cambridge corrected her.

"The wolf?"

"The Market Consortium. Surely you've realized by now that they run this civilization."

"I only spoke with a few of them tonight, but certainly more of their representatives than the presider's advisors," Janeway said.

"These people are hungry, but they are only permitted to eat what they kill. They have success but no real security. It's a tough way to live."

"Chakotay," Janeway said, "I'd like to have the counselor transferred to my team for the next few weeks. Can *Voyager* do without him?"

"We'll muddle through," Chakotay assured her.

"Excellent. I'll see you in the morning, Counselor."

"Good night, Admiral, Captain," Cambridge said, raising his glass to both of them as he departed with it still in his hand.

As soon as he had gone, Janeway moved to the room's sitting area, two small sofas separated by a table, and motioned for Chakotay to join her. When they were both settled, she put her feet up and asked, "Is he a little more surly than usual?"

Chakotay nodded. "He's worried about Seven."

Janeway tipped her head back and rolled her neck gently from side to side. "He's not the only one."

"Hugh and Seven began a relationship a few months ago."

"I thought he was her counselor."

"He was. Now he's more. He thinks she won't come back once she is reunited with Axum."

Janeway seemed to consider this. "I don't think that's likely."

"You don't have as much to lose as he does if you're wrong."

"That's not true either. I'm already missing her perspective and it's only been a few weeks."

"How are you doing otherwise?" Chakotay asked.

Janeway inhaled deeply and released the breath slowly.

"That well?"

"I'm trying to keep an open mind," she said.

"Part of the job, right?"

Janeway shrugged. "I suppose. But if we'd made this contact when we were out here the first time, we'd already have resumed our course for home by now."

"You think so?"

"Presider Cin is a lovely person. I think she genuinely cares for her people. But I have a feeling that the differences between us go a lot deeper than economics or technology."

"The same can be said of many Federation members and allies."

"True," Janeway said. "They control more space than any group in the Delta Quadrant we've encountered aside from the Borg. They're civilized, technologically advanced, have a stable, representative government; in theory they're an ideal ally for us."

"Is Command pushing you to form this alliance?"

"They could use some good news. It would also ensure the fleet's position. But I won't make a deal with the devil."

Chakotay smiled at a memory. "I thought those were sort of your specialty."

Janeway punched him playfully. She then moved closer and settled herself beneath his arm. "Who did you talk to tonight?"

"I'll tell you in the morning at the briefing," Chakotay replied.

Janeway crooked her neck to look at him. "Do I need to remind you that I'm your commanding officer?"

"Only if you plan on spending the rest of the night letting your pips keep you warm."

She smiled, and Chakotay felt the last of the tension he'd been holding begin to vanish.

"I missed you so much," she said.

"I missed you too, Kathryn."

She moved her face closer, and for a moment, he considered forgetting the last few weeks.

But only for a moment.

"We haven't gotten off to a great start since you've been back," he reminded her.

"No," she agreed. "But we've always managed to work through our differences in the past."

"If I'm remembering the same timeline you are, most of those differences were resolved by you doing whatever you thought best. If I happened to agree, there was less conversation."

Janeway's back stiffened visibly. "Do you think this is a bad idea?" she asked.

"Nope," he replied. "I just think we both need to agree about how this is going to work going forward."

"I have always respected you and your opinions," Janeway insisted.

"As have I yours," Chakotay replied. "And as the officer in command of this fleet, I understand that sometimes you are going to have to make tough calls. But we're more than fellow officers now. There's no way to take it back, no matter how it might complicate our working relationship."

"I have no intention of taking it back."

"Then we have to be on the same page."

"What does that mean?"

"You need to tell me what happened to you in the last three months. You've changed, Kathryn. I sense you're more at peace, but I don't know how you got there. And I also need to know that when things get tough, you're not going to retreat behind your rank."

Janeway stared at him, a faint smile playing over her lips.

"You've changed too," she said.

"I guess I have. I know now that here, by your side, is the only place I ever want to be. And as long as you want the same thing, I'm going to do whatever it takes to make sure we don't mess this up. We both deserve as much happiness as the universe will grant us."

"What do you need from me that you don't already have?"

"Your trust. That's always going to be more important to me than your respect."

Janeway nodded. "Okay."

"So tell me about Earth."

For the next few hours, they talked.

She told what she'd learned of Admiral Montgomery and how close he'd come to ending the fleet's mission in the Delta Quadrant. She told him of her newfound confidence in Admiral Akaar's judgment but noted the scrutiny under which every move they made would be reviewed. She told him about the many happy hours she'd spent with her mother, and of her sister's disappointment in her choice to return to duty. She spoke of the time she'd spent with Counselor Austen and all she'd learned of letting go.

Finally, she told him that, through it all, she had never doubted the promise of their future together, knowing that whatever came to pass, they were meant to be with one another.

They found time for a few hours of sleep before Chakotay slipped from her quarters and made his way to the shuttlebay. His fears relieved, he blessed again the gods of his fathers for bringing Kathryn back to him. He refused to think too far ahead. He'd already learned that to live in the future was folly, especially when the present held everything for which he could ask.

Chapter Six

Despite the lateness of the hour when Doctor Sharak had finally settled into his temporary quarters, he was up early and back at Starfleet Medical at first light. Assured of Seven's safety, at least for now, he intended to devote himself entirely to the work Doctor Frist had given him; evaluating the spread of the catomic plague.

Frist was already at her station when he arrived and bade her good morning. She introduced him to Doctor Greer Everett, a civilian from the Federation Institute of Health, who was taking point on their efforts to assist with stemming the plague's spread. She gave him a thorough tour of the facilities and introduced him to his new associates.

When they had returned to his workstation and Frist was prepared to attend to her own duties, Sharak asked if she would introduce him to the Commander.

"The Commander is in the quarantine area, and we do not disturb him," Frist replied. "If he has questions for us, they are immediately forwarded to our attention, but that is rare."

"Does the Commander . . ." Sharak began, then asked, "I'm sorry, is he a hologram?"

Frist seemed shocked by the notion. "Why . . . what?" she asked.

"No one has ever referred to him as anything other than 'the Commander.' I wondered if, like *Voyager*'s former EMH, the Doctor, this Commander simply doesn't have a name."

Frist nodded her comprehension. "Ah, no. He is Commander Jefferson Briggs, one of the most ingenious and inventive medical researchers Starfleet has ever produced. His thesis at the Academy on the discovery of the unique genetic profile of the Planarians was celebrated to the ends of the Federation as a dramatic theoretical breakthrough. It established him as a preeminent authority on genetic manipulation. He then devoted himself for the next several years to curing the *Lernk* virus, a feat he achieved where many others had failed. He has reached a status among his peers to which few of us can even aspire. We are certain he will resolve this catomic plague and likely advance our understanding of catoms significantly in the process."

"It sounds as if we are all in good hands," Sharak said.

"The best," Frist agreed.

"I would like to speak to Commander Briggs," Sharak went on. "I wish to make sure he is aware of my perceptions of Miss Seven, as her physician."

"We received her records before you arrived, Doctor, and no doubt the Commander has committed them to memory by now."

"Does he not like his name?" Sharak asked.

Frist smiled benevolently. "The Commander has instituted a unique organizational structure among his team members. Once assigned to his group, the members eschew addressing one another by their names. They use ranks or titles he assigns denoting their specific duty among the team."

"Doesn't that get confusing?" Sharak asked.

"It is intended to emphasize the reality that those who work with his team are performing a duty that is beyond their individual identity. In casual conversation modes of address are less formal, but while on duty all observe the designations he gives them. In this way they become distinct parts of something greater. They are as much a representative of a 'position' as a person. It's helpful when navigating issues of ethical nuance to think of oneself, not as an individual, but as a significant part of a larger whole."

"I see," Sharak said. "However, I would suggest he not assign such a designation to Miss Seven. She is very particular about modes of address, given her unique heritage and the unusual lengths to which she has gone to clarify her identity."

"I have no doubt that once she gets to know the Commander, she too will realize how lucky she is to be part of his team."

"I would pass along my recommendation nonetheless," Sharak suggested.

"Of course. Thank you, Doctor," Frist said.

"What does this suggest?" Axum asked.

Seven stared at the images of subatomic scans Axum had done of his own catoms. The tags the Doctor had first discovered were visible, but otherwise, nothing in the arrangement of the particles revealed anything new to Seven. Had she not known she was looking at catomic particles, she would have concluded she was looking at organic ones.

"I don't know," she finally admitted.

Axum stood patiently beside her. "Are you sure?" he finally asked.

"I would not have said so otherwise."

Frustrated, Seven turned away from the display and crossed to the lab's doorway. Axum had obviously intuited something that eluded her. He clearly had his reasons for wishing her to grasp the concept on her own. The feeling that she was being tested, however, was intensely annoying.

Beyond that, Seven could not dismiss the uncomfortable sensation that she *should* be elsewhere right now. Axum was recovering well. There was much she wished to share with him when this crisis had passed, including the fact that her personal life and commitment to Counselor Cambridge made the future relationship Axum was obviously contemplating impossible. But now was not that time. She needed to speak with the Commander. She needed his most current research on the catomic plague. She needed to begin working to solve that problem, rather than the one Axum seemed intent upon placing before her.

Wondering if the Commander's residence might be one of those adjacent to the patio, Seven moved toward it. Even if this wasn't his, by engaging the other researchers working there, Seven might get some of the information she required. Though there were at least a dozen separate units visible, none of them showed signs of life, despite the fact that the sky above had darkened hours before.

Axum moved silently to her side. "You're angry with me," he said.

"No," she said.

"Then let's approach this another way," he suggested.

Intrigued, Seven nodded.

Taking one hand, Axum led her to a table on the patio and moved two chairs to face one another. As Seven sat, a riot of pleasant, exotic fragrances assaulted her. She had seen many blooms filling the patio by day, but she only now understood how completely they transformed the otherwise sterile space.

Seven closed her eyes, allowing the smells to wash over her and clear her mind. She knew that simply staring at a problem from the same place incessantly rarely produced results. A change of perspective might help.

Annika?

Seven jumped as a rush of adrenaline poured into her system and her heart began to race. The fear must have been obvious on her face. Axum took both her hands in his and with gentle pressure kept her seated.

"Was that you?" she demanded.

"Yes. Why does it frighten you so?" he asked.

Seven indulged in a few long, deep breaths to calm her body's frantic systems. When she felt steady enough to speak again, she did.

"For many months after the Caeliar transformation, I lived with the presence of a voice in my mind. I experienced several waking 'dream' states where I was able to visualize the source of the voice. She was a sort of amalgam of my human and Caeliar natures; a child who hated the Borg. It took a great deal of effort for me to embrace her message and silence her. The sensation of hearing you in my mind frightened me because I thought for a moment she might have returned."

Axum nodded thoughtfully. "Obviously, the transformation affected each of us who remained outside the gestalt differently. Perhaps because I was still part of the Collective at the time, I did not share that experience. I don't think I truly grasped reality for a long time before or after the transformation. I had been living in torment for so long. When I finally experienced absolute silence, I thought it might mean that I was dead. I welcomed it."

Seven raised a hand to Axum's cheek. He placed his over it and they sat for a moment, grieving one another's pain. Finally Seven said, "Why did you initiate telepathic contact?"

"My people, the Mysstren, shared low-level psionic abilities. I never had a chance to develop mine before I was assimilated. But when I began to find you in my dreams, I started to wonder if these catoms might have awakened or enhanced my latent abilities."

"We shared those dreams because our catoms were mingled," Seven said.

"Did we?" he asked. "The *dreams*, perhaps, but this?"

Seven considered his words.

"Again," she said.

You hear me, Annika. You hear my thoughts.

"I do," she said, nodding.

Respond to me with your thoughts, he asked.

"I don't think I should. Twice now, I have experienced telepathic communications enhanced by my catoms. In the first instance, a known telepathic species reached out to me. The second time, a transformed former Borg, like us, initiated the contact. Both events resulted in degradation of my neural tissues that required medical intervention to heal."

You're in the middle of Starfleet Medical. I'm sure someone here will rush to attend you should your health be in jeopardy.

Seven considered the argument. It seemed a risk worth taking. She had also been advised by the Doctor that her catoms had actually repaired the damage to her neural tissues, creating new ones as needed.

Very well.

Axum smiled. *That wasn't so hard, was it?*

Seven felt her heart begin to flutter again.

You heard that?

I did.

How?

This is my point. We're not going to learn what we need to know about our catoms by studying them under a magna-scan. We must use them. Test them. Discover their limits through experimentation.

That will not help us cure this plague.

How do you know?

Seven had to admit, she didn't. *Even if our catoms permit us to speak with one another and other telepathic species in this manner, it brings us no closer to understanding* how *they can do this.*

Of course it does, Axum insisted.

How? Seven asked.

There are a number of possibilities, but the one I find most intriguing is this: Catoms do not seem predisposed to function independently. When they mingle, or sense one another, there is an inherent desire to connect. Is this desire ours? And do the catoms just make it possible for us to realize them? Or are they functioning according to their own imperatives, separate from our wishes? We experienced briefly the Caelier gestalt. Did this gestalt exist because the Caelier were catomic beings? Can catoms exist without a coincidental gestalt?

We did not join the gestalt.

But are we now on our way to creating a new one of our own?

Seven pulled her hands free from Axum's and sat back. She felt no physical discomfort from their communication. But it wasn't hard to pinpoint the emotional distress she was suddenly experiencing.

What's wrong?

"Stop it," she said.

"Annika . . ."

"Stop it," she said again. "We both risked our lives once to free ourselves from the hive mind. Would you have us willingly re-create it? Does your individuality mean so little to you?"

"Simply because we *can* do a thing, does not mean that we *should*," Axum agreed. "But it is in both our best interests to learn if our catoms are going to give us a choice in that matter."

"Then let's try that experiment, now," Seven said, a bit harshly. "You obviously knew before I did that what I was experiencing as dreams were intentional communications on your part. You initiated intimate physical contact in those dreams."

"You didn't seem to mind," he said, stung.

"I had my own reasons to wonder at the source of the dreams. It took time for me to realize what was really going on, and by the time I did . . ." She trailed off. She had no wish yet to share with him exactly how those dreams had complicated and compromised her private life.

"Had I thought for a moment you did not want to be with me there, I would never have dared," Axum said. "At first, it was almost a reflex. I had been alone for so long, and when I sensed you again, my need was all-consuming. I guess I didn't think."

"No, you didn't."

"I'm sorry, Annika."

Genuine anguish washed over his face. As angry as she was, Seven could not bear to see it.

"Axum, you and I have never had a chance to know one another in the real world. Every touch we shared until now happened in some alternate reality created by nanoprobes or catoms. You say you want us to have a future together. How am I to know what that would feel like if you keep forcing us back into our past ways of relating?"

Axum lowered his head, trying to collect himself. Finally he said, "You are right. I have violated you. Please believe me when I say that was never my intention."

"I know," she said. "And I understand. Both of us will have to work to unlearn so much of what we once knew. It no longer applies in this new world. I have moved on. I have experienced

many things since we were last in contact. You have suffered ter-
ribly. I want to help you, but not like this. You need to stay out
of my mind."

Axum started to speak, but finally he just nodded.

A flash from the corner of Seven's eye caught her attention.
Turning her head, she saw that a light had just gone on in one
of the units above those adjoined to the patio. A small balcony
extended out from it, but Seven could not see motion or shadow
beyond the balcony, given her position relative to it.

"Someone's home," she said softly.

Axum stared at her, his eyes filled with longing and regret.

Cadet Icheb had no idea where Seven or Doctor Sharak were
spending their days at Starfleet Medical. It did not seem likely
after the previous evening's encounter that Doctor Sharak would
provide him with this information. Even if he knew where they
were, his assigned duties did not permit him to seek them out.
He had been given a very specific task in the administrative
offices, one that was actually an excellent use of his skill set.

It was also incredibly boring.

For three hours, two evenings per week, Icheb reviewed
inventory and material requisitions. Where matches existed in
stock, he allocated them appropriately. Where they did not, he
placed the necessary orders.

He would have been grateful for the fact that this assignment
was not mentally taxing in the least, had it not been for Seven's
circumstances. He could easily complete his assigned work in
less time than he had been granted and use the extra hour to
attend to his other studies. As it was, he found his attention constantly shifting from the task at hand to concerns about Seven
and, as a result, filling all of his allotted time.

Near the end of this day's work, he paused over an unusual
requisition: an order for additional gloves that were standard to
biohazard suits. He noted the source of the request, a department designated CLCP-119. He then ran a quick search of the
database for other requisitions from this department. Many of

them were standard, but among them were several for items that would be used only in work with highly dangerous infectious or toxic substances.

On a whim, Icheb asked the main computer to display the department's physical location within Starfleet Medical.

To his surprise, it did.

The first day of mediation ended with the two parties nowhere near a potential compromise. Tom Paris spent a fitful night, tossing and turning. When he managed to drift off, Paris was tormented by dreams of B'Elanna and Miral calling to him from the end of a distant tunnel that seemed to grow longer the more Tom struggled to reach them.

As Paris entered the chamber for day two of the proceedings, he was a knot of nervous energy. He needed a physical release of some kind. As soon as this session adjourned, he promised himself a visit to the gym, where he planned to punch something repeatedly as hard as he could.

His mother was as composed as ever. Thinking back, he remembered that this had always been the truest barometer of her level of anger. Where his father would rage and thunder, Julia's ire was at its peak when she was the most contained.

Lieutenant Shaw seemed relaxed, and he greeted Paris with a firm handshake and a reassuring clap on the shoulder as he took his seat. It filled Paris with faint hope to note that his mother's counsel, a man Shaw had identified as Admiral Clancy, an old friend of Tom's father, sat with his head bowed. Paris couldn't be sure, but it looked like Clancy might be napping.

Ozimat opened the session, as he had the previous day, addressing himself to Julia. "Yesterday, we began our discussion with the events that directly precipitated your choice to bring this case, Mrs. Paris. Perhaps today we should delve deeper into other incidents you cite in your complaint as having direct bearing on your choice. Perhaps if Commander Paris can shed a little light on his thinking at that time, it might put your concerns in a clearer context."

Julia nodded, smiling with pained gratitude at Ozimat before leveling her gaze at her son.

"Obviously Your Honor is already aware of the grave and serious nature of the incidents that led to my son's incarceration a few years after being separated from Starfleet Academy. Although the accident that claimed the life of three of his fellow cadets, young men and women he thought of as dear friends, was truly, I believe, an *accident,* his poor judgment in lying about the series of events that led to their deaths, when seen in the light of his more recent choices, remains troubling. His choice to offer his skills as a pilot to the Maquis, a known terrorist group responsible for the deaths of many Starfleet officers, was another.

"But I hoped that the loss of his commission and the subsequent loss of his freedom served their purpose. My son's service record aboard the *Starship Voyager* seemed to show that rehabilitation is possible where an individual is willing to acknowledge his mistakes and work diligently to avoid making them in the future.

"That said, I first began to question his and his wife's choices when Miral was only a few weeks old. Tom told us that B'Elanna had decided to undertake an archaic Klingon ritual to honor her mother who, *I was told,* was presumed dead at the time."

Paris was pleased Shaw had already raised this issue. It kept him from flying across the table and attempting to shake some sense into his mother. He looked to his counsel, who was already staring at him. Shaw's face betrayed nothing, but Paris still read the clear warning to say nothing he would later regret.

"The first days and weeks of a child's life are so incredibly important. The bonding that goes on lays the foundation for all of the challenges to follow. My son rose to the occasion admirably. I saw him and Miral a few times during those weeks and could see how clearly he doted on her. He did the best he could. What troubled me then, and now, was the fact that he was put in this position at all.

"At the time . . ." Julia continued, but her eyes began to glisten and she paused to collect herself.

Paris suspected that his mother might have taken acting lessons since they'd last met. A bucket of onions couldn't break her under normal circumstances.

"I'm sorry, Your Honor," she went on, "but that night is still so vivid in my memory. Miral was all of two weeks old and crying that infant cry that only means one thing—*I need my mother.* My son told us that B'Elanna had chosen to perform something called the Challenge of the Spirit. It was a Klingon ritual that often as not resulted in the death of the participant. I looked it up," she noted, with a sad shake of her head.

"But that was a lie. B'Elanna had found a note among her mother's personal effects that indicated that Miral Torres was somewhere out in the wilds of Boreth waiting for her. Ms. Torres apparently made this choice after she shared some sort of vision or dream with B'Elanna. She wanted her daughter to embrace her Klingon heritage and, like a dutiful daughter, B'Elanna wanted to oblige her.

"Tom didn't tell his father or me about this at the time."

"My wife asked me not to," Paris interjected coldly. He couldn't help himself, but a meandering glance in his direction from Shaw calculated to appear casual silenced him.

"Of course she did," Julia continued. "She knew that even the most basic scrutiny would reveal the lunacy and selfishness of her choice."

Paris clenched his hands into fists, focusing on the tension there rather than the words trying to force their way out of his windpipe.

"Let us accept the notion that B'Elanna's mother actually experienced this vision. Miral Torres left the safety of the monastery on Boreth and journeyed alone into a wilderness known for its extreme climate and filled with deadly animals, almost two years before *Voyager* returned home and, frankly, dozens of years before even the optimists among us expected *Voyager* to return. She intended to wait all that time for B'Elanna to come after her. Was this the choice of a rational person? And did B'Elanna, by all accounts a brilliant engineer, not consider the statistical probability that her mother was no longer alive *two years later* before abandoning her infant daughter and embarking on a quest she was not likely to survive?

"Who does this? If Miral Torres wanted so badly for her daughter to embrace her heritage, why did she not simply wait until B'Elanna returned home and then invite her to Boreth and discuss it? Or take the challenge with her? Why the secrecy? Why the lies? And why did B'Elanna risk her life and her daughter's future by agreeing to such a thing? If she believed her mother was alive, any Starfleet vessel could have performed rudimentary scans that located her mother, a lone Klingon life sign in a vast wilderness, and she could have simply transported down to have this crucial conversation.

"Were she not married and a mother, B'Elanna would have been free to follow her heart. But her choices to marry and to bear that child placed responsibilities on her. They eliminated the right she had to put her own needs, or her mother's, before those of her child.

"This was the truth B'Elanna did not want to hear. So she lied and demanded you do the same. It seems any time she is faced with a difficult decision, her default choice is to lie to avoid confrontation and to simply beg forgiveness and understanding later.

"Would you condemn your daughter to a lifetime of such lies? This is not an isolated incident. It is now an established pattern of unacceptable behavior."

Ozimat's and Shaw's eyes fell upon Paris. He knew what was expected of him, and for the love of his wife and children, he did his best to rise to the occasion.

"It is inappropriate for you to level accusations at my wife based entirely upon your own cultural ignorance," Paris began. "B'Elanna has lived most of her life divided between the demands of her human and Klingon heritages. It is a chasm even the Federation has yet to fully bridge. The Klingons are our allies, but how often do we still question one another's motives and choices? How close are we, even today, to an incident that could shatter the fragile peace that exists between us?

"B'Elanna has lived that war internally. To be the mother that Miral needs, she had to make peace within herself. Her mother's actions provided B'Elanna the opportunity to do that. It was too important for her to pass up. She returned from that experience more centered, and more at peace with herself, than in all the time I have ever known her. It was worth it. And since then, she has done nothing but sacrifice her own needs for Miral's. She has loved her, protected her, educated her, and provided her with a solid foundation and security, even while the galaxy has been tearing itself apart all around her."

"Begging your pardon, Commander Paris," Ozimat said, "but was not your wife Miral's sole caretaker when she was kidnapped?"

Paris had tried. He really had. It was a victory of sorts that his response was limited to "We're done here for the day," before he rose from his chair, toppling it backwards onto the floor. He ignored it as he stalked from the room, allowing the chamber door to slam behind him.

Chapter Seven

Despite the sleep sacrificed on the altar of diplomacy the previous evening, everyone assembled in the *Vesta*'s conference room the following morning appeared eager and ready to face the new day.

Admiral Janeway sat at the largest table's head. To her right was her aide, Lieutenant Decan. To her left sat *Voyager*'s officers: Captain Chakotay, Fleet Chief Torres, acting first officer Lieutenant Harry Kim, Counselor Cambridge, and Lieutenant Lasren. Both Commanders O'Donnell and Fife had come from *Demeter*. Commander Glenn was the sole representative of the *Galen*. Captain Farkas closed the circle, sitting to Decan's right.

"I would like to commend all of you for your work last night," the admiral said. "Each and every one of you made me proud, which was no less than I expected. I am sure that many of you have already begun to form opinions of a potential alliance between the Federation and the Confederacy based on your experiences with them, but I encourage you to keep an open mind over the coming days.

"I have read all of the brief reports each of you submitted last night. I found your experience, Lieutenant Kim, particularly troubling."

"What happened?" Chakotay asked.

"The woman I was seated next to at dinner last night tried to steal my combadge," Kim said.

"How?" Cambridge asked.

"She put her arm around me. She had an accomplice who tried to distract me. But you have to get up pretty early in the morning to get something like that past a security chief," Kim added. "She actually damaged it in the attempt. I had to replicate a new one."

"Who was she?" Chakotay asked, biting back his amusement.

"We don't know," Janeway replied for Kim. "I made a request of the first consul an hour ago to identify her and her affiliation. Apparently no one named Ligah was on the official guest list."

"Then how did she end up at one of the reserved tables?" Kim asked.

"The first consul is lying, Lieutenant," Cambridge said.

"Obviously," Janeway agreed. "Two things to file away for future reference: No one with whom you will be interacting over the next few days can be trusted completely, and it is possible that high-ranking members of the Confederacy government assume we are quite stupid."

"We should correct that assumption sooner rather than later, Admiral," Commander Fife piped up.

"I think that problem will take care of itself in due time," Janeway said.

"Until then, it gives us a potential advantage," Chakotay noted.

"It does," Janeway agreed.

"How?" Fife asked.

"The dumber they think we are, the more likely they will be to relax their own security. We'll learn a lot more by keeping our mouths shut than we will by getting into a pissing contest with them," Cambridge explained.

"Admiral?" Torres interjected.

"Yes, Commander?"

"Did you note the comments in my report regarding the status and advancement of Confederacy women?"

"I did," the admiral replied. "And while I too found it disturbing, it's important to remember that every culture develops its priorities based upon their past. While the treatment of the

Confederacy's women during their fertile years is difficult for us to accept, it's also worth noting that their current presider is a woman."

A flush of anger tinged Torres's cheeks. "So, they're fine? Nothing to worry about?" Torres asked.

"Commander," Chakotay chastised her gently.

"You don't believe this cultural difference significant enough to warrant abandoning the negotiations?" Torres demanded of Janeway.

"At this stage, they warrant further investigation. Should we learn that the vast majority of women within the Confederacy chafe under the burdens their society places upon them, that would be one thing. If they accept it as part of their cultural identity . . ." The admiral shrugged.

Torres did not appear mollified, but she did not protest further.

Janeway continued: "I have received a number of proposals from the Confederacy diplomatic liaison. Based on these proposals, I have your next assignments."

Turning to Chakotay first, she said, "*Voyager* will depart this afternoon and accompany the *Twelfth Lamont* to a planet called Lecahn."

"The manufacturing center?" Chakotay guessed.

Janeway nodded. "I need you to get the best sense you can of the Confederacy's current technological capabilities. We already know they don't have universal translators or transporters other than the protectors. I'm guessing they don't have replicators, but that's just a guess. The liaison was vague about what exactly Lecahn produces, and I'm assuming it isn't military, but the journey will take a few days and any readings you can get on *Lamont* will be helpful."

"I've been toying with some modulated scanning frequencies. They'd be passive, and not as accurate as we'd like, but they're also less likely to be detected," Kim said.

"Good. I will be depriving *Voyager* for the duration of her counselor and operations officer," Janeway went on. As soon as she said this, Lieutenant Lasren's large black eyes widened visibly. "I understand you had a rough time of it last night, Lieutenant," Janeway said to Lasren. "I want you to work closely with Counselor Cambridge. Both of you will attend all of my meetings to help me read the participants, but I won't have you putting yourself at unnecessary risk. Just do what you can, understood?"

"Yes, Admiral," Lasren replied.

"General Mattings suggested an officer exchange during this trip," Chakotay said.

"I saw that proposal," Janeway said, and she was inclined to agree, as it opened up all sorts of possibilities for intelligence gathering.

"It's not one I want to accept at the moment," Chakotay said.

"Why not?"

"There's a lot we aren't telling them yet about our capabilities, and those things will be harder to hide from anyone aboard *Voyager*," Chakotay replied.

"You're right," Janeway said. "But still . . ."

"Mattings tentatively agreed to a one-sided beginning," Chakotay went on. "I think he'd let me place an officer with him without demanding that I take one of his in exchange."

"Who did you have in mind?"

"Lieutenant Kim," Chakotay said.

"He's your first officer and chief of security," Janeway said.

"Who has trained his security staff exceptionally well. And Lieutenant Patel is coming along nicely as a potential second officer. We can make it work for a few days."

"Then do it," Janeway said. Turning to O'Donnell, she continued: "The *Demeter* will be accompanied by the *Fourth Jroone* to a place called Femra."

"One of their more recent success stories," O'Donnell said.

"You've heard of it?" the admiral asked.

"I spent two weeks with Overseer Bralt before you returned, Admiral," O'Donnell said. "When it comes to his department's achievements, he does not suffer from an overabundance of humility."

"Obviously, we have no idea yet if an alliance will be possible," Janeway said. "I want you to look at what they have, with an eye toward improving it, should we come to some agreement. Enhanced productivity seems to be their greatest concern."

"And the greatest example of their shortsightedness," O'Donnell said. "They don't need more. They need to diversify what they have. Their lack of regular crop rotation rapidly depletes their soil's nutrients. There are, of course, many synthetic means of correcting the imbalances, but, over time, continued use of those chemicals builds resistance and ultimately you are left with a mess, at which point all of that productivity will quickly become a fond memory."

"I assume you have developed safer methods of reinvigorating depleted soil?" Janeway asked.

"One or two," O'Donnell replied, clearly estimating on the low side.

"Go, see if anything surprises you," the admiral ordered.

"I look forward to being surprised, Admiral," O'Donnell said flatly.

"Commander Glenn, for the next few days, *Galen* will be the only fleet vessel in orbit of the First World. You have been invited to tour several of the capital city's medical facilities. My staff will also require accommodations on your ship for the duration."

"I'll see to it at once, Admiral," Glenn said.

"Where are we going?" Farkas asked.

"Another Confederacy vessel—the *Sixteenth Hadden,* I believe— will escort the *Vesta* to an area near the entrance to the Gateway. They recon the ships that have begun to make noise out there," Janeway replied. "I want you to train every sensor we have on any ships you find. I want to know what they're having for dinner."

"You want to know what could possibly bring together the Turei, the Vaadwaur, and the Devore," Farkas clarified.

Janeway nodded. "I also want you to become as close as you are comfortable with your counterpart on the *Hadden*. I want to know what they really think of these attacks and what they are prepared to do about them."

"Understood, Admiral, but . . ." Farkas began.

"Aren't you leaving yourself vulnerable, Admiral?" Chakotay finished the sentence for her.

"The *Galen* has a full security detail in the event she was to be boarded," Janeway said.

"Eighty percent of them are holograms who haven't seen a great deal of use," Glenn noted.

"Which is why I will ask Captain Farkas to provide me with an extra detachment from the *Vesta* to accompany my team to and from the First World," Janeway said.

"I'm going to wake Lieutenant Psilakis up and ask him to lead that detachment," Farkas said. "And I would suggest that, as an additional precaution and cover, we assign Lieutenant Lasren temporarily to security."

Lasren appeared confused. "I've had all the standard training, Captain," he said, "but I don't know how much help I'd really be in that position. Obviously I will do my best, but . . ."

"If the admiral takes two special assistants plus Lieutenant Decan with her to every meeting, it's going to raise suspicions," Farkas said. "It will be clear that at least one of you is more than an advisor. A ship's counselor makes sense. An operations officer is harder to justify, as you have nothing to operate down there."

Lasren nodded as the light dawned.

"An excellent suggestion. Thank you, Captain," Janeway said. "Anything else?" she asked.

"We're working now under a complete transporter blackout," Chakotay said. "Every communications transmission we send is being monitored. Once we separate, that might become more than inconvenient."

"Agreed," Janeway said. "Obviously you are permitted to use transporters in an emergency situation. I will rely on your discretion. Is there anything we can do to secure a channel they won't be able to detect?"

"Not really," B'Elanna said. "We can encrypt whatever we want, but just knowing we're speaking privately is going to breed distrust."

The admiral nodded thoughtfully. Finally she said, "I'm going to institute a special emergency protocol for all fleet vessels. Before we separate, we will establish a rendezvous point far beyond Confederacy space and within range of our communication relays. Should any vessel come under attack by the Confederacy, or anyone else while we are here, you are to disengage as safely as possible, engage your slipstream drives, and report to the rendezvous coordinates. Should any ship fail to report in as scheduled, and you cannot verify their status, the same rule applies. Transmit a full report to Admiral Montgomery at Starfleet Command and await further orders before taking any actions, beyond ensuring your own safety."

Each of the commanding officers nodded their understanding of her orders.

Turning to Farkas, Janeway went on: "Before you go, the *Vesta* is going to host a small tour of delegates, including the First Consul. I will lead the tour, and as soon as it's done, my team will head over to the *Galen* and you'll be on your way."

"Aye, Admiral," Farkas said.

"If there aren't any further issues, we're done here," Janeway said, bringing the meeting to a close.

As Chakotay moved toward the door, Admiral Janeway pulled him aside. Pitching her voice low, she said, "The first time I asked you if you trusted our potential new allies, you said, 'for the most part.' Has something changed your mind?"

Chakotay considered these words carefully before responding. "It's complicated. I don't want to blame them for the actions of their ancestors: the way they raped those star systems, tearing entire planets apart. But experiencing it from the protectors' point of view was painful. I have yet to hear anyone acknowledge the magnitude of that transgression. To a person, they accept it as what had to be done. They don't regret it."

"Which means they'd do it again," Janeway said.

"In a heartbeat." Chakotay nodded. "What I've seen of Mattings, thus far, I want to like. He's a fascinating man, and I sense nothing from him but a genuine desire to do his best by his people. He's one of the few who aren't coming at us with a definite air of superiority. He's seen our slipstream drive in use. He knows there's a lot we aren't sharing, and the longer we withhold, the less he's going to trust us."

"I feel the same about the presider. She cares about her people. I just don't know how much power she has here," Janeway said.

"The one thing I won't do is allow my personal regard for any individual to blind me to the threat they pose as a civilization. We have speed and the element of surprise. They have numbers. I know what you want to achieve here, for the Federation. But we're still a small group a long way from home. We take care of ourselves first."

"Agreed," Janeway said. "Thank you, Chakotay."

Lieutenant Kim was waiting for his captain when he stepped outside the briefing room. As they made their way to the shuttlebay to return to *Voyager,* Kim asked, "Is there anything in particular you want me to focus on while I'm on the *Lamont,* Captain?"

"I'd love to know the specs on their defenses," Chakotay said, "but don't put yourself at risk trying to get them."

"I've been talking to Lieutenant Conlon about that. She's going to work with B'Elanna on enhancing our scans. We have logs of the battle between the Confederacy ships and the alien armada at the Gateway. Conlon has already started analyzing those."

"Good," Chakotay said.

"If you don't object, I'd like to learn more about the ways the Confederacy uses the protectors."

"That request doesn't surprise me," Chakotay said, nodding grimly. "We know that the Confederacy uses the protectors to reinforce the streams. Mattings hinted that, in addition to transport, they can use them as some sort of rudimentary cloaking device. He also told me that the protectors they use now are usually destroyed after a short time in use. I don't think they're like the ones we encountered. They aren't active long enough to develop the memories or make the intuitive connections the proctors and sentries did."

"Using them to cloak a ship involves a minor harmonic adjustment," Kim said, "similar to the design for the cloaking matrix. That's not my question. I asked Commander Fife to send me *Demeter*'s logs from the first few minutes they were in Confederacy space."

"Why?"

"Commander O'Donnell said that the protectors that accompanied *Demeter*—the ones that saved us during that battle, and then somehow secured safe passage for *Demeter*—disintegrated just after they arrived in Confederacy space."

"We knew they were damaged during the battle."

"Yes, but once they stopped taking fire they should have been able to sustain whatever was left of them. Unless journeying through the Gateway damaged them further," Kim mused.

"You have a theory?"

"Yes," Kim said. "But I'm not even going to suggest it until I have more information."

"Fair enough," Chakotay said.

As they entered the shuttle, Counselor Cambridge had to squeeze past Kim and the captain to reach his seat in the rear. The shuttle was well on its way back to *Voyager* before the counselor tapped his combadge and said, "Cambridge to Lieutenant Kim."

Kim reached automatically for his chest and was surprised to find it lacking the small metal insignia. Looking back he saw the counselor holding his combadge in his hand. With a wry smile he tossed it back to Kim. "What time did you get up this morning, Lieutenant?" Cambridge teased.

"I'm never going to live that down, am I?" Kim asked.

"No," Chakotay said, shaking his head vigorously.

VOYAGER

As soon as Commander Glenn had returned to the *Galen* the previous evening, Lieutenant Reg Barclay had boarded a shuttle bound for *Voyager*. Upon his arrival, he had set to work freeing space and installing the programs required by the Doctor. He had also examined the results of the self-diagnostic he'd asked the Doctor to perform. It had shown no malfunctions. But as far as Barclay was concerned, the matter was far from settled.

The Doctor's odd memory lapses might indicate any number of problems. Most likely he was looking at some minor degradation in the Doctor's short-term memory buffers. That was easy enough to repair.

At the back of his mind, however, was the strange file he'd found during the Doctor's last level-ten diagnostic, a message sent by the Doctor's creator and aging doppelganger, Lewis Zimmerman, for Admiral Janeway's eyes only.

Barclay didn't want to know what that message said. If Zimmerman really wanted him to know, he would have told him in spite of Reg's pleading not to be asked again to keep secrets from the Doctor. He had done that once and the results had been devastating. The Doctor had taken what was meant to be help as a betrayal, and in the process a powerful menace had been unleashed in the form of Meegan. Barclay wasn't going down that road again.

But if there was really something wrong with the Doctor . . .

Barclay had completed the installation and returned to *Galen*. A few hours of light sleep populated by dreams of the Doctor vanishing before his eyes, piece by piece, brought him back to *Voyager* less than an hour before it was scheduled to depart on its new assignment.

He found the Doctor multitasking: a good sign. Every data screen the sickbay possessed was displaying different programs the Doctor had initiated. He moved among them like a conductor, analyzing, tweaking, and integrating the data faster than any human could. He did not even realize Barclay had entered until he placed himself between the Doctor and one of those screens.

"Hello," the Doctor greeted him. "I didn't expect to see you again so soon. The new systems are performing perfectly, Reg. I can't thank you enough."

"Have you been running continuously since I departed?"

"Of course," the Doctor said.

"Great," Barclay replied. "Keep doing what you're doing. I just want to check a few things. We'll be out of touch for several days and I don't want your progress to be slowed by any bugs in the system."

A faint smile lit the Doctor's face. "That's very considerate of you, Reg. Thank you."

"My pleasure, Doctor."

Technically, it wasn't a lie. The Doctor assumed the systems he was referring to were those Barclay had just installed. Instead, Barclay pulled up the master files of the Doctor's matrix and initiated a level-six diagnostic, one that was specifically designed to analyze his memory centers.

Once the program had started to run, Barclay said, "What progress have you made thus far?" Part of the test included analysis of the integrity of the memory buffers with their corresponding vocal subroutines. Barclay could test this no matter what subject the Doctor spoke about, and there was nothing the EMH enjoyed so much as sharing his experiences, however minute.

"You really want to know?" the Doctor asked.

Barclay had to be careful not to overplay his hand. For months he had been a lousy conversationalist, and both of them knew it. His focus had been singular and obsessive. The Doctor had taken him to task several times for it.

"I do," Barclay said, searching his own memory for the words Counselor Troi might have suggested for such a moment. "Part of being a good friend is showing interest in another's work. I have not been a good friend to you lately, Doctor. It's time I started to correct that."

The Doctor beamed at him. "You are a good friend, Reg. You always will be. And, thankfully, you are one of only a few individuals I can speak with openly about my current work."

Barclay understood. In some ways, he was the Doctor's *doctor*. As the fleet's resident holographic specialist, he was authorized to access every file and subroutine in the Doctor's program. The Doctor couldn't hide anything from Reg, even if he'd wanted to. It was understood that for Barclay to perform this essential function, there could be no secrets between them. Data on the Doctor's patients, though confidential, had to be retrievable by someone should the Doctor's program fail. As a result, Barclay was already privy to many sensitive subjects, including the Doctor's work on Seven's catoms, his treatment of Axum, and the classified catomic plague.

"So . . . ?" Barclay prodded.

"I began my analysis with the records I was given of the first hundred plague victims on Coridan," the Doctor began. "Of those hundred, forty-five were Starfleet officers who came in direct contact with Borg debris just prior to the Caeliar transformation."

"How?" Barclay asked, as he checked the progress of the diagnostic and noted that several key memory centers were already showing slight variances from normal. They were within tolerances, but they had not appeared on any previous diagnostic Barclay had run since the fleet's launch.

"There was a great deal of fighting above Coridan. Three Starfleet vessels engaged six Borg cubes. At least two of the cubes took heavy damage, and several large pieces of them, some with functioning drones, were found on the surface. Teams of our officers were dispatched to engage them."

"I see," Barclay said, not caring one bit.

"The interesting thing is that none of the victims died from a single or similar cause. Most suffered from treatable conditions, or genetic issues that were exacerbated by injuries they sustained. For reasons that are still unclear, these conditions led to massive systemic failures within hours. The range of their diagnoses made categorizing this 'plague' as such almost impossible, initially."

"That sounds terrible," Barclay said, hoping it did. A few scattered memory files showing variances had turned into hundreds in the time it had taken the Doctor to explain this much.

"It was," the Doctor said, nodding. "Causes of death ranged from multiple massive aneurysms, heart failure, the sudden emergence of antibiotic- and antiviral-resistant infections, neurological collapse, complete autoimmune failure, toxic shock, and sepsis. It's like something caused these people's bodies to turn against them."

When the Doctor paused for too long, Barclay looked up. The diagnostic was almost complete and the affected files had hit a thousand. The Doctor was staring at Barclay but in a way that suggested he wasn't even seeing him.

"It's a virus," the Doctor said.

"Are you sure?"

"It has to be; a virus that somehow adapts to target each patient individually and attacks them wherever they are weakest. It must also be able to adjust its mode of transmission. Hundreds were affected following these first cases that had no direct interaction with Borg debris, including some of the first physicians to treat them. It became airborne, probably within hours, but could also spread through direct contact."

"Can a virus do that?"

"Many viruses can mutate and alter the ways in which they spread. But most that kill this quickly don't have time to do that," the Doctor mused. "They're too busy devouring their hosts."

"Okay," Barclay said, his mind running through all of the possible things that could account for the new variances in the Doctor's memory centers. He quickly eliminated all of them but one.

"If a virus could somehow be imbued with catomic properties, the ability to customize its destructive potential to each host as soon as it entered their body the same way catoms take their input from surrounding cells and adapt to augment them, that would certainly explain what we're seeing here," the Doctor said. "But I've already reviewed the blood work from each of the first hundred patients and none of the particles show catomic tags."

"So it's not catomic?" Barclay asked.

"I don't see how it could be. But nothing else suits the evidence so perfectly," the Doctor replied.

"Doctor?" Barclay said.

"Hmmm . . . ?"

"Doctor?"

The Doctor fixed his gaze on Barclay. "Sorry, Reg. I was just thinking."

"When was the last time you spoke to Doctor Z?"

"It was . . ." the Doctor began, but he paused in midthought. Barclay watched in horror as one of the slight variances in a memory file only recently shifted from short term to long term increased by a factor of twenty. Looking again at the Doctor's face, Barclay noted a blankness relax his features, quickly replaced by his more normal alert presentation.

"It was just before the fleet launched," the Doctor said, and he seemed unaware of the length of time it had taken him to find this response.

Looking again at the diagnostic, Barclay noted that the file in question had now returned to a more or less "normal" variance range.

For better and worse, Barclay had the answer he had come here seeking. The Doctor had just lied to him. And he didn't seem to realize he had done it.

"Why do you ask?" the Doctor inquired.

"I was just curious," Barclay said as he quickly copied the diagnostic results to his padd and deleted them from the sickbay's files.

"Are you finished?" the Doctor asked.

"Everything looks good for now," Barclay said, hating himself for betraying the Doctor's trust again so soon after swearing not to. "I don't see any system integration errors."

"Good."

"I have to get back," Barclay said, relieved to be in the land of truth again.

"Take care of yourself while I'm away," the Doctor said.

"I promise," Barclay said.

"I'm sure the next time I see you, I'll have made considerable progress."

"I don't doubt it."

Barclay departed, knowing that Doctor Zimmerman was the only person in the universe other than himself who could have intentionally altered the Doctor's memory centers. The file sent to Admiral Janeway suggested it had happened recently, as Admiral Janeway had been presumed dead until a few months before and there would have been no reason for Zimmerman to encode a message to a dead admiral.

But what exactly had Zimmerman done and why? Had he created some new subroutine that gave the Doctor more autonomy over his ethical subroutines? Or had he discovered some degradation in his memory files that had eluded Barclay's standard tests?

Barclay had told the admiral the last time they spoke that he didn't want to know what was in that file unless the Doctor's program was seriously compromised. Thus far, that wasn't the case. The variances were within tolerable limits and were not a serious threat to the Doctor's program.

The engineer just wished he knew how soon that might change.

VESTA

"First Consul Dreeg," Admiral Janeway greeted him, "a pleasure to see you again."

"And you, Admiral Janeway," Dreeg said cordially as the members of his party stared openmouthed at the shuttlebay around them. Their transport ship was smaller than the two runabouts stored in the *Vesta*'s auxiliary bay. It was hardly the largest bay the *Vesta* had, but it was clearly imposing to their Confederacy guests. A few security officers strolled along the catwalks above, monitoring the Confederacy representatives while giving the appearance of attending to other, nonrelated duties.

Dreeg turned and cleared his throat. All but one of his people promptly shut their mouths and focused on him. Only one, a tall male humanoid in a reserved gray suit with a skull nearly twice the size of the Djinari and Leodts, continued to study his surroundings, unabashed.

"Bridge to Admiral Janeway," the voice of Commander Roach, *Vesta*'s first officer, said over the comm.

"Go ahead."

"A second Confederacy shuttle is on approach. I have cleared them to land in bay three."

"Acknowledged," Janeway said, turning to her aide.

"We were advised that only one shuttle would be arriving this morning," Decan said.

"You were not misinformed," Dreeg said quickly. "If you will excuse me for a moment?" he asked.

"Of course," Janeway said. Turning to Farkas, she added, "Would you please greet those arriving in bay three?"

"Right away, Admiral," Farkas replied. Counselor Cambridge stepped closer to Janeway as she departed. Lieutenants Lasren and Psilakis continued to monitor the arrivals from a greater distance.

"What species is that?" Cambridge asked softly, looking toward the man in gray.

"I don't know," Janeway replied.

"He's studying the bay like he's trying to memorize its design."

"For all we know, he is," Janeway said with a shrug.

Dreeg strode quickly back down his shuttle's ramp. He appeared agitated. He opened his mouth to address Janeway but promptly closed it as Captain Farkas reentered the shuttlebay. Presider Cin was by her side, inclining her head graciously to speak with the much shorter Farkas. Settling his face again into composed lines, Dreeg said, "As you can see, our presider has chosen to make an unexpected gift of her presence to us."

"I'm honored," Janeway assured him as she turned to offer her hand to Cin. "It is a pleasure, Presider Cin, to welcome you aboard the *Vesta*."

"Please forgive the disturbance my presence has created," Cin said. "I did not have time to advise the first consul of my desire to join him this morning."

The look on Dreeg's face suggested that he knew this was a falsehood, but he did not dare accuse his presider of it publicly. Instead he simply said, "We exist to serve your needs, Presider. Your presence is never a disturbance."

"I wonder if you would introduce us to the rest of your party, First Consul," Janeway requested. "I'm sure you remember our Captain Farkas, Counselor Cambridge, and my aide, Decan."

"I do," Dreeg said. "This is my secretary, Yent; Consuls Elvoy, Raniet, and Mistoff of the Consortium; Overseer Peene, a civilian starship expert; and Grish," he finished, nodding toward the only member of the party who was not Djinari or Leodt, the man in gray.

"Who does Mister Grish represent?" Janeway asked.

"He is my personal translator," Dreeg replied. "In the event your translation system fails, I wanted to make sure our communication did not."

"A most thoughtful precaution," Janeway said. "Welcome, one and all. You are standing in the *Vesta*'s auxiliary shuttlebay. With your permission, I'd like to escort you now to our first stop on the tour, the *Vesta*'s mess hall. We've prepared refreshments for you and invite you to partake before we begin the tour. I warn you in advance, we'll be doing a lot of walking today."

"That sounds wonderful, Admiral," Cin said.

The group fell into two lines, Cin walking by Janeway's side. Dreeg walked beside Farkas and began peppering her with questions the moment they entered the hall outside the bay. The presider seemed content to simply walk in silence, taking in everything around her.

Over "brunch" Janeway introduced their guests to the ship's replicators. She had decided in advance that this would be the first of two sensitive technological miracles she would show the representatives, though in describing them, she limited her explanation of their uses to those they could see: food and other basic essentials, like clothing.

Presider Cin clapped her hands in delight when a cup of hot tea was replicated for her. "It is like magic," she said, sipping the tea and judging it delicious. "Is all of your food prepared in this manner?"

"Most of it," Janeway said, "although the *Demeter* also grows many edible fruits, vegetables, and grains for the fleet's crew to enjoy from time to time."

"Officers that serve our interstellar fleet enjoy the freshest food and produce our planets can provide," Dreeg noted. "Their needs are met before a mouth on any of our planets is filled. Our ships are also stocked with supplement packs and dried foods that can provide emergency sustenance as needed."

"We have those too." Janeway smiled. "We call them rations, but in our case, none of our crew members look forward to eating them."

"With these replicators at your disposal, I'm surprised they would have to," Cin said.

"As with everything aboard our ships, they require energy. If our energy supplies are unexpectedly diminished, we do without them," Janeway said.

"You mean during battle?" Dreeg asked pointedly.

"Among other things," Janeway replied.

As the group moved through the arboretum and the main medical bay, the admiral provided them with a brief history of the founding of the Federation and a description of some of the larger and longest-standing member worlds.

"Have your people ever encountered the Borg?" Cin asked, as the group moved toward holodeck one, where Janeway had requested a program re-creating the main chamber of the Federation Council to be run.

"We have," Janeway replied. "Our first contact with them was made by the Federation's flagship more than fifteen years ago."

"How fortunate for you, that you have only had to reckon with them for such a brief period of time," Dreeg said.

"When I led the *Starship Voyager* on our long journey home through this quadrant, we encountered them several times."

"It is amazing to me that you survived those encounters, Admiral," Cin said.

"It is a testament to *your* people's fortitude and resourcefulness that you were able to save your civilizations in spite of their aggression," Janeway said, hoping to drop the subject. It was far too soon in their relationship for her to consider sharing the truth of the Borg Invasion of the Alpha Quadrant, or the actions of the Caeliar in ending the Borg's reign of terror.

Their entrance into the holodeck was met with several gasps from the Confederacy guests. The Federation Council chamber appeared to be larger than the shuttlebay.

"Don't be alarmed," Janeway said. "This room is called a holodeck. Its actual size conforms to that of the other rooms on this deck. However, our holographic technology makes it appear to be larger. Holographic emitters create everything you are seeing. This is one of thousands of potential locations our holodecks can re-create. They are used primarily to enhance the variety of the crew's recreational activities during long missions."

Dreeg moved to the podium at the head of the chamber, from which the president usually addressed the council, and rapped his fingers on the wooden surface. "But this is solid," he said.

"A convincing illusion," Janeway said. "This is a representation of our main Federation Council chamber. Every seat in this room is filled by the duly elected or appointed representatives from every Federation member world and our allies. This is where our government does their work."

"It is beautiful," Cin said. "How often does your president consult with this Council?"

"Most days," Janeway replied. "There are smaller committees that tend to specific issues, but legislative sessions run consistently with short breaks for our representatives to return to their own worlds, as is required by the Federation Charter."

"And this Federation has only existed for a little over two hundred years?" Dreeg asked.

"Yes," Janeway said, nodding. "But we hope to one day claim to have thrived as long as your Confederacy."

"You will," Cin assured her.

"Your ship must have a centralized operations facility," Dreeg said.

"Our bridge, yes," Janeway said.

"We would very much like to see it," Dreeg said.

"Very much," Cin echoed.

"Of course," Janeway said. She had expected the request and was already prepared to make this visit a brief one.

The moment the turbolift doors to the bridge slid open, Janeway felt movement behind her as the Confederacy representatives strained to see past her and Presider Cin. As Janeway had ordered, there was a sense of controlled chaos under way. Although each post was manned as required, several crewmen moved about inspecting open panels and apparently in the thick of making numerous repairs.

Janeway turned to Captain Farkas as if this were an unexpected sight and said, "Captain?"

"A moment, please, Admiral," Farkas said, slipping past her and moving to Commander Roach, who stood beside the center seat. "Commander Roach, report," Farkas said sternly.

"I apologize, Presider Cin," Janeway said. "I thought our senior staff would be prepared to receive you, but obviously . . ." she trailed off.

By then Farkas had returned to the turbolift. She whispered a few words in Janeway's ear, and with a theatrical sigh, Janeway said, "The *Vesta* was upgraded and refitted just before we journeyed to the Confederacy. It seems a number of systems require attention now. It would not be safe to tour the bridge at this time, but I would be happy to reschedule this portion of your visit as soon as possible."

"Thank you, Admiral," Cin said. To see the Federation crew in such a state obviously pleased her and restored some of her pride in her own people, who clearly would never have presented such a spectacle of disarray to guests.

"I appreciate your understanding," Janeway said as the turbolift doors slid shut. The moment they had, Janeway knew that the additional crew would collect their things and return to their normal duty posts. The *Vesta* was functioning just fine, but this little ruse made it possible for her to limit the Confederacy's exposure to critical systems.

"Our next stop will be on deck three," Janeway said, finally escorting them out of the cramped space. "These are our standard crew quarters."

As Janeway turned to open the door to an unassigned room, she noted Lieutenants Psilakis and Lasren approaching from the opposite side of the hallway. Between them walked Mister Grish.

"Lieutenant Psilakis?" Janeway asked, as Mister Grish rejoined the larger group.

"We found him wandering around on deck sixteen," Psilakis said.

"My apologies, First Consul," Grish said. "When the group left the holodeck, I remained behind just for a moment. I was marveling at plaques posted at each seat, indicating the names of the member worlds assigned to them. By the time I emerged, the group was no longer in sight."

"I'm glad our security team found you, Mister Grish," Janeway said amiably. "It's a big ship. You're not the only one ever to lose their way while aboard her."

Cin appeared equal parts mortified and angry. "It will not happen again," she offered apologetically.

"Of course not," Dreeg said. Janeway's eyes met those of the first consul. Apparently she wasn't the only one engaging in polite deception.

Chapter Eight

"Miss Seven, how good to see you," Doctor Sharak said the moment she appeared on the viewscreen before him. She looked well rested, but there was concern in her eyes.

"Thank you, Doctor," she said. *"How is your research progressing?"*

"Very well," Sharak replied. He took it as a sign of her continued good health that she bothered to inquire at all. "If my calculations are correct, we might see an end to this plague sooner than expected."

Seven cocked her head to one side, an old tic Sharak rarely witnessed. *"Explain."*

"For now, my studies have been limited to Coridan, specifically the capital city and its surrounding environs. The early infection patterns were what you would expect from an aggressive airborne agent. Proximity to known victims was the clearest indicator of potential infection, and as there were many large public gatherings in the immediate aftermath of the attack on the planet, the spread went unchecked. Quarantine procedures were not put into effect for almost two weeks. The bulk of the casualties came from this period. Following the quarantine, the spread of the illness was immediately reduced. It was several weeks before large numbers of new cases were detected. But even now, new cases are found daily. However, the positive sign is that they arrive in groups of no more than ten to fifty at a time."

"*Then you believe the quarantine is proving effective?*" Seven asked.

"It clearly is," Sharak replied. "Our quest now is to determine where these new cases are coming from. It is difficult to trace the activities of every individual who has been exposed, but most of them are too far removed from the red zone to have contracted it there."

"*Coridan remains an important center of mining operations for the Federation,*" Seven noted. "*The constant traffic over the planet's surface and beyond must limit the quarantine's effectiveness.*"

"It does," Sharak agreed. "However, the restrictions put in place by the Federation Institute of Health are arduous. I believe their quick work has done much to protect the public's health."

Seven nodded in response.

"And how is your friend Axum?" Sharak asked.

"*He is well,*" Seven said. "*His recovery has been astonishing. More work will be required on everyone's part to better understand how the catoms we were given by the Caeliar have restored him.*"

Sharak paused. "Surely that is not your focus at this time?" he asked. "It was my understanding that you would be working directly with the Commander's team to better understand the nature of the plague."

"*The Commander's team works diligently toward that end,*" Seven said. "*The samples I was able to provide have aided them in their efforts. For now, the majority of my time has been spent with Axum.*" After a long pause she added, "*I do not see it as effort wasted.*"

"I did not mean to imply otherwise, Miss Seven," Sharak said kindly. "Do you have any idea how soon you might be able to leave the restricted area? Cadet Icheb made contact with me and is anxious to speak with you."

"*Icheb?*" Seven asked.

"Yes," Sharak replied, determined not to reveal over an open channel Admiral Janeway's efforts in securing the cadet's current assignment in the event Miss Seven was unaware of it.

"*It may be some time until I am able to contact him,*" Seven said.

"I understand," Sharak said. "I will advise him accordingly."

"Thank you, Doctor."

With that, she signed off.

It was clear to the doctor that Seven was still choosing her words carefully during their communications. This was difficult to understand given that everyone working in both the restricted and open labs dedicated to the plague was striving for the same goals. Perhaps her concerns were directly connected to Axum and she was reluctant to share more personal matters over an unsecured channel. Sharak did not doubt that, eventually, he would learn more.

Until then, *Lemross. His burden heavy.*

Returning to Axum's private lab, Seven studied the results of the latest test programs she had created. She agreed with Axum that, for the time being, the only progress she could make would be in further developing her understanding of catoms. As long as the Commander refused to see her, there was little she could do to address the virus directly. But when that time came, she intended to be able to provide essential data that would prove his error in keeping her secluded from the rest of his team.

She wished that the Commander's unwillingness to have her as a contributing member of his team had come as a surprise. Given the Doctor's experience with Doctors Mai, Frist, and Everett, it was not completely unexpected. They believed that they already had the finest minds in Federation medical science addressing the issue. It was true that medicine was not Seven's area of expertise, but the fact remained that she was Borg and retained the collective brilliance of billions of minds. She was also living daily with Caeliar catoms in her body and had discovered many unexpected uses for them. All of this, the Commander must know. He had accessed all of the Doctor's records of her before she had even arrived. What he clearly did not know was that, given enough data, most subjects of inquiry put before Seven, regardless of her prior exposure to them, were quickly added to the long list of items she had mastered.

He underestimated her. That might result in the unnecessary

prolonging of this plague. But until she was given a chance to prove her abilities, Seven was not going to change his mind.

However, her usefulness as a provider of unique catomic material to his efforts had granted her access to Axum. And for that she was grateful.

The specific task upon which she was presently focused was to move beyond the catomic molecules she could now visualize and attempt to unlock the programming that defined them. This was not a simple task. But it was a mathematical one, which meant that, however obscure, the answer existed somewhere within the organization and actions of the catoms themselves. It would not elude her.

Unfortunately, the models she had already created showed multiple errors.

"You don't understand."

Seven's heart quickened. The voice was Axum's. She had expressly forbidden him from speaking again into her mind.

"That is not possible."

Seven took a deep breath and shook her head. He had not betrayed her trust. He was in his own room, and the doors between it and the shared living space and the lab were all open.

But to whom was he speaking?

Seven moved silently to the lab's entrance and peeked into the common room. Urgent whispers came clearly through the door to Axum's room but he had lowered his voice, possibly intentionally.

"I will," she heard distinctly.

The sounds of movement met her ears; the soft fabric of his pants and tunic brushing metal as he rose from a chair that had its own particular squeak, followed by gentle footfalls.

A sudden, unfamiliar anxiety washed over her. She began to retreat back into the lab but stopped herself. Axum's mental health was as important to her as his physical health. He had yet to share with her his experiences following the destruction of Unimatrix Zero or the personal hell the Borg queen had created for him prior to the Caeliar transformation. She knew the broad strokes from the Doctor's reports. As she was withholding significant personal information from Axum, however, she could not fault him for not opening up to her.

Still, she would not hide her concerns.

He stepped into the common room, obviously in the process of relaxing his face into the composed lines Seven was growing accustomed to seeing.

He doesn't want me to see his pain, she realized.

She moved toward him. "Are you all right?" she asked.

Axum nodded.

"I heard your voice. To whom were you speaking?"

A wince confirmed her suspicions, but she still wanted to hear it from him.

"I spent many solitary months on the shuttle that eventually brought me to Starbase 185," he said. "I'm afraid I picked up some lonely habits."

Seven nodded. "I understand. It was incredibly difficult for me to adjust when I was first severed from the Collective. And I did so under the patient care of *Voyager*'s crew."

"I was not that lucky," Axum said.

Tell me, she wanted to say.

Instead, she simply nodded.

"Hello, Jefferson."

"Good afternoon, Naria."

Her eyes betrayed no fear, but her flesh was a warmer shade of purple than he usually found when they greeted one another.

She's sensing your frustration, the Commander chided himself, as he extracted the hypospray from its case.

"Please lie down," he requested.

Bowing her head, she raised her right hand and used it to sweep her long, straight black hair over her shoulder. He automatically lifted a gloved hand behind her, supporting her as she reclined.

"This won't hurt, will it?"

"I don't believe so," he replied, forcing more confidence into his voice than he felt.

The Commander raised the hypospray to her neck, and a

soft hiss accompanied the transfer of matter into her body. He braced himself for the sound of alarms.

Instead, he heard a soft keening sound from Naria. She had raised her left hand and stared at it in confusion. The Commander watched the back of it ripple unnaturally, as if it had suddenly been transformed to a liquid state.

"Jefferson?" Naria asked, wide pleading eyes meeting his.

"Wait," he said. The room's bioscanner was starting to trill, but its warning was not urgent. The Commander watched Naria's hand settle again into its normal, solid state.

The Commander smiled, bending directly over Naria to be sure she could see his relief. Her eyes lost their terror. The corners of her mouth began to tip upward.

Suddenly, they drooped. The momentary shared delight in her eyes shifted to confusion, then fear.

The flesh of her face began to darken as it slid away from the bones beneath it. Obsidian lips opened wide, but what should have been a scream was reduced to a sickening gurgle.

Every critical system warning alarm began to blare at once.

The Commander did not hesitate. He moved back through the airlock to the room's exterior controls. There he entered his personal code into a padd beside a transparent steel case and quickly depressed the single large control mechanism it contained.

A muffled boom met his ears as the room in which Naria lay dissolving was filled with instantaneous sickly orange light.

The Commander looked away, trying to calm his ragged breathing. When he looked back, fine black dust was scattered over the surface of the bed where Naria had greeted him only moments before.

Axum extended his left hand to Seven. She took it in both of hers and wordlessly raised it to her cheek, relaxing into the caress. She was surprised by the warmth she felt radiating from it. Clearly there had been recent advances in prosthetic limbs of which she was unaware.

Curious, she pulled it from her face and began to study it.

Resting it in her right hand, she touched his palm gently with the fingers of her left.

As soon as she did so, she felt a curious spasm in her hand. Her fingertips began to tingle, but only briefly. Invisible fire shot upward through each finger and she turned her palm up automatically as her hand involuntarily stiffened.

The pain was too intense to scream. It simply enveloped her as her entire existence seemed to shrink to the size of her left hand. A deep groan escaped her lips.

"Annika?" Axum asked.

For an instant the heat of the fire expanded. It was as if she had been standing in the path of an explosion's shockwave.

As soon as it had come, it vanished. Thankfully, it took the agony in her hand with it.

"Annika?" Axum asked again.

Seven started to fall, but Axum's arms held her, lifting her with ease as she curled into his chest.

MONTECITO, CALIFORNIA

This is a mistake.

Tom Paris knew it. He'd made enough of them in his life to recognize the sick twist of his stomach combined with the odd clarity of his mind. It was the absolute certainty that made him pause. The worst mistakes he'd ever made had all been precipitated by precisely this cocktail of sensations.

So take a minute, a new, faint voice suggested. It might have been B'Elanna's; Paris couldn't say for sure. But in a radical departure from tradition, Paris stepped back from the front door of his mother's home and moved to the large front window to its right, through which the family's dining room was clearly visible.

The room was dark, but ambient light coming from the connecting hall to the kitchen cast the oval table that could easily seat a dozen in faint relief.

A shadow passed across that light. Straining, Paris thought he could hear his mother's voice. It was impossible to make out her words, but as the light dimmed again, he realized she was pacing to and fro, likely addressing the comm panel she'd had installed on the stone island that occupied the center of the kitchen. He could remember her passing in and out of the panel's camera sight as she prepared dinner while checking up on him when he was at the Academy, a lifetime ago.

"Kathleen!" his mother said clearly.

She was talking to his older sister, the professor.

Paris hadn't made contact with either of his sisters. Shaw had ordered him not to. Truth be told, he had a hunch where their sympathies would lie in this case and he didn't really want that confirmed.

Still, it rankled. She didn't need to talk to Kathleen. She needed to talk to her son, the one whose life she was trying to destroy.

Indignant, Paris walked back to the front door. As he raised his hand to ring the bell he was suddenly conscious of motion behind him. His arms were grabbed in viselike grips and a hand was thrown over his mouth as he was pulled, none too gently, from the porch.

Naturally he struggled. Had his attackers been smaller or less intent on their purpose, he probably still wouldn't have stood much of a chance, given their brute strength. His feet did not touch the ground until he had reached the far end of the large front lawn and been shoved unceremoniously through the natural wood gate that bordered his mother's property. Roughly, the hands turned him to face a single, slight figure stepping from the shadows thrown by a large tree at the front edge of the yard.

The face was difficult to make out in the faint light of the moon. The voice, however, was familiar.

"Are you out of your mind?" Lieutenant Garvin Shaw asked.

Paris's shouted response was muffled by the hand still covering his mouth.

"Quiet!" Shaw hissed.

It took a few moments for Paris to relax, but finally he did. A nod from Shaw freed his mouth. Paris looked briefly at the hulking officers still holding his arms before turning his fury on Shaw.

"What are you doing here?" Paris asked.

"Your personal file acquainted me with your predilection for rash idiocy, Commander," Shaw replied. "Frankly I'm a little surprised it took you this long to try such a boneheaded move."

"I can't talk to her in front of Ozimat. I can't say what I need to say if I have to weigh every word. It just comes out wrong," Paris said.

"And what were you planning to tell her tonight?" Shaw asked.

Paris paused. It surprised him to realize that, even now, he wasn't exactly sure.

Shaw looked to the large man on Paris's right and said, "It's all right now. Let him go. And thanks, guys."

The two men did as Shaw had asked but continued to stand at attention beside Paris.

"Do these two work for you?"

"From time to time," Shaw replied. "I engaged them the moment I was assigned your case. You should know that they'll never be far behind you as long as you're on Earth. Try as hard as you like, Tom. I'm not going to let you screw this up."

"The JAG corps really is a full-service branch, isn't it?" Paris asked.

"Let's take a walk," Shaw said, ignoring the barb.

The Paris family ranch was located in a secluded valley. Familiar tree-lined paths snaked throughout the forest surrounding the house that had been cleared centuries earlier. Shaw's goons didn't follow too closely behind, but Paris was still conscious of their steps in the distance as he and his attorney melted into the forest.

"You could have just transported in and stopped me yourself," Paris said, still smarting from the humiliation of the last few minutes.

"I'm fifty-seven kilos dripping wet with two rocks in my pockets, Commander," Shaw said. "I know my limits."

Shaw's honesty took Paris by surprise and he laughed before he could stop himself.

"I know this is tough for you," Shaw continued. "But you have to trust me. This isn't the way. You go after your mom outside of mediation and Ozimat is going to find for Julia before we even finish making our case."

"She's winning," Paris said softly, finally giving voice to the fear that had brought him to his mother's door.

"Are you a lawyer now?" Shaw asked. "You don't know that."

"She's winning because she's right."

Shaw stopped and turned to face Paris. "See, if you were a lawyer, you'd know that doesn't matter."

"I try to do the right thing," Paris said, as if he hadn't heard. "I try to follow orders. I try to live up to my own expectations, now that I finally know what those are and how good it feels to meet them. But she's right: Too many times in my life I've come up against problems the truth won't solve. I have to do what my conscience, or my fear, or my heart demands, and damn the consequences."

"Everybody does that, Tom," Shaw said.

"Maybe. But not everybody ends up in jail, or in the brig for thirty days, or staring at their mother across that damned table. It's like I have a special gift for screwing things up."

"What you did to protect Miral was not wrong," Shaw insisted. "The problem is it came after all those other choices that were less defensible." After a moment, Shaw asked, "Why didn't you tell your parents what B'Elanna was really doing on Boreth?"

"She asked me not to."

"Didn't she trust them?"

"She didn't even know them at that point. And in fairness, I hadn't painted the best picture of them for her. She didn't want them to see her weak. She barely lets me see that. And the issue with her mom, it had been building her whole life. She had to confront it when and how she did. But there's no explaining that to my mom. It's a Klingon thing."

"I dated a Klingon woman once," Shaw said. "She was amazing."

Paris laughed again. "You don't say. What happened?"

"She left me. Got tired of sending me to sickbay. It was probably for the best."

"If you say so," Paris said. After a long pause, he added, "B'Elanna's pregnant again."

"What?"

"She's going to have our son in about six months."

Shaw's silence grew unnerving in short order. Finally he said, "No wonder you're such a wreck."

"Actually, this is pretty much just me," Paris said.

Shaw cracked a smile and shrugged. "This helps us. You should have told me sooner."

"I hoped this wasn't going to take more than one meeting with my mom."

"How many friends do you have around here these days?"

"Not many," Paris replied, wondering at the abrupt change of subject.

"I need some good character references for you."

"That's going to be a challenge. For *good* references you have to go to the Delta Quadrant," Paris said.

"Make a list. Don't contact them yourself. Give it to me and I'll do that."

"Okay."

"Tom?"

"What?"

"Don't contact them yourself."

"I won't."

"You're sure?"

"Yes."

"I also told you not to contact your mother outside of mediation."

"I remember."

"But here we are."

Paris sighed. "Don't worry. I'm done thinking."

"Good."

"But you'd better be right about this," Paris added. "My wife is only half-Klingon, but she won't put me in sickbay. She'll put me in the morgue."

Chapter Nine

Counselor Hugh Cambridge had begun to sense the shift in the Confederacy's representatives several days before. Until then, the presider and her people had lived secure in the knowledge that they rested atop the pinnacle of social, cultural, and technological achievement. The Federation had been viewed as little more than an amusing, if slightly backward, distant cousin. Initially, the Starfleet officers who engaged their diplomats were met with unfailing hospitality, great courtesy, and polite condescension.

The ground had begun to shift as soon as the *Vesta* had entered orbit around the First World. Cambridge had monitored the public news feeds. They had wasted no time in beginning the comparison game, all of which inevitably concluded with conviction of the Confederacy's superiority. They seemed blissfully ignorant of the fact that they were the only ones engaging in this debate. Starfleet didn't contact alien species to feather their own nests or bolster their self-esteem. They did it to expand their knowledge of the universe. To encounter a species or civilization more advanced than the Federation was not a source of humiliation; it was simply another wonder to be studied and, when possible, embraced.

The tour of the *Vesta* had cemented the sea change, at least as far as the delegates were concerned. Naturally, they did not rush to public microphones and proclaim their astonishment at the technology of the Federation. For now, it remained a dark and festering secret. The saddest part was that the admiral had chosen to reveal relatively little of the Federation's true technical capabilities. Cambridge could only imagine how it would wound the Confederacy to learn of their transporters, transphasic torpedoes, their role in the transformation of the Borg, or their fledgling attempts to understand catomic matter.

The presider seemed determined, however, to regain sure footing in the eyes of her Federation guests. The morning had been spent walking the wide halls and standing beneath the vaulted ceilings of the capital city's largest museum and central library. A wide variety of fine and decorative arts was on display, and while they weren't the most interesting or beautiful Cambridge had ever seen—their paintings, sculptures, mosaics, and collage constructions shared a flat, realistic preoccupation and their furnishings tended toward the baroque—they certainly possessed intrinsic beauty and were worthy of admiration.

Dreeg accompanied the group, along with his translator, Grish, but kept his own counsel as the presider regaled Admiral Janeway with the story of the Confederacy's beginning. Decan walked behind them, beside Cambridge, with Psilakis and Lasren bringing up the rear. The Betazoid lieutenant was clearly learning quickly to regulate his empathic input. He seemed calm and focused as Cin spoke.

"Was it difficult for the Djinari and Leodt to set aside their previous grievances and work together?" Janeway asked.

"Less so than you might imagine," Cin said, "at least if our records of that journey are to be believed. What we learned when we joined our efforts against a common enemy was that in many ways, even after years of conflict, we were one people at heart."

Cambridge had already surmised that this was the case. Although the physical similarities between the two species were few, their DNA was another matter. It was likely that hundreds of thousands of years earlier, these two disparate peoples had shared a common ancestor, which made one thing very difficult for the counselor to understand. He had yet to meet a single Djinari or Leodt of mixed heritage.

"I would guess, Presider Cin, that when your people began their journey, the issue of rebuilding a sustainable population was not at the forefront of their minds, but once the Great River was discovered and its streams led you to the First World, that must have changed," Cambridge ventured.

"It did," the presider said, nodding. "Our reproductive rates plummeted aboard the colony ships. They traveled for more than forty years, and although procreation was encouraged among any and all willing to accept the inherent risks, very few of those brave women managed to carry their children to term."

"Were attempts made to mingle your gene pools?" Cambridge asked.

"It had been accepted biological fact for centuries that the Djinari and Leodt were not compatible in that way," Cin replied. "I cannot state to a certainty that some did try," she said, smiling demurely, "but our species cannot reproduce with one another even to this day, nor have there been any productive intermarriages between our people and any of the other species that have since joined the Confederacy."

"Is that something your people would like to change?" Janeway asked.

Cin shook her head again. "Thank the Source, it is not necessary. In fact, though many had come to believe that a higher power was leading us to our salvation, it was not until we arrived on the First World that we knew this to be true."

"Your people did not worship the Source before they arrived here?" Cambridge asked.

"It is said that the first to travel the Great River were the first to know the Source. As soon as the streams were discovered and began to carry us far from the reaches of the Borg, many began to tell stories of dreams in which the Source spoke to them. But few embraced the Source until we discovered the First World. The Source revealed itself to us in all of its glory. Only then did its purpose in saving us become clear."

"How did it do that?" Janeway asked.

"The first people to land on this world knew that it was unique. It was the first planet suitable for colonization we discovered where no evidence could be found of other sentient life ever inhabiting it. Given its age, that puzzled our scientists. Now we understand that it was created for us."

"Did the Source tell you this?" Cambridge asked.

"In a way," Cin replied. "In the five years prior to our arrival here, the few children conceived of either Djinari or Leodt parents carried to full term were stillborn or died within hours of their birth. Despair had poisoned them. Our people had struggled for so long to find a new, safe world on which they could rebuild their civilization. But that hardly mattered if no future generations would exist."

"Let me guess," Cambridge said. "Once you reached the First World, your reproductive issues vanished?"

"Almost overnight," Cin said. "Our colony ships came to rest here with an eye toward replenishing our supplies and moving on. Some argued, however, that this might be a good place to make our permanent home. Two months later, as the ships were preparing to depart, the Revered Mother, Isandala, gave birth to the first healthy Djinari daughter born in years."

"And her Honored Sister, Malamai, followed her example six weeks later, giving birth to a Leodt son," Dreeg added.

Cambridge knew that these miracles probably had more to do with clean air and fresh water than a god who had chosen these species to worship it, but he also knew that for the ancestors of Cin and Dreeg, that hadn't mattered. Pity that it had meant the destruction of dozens of other worlds, once the First World was designated as sacred.

"So they chose to stay," Janeway said.

"Is it really a choice when the truth of divine design is so clear before you?" Cin asked. "The Great River had carried us beyond the reach of our enemies. The journey had made us one people. The First World had been given to us and only here could we survive beyond a single generation. The Source knew better than we did what the people needed. All we have done since honors the Source. Our gratitude to it knows no bounds, and that gratitude has informed our choice to embrace the other worlds connected through the Great River to this secluded area of the First

Quadrant. Many of the worlds that now comprise our Confederacy once believed themselves to be alone in the universe. Now they are part of something greater. Now they know the Source and its many gifts. Our ancestors were noble people, but they had fallen into darkness and strife. We have learned from their example. We could never have done all this without the guiding hand of the Source or its infinite wisdom."

"And what about the worlds sacrificed so that you could rebuild here?" Cambridge asked.

"You speak of the *lemms*," Cin said.

"The *lemms*?" Janeway asked.

"Our ancestors feared to disrupt the bounty of the First World. As a gift of the Source, preserving it in its natural state was required. Obviously, we have developed an advanced infrastructure here, but we dig only as deep as we must. To harvest the resources of the First World to build all that we required would have destroyed it, and insulted the Source, and that we could never do. We sought out worlds that did not contain other sentient life—what we call the *lemms*—and sacrificed them to the Source."

"With the help of the ancient protectors?" Cambridge asked.

"They were a gift of the Source. Ancient technology was discovered on a distant planet, far from the First World but near enough the Gateway to make regular access possible. Once activated, that technology gave birth to the ancient protectors. It took decades to determine how many uses they had, as well as their symbiotic relationship to the streams. But as a gift, we knew they were ours to do with as we required. Without them, we could never have built what you see here. Once they began to resist our efforts, we knew the Source had placed a limit on our expansion. We honored the ancients' compassion for the *lemms* and left them in peace to tend to their own."

Janeway nodded, though Cambridge thought he saw her eyes glistening. That the presider could paint such a pretty picture over wanton destruction was no solace. It was willful denial and its results, no matter how aesthetically pleasing, could never hide that truth. Had the Djinari and Leodt abandoned the *lemms* and the ancient protectors because they believed it was ordained by their god, or because the protectors had become more of a nuisance than they were worth? The Leodt and Djinari would only ever admit to the first answer. Cambridge suspected the admiral grieved, because she believed that it was the second.

CIF TWELFTH LAMONT

"Welcome to the command center, Lieutenant Kim," General Mattings greeted him from within a waist-high circular bank of control panels.

"Thank you, sir. It's an honor to be here," Kim replied. He had already been briefed on the configuration of the *Lamont*'s bridge by Chakotay. The general stood at the heart of the center. Every Confederacy Interstellar Fleet's commanding officer was required to stand while on the bridge, as was every other officer. That rank did not earn one a chair was likely as much a reflection of the value placed on "readiness" by officers of the CIF, as the reality that their reliance on the streams gave them access to much of their territory in a matter of hours.

The ship had a large viewscreen stationed directly ahead of the central controls. A few meters before it rested a long series of panels where three officers worked, dividing the duties of operations, navigation, and engineering among them. The port side of the bridge held interfaces for two armament, or tactical, officers. The starboard side was manned by two sensor operators.

Behind the general, six junior officers stood at attention, three on either side of a large door, the command center's only entrance. Every bridge officer, from Mattings on down, carried a sidearm secured to their belts.

Uniform color denoted specialty and rank. The general wore white. The forward bridge officers were clad in shades of blue, tactical in red, and sensors in green. The rear guard wore gray. Like everything the Confederacy did, the uniforms were ornate, both in design and insignia. They reminded Kim of some of Tom Paris's more ancient naval holodeck programs.

"JP Creak, let's show our guest where we're going," the general ordered, gesturing for Kim to stand beside him, just outside the control ring.

The lieutenant looked toward the main viewscreen where a relatively crude astrometrics display was rendered. Several long blue lines streaked through it.

"Are those the streams, General?" Kim asked.

"Chakotay said you were a quick study," Mattings noted. "They are, son. They're but a fraction of the Great River. Those are the significant ones within five thousand light-years of our present course." After giving Kim a moment to absorb this, the general asked, "Can you identify our destination, Lieutenant?"

Kim could not read the alien script that dotted the display, but he and Chakotay had already reviewed the flight plan to Lecahn.

"Sector 361, Grid 19," Kim said.

"That's right," Mattings said, a little surprised.

"General," Kim said, "didn't you say it would take two days for us to reach Lecahn?"

"Yes."

"Begging your pardon, sir, but isn't that a stream running through Sectors 269 to 361?"

"It is."

"Is there some reason our course does not utilize that stream?" Kim asked.

"We could." Mattings nodded. "But then we'd arrive at Lecahn in less than five hours. We're taking the long way. Give us a little time to get to know one another."

"I look forward to it, General," Kim said.

"As do I," Mattings said.

After a long pause, Kim asked, "Was the *Twelfth Lamont* the first ship to register *Demeter*'s access of the Gateway?"

"She was," Mattings said, nodding. "I came within a *monkar*'s tail length of destroying her."

"But they were accompanied, sir," Kim said. "I thought the presence of the ancient protectors saved them."

"It did," Mattings said. "But those ancients took the Source's sweet time identifying them as friendly."

"To the *Lamont*?"

"To the other protectors inside the stream, who then transmitted their acceptance to the *Lamont*."

"Do you still have records of that encounter?" Kim asked.

"Creak?"

A young, wiry Leodt in a dark green jacket replied, "Affirmative, General."

"May I see them?" Kim asked.

"Of course," Mattings said. "Creak won't bite," he added with a chortle, gesturing for Kim to approach the sensor station.

"General," a low voice called over Kim's shoulder as he made his way around the command center's rear arc, "all data regarding Federation contacts remains restricted."

The general looked toward the voice's source, a stout Leodt wearing scarlet. "You think Lieutenant Kim doesn't already know his fleet ships inside and out, JC Eleoate?"

"Our protocols are sure to be new to him," Eleoate replied.

Mattings sighed. "If you're worried that it'll take Kim here only two days to do our jobs better than we do, I'll take that bet. But our purpose is to exchange information with our new friends. He hasn't been here five minutes and you're already at threat level nine."

"I did not mean to suggest—" Eleoate began.

"Your concern is noted," Mattings said. "Creak, show Lieutenant Kim whatever he wants to see."

"Immediately, General," Creak replied.

Kim noted that Eleoate's eyes remained fixed on him as he reached the sensor station. As a tactical officer, Kim understood Eleoate's reservations. He could only hope that the vast majority of those serving with Eleoate did not share his fears.

VOYAGER

The large display screen of the astrometrics lab looked like a playbook for parrises squares. Captain Chakotay had never seriously studied the game, but a roommate at the Academy had been a champion and spent many a long night poring over the patterns he and his teammates had designed. Several bright stars dotted the screen before him like team members. Running through the display in hues of blue, violet, and red were long lines connecting and dividing the territory or indicating patterns of movement through it.

"Captain," Commander B'Elanna Torres greeted him as he approached her position at the main data interface panel that bordered a wide platform separating it from the massive screen.

"Good morning, Captain," Lieutenant Nancy Conlon echoed.

"What have we here?" Chakotay asked.

"It's taken a little time," Torres began, "but Nancy and I finally identified the particular subspace glitch common to the corridors or streams the Confederacy uses."

"Glitch?" Chakotay asked.

"The proper term is 'subharmonic particulate manifold variance,'" Conlon said.

"'Glitch' is fine," Chakotay said, smiling.

"It also might be more accurate," Torres added. "The first time one of these corridors was created, no one with a rudimentary grasp of physics or quantum mechanics would have called it anything but a mistake. These streams are not naturally occurring. They are not the byproduct of interstellar travel or weaknesses in the fabric of subspace. The energy necessary to carve out even the most unstable tunnels or corridors through subspace is violent and usually very destructive to local surrounding normal space."

"Unstable?" Chakotay asked. "The Confederacy has been making use of them for five hundred years."

"And the Vaadwaur were using something similar to them at least three hundred years before that," Torres said. "When *Voyager* visited the Indign system and its surrounding sectors, you were also right on top of another system of subspace corridors."

"I was still a guest, but I don't remember anyone mentioning them during the briefings I attended," Chakotay said.

"*Hawking* took the best readings and referred to them as

subspace instabilities," Conlon noted. "They thought they had detected old transwarp tunnels. We had our hands a little full to investigate further, but now that we have data on so many examples of these corridors, it's easier to find the appropriate correlations. Transwarp leaves unique signatures, just like warp trails. The streams don't work quite the same way. One of the instabilities *Hawking* detected was definitely transwarp. But none of the others show the same signature.

"What's more interesting," *Voyager*'s engineer went on, "is that the Turei told you the corridors they used were unstable. They had devised means to reinforce them, but constant use degrades them quickly. The corridors near the Indign system had obviously fallen out of use, and many were collapsed or on the verge."

"The Confederacy seems to have realized early on that the corridors were unstable and uses the wave forms to keep them open," Torres added.

"But they rotate individual wave forms constantly throughout their corridors, don't they?" Chakotay asked.

"If we're taking their word for it," Torres said, nodding. "I'm guessing that they didn't institute that precaution until the ancient ones turned against them. They no longer seem willing to run the risk of allowing them to grow beyond very limited parameters."

"These are all of the corridors present in how many sectors?" Chakotay asked.

"Ten," Torres replied. "The deeper we get into Confederacy space, the more we'll be able to map. I'm adding some new protocols to our long-range sensor sweeps to pick up as many as possible. But look at this," Torres said, magnifying a small section of the screen.

"That's our current route to Lecahn," Chakotay realized.

"And there's a stream running right beside it," Conlon pointed out.

"They don't want to use it," Chakotay said softly. "Why?"

Torres shrugged. "Each stream, like the Gateway, has a particular harmonic resonance that pulls it into normal space to allow ingress. Sometimes the resonance range is large enough that any ship moving at high warp could accidentally access it, but most require a key, like the one the proctors gave us for the Gateway. However, once inside, as long as you know what you're looking for, the resonance is easy to detect."

"So if we use them once, we can always use them," Chakotay said. "The Confederacy probably doesn't want us to know."

"I wouldn't if I were them," Torres said, expanding the map again.

"There's one more thing you should see," Conlon said, directing Chakotay's attention to another area of the grid, where the bright lines denoting corridors were noticeably absent.

"Is that a border of Confederacy space?" Chakotay asked.

"No," Conlon replied. "Long-range sensors are just beginning to render it, but it looks like another small void."

"Something they're hiding from us?" Chakotay mused.

"Could be," Torres agreed. "But according to the charts the Confederacy provided of their territory and aligned planets, it is surrounded by several members."

"Maybe they haven't expanded there because there are no corridors present to access it," Chakotay suggested.

"But look at the rest of it," B'Elanna said. "This area around that void is filled with corridors. What happened there?"

Chakotay agreed it was odd. "Maybe I'll ask Mattings the next chance I get." After a moment he asked, "Do we have any idea how these are created?"

"None," Torres said.

"But give us a little more time," Conlon added, smiling.

"Good work, you two," Chakotay said. "B'Elanna?"

The fleet chief engineer nodded, following Chakotay to the door. Once they were outside, Chakotay asked, "How's Miral doing?"

Torres's face hardened. "She's fine."

"B'Elanna?"

Finally she looked up at the captain, her sadness plain to see.

"I'm sorry," Chakotay said. "I'm not trying to pry. You've got plenty to keep you busy. But with Tom gone and Harry *studying abroad* for a few days, I don't want to lose touch with the crew."

"It's okay," Torres said. "She misses her daddy. I do too. Nancy and I are running in circles trying to keep her distracted. So far, it seems to be working."

"And the baby?"

"He's a busy little guy already," B'Elanna said, smiling faintly.

"Are you settled in to your new quarters?"

"Miral loves them. She's never had her own room before. Thank you again."

"It was nothing."

"Tom told me you lied to Admiral Janeway for us," Torres blurted out.

"It was a reflex," Chakotay said. "Not one I'm particularly proud of."

"I know what that must have cost you," Torres said. "But your instinct was right. Wild *targs* couldn't have dragged me to the Alpha Quadrant for that mediation."

"I don't care what the court decides," Chakotay said.

"That makes two of us," Torres agreed.

"Tom will make this right. He'll make his mother understand."

"Or he won't." Torres shrugged. "Either way, it doesn't matter."

"No, I guess it doesn't."

The Doctor was frustrated. In less than a day he had isolated dozens of viral agents found in the bloodstreams of ten of the first plague victims. In each case, any of the viruses might have caused the systemic damage that ultimately killed them, but none of them showed the telltale catomic tags that would have made the speed with which they attacked and killed their hosts directly attributable to catomic material. And no single virus yet detected possessed other properties that could account for the incredible mutability or effectiveness of his theoretical "catomic virus."

The Doctor still had hundreds of samples to process. He would find it eventually. But "eventually" might come too late.

"Good morning, Doctor," a familiar voice said, pulling him from his processing.

"Captain," the Doctor said, looking up from the screen in his office, a space he did not remember being as small as it actually was. "Please state the nature of the medical emergency."

Chakotay laughed. "I really don't miss that," he said. "Harry mentioned that Lieutenant Barclay has been here a few times since you transferred."

"He was assisting me in upgrading the systems," the Doctor said.

"*Voyager* wasn't brought up to current specs during the last refit?" Chakotay asked.

"Current specs for Starfleet, not for *me*," the Doctor replied.

"How goes the battle?"

"Slowly," the Doctor conceded. "When a premise is impossible, looking for evidence to support it seems like a waste of time. But when nothing else seems possible . . ." The Doctor trailed off.

Chakotay watched as a strange calm settled over the Doctor's face. It was an oddly *human* expression, one that in anyone else might have indicated conflicting thoughts or emotions. But human as the Doctor appeared, and despite his growth, he had always retained a few subtle "tells" that, to a familiar eye, betrayed his holographic nature.

"Doctor?"

"I'm sorry, Captain," the Doctor said, focusing his attention again. "Was there something you needed?"

"Not really," Chakotay admitted. "But you and I haven't talked much since you got back."

"Do you wish to take me to task for betraying Seven?" the Doctor asked defensively.

The walls rose so quickly, Chakotay was stunned. "No," he said. "My understanding from the admiral was that you were ordered to turn over your records regarding Seven. You saved Axum's life, for which I know Seven is grateful."

"But you're still in love with her," the Doctor said. "Surely you blame me for her separation from the fleet."

Chakotay leaned forward. "Doctor, Seven is a dear friend, but she hasn't been more than that to me for years."

Concern creased the Doctor's brow. After a moment he said, "Of course she hasn't. I'm sorry, Chakotay, I don't know where that came from."

"Doctor . . ." Chakotay began.

"Please don't suggest I run a diagnostic," the Doctor said. "Reg had me perform one yesterday and he was satisfied with the results."

"Okay," Chakotay said. "But that was weird."

The Doctor struggled to speak for a moment. Finally he said, "It's the strangest thing. Most of the time my program seems to be functioning normally. I sense nothing out of the ordinary. But from time to time now, my mind just wanders, as if I can't access the appropriate subroutine or memory file as quickly as I used to."

"Is that unusual?"

"Very," the Doctor stated. "If I didn't know it was impossible, I'd associate it with the normal lapses of the brain consistent with the aging process."

"Holograms don't age," Chakotay pointed out.

"They usually don't achieve sentience, either."

Concerned, Chakotay said, "We're in the middle of a complicated first-contact situation. You are our chief medical officer. The *Galen* is at the First World; if we lose you, we're really in trouble."

"I will monitor the situation as best I can, Chakotay," the Doctor said. "If I believe it is affecting my ability to serve in the capacity required, I will advise you at once."

"Thank you, Doctor," Chakotay said, rising. "You know my concern is not just professional."

"I do," the Doctor said. Once the captain had departed he turned back to his workstation. It was difficult to focus on the viral properties before him. Odd, random memories interrupted his normal processes: Counselor Cambridge emerging from Seven's bedroom, Seven's face as she—

The visual record of Seven's face vanished, like a screen going black. As it did so, a sense of absolute calm poured through the Doctor. Once it had passed, the images of the various viruses he had been studying engrossed the Doctor completely. His concerns of only moments before, along with Chakotay's, no longer resided in his short-term memory buffers. They vanished into long-term ones that were now veiled by a vast, dark curtain. That curtain was growing incrementally larger each day, and with it, precious experiences accumulated by his program were more difficult to access. Wrong as the Doctor knew this was, he could not bring himself to care.

There was simply too much to do.

FIRST WORLD

"Do you smell that, Lieutenant?" Commander Glenn asked.

The *Galen*'s tactical officer, Lieutenant Ranson Velth, took a short sniff, then followed it with a deeper inhalation. Finally he said, "What?"

"Fresh air," Glenn said, smiling.

Velth nodded, though he might not have called the wide variety of fragrances around him "fresh." It was, however, a vast improvement over the last five hours. In Velth's experience, no matter what quadrant of the galaxy you were in, every hospital had its own unpleasant odor that was only made worse by some universal antiseptic solution.

Velth and Glenn had just departed the capital city's Central Medical Service. Their tour had begun at noon, local time. Five hours later, they broke for dinner. The Starfleet officers had been invited to join the doctors and staff. The facility boasted six separate eating establishments, and Commander Glenn had been issued enough local currency to purchase anything they would have desired. But *Galen*'s captain had other plans, and Velth hadn't argued. Another universal truth: Whatever consumables hospitals served, they should not be confused with *food*.

After thanking their guides profusely, Glenn had asked if it would be possible for her to leave the hospital grounds for dinner. She assumed that several other local eateries could be found nearby, and Glenn sincerely wanted an experience of the native cuisine.

Neurological Specialist Piron had suggested a small establishment that was famous for its vegetarian dishes. By the time he'd finished describing the signature soup, Glenn was sold. Piron had offered to escort them there but settled for giving them directions when he was called to an emergency consult. Glenn had thanked him, and she and Velth had slipped out of the hospital for a little freedom. As a tactical officer, Velth instinctively took note of their surroundings, but even after several minutes of walking he had not noted anyone following them.

Their destination was off the main thoroughfare, several blocks ahead. They walked down a wide paved sidewalk, occasionally jostled by natives, most of whom moved at a hurried pace. Some stared. A few raised small devices Velth assumed were cameras of some sort, but most settled for a nod of greeting as they passed.

The street was lined on both sides by tall edifices of metal and glass. Random small storefronts were sometimes sandwiched between them. Most bore discreet signage Velth could not read, but their window displays easily solved that problem. Glenn had paused at one offering several complicated items of clothing suspended as if in midair. Velth wondered if the commander was tempted, but she settled for a quick look before continuing.

The street side of the sidewalk was lined with tall potted plants with large blue and orange fronds forming a hedge. Beyond them, several small vehicles traveled down the main road with no discernible emissions. Exotic spices assaulted Velth briefly, their source difficult to pinpoint.

Glenn seemed to relish every step.

"You didn't get as much downtime as the rest of us when we were home," Velth suddenly realized.

"No," Glenn said. "I hope you made the most of it."

"I spent a couple of weeks with my sister and her kids," Velth said. "I didn't mind when we were recalled early."

"Velth," Glenn said, clearly offended for his sister. She punctuated her disapproval with a backhanded smack to his upper arm. Velth was a little surprised by the strength behind it. Glenn was tall and thin, but her lithe frame belied her apparent muscle tone.

"You've never met those kids," Velth insisted. "They're monsters."

"But when you were their age, you were a perfect little angel?" Glenn teased.

"I can't have been that bad. They run Shirin wild and they're always at each other's throats."

"They're children, Velth. That's their job description."

The tactical officer would have continued to argue his case had he not caught sight of what he believed was their destination. A long line of patrons extended out the small café's front door, and several people were seated outside. Most were reveling in bowls of a deep green soup filled with large chunks of *feon*, a root Piron had made sound much like a sweet onion.

"This is it," Glenn said, turning the corner and making a beeline for the queue.

As they settled themselves behind a tall Leodt male in a stark black suit, Velth said, his voice pitched low, "Were you surprised by anything you saw this afternoon?"

"Pleasantly," Glenn said, keeping her voice down. "Their facilities were exceptional. Their staff is well trained and professional. Their technology is obviously designed to handle the unique physiology of the species they most often treat, but I'd say, in general, it is on par with the Federation."

"So if whatever we have for dinner doesn't sit right, I'm in good hands?" Velth asked.

"Yes," Glenn said. "*Mine.*"

"Did anything bother you?"

"Not so far," Glenn replied, as a look of concern contorted her face. In the distance, the sound of voices raised in anger cut through the buzz of normal activity around them.

Searching automatically for the voices, Velth began to study the details of the café's immediate surroundings. All of the businesses on this block were small storefronts. There were several carts standing before high walls offering a wide variety of fresh fruits, vegetables, flowers, and plants, and local handcrafted items. Foot traffic became congested as people moved at a more leisurely pace into the open-air market. Velth noted that most of the patrons were female, and several carried or held young children by the hand.

He was about to comment on how well behaved most of the youngsters were when several loud cracks met his ears. Velth immediately grabbed Glenn around her waist and pulled her to the nearest wall, listening for more but still unable to determine the direction from which the sounds had come.

To his surprise, none of the other patrons seemed worried by the unusual sound. They continued to eat and talk as if they hadn't heard it.

The next sound was unmistakably bad, however. A wail of distress began to bounce off the walls around them.

"Come on," Glenn said, weaving through the crowd outside the café and rushing toward the plaintive shriek as it grew in intensity. A single word was now clear. "Jent! Jent!" By now a few of the locals seemed curious and some started to move along with Glenn and Velth.

The market continued for several blocks. Glenn ducked onto a smaller side street, an alley between the larger buildings they had passed on their way from the hospital. A few stationary vehicles were present, most near the rear entrances to the tall towers.

Once they'd entered the alley, they had to force their way through the crowd that was forming around a Djinari woman who knelt on the ground, keening and rocking. Her back was to them as they approached, but soon enough Velth saw the source of her distress. A small figure was splayed in her lap, another Djinari, a young male.

A few meters beyond, four CIF security officers were physically restraining two young Leodt males who were gesticulating angrily at the woman and boy. The officers seemed decidedly uninterested in the woman or the gathering crowd.

"Velth, move these people back," Glenn ordered as she knelt before the woman and said softly, "What happened?"

This only made the woman's cries intensify, so Glenn busied herself examining the young man. A sticky whitish fluid was seeping from a large, fresh opening in his chest. His face was contorted in pain, and the short tentacles that flowed from the base of his neck moved in jerking spasms.

Glenn wasted no time. Turning to the nearest guard she shouted, "This child needs medical attention!"

The security officers did not turn to answer her call. Moments later, however, the crowd's attention was diverted by a loud mechanical screech. A vehicle came to rest well clear of the throng, bearing the insignia of the Confederacy Medical Service.

"No!" the woman shrieked. "No, please." She moved as if to lift the boy but was unable to carry his weight. As the medics exited the vehicle she settled for holding him tightly to her chest.

"My boy. My Jent," she begged those surrounding her.

Velth watched as two young Djinari males, faces set in grim lines, pushed their way forward. One lifted the boy, cradling him in his arms, and the other helped the mother to her feet.

Glenn protested immediately. "What are you doing? He's wounded. You could do serious internal damage if you move him like that."

The two men paid her no heed. They merged into the crowd before the medics got within twenty meters of the scene.

"The medics are almost here!" Glenn shouted after them. Velth noted that these words seemed to quicken their pace.

"What the . . . ?" Velth asked of Glenn.

"With me, Lieutenant," Glenn replied, as she began to force her way past the spectators, following those who had taken the boy and his mother.

Chapter Ten

Tom Paris was surprised upon entering the mediation chamber bright and early the next morning to find Shaw already speaking quietly with Ozimat. Clancy stood on Ozimat's other side, looking lost.

His mother looked at him with eyes of sapphire stone. Her cheeks were ruddy and her lower lip quivered visibly. Force of habit brought the question, "Mom?" from Paris's lips.

Shaw turned immediately and called, "Commander."

Paris moved dutifully to join Shaw, who resumed speaking to the mediator. "Under the circumstances, it is necessary that Mrs. Paris demonstrate adequate ability to care for both children."

Ozimat glared at Shaw before nodding grudgingly. Shifting his eyes he said, "It appears congratulations are in order, Commander Paris."

In a flash, Paris understood. Turning back to his mother, he realized that despite all she was now inflicting upon her son, she still expected that *he* should have been the one to tell her of the impending arrival of her first grandson. Her right hand covered her mouth, surreptitiously wiping away the tears that glistened in her eyes before they could fall.

Had Paris believed they were tears of joy, he would have gone to her, Shaw be damned.

As they weren't, Paris simply said, "Thank you, Your Honor."

"Is there a reason you did not inform us of this happy news until now, Commander?"

A warning glance from his counsel and the memory of two sets of strong arms carrying him over shrubbery silenced him.

"Commander Paris informed me as soon as he determined it was relevant to the proceedings," Shaw said. "We both believed that, long before now, Mrs. Paris would have realized that her case is entirely without merit. Her persistence in continuing with this frivolous claim has forced us to formally advise Your Honor, as it is now material to the case. Naturally, Mister Paris wished to inform his mother privately that his wife is expecting again, and had his mother been more understanding of his position, he would have gladly done so. However, we must insist that she show competence and ability to provide appropriate care for her three-year-old granddaughter *and* an infant grandson before we continue—unless she does not intend to pursue the same claim regarding her grandson."

Ozimat nodded. "Agreed." Turning to Clancy, he said, "You will prepare the appropriate revisions to your client's claim and I will instruct a case specialist to visit Mrs. Paris's home at the earliest conceivable moment. These proceedings will stand in recess until then."

"Yes, Your Honor," Clancy said before returning to Julia's side and beginning to whisper in her ear.

"Gentlemen," Ozimat said before disappearing into the room's antechamber.

Paris followed Shaw to the entrance, only glancing back once at his mother. When they were alone outside the closed doors, he said, "Did you really have to do that?"

"Do you want custody of your children?"

Paris's jaw clenched.

"Your mother is almost eighty years old. Caring for a child Miral's age is one thing. Providing for her *and* a newborn, especially when she intends to bar him from the presence of his natural mother, is something else entirely."

"She'll just get help," Paris said.

"She can fill her house with warm, capable bodies," Shaw said, "but proving that they are a better choice than you and

B'Elanna is a tall order, given that your wife hasn't ever physically harmed you, herself, or Miral, nor demonstrated neglect. The court doesn't like to take children away from their parents, *especially* newborns, nor is it likely to separate siblings."

When Paris didn't respond, Shaw said, "Plus it might give her second thoughts. All this time, she's only considered caring for Miral. Adding a newborn to the equation might make her reconsider."

Paris shook his head slowly. Finally he said, "You really don't know my mom. The only thing she ever wanted more than a grandchild was a *grandson*."

Seven did not know how long she had been resting in Axum's arms. She had floated for some time beneath a star-filled sky on a warm, crystal sea. Eventually her feet found solid ground and she began to make her way lazily toward the shore. There were no waves to force her forward. With each step, the water receded until she found herself nestled beside Axum. They were alone on the patio. A long, low chaise with its back tilted upward held them both. The sky above was filled with dark clouds that hid the stars.

She was pleasantly warm. Lifting her face, she saw Axum staring down at her. His eyes had lost their ghosts. This was as close to happy as she had ever seen him.

Seven tried to pull herself up, but Axum said softly, "Please."

She searched for the will to refuse him. She was still looking when he asked, "How is your hand?"

Memory of the pain returned, but nothing more.

"Better," she said.

Axum nodded.

"Has this happened to you since you've been here?" Seven asked.

"No."

"Did you call for medical assistance?"

"No."

"Why not?"

"I already knew that you were recovering."

Seven shifted her shoulders to meet his eyes on a more even plane.

"How did you know?" she demanded.

Axum looked away. "I promised never to enter your mind without your consent, and I did not mean to do so. But the moment you cried out, I found myself sharing your thoughts. I did not feel your pain. I watched as it took you and released you, and I saw your catoms moving to repair what had been done." After a moment, he added, "I am sorry."

"It was not intentional," Seven said.

"Do you want me to call for someone now?" he asked.

"It is no longer necessary," she replied.

After a long silence, he said, "When we were together in Unimatrix Zero, we promised each other that we would never ask for more. We knew it was impossible, and to waste time wanting it to be so squandered what time we'd been given."

"I wish I remembered," Seven said.

"I wish I didn't."

Stung, Seven asked, "Do you mean that?"

"When I brought you back to Unimatrix Zero, I told myself it was for the good of all of us. There was no other way to stop the queen from destroying us, from stealing the last of our individuality. I knew you would never remember us. I didn't want you to. I had already grieved what we'd lost for both of us."

"But I did remember you," Seven said. "Not everything we had shared, but *you*."

"I was surprised," Axum said. "And then I was angry for a very long time."

"At me?"

"At myself. Had I left well enough alone, Unimatrix Zero might have been lost, but I would never have known. To live again in the real world as myself, even with the voices of the Borg, might have been bearable if I'd had nothing with which to compare it. But I did. It would never be enough to claim a small victory over the Borg, to free myself and the others by destroying our vessel. Nothing would ever be enough until I found you."

Seven smiled bitterly. "I wanted the same thing at first. But it was impossible."

"Not anymore."

This time, Seven looked away.

"You are in my arms again, but you may as well be lost in the Delta Quadrant," Axum said. After a long pause, he added, "Who is he?"

Seven did not bother to ask how he knew. With each moment that passed, it was growing harder to find a place inside her that he did not share.

"He was my counselor," she began. "The inner voice the Caeliar left behind was terrifying. I had worked so hard for so long to become an individual. I had learned to cherish the silence in my mind. I had adapted. But after the transformation, I feared I would never know that silence again."

"He helped you find it?"

"He helped me to see that my struggle was not with the Caeliar but with myself. He gave me the courage to face it and to accept it."

"But he is more than that to you, isn't he?"

"Yes."

Axum nodded. "Does he know that when you were a girl, you loved to nap among the wildflowers around your house?"

Seven shook her head.

"Does he know the names you gave the trees before your father forced you to memorize the proper ones?"

"No," Seven admitted.

"Have you told him about Skiria, and how she used to taunt you?"

"No."

"Does he know how long you dreamed of dark monsters?"

"Because he loves me, I dream of different things now."

"You love him?"

"Yes."

"You're sure?"

"Yes."

"Then why are you here?"

Seven paused. "I came because you needed me. I will always come if you need me."

"I need more than your concern, Annika."

"It is all I have to give."

Axum bent his head to hers. She knew better than to allow it. In her dreams, she had not thought to refuse him. But this was not a dream.

Their lips met gently, barely a touch. In that instant, she glimpsed something she had never thought to have or lose. Her mind rebelled, but her body overruled it. Something she had refused to acknowledge until this moment demanded her response.

Long before, she had made a conscious choice to be Seven. But Annika didn't care. Before Seven had given herself to Hugh, Annika had belonged to Axum.

Annika was human. She was a child whose life had been stolen by dark monsters, but she'd hidden her true self from them in Axum's heart. He had kept her safe. He had kept her alive. And *his* was the only touch she had ever desired.

Seven returned to the crystal sea as Annika opened her lips to Axum and pulled him closer.

Doctor Sharak had worked into the early evening hours without word from Miss Seven. It was the first day since they had been separated that she had not made contact. Sharak had asked if it was possible to forward any communication from her to his personal terminal in his temporary quarters. Doctor Frist had refused to risk compromising the lab's security to accomplish this. But surely, by now, he was satisfied that she was in no physical danger? Exhausted from hours of calculations that had yielded disquieting results, Sharak succumbed to his need for rest and left the lab.

As he approached the secured entrance to Starfleet's temporary housing facility, he barely took note of the solitary figure seated on a bench where those seeking clearance were made to wait. The individual rested against the wall, slumped over, face concealed beneath a hood, and body by a long, dark cloak.

Sharak had almost reached the turbolift when a stern voice said, "*Enceth. Far from home.*"

He turned instantly. The hooded figure had stolen behind him without betraying her presence.

"Ratham?" he asked in disbelief.

She removed the hood and smiled up at him. "*Pirakee, when the clouds parted.*"

Sharak lifted his right hand to his forehead, saying, "*Pirakee, the sun blinding.*"

Ratham repeated the gesture as Sharak bent to embrace her. Their cheeks touched side by side as she added, "*Chatha. Her journey long.*"

"*Chatha and Terubim. The fire warm.*"

Sharak released her. Her eyes were glistening, as were his. It was more than a year since he had seen another Child of Tama. He had not allowed himself to regret it until this moment. Ratham had made the journey with him to Earth years before but had yet to master Standard to the degree necessary to secure her a Starfleet post.

The duty officer tried and failed to hide his interest in this exchange. Sharak said simply, "An old friend, Ensign Ult."

"Have a good evening, sir," Ult replied as he offered Ratham a temporary access pass.

As Ratham removed her cloak to affix the pass to her tunic, Sharak noted the *kwells* adorning her sash. He had kept his— symbols of achievement, remembrances of those who had once walked beside him, and guides in times of confusion—but had not displayed them since the first day he had donned his Starfleet uniform. He wondered if she would chastise him for this lapse.

She did not. In the brief ride to his quarters, she spoke only of her happiness to have found him and recent contact with a few mutual acquaintances.

"*Solotep at midday?*" Sharak asked once she was seated at

the small table where he ate his solitary meals and created his personal logs. His bedchamber was a separate, smaller room containing two bunks, though the second had been unassigned since his arrival.

"Solotep at day's end," Ratham replied.

Sharak quickly replicated light fare, two bowls of soup and glasses of water. Ratham sniffed the soup warily when he placed it before her.

"Ishika. In winter," he chided her.

"Callimas at Bahar," she replied, chagrined, then lifted the bowl to her lips. After a few sips she said, *"Hammat dancing."*

"Emnis. His sight restored," Sharak teased.

They drank for a few silent moments. Finally Ratham said, *"Kira at court. The court filled."*

Sharak started to reply, *"Canthu at Belren,"* but stopped himself, asking instead, *"Ratham. The winds fair?"*

"The ocean still," she replied.

"Then perhaps you should continue to practice," Sharak said.

"I practice all day, just as I have every day for the last three years," Ratham said. "And you do not require practice."

"But you do."

Ratham sighed. "As you wish. Tell me of the day."

"How was your day?" he corrected her gently.

"Zinda—" she began.

"The river Temarc." He smiled. "My day was difficult."

"The cause?"

"I am not permitted to share the details with you," Sharak said. "The project is classified."

"Lianna. Her arms outstretched."

"Ratham."

"You know that you can tell me without fear," Ratham said.

"My oath forbids it," Sharak insisted. "But my work today led me to an unusual conclusion."

"How?"

What would have been more precise, but Sharak let it go. "Many I am working with believe one thing to be true. I no longer share their belief, but I cannot access the data I require to convince them that I am correct."

"Where does the data live?"

"Another planet, several days journey from here."

"Mirab, his sails unfurled."

"It is not that simple. I do not have a vessel of my own, nor could I pilot it safely if I did."

"Glenarat of Miwandi."

"I chose to be a healer. I would have made a poor pilot."

"Glenarat. His hands empty," Ratham said, smiling.

"My only regret is that I am not better understood among my peers."

"Uzani?"

"I do not seek glory for glory's sake," he corrected her. "To be understood is to be trusted. They do not trust me yet."

"Kinla in . . ." Ratham began, but stopped herself. "You cannot make them trust you. You must earn their trust by action."

"There is another here who needs me. I cannot leave her unattended. Her care is my primary occupation."

"Ubaya of crossed roads."

"Sallana. Her pack full. I do not resent my duty. But yes, it is difficult to know the wisest course."

"Have you asked the *kwells?*"

"Fendit in silence."

"Fendit refusing the flame."

"I have not thrown *kwells* since I was a child," Sharak said. "This decision is too important to leave to chance."

"For you know better than Tama?"

"Tama is ever silent."

Ratham stared at him for a long time. Finally she said, "Silence is an answer too. You already know what you must do."

"Shaieen. In darkness."

"Shaieen, the wind rising," Ratham challenged. *"Sharak on the ocean."*

Sharak bowed his head.

"I have missed you, my good friend," he finally said.

"I will still be here when you return," Ratham said.

"Jeral at rest."

"Jeral. Her arms weary."

"Jeral. Her eyes uplifted."

Ratham reached for his hand and squeezed it gently. "Today and every day," she assured him.

Tom Paris was surprised when the computer alerted him to an incoming transmission. He half hoped, half feared it would be his mother. It wasn't.

"I trust I am not disturbing you, Commander," Lieutenant Vorik said evenly. Paris had not spoken to his former *Voyager* crewmate, an old rival for B'Elanna's affections—at least if Vorik was the one telling the story—since the memorial ceremony on New Talax. Paris had been relieved that Vorik had survived *Hawking*'s entry into the Omega Continuum and assumed once he heard that Starfleet was sending the *Vesta* that Vorik would be aboard her. That had not happened. Vorik had requested transfer and Captain Farkas had granted his request.

"Never," Paris said sincerely. "It's great to see you." Paris and Vorik hadn't been the best of friends, but, after the last week, Paris welcomed any port in a storm. "Where are you?" he asked.

"Utopia Planitia. They always need capable engineers."

"They do," Paris agreed. *But so did the* Vesta.

"My shift begins shortly," Vorik said. *"I received word from a Lieutenant Shaw yesterday, asking if I would return to Earth to speak on your behalf at a custody hearing. That request was most disturbing."*

Vorik was Vulcan, so he would have used the same deadpan tone had the news been the happiest he'd ever heard.

"Oh," Paris said. "Yes, that's right."

"Who is seeking custody of Miral?"

"Shaw didn't tell you?"

"He left a message. I did not wish to speak to him until I reached you."

Paris had taken Shaw's instructions to heart, but this was

Vorik. There was no way he was going to side with Julia Paris against B'Elanna.

"My mother," Paris said. "But I'm not allowed to discuss the specifics of the case with anyone who might be called as a character witness. Shaw is looking for people who know B'Elanna and me well enough to speak on our behalf. If you can make the time, I would appreciate it, and I know B'Elanna would as well."

Vorik's face was, as ever, inscrutable. Finally he said, *"I do not think that it would be wise at this time for me to agree to that request."*

This struck Paris with the force of a fist to the gut. A million questions rose to his lips. He counted to ten and said, "You should do what you feel is right, of course."

"Thank you, Commander. If there is nothing else . . ."

"Why didn't you rejoin the fleet?" Paris asked quickly.

Vorik's eyes left Paris's for a few moments. When they met his again, Vorik said, *"I have had my fill of the Delta Quadrant."*

"I hear you," Paris said, but he also sensed that Vorik was holding out on him. "But the fleet could really use you."

"Starfleet chose to assemble a fleet without sufficient experienced personnel to ensure its safety. As a result, almost a thousand officers are now dead, including Captain Itak. To continue to serve that fleet is to silently condone Starfleet's reckless actions, including their decision to give command of the fleet to Admiral Janeway."

That punch to the gut was followed by a right hook.

"We're talking about the same Admiral Janeway, right?" Paris asked.

"We are."

"The woman who brought all of us home in seven years when the journey should have taken seventy?"

"But at what price?" Vorik asked. *"You may be willing to allow your personal regard for the admiral to blind you to the consequences of her choices, including the one that brought us home, but I cannot. Starfleet could have chosen to retire her, with honors if need be, but to give her command again is to court further disasters."*

Paris considered Vorik's words. He had seen the depth of emotion of which Vorik was capable and which he worked diligently to mask. For him to speak this way about the admiral suggested that whatever he felt was more powerful than Vorik's mating instinct.

"I don't agree," Paris finally said. "Admiral Janeway had no way of knowing or even guessing that destroying that transwarp hub would have had the results it did. And I don't remember you voicing that concern when she asked all of us if we agreed with her decision."

"I was not asked," Vorik said. *"I was not senior staff at the time."*

Paris winced. He'd grown so accustomed to seeing Vorik running *Voyager*'s engineering in the years leading to the Borg Invasion that he'd forgotten that the Vulcan wouldn't have been in that meeting.

"But had I been, I would have counseled the captain to follow her first instinct upon discovery of the hub. She should have retreated."

"But the Admiral Janeway who came from the future—" Paris began.

"Had no business being there," Vorik finished for him. *"Nothing she said should have been taken into account. The only meaningful effort made in regards to that Admiral Janeway should have been to attempt to return her to her own timeline."*

Paris bowed his head. Vorik was adhering to the strictest possible interpretation of the temporal Prime Directive. But in Paris's experience, such fundamentalism had little value beyond academic discussion.

"Obviously you have to make the best choice for you," Paris said.

"Yes."

"Good night, Vorik."

"Peace and long life, Commander."

Once he'd signed off, Paris said softly, "You didn't mean that, did you?"

The conversation had left Paris queasy. Wondering what the quickest relief might be, he rose to access his replicator. As he did so, his door chimed.

"Enter."

The door slid open to reveal Doctor Sharak.

"Hello, Doctor," Paris said. "Welcome, come in, please."

"Thank you, Commander."

"Where is Seven?" Paris asked.

Sharak seemed to struggle for a moment, and as he did so, Paris's stomach soured further.

"Seven is well," Sharak finally said.

Paris sighed in relief. "Don't do that, Doctor," he chided the Tamarian. "I thought you were going to tell me she'd died or something."

"Forgive me," Sharak said, opening his hands. "I have spoken with her every day this week except today, and she seems to be in excellent health, though I believe she is keeping the particulars of her current circumstances to herself for the time being."

It suddenly occurred to Paris that, as the senior officer on this extended away mission, he should have contacted Sharak himself on a daily basis to check in.

"Aren't you working with her?" Paris asked.

"The medical facility is divided. Those who work directly with the virus are quarantined from the rest of us."

Paris didn't like the sound of that. "But Seven is helping them, right?"

"The last time we spoke, she indicated that she had not been requested for that duty," Sharak said. "She has confined her efforts to assisting her former friend, Axum."

"If they didn't need her, why did they call her back from the Delta Quadrant?" Paris demanded.

"They needed her catoms," Sharak replied. "Beyond that, I cannot say if her current status is their choice or hers."

Paris spared a moment of regret for Hugh Cambridge but quickly shook it off. Seven had every right to make her own choices, though this one surprised him.

"Well, if they don't need her further, I'll put in a request for us to return to the fleet as soon as my hearing is done."

"When will that be?" Sharak asked.

"I honestly don't know."

"More than a few days?"

"Maybe. Why?"

"I have come because I require your insight."

"You'd be the first, but go ahead," Paris said.

"I need to go to Coridan," Sharak said. "I cannot tell you why. But I believe the trip to be necessary if I am to complete the work I have been assigned."

"Tell your superiors at Starfleet Medical," Paris said. "I'm sure they can accommodate you."

"I do not believe they will. The data I require is there, and it cannot be accessed remotely. However, those in charge of the project have already resolved the question I seek to answer to their satisfaction, and I doubt they would appreciate my questioning them. I do not believe they think me capable of offering significant insight. I believe they are assigning me a task that will occupy my time while they continue to hold Miss Seven."

"That's quite an accusation," Paris said.

"It is my belief. But despite their assessment, I know my capabilities and I know what I must do. The question is: Can you help me get to Coridan?"

"I'd take you there myself if it weren't for this damned hearing," Paris replied. "But I don't know . . . wait," he said.

"Commander?"

Paris smiled. "I take it back. I know exactly who can get you there. Just give me a minute to contact her. Take a seat."

"Thank you, Commander."

As Paris moved back to his comm station, he suddenly realized that sending Sam Wildman to Coridan with Sharak might make her unavailable to testify on his behalf. Hers was the first name on the list he had given to Shaw. But there was no one else Paris could trust with a request like Sharak's, no one else he knew would understand.

"Just promise me one thing?" Paris asked.

"Of course."

"Hurry back."

"If you will agree to check in with Seven daily while I am gone."

"Consider it done," Paris said.

Chapter Eleven

Captain Roberta Farkas didn't like speaking over a comm channel, even an encrypted one, with her counterpart on the *Sixteenth Hadden*, General Deonil. The Leodt officer had assured her that the cloak provided by the protectors surrounding both of their vessels hid them completely from the sensors of the ships they had come to recon. When their comm channels were open, the protectors merged, adding an extra layer of stealth. Still, Farkas couldn't help but think that if she were playing for the other team out here, any strange signal would have been cause for investigation. Captain Chakotay's reports spoke to the effectiveness of the ancient protectors' cloaking mechanisms, but it had taken *Voyager* less than half an hour to detect them. The alien armada reassembling at the Gateway must suspect by now that they were being monitored, and an open comm channel could easily betray the *Vesta* and the *Hadden*.

Farkas's only comfort was the fact that her ship and the *Hadden* were almost a light-year away from the Gateway. *Vesta* had spent the better part of the day traveling a dizzying course through more than fifteen streams before emerging within two light-years of their present position. She'd had no idea that there was another access to Confederacy space anywhere near the Gateway. The ingress point of the final stream they had traveled was as well reinforced on the Confederacy side as the Gateway, but only because of its proximity to the network of other streams. Dozens of CIF ships held position there, but no inhabited planets or systems were near its entrance. Deonil had advised her that they would return to the First World when their mission was done via an alternate route. Several of the streams they had used to get here flowed efficiently in only one direction, so no alien force could simply retrace their footsteps. A successful attacker would have to possess an accurate map of the Confederacy streams.

That didn't mean she felt any less naked.

"We confirm nine ships grouped within ten million clicks of the Gateway, Captain Farkas."

A nod from Jepel at ops told Farkas that Deonil's count was right.

"Two of the nine are Turei," Farkas said. "One is Devore. But I don't recognize the other six."

"Three are Karlon," Deonil advised. *"They are tenacious in battle, but their weapons do not possess sufficient range or power to pose a true threat."*

"Jepel?"

"I have added the Karlon specs to our database, Captain."

"Good," she said. "What about the big fellow in the middle?" Farkas asked.

"The Skeen," Deonil replied. *"Lack of maneuverability in close quarters is their greatest weakness."*

"Thankfully, an issue we do not share," Farkas said, though the Skeen vessel was almost as large as the *Vesta*.

"The last two are new additions to their forces," Deonil said. *"Perhaps we will pick up a designation in the next few hours."*

"I'd like more than that," Farkas noted, "but we'll take whatever we can get."

"Agreed," Deonil said, his mouth widening in what Farkas hoped was a smile. In her limited experience, the happier a Leodt was, the more he looked ready to bite you.

"How often have you engaged these folks?" Farkas asked.

"For most of my career with the CIF, it was rare for any alien vessel to approach the Gateway, let alone breach the stream. A year or more could go by with no contact. Occasionally, someone who knew us and knew what to look for would make an attempt to enter the Gateway.

I've studied encounters from the first three centuries of the Confederacy's existence where outsiders were brought by the ancient protectors, but none of them proved their worth as allies or potential members.

"That changed about a year ago. Small groups of vessels, two or three at the most, began to appear and work diligently to open the Gateway. None were accompanied. But it has only been in the last three months that we've seen numbers like what we have here."

"How recently did the Turei, the Vaadwaur, and the Devore join these hostiles?" Farkas asked.

"Their specifications were first added to our databases approximately two months ago," Deonil replied.

"To what do you ascribe their actions?" Farkas asked. "What do you want?"

"Access to the streams, possibly the Source," Deonil replied.

"But no one has ever seen the Source, have they?" Farkas asked.

"No. But it would not surprise me if those attempting to breach the Gateway had experienced its power in some limited capacity. They might be pilgrims. But if they truly understood the Source—if they were of it, as we are—they would know that knowledge does not come through force. It cannot be taken, it can only be freely received."

"You don't think they've heard of the wealth of your Confederacy and might be looking to share that?" Farkas asked.

"To steal it, perhaps," Deonil acknowledged.

"You've never just asked?" Farkas asked.

"Our government has chosen not to open diplomatic relations at this time. They do not pose sufficient threat to warrant the risks involved."

That sounded incredibly shortsighted to Farkas, but she held her peace. "Worst-case scenario, General," Farkas asked. "If these invaders could assemble sufficient numbers to force access to the stream, how would the Confederacy respond?"

"We have the capacity to destroy the Gateway," Deonil replied. *"To preserve the First World, we would not hesitate to do so."*

"The First World is ten thousand light-years away, but obviously there are other streams that can get you there. Would you destroy all of them?"

"*We will do whatever is necessary to defend ourselves against these aggressors.*"

Farkas took that as a yes.

"Captain," Jepel said.

"Yes?"

"I'm picking up some comm traffic between the Turei and the Skeen."

"Anything useful?" Farkas asked.

"I'm going to need some time to clear up the signal."

"Do it," Farkas said. "We're not going anywhere for a while. As soon as we have anything solid, General, we'll be in touch."

"*Thank you, Captain.* Hadden *out.*"

Farkas rose from her seat and crossed to the ops panel. "If you get even a hint that they have detected us . . ." she began.

"Aye, Captain," Jepel said, understanding her perfectly.

DEMETER

"Well, Atlee?" Commander O'Donnell asked as his first officer returned to *Demeter*'s bridge, after six hours spent on Femra, the planet Overseer Bralt had been most anxious for the Federation's preeminent botanical geneticist to see. O'Donnell had been grateful, for one of the few times in his career, that Starfleet regulations made it possible for him to refuse Bralt's request to join the rest of the away team. Nothing would have ended the hopes of an alliance as quickly as six uninterrupted hours in Bralt's company. Commander Fife, on the other hand, seemed genuinely thrilled by his experience on the planet.

"It will take me several hours to complete my formal report, Captain," Fife replied.

"Were you impressed?" O'Donnell asked. It wasn't a huge leap. Fife's eyes were lit with first-contact infatuation. O'Donnell had never seen the condition listed among communicable illnesses by Starfleet Medical, but it should have been. For those with little experience of alien cultures, a day spent touring their natural and technological wonders nearly always produced this heady effect. Even the most hardened Starfleet officer usually listed "exploring the unknown" at the top of the list of reasons they entered the service. Atlee had just learned why.

"I was, sir," Fife replied. "Nearly every square meter of arable land has been efficiently allocated to optimize production of *yint* and *hrass*. Their infrastructure for transporting the raw grains to their local processing facilities is state of the art, as are the refineries. The producers and technicians take great pride in their work. They enjoy a standard of living comparable to those on the First World. Their weather-control satellites mitigate unfortunate natural occurrences and have brought the rate of loss below one percent each season. I cannot speak highly enough of the people I met today, or the work they do for the greater good of the Confederacy. They are exceptional."

O'Donnell nodded. "What percentage of land is devoted to the production of *yint*, Commander?"

"Seventy-two percent," Fife replied.

"And what is *yint* used for?"

"The manufacture of cloth."

"Any old cloth?"

"Sir?"

"Do Confederacy citizens wear clothing made from *yint* every day?"

"No, sir," Fife said, understanding. "When properly refined, *yint* yields a fabric of surpassing beauty. It appears almost liquid to the naked eye."

"And those who purchase it pay quite a premium for it, don't they?" O'Donnell asked.

"It is exported to fifty of the fifty-three worlds of the Confederacy."

"Would you consider it a necessity?"

Fife sighed. "No, sir. It is definitely a luxury item."

"Which explains the quality of life of those who produce it?" O'Donnell asked.

"It does, sir."

"And what is *hrass*?"

"A less nutritious grain, used mainly for the sustenance of livestock," Fife said. "Several developed worlds in the Confederacy still make use of beasts of burden. The *hrass* is a necessity for them, particularly in times of extreme weather variances."

"Drought?"

"Or flooding, yes," Fife said.

"Does anybody on Femra, one of the Confederacy's most productive agricultural centers, grow anything *people* can eat?"

Fife considered the question. "Not that I saw," he finally replied.

"So where does their food come from?"

"I," Fife began, then admitted, "I don't know."

"It comes from the Consumables Exchange, a very profitable branch of the Market Consortium," O'Donnell said. "Were the soil here fit for growing nothing other than *yint* and *hrass*, it would make sense for the residents to trade with other worlds for the resources they need. But for tens of thousands of years before Femra joined the Confederacy, they did not engage in trade. They sustained themselves by conserving their own livestock, fish, and fowl, and growing their own produce."

"But the markets for *yint* and *hrass* are more profitable than any other products they could grow," Fife said. "Why shouldn't they devote the majority of their resources to the product that will reap them the greatest rewards?"

O'Donnell shrugged. "You tell me."

Fife considered the question. "If supply lines were cut off for any length of time, it could leave the residents in difficult circumstances, depending on how much stored food they hold in reserve. Rationing might be necessary."

"Think bigger," O'Donnell suggested.

Fife took a moment to do so. "I can't see the market for *hrass* falling for any reason. It is essential to the existence of too many member worlds."

"Various breeds of livestock survive because of ready access to plentiful food sources. A drought or flood can do some damage, but it's not going to wipe out entire populations. It would take planet-wide catastrophes to do that, in which case there probably wouldn't be enough people left to worry about feeding their animals," O'Donnell said.

"But even if the market for *hrass* failed, *yint* is in high demand," Fife said.

"For now," O'Donnell agreed. "Do you know what the well-heeled Confederacy citizens wore before *yint* was all the rage?"

"I don't, sir," Fife replied.

"Vincent, open a channel to the *Fourth Jroone*," O'Donnell ordered.

"Aye, Captain," the ops officer replied.

Within seconds, Overseer Bralt's teeth filled the screen.

"Commander O'Donnell, so good to see you again."

"And you, Overseer," O'Donnell said. "Commander Fife has reported that his visit to Femra was both instructive and impressive. I look forward to reading about it in its entirety."

"You do us great honor," Bralt said.

"In the meantime, I wonder if you and the *Jroone* would show us another agricultural planet your office manages."

"If we have the time, I would be delighted to accommodate you," Bralt said.

"I don't think it's far, Overseer. I'd like Commander Fife to see Vitrum."

Bralt's face betrayed obvious discontent. The bony ridge above his eyes crept upward with surprise and most of his teeth disappeared into his mouth.

"Vitrum is not on our schedule, Commander," Bralt said. *"The local officials would have to be apprised and it would put them to great difficulty to accommodate our party. Without notice, I feel it would be an unfair imposition."*

"No advance arrangements are necessary, Overseer. You've already wined and dined us off our feet. Your generosity does you great credit. But Vitrum is one of your larger food producers. I'd like Fife to see how those operations compare to Femra's." When Bralt appeared ready to refuse, O'Donnell added, "It is my understanding that should our alliance progress, you intend to petition the Federation to review your entire agricultural portfolio with an eye toward increasing productivity."

"That is true, however—" Bralt began.

"The reports I've read of Vitrum suggest they might be an excellent candidate for increased productivity."

A low hiss escaped Bralt's mouth.

"Thank you, Commander. I will ask EC Irste to plot a course and we will transfer it to you as soon as possible."

"Thank you, Overseer. You are, as always, generous to a fault."

When the image on the main viewscreen was replaced by Femra, O'Donnell turned to Fife.

"What's on Vitrum?" Fife asked.

"Another world," O'Donnell replied grimly.

GALEN

As soon as Admiral Janeway's shuttle docked, she dismissed Counselor Cambridge and Lieutenant Lasren for a few hours of rest. Decan accompanied her to the bridge where she found Lieutenant Cress Benoit, *Galen*'s chief engineer, still in command.

"Admiral on deck," Ensign Drury, the ops officer, announced as soon as the lift doors had opened. Benoit rose as Janeway stepped the few meters necessary to stand directly in front of him on the small bridge.

"Where is Commander Glenn?" the admiral asked.

"She is still on the surface of the First World with Lieutenant Velth," Benoit replied. "She is due to return within the hour."

"Very good," Janeway said. "Notify me as soon as the commander returns."

"Aye, Admiral," Benoit said.

"We spent some time today touring the capital city's central library. The presider has agreed to allow us to access every public record within that library in order to better acquaint ourselves with the Confederacy's history."

Benoit nodded, clearly not understanding what the admiral was getting at.

"Among those records is what the Confederacy calls their 'material ownership decrees.' We call them 'patents.' Contact the library's administrator at once and establish an interface that will allow us to research those decrees. They'll give us the best possible sense of current Confederacy technology and what they might have in the works."

"Aye, Admiral," Benoit said.

"Assign as many engineers as you can spare to review them," the admiral ordered.

Benoit hesitated. "If you mean actual living engineers, Admiral, at least aboard the *Galen,* there's only me and three others."

"Your duties to the *Galen* take priority, Lieutenant," the admiral said. "When the *Vesta* returns, I'll ask Captain Farkas to provide us with extra eyes. Until then, automate as much of the process as you can.

"I'll be in the commander's ready room if you need me," Janeway said. "Decan."

Glenn's ready room was small, like everything else aboard the *Galen.* The furnishings consisted of a desk and two chairs placed before it. Janeway looked automatically for a replicator—a cup of coffee was definitely in order—but did not find one. The only personal touch present in the room was a small mat tied in a roll in a corner behind the desk.

"Decan?"

"I will report immediately to the mess hall and return shortly," her aide stated. In their years together, the Vulcan had never admitted to extraordinary telepathic abilities. He simply displayed them flagrantly on a daily basis. "Will half a pot suffice?"

"For now. Thank you," Janeway replied. "Remind me where we're scheduled to go next."

"Evening observation," Decan said. Off the admiral's puzzled brow, he clarified: "Church."

Chapter Twelve

"I f you'd like to catch some sleep, there are three bunks in the back. Feel free to take your pick," Lieutenant Samantha Wildman suggested to Doctor Sharak as soon as she had engaged her small vessel's warp engine. "We're a good nine hours out from Coridan."

"You are most kind, Lieutenant Wildman," Sharak said. "I am sufficiently rested at this time."

The soft-spoken lieutenant, who Sharak had learned was a xenobiologist, wore her shoulder-length blond hair loose. Unruly strands obscured the side of her face, so it was hard to tell if the glance she shot toward him in response was one of acknowledgment or trepidation.

"You must be a very good friend of Commander Paris," Sharak said.

"We served together on *Voyager* for seven years," Wildman said. "We've been through a lot together."

"It is good fortune to serve for so long with those you respect," Sharak said.

Wildman's face scrunched in confusion. "I would not call being stranded in the Delta Quadrant good fortune, Doctor."

"No, I did not mean . . ." Sharak began, then sighed. "I do not envy the circumstances that brought you together." One achingly pleasant conversation with Ratham had temporarily realigned his divided mind. For a brief time, his thoughts and words had been one. Now he must force them again into opposing camps.

"I'm sorry," Wildman said, clearly regretting her tone. "I've never had the pleasure to meet a Tamarian before. I understand our language does not come easily to you."

Sharak smiled. "But like every new experience, it brings its own rewards."

Wildman smiled shyly.

"This ship has such a lovely name. It is more poetic than most given to Starfleet vessels," Sharak said.

Wildman's smile widened. "It's not a Starfleet ship anymore. It was decommissioned before my husband acquired it and renamed it."

"Your husband does not serve Starfleet?"

"He did. Gres—Greskrendtregk," she clarified, carefully enunciating each syllable, "is also a scientist. He specializes in evolutionary biology. When *Voyager* returned to the Alpha Quadrant the first thing we decided was that we were never going to be separated again by our jobs. He resigned his commission and works with several civilian labs. He still travels from time to time, but only when he chooses to. For the most part, we spend our time on Earth, where I'm stationed, so we can both be close to our daughter, Naomi."

"How old is she?"

"She's almost twelve, but for a Ktarian, or half-Ktarian in Naomi's case, that's more like eighteen human years. She's in her first year at Starfleet Academy."

"You must be very proud."

"We are." After a short pause, Wildman added, "Gres named this ship for her."

"Goldenbird is his pet name for her?"

"A nickname. It comes from a Ktarian song—from my husband's homeworld—a really beautiful one, particularly when played on a *lal-shak*. Gres missed the first years of Naomi's life. Since then he's tried to teach her about the Ktarian part of her heritage. She resisted at first. It was a lot of change to accept at one time. But she fell in love with *The Song of the Golden Bird*. It brought them close."

Sharak was oddly touched. He had listened for so many years to the words of people of the Federation. Few had taken the time to tell him their stories. Those he'd had to seek out on his own. They were readily available in written form, less frequently simply shared.

"Thank you, Lieutenant Wildman," he said.

"For what?"

"The Children of Tama are taught to think and speak in stories. Proper nouns followed by descriptions of locations or actions provide all of the information required for communication. Many of your words are impossible to translate into Tamarian. But the lovely story you just shared with me would do so beautifully."

Wildman smiled again. "How?"

"*Greskrendtregk of Ktaria. Greskrendtregk and Naomi. The Song of the Golden Bird.*"

"Oh, I see," Wildman said, her eyes dancing in delight. "You're right. That's lovely. I must remember to tell Gres."

"Humans also tell a story of a golden bird. Do you know it?"

"No."

"It is quite ancient. I first began to learn your language by reading your myths and legends. I believe this one is a fairy tale."

"About a golden bird?"

"It is about a young prince, the youngest of three brothers, who is sent to find a golden bird that has stolen precious golden apples from his father's orchard. Several times, he meets a wise fox. The fox always speaks the truth to him, and when he follows the fox's words, he succeeds. When he does not, he fails."

"Does he ever find the golden bird?"

"Yes, and much more. He finds his life. He finds that to live, he must heed wisdom, even when it is found in unlikely places or contradicts the counsel of his heart."

"The moral of the story is to always listen to the wise fox?" Wildman asked.

Sharak nodded.

"I think Gres would like that story too," Wildman said, smiling. Turning her seat to face him, she said, "Tell me more."

"*Temba. His arms wide.*"

"What does that mean?"

"What do you think it means?" Sharak asked.

Wildman smiled in faint self-deprecation. But after a moment, she rose to the challenge. "I don't know who Temba is. But, *his arms wide.* He could be reaching for something." The lieutenant extended her arms as if to reach but quickly realized they were too close together. "*Temba. His arms wide,*" Wildman repeated. Opening hers, it suddenly hit her. "Temba is ready to receive something." Slowly she closed her arms until her hands rested over her heart. "Give me something? Tell me something? *Tell me more,*" she said, nodding.

The next nine hours went by much too quickly for both Sharak and Lieutenant Wildman.

STARFLEET MEDICAL

Twenty-eight code variations had been translated into program-mable algorithms. None of them had altered a single catomic molecule. As she began her work on number twenty-nine, Seven pondered futility.

She did not consider herself to be a quitter. Many times since she had been severed from the Collective their paths had crossed, and they had promised that resistance to them would prove futile. Each time the Borg uttered these words, they believed it to be a statement of fact. No matter how many times they had been proven false, the words retained an eerie power: a suggestion that no matter how any particular encounter ended, eventually, the Borg would prevail.

They hadn't. But they had slaughtered billions of life-forms on their way to learning that lesson.

Seven wanted to believe that her effort to unlock the program-ming of her catoms was not destined to end with a similar body count. But each day that passed with no word from the Com-mander cemented her belief that nothing she did here was going to be of consequence when it came to curing the catomic plague.

She needed to speak to the Commander.

Axum murmured quietly in his room. This behavior did not trouble her anymore. She knew his loneliness now in a way she could not have imagined when he had only spoken of it.

Physical intimacy was no longer a mystery to Seven. Her first true experience of it had been with Hugh. Those instances, while intensely pleasurable, had not prepared her for sexual relations with Axum. With Hugh, she was conscious of her body's responses to him. Though his might be inferred from the satisfaction she saw on Hugh's face, as well as his verbal assurances, she was forced to accept on faith that he enjoyed their coupling as much as she did.

With Axum, there were no questions. She did not know if their catoms somehow heightened the experience. But they must be responsible for the many new layers of sensation that flooded her body when they initiated physical contact. As powerful as her responses were, they paled in comparison to Axum's. To be with Axum in that way was to feel his need, his hunger and his release along with her own and *as if they were her own.* It was the same for Axum. Her fears, doubts, and, yes, desires *became his*, even as they tempered his. There was nothing for them to learn of one another. Everything thought, every breath, the slightest touch moved seamlessly into the next, propelled by absolute certainty of one another's desires. Complete satisfaction was a foregone conclusion as they moved deeper into one another, beyond their bodies and into a place where they alone existed, perpetually intertwined, woven together into one being. As a Borg, Seven had sought perfection. As a human, she had recognized the futility of such a pursuit. Hugh had once said that it must be awfully boring once achieved. She had thought him wise. Only now, as something not Borg, not human, and not quite Caeliar, did she understand that perfection sustained might be impossible, but experiences on a regular basis with another who could also understand it as such was, at the very least, intoxicating.

She wished she had anticipated this possibility when she had last spoken with Hugh. She had never intended to deceive him.

Seven knew well that what she had now experienced with Axum was a betrayal of Hugh, one for which she could not expect, nor would she ask, forgiveness. But in the strangest way, her life now seemed entirely separate from her previous existence. Some part of her knew that someday she would be forced to leave this place and that when she did, Hugh would still be there for her. She could not imagine being without Axum any more than she could imagine willfully choosing not to breathe. In this place, that was true. But somewhere else, she still belonged to Hugh.

These thoughts were not constructive.

She needed to speak to the Commander.

Abandoning the workstation she had made her own in Axum's lab, Seven moved to the patio. The night air was pleasantly cool. A single light now burned consistently in the quarters above that balcony. But no one had ever accessed the balcony, so Seven had no idea to whom those quarters belonged.

A strange determination flooded her. The Commander might not wish to speak with her. But his were not the only feelings that deserved consideration.

Seven reentered the quarters she shared with Axum. There were three doors accessible from the living area. One led to the lab. The second led to Axum's bedroom. The third . . .

That's the 'fresher.

Axum's soft warning the first day they had been reunited returned to her.

But it couldn't be. If it was, the only access to the rest of the facility would be the patio, and there were no doors present at ground level there.

Confused but undeterred, Seven moved to the third door. It did not open when she approached, nor did it move when she applied pressure and attempted to slide it open. A small control panel was embedded into the wall at the door's right. She tried several codes, but none of them worked. Finally, she pressed her hands onto the door's surface and attempted to slide it open manually. A faint alarm began to sound. Seven increased the pressure of her hand and, seconds later, the door slid open.

Seven immediately stepped into a hallway with unadorned gray walls. To her right, it ended after a dozen meters. There were no other doors present in that direction. None were visible to the left either, but, given the lighted balcony's location in relation to her current position, she knew that she must go left if she hoped to reach it.

Following her instincts she soon came to a T-junction. Again she turned to her left. A few meters beyond she was surprised and delighted to find a flight of stairs leading up. She took them and found herself in a wider hallway, this one bearing several doors on either side.

The area felt deserted. She had seen no one since she had left Axum's quarters. But the first door she came to on her left should have led to the lighted room.

When she reached it, the first thing she realized was that there was no control panel on the outside she might use to alert the occupant of her desire to enter. She raised a hand to knock but, as she did so, the door slid open.

Why her heart began to pound as she crossed this threshold, she did not know. Ignoring it, she stepped into yet another hallway, this one dimly lit. The only source of light came from the wall, several meters ahead. When she reached it, she understood the odd effect. It was not an open doorway but rather a window—transparent aluminum unless she was mistaken.

Beside the window was a single door, but peering through it she saw that this door was the first of two. There were two rooms visible to her. One contained a large control panel with several unusual manual configurations. Beyond it, visible through a second window and accessed by a second door, was some sort of exam room.

An individual in a biohazard suit stood in that room. Lying on the room's only biobed was an alien female. Her skin was a light shade of purple. Long black hair flowed down over the side of the bed.

Seven watched as the individual in the suit placed a small case on a shelf beside them and removed a hypospray from it. The woman's lips moved at this, but Seven could not hear her words. She must have received a response because her features settled as she was injected with the hypospray.

For a moment, nothing happened.

The woman's head turned and she appeared to see Seven standing there. An odd smile, almost of recognition, crossed the woman's lips before they parted in a silent scream.

Seven stepped back automatically. The flesh that Seven could see on the woman's face and arms contorted strangely. Dark black lines began to streak down it as it continued to ripple and then melt away from her bones.

Seven looked at the backs of her hands and saw the same odd rippling effect begin. The tingling she had experienced before returned. She thought she knew what would follow, but she was mistaken as not just her hands but, instead, her entire body was suddenly clenched in a spasm of agony. There was nothing to reach for, nothing Seven could use to steady herself. She took a few steps back as her body folded into itself, searching for a place to hide from the pain. Her spine hit the wall behind her as her feet came out from under her.

Then, as it had before, the pain was lost in a wave of fire so fierce it should have incinerated her on the spot.

She could not remember beginning to scream. She knew only that when a pair of strong hands found her and began to lift her from the floor, she was still screaming.

There was only one way for Icheb to access the quarantine area in which Seven was located. Over the last few days, while he waited in vain for Seven to contact him directly as he had requested, he had assessed the operating procedures for inventory control and formulated a relatively simple plan to use them to reach Seven. Acting on that plan would be to step firmly outside of the stark lines that proscribed the limits of acceptable behavior for a Starfleet Academy cadet.

Icheb did not feel he had a choice. Seven had not contacted him. Icheb could not shake the sense that once Sharak had apprised her of his wishes, Seven *would* have done so had she been able. *Something was wrong.* Still, Icheb had not settled on his present course of action until he learned that, as of this morning, Doctor Sharak had been granted several days of leave from Starfleet Medical. He was no longer available to assist Seven, should she require aid.

That was now Icheb's responsibility.

Icheb had been disheartened to learn that supplies were not forwarded to the quarantine area manually. Like many organizations as vast and complex as Starfleet Medical Headquarters, many mundane tasks were automated. Inventory dispensation was done by transporter. The central computer system performed transports that were deemed hazardous, and any item coming in or out of the quarantine area was designated as such. As many transports contained living organisms, even cargo transporters within the facility were rated for human use.

Locating an appropriate transport vessel had not been an issue—he had chosen one used for the transport of biohazard suits—nor had installing biometric shielding that would prevent the computer's sensors from detecting him within the suit. It was more complicated to program the shield to emit scans that would identify the contents as requisitioned items of the appropriate weight, but this certainly was not beyond his abilities. He had records of everything that had been requested by the classified division over the last several days and he was able to prepare a falsified manifest. The last step was to enter the container into the queue for inventory transport, don the suit, position himself inside the container, and wait as it was picked up by the appropriate duty officer and taken to central inventory control. He anticipated it might take several hours for this to transpire. To his relief, he had waited within the container for less than twenty minutes before he felt it being lifted onto an antigrav unit.

The only question was whether or not anyone would be present to receive the transported items or if they would be automatically routed to the appropriate storage room when they arrived. That challenge he would deal with once he knew the answer.

He had drifted into a light doze when he felt the familiar sensation of transport take hold. A check of the suit's chronometer indicated that less than two hours had elapsed. As soon as he rematerialized, he felt the container being lifted by an automated control arm and removed from the transporter padd. He immediately stilled his breath to eliminate the reverberations of his own respiration. The indistinct sound of conversation confirmed that officers were indeed present and coordinating receipt from their end. Less than half an hour later, the container was again moved, and this time, when it came to rest, it remained undisturbed for more than an hour and the sound of voices had vanished.

If all had gone as planned, the container was now at rest within storage room CLCP-004. Gathering his courage, Icheb released the container's internal locks and emerged into a dimly lit room lined floor to ceiling with shelves containing numerous boxes of various shapes and sizes. He quickly removed the biohazard suit and returned it to its container. Only then did he activate his tricorder and scan the adjacent hallways.

Once he had satisfied himself that they were clear, he grabbed a small box from the nearest shelf and left the storage room.

He moved at a sedate pace, hoping to attract as little attention to himself as possible. Everything depended on him looking like he belonged there. A right turn at the next juncture and an immediate left should take him to the living quarters for the quarantine area.

His second turn brought him face-to-face with a Bolian female. Her eyes narrowed as she studied him.

"Who are you?" she demanded.

Icheb tried to swallow the lump that had just appeared in his throat.

"Um . . ."

That was when the screaming began.

Seven?

A breath later, an alarm klaxon began to shriek directly above him.

The woman turned, and Icheb took that as his cue to begin running toward the screams.

Despite the care with which he had planned this mission, he never really had a chance.

Liaison did not possess a face well suited to subterfuge. The moment she entered the clean room where the Commander was quickly discarding his biohazard suit, she knew *he knew*.

"What the hell is going on out there?" he demanded.

"An intruder," Liaison began.

"In quarantine?" the Commander asked in disbelief.

"We don't know how he entered the area. He swears he got lost. I don't believe him."

"Why not?"

"He is an Academy cadet assigned here for his first-year internship, but he is also a friend of Seven of Nine. His name is Icheb."

Tension rippled over the Commander's jaw.

"He requested that she contact him several days ago," Liaison added.

"Did she?"

Liaison shook her head.

"He knows her very well," Liaison apologized.

"Where is he now?"

"Decontamination. From there he will be returned to the Academy under guard," Liaison replied.

The Commander nodded. "It doesn't matter. Seven's catoms have proven completely resistant to programming. We'll likely have more success with our new arrivals." After a moment, he added, "Return to data management, Ensign."

"Sir?" the ensign said, as a rush of blood rose to her cheeks.

"We will have to assign a more skilled Liaison."

The ensign refused to allow her chin to fall. The Commander believed weakness to be almost as great a sin as failure.

"Understood, Commander."

"Dismissed."

Chapter Thirteen

The Doctor stood on the precipice of greatness.

The fact that none of the viral agents the Doctor had detected thus far possessed Caeliar molecular tags was a minor detail. With painstaking effort, the Doctor had completed a genetic analysis of each virus and found twelve likely candidates for the plague. The key now was to determine how known catomic molecules would react in the presence of these devious little organisms. He suspected the virus would integrate the catoms, enhancing its effectiveness.

The Doctor's supply of catoms that Seven had provided had dwindled precipitously, given the amount he had transfused into Axum. Those that remained had maintained their neutral state in the absence of organic material. That was about to change.

Given the nature of the virus, at least as he theorized its functioning, the Doctor had chosen to make an unusual request of *Voyager*'s crew. Several dozen crew members had donated blood for him to use in his tests. He could have replicated the necessary tissue, or taken some from the sickbay's reserve stocks, but it was essential for him to have complete baseline readings on all of the donors prior to beginning. Only six samples would be used for this initial experiment.

Each blood sample was free of any viral or bacterial agents. Each sample was injected with a replicated version of one viral candidate based on the initial victim's records. Each was then injected with a single catom from Seven.

The reaction upon injection was instantaneous and unexpected. Once the Doctor had confirmed his results he repeated the procedure with six additional candidate viruses.

The results were identical. In each case, Seven's healthy catomic particles immediately took the form of healthy blood cells, and the response of those cells to the presence of the virus was aggressive, to say the least. Every single viral candidate was neutralized within seconds.

Perhaps greatness was going to take a little more time.

FIRST WORLD

Within a few blocks of the market, the streets of the capital city changed subtly. Commercial buildings gave way to dwellings. Most of them were tall, multiunit constructs and well maintained, though quarters were definitely close. Foot traffic had dwindled to almost nothing, making it relatively easy for Glenn and Velth to follow the men carrying the injured boy, but that changed as they entered another small public square.

Here dozens of men and women meandered past more small carts. None of the displays were as appetizing as those Glenn had seen near the café. There was more good-natured shouting, as vendors hawked their wares and the locals bartered for better prices. The area had a rough feel to it. The stares Glenn noted as she struggled to keep pace through the jostling crowd were harder and warier.

Finally the small group she was trailing ducked into a wide alley. A deep scarlet sun sat low on the horizon, blinding Glenn temporarily as she turned the corner. She shielded her eyes from the glare in time to see them entering a large double doorway beneath a low, metal awning.

Glenn felt Velth's hand grab her upper arm as she moved toward the doorway.

"Where do you think you're going, Commander?"

"That boy needs medical attention," she replied.

"His mother didn't want that. You saw the way the medics scared her. This is her problem to solve, not ours."

"I know my duty as a Starfleet officer and a doctor," Glenn said. "If they refuse my help, that's the end of it."

"You don't even have a medkit on you, sir, or a tricorder," Velth said. "You know you can't transport one down."

"You think *that's* what it takes to practice medicine?" Glenn asked as she moved toward the doors.

Glenn stepped back as they swung open. One of the Djinari men who had carried the boy brushed past her without comment. His vest was covered in viscous white fluid. Glenn started to call after him, as Velth said, "Commander."

Now that the interior of the building was visible, Glenn understood. She stepped into a very large open room. To her right, dozens of Djinari, Leodt, and unidentifiable aliens nursing a variety of ailments stood along the walls, sat restlessly on low metal benches, or lay on the dirt floor. Along the far wall, five tables were staffed by men and women in plain clothing. Long lines formed before each table.

Several official-looking individuals in gray smocks moved among the assembly, checking the status of the waiting, directing them to lines or toward a wall of partitions that began to the left of the waiting area. Moans, sobs, and the occasional scream punctuated the low din of conversation. Infrequent loud shouts came from the partitions, which Glenn concluded must be examination or treatment rooms. The partitions were rudely constructed of thin wood and, in some cases, curtains suspended from rods attached to the ceiling.

"Is this a hospital?" Velth asked in dismay.

"I think so," she replied. Searching among the faces, Glenn caught sight of Jent's mother. She stood at the end of one of the longer lines, holding herself with arms crossed over her chest. Her face was a mask of shock, but the tendrils extending from the back of her neck jerked and flailed in a motion Glenn now associated with physical or mental distress.

Jent was nowhere to be seen.

Glenn picked her way carefully through the crowd. Few were in any condition to glance at her, let alone question her. When she reached the woman she placed a gentle hand on her upper arm. The woman looked up slowly.

"You?" she asked.

"Yes," Glenn said. "My name is Clarissa Glenn. I'm a doctor, visiting your world. Is Jent being cared for here?"

The woman nodded. "He didn't do anything to those boys," she said. "We were just walking down the street."

"I'm sure he didn't," Glenn said kindly. "When we were in that alley, medics arrived. They could have taken your son to the central hospital immediately, but you ran. Why?"

"We're *nonszit*." The woman shrugged.

"I don't know what that means," Glenn said.

"We're not cleared for medical care. They didn't come to help him," she added.

"Why did they come?"

"To get him off the street. To shut him in some dark room so no one would hear him die."

Horrified, Glenn asked, "What's your name?"

"Neecah."

"Neecah. That's lovely."

The line began to move and Neecah shuffled forward.

"We need to go, Commander," Velth said softly.

Glenn's face set into hard lines. "We came here to tour the First World's medical facilities, Lieutenant. And that's exactly what we're going to do."

"We gather together in the sight of the living Source and invoke its blessings on all those who seek out the streams."

Kathryn Janeway stood next to Presider Cin in a secured area at the front of a vast, ornate hall. Cambridge stood beside her. Decan was in the row directly behind her. First Consul Dreeg was conspicuously absent. The contemplative energy of those who had assembled for evening services filled the space with quiet dignity.

The presider's personal guards stood at either end of the rows designated for Cin and her guests. Two of Psilakis's men stood behind them. Psilakis and Lasren had been stationed at the rear of the hall, nearest the doors. Seventy rows filled with worshippers stood between them, their heads bowed.

"We gather to acknowledge all that the Source has given us. We gather as one people who were divided in space and time until the Source, in its wisdom, carved the Great River that carried us to one another. We gather to give thanks."

As the celebrant continued to list the many accomplishments of the Source, Janeway allowed her eyes to wander. The walls and ceiling were decorated with luminescent mosaics of glass in rich hues. Directly behind the celebrant, a massive, perfect circle of gold against a black field obviously represented the Source. From its outer edge, hundreds of individual streams extended: first white, but breaking into various reds, oranges, yellows, greens, and indigos as they flowed into the obsidian field, dispersing into blackness. The effect should have been enchanting.

Why such fine and careful artistry left the admiral cold, she could not say.

As Glenn and Velth began to pass through the lines toward the partitions, few bothered to glance at them, let alone speak to them. Everyone who had a job to do was clearly overwhelmed, and patients who had come to utilize this crude facility's services were in too great a need to care.

When they reached the first set of partitions, Glenn stepped past the open doorway and listened for a few moments as the patient inside spoke to the nurse attending him.

"The wheel came loose before I could move my hand," the man said. He groaned loudly as the nurse applied gentle pressure on the limb.

In the next partition a Djinari woman struggled alone, clearly in the throes of heavy labor. Another nurse brushed past Glenn as she entered and wordlessly sat at the end of the cot and checked the woman's progress.

Several partitions down the row, an urgent voice shouted, "I need a donor, Djinari, Type 6G-alpha, and a pair of hands!"

Motioning to Velth, Glenn moved quickly toward that voice.

"The streams of the Great River flow endlessly from the Source, like blood flowing through our body. All that we have is a gift of the Source. All that we are reflects its bounty. All that we do repays its generosity. The Source calls us to remember that, as individuals, we may toil, but unified by the power of the Source, we will achieve our true potential."

As the celebrant droned on, Lieutenant Lasren tried to keep his eyes focused on the bright, beautiful image before him. But as he opened his empathic senses to those nearest him, he found his gaze drifting to the black sphere within the golden circle as a pit slowly opened in his stomach.

Initially, the sensation was all too familiar. The fear was a living thing in the center of almost everyone he had encountered on the First World. It began as a hunger and inevitably grew to something that could not be filled, a darkness that seemed determined to wipe him from existence.

Forcing his breath to slow, Lasren leaned his back against the rear wall, noting the worried look Psilakis threw in his direction. Closing his mind to the darkness, Lasren forced a vivid image into his consciousness: a *mect* tree that had stood near his family home on Betazed for more than a thousand years. As a boy he had often tried to embrace its trunk, but the width of his outstretched arms barely spanned a tenth of its circumference. His face lay against rough, lavender bark. The lowest branches were fifty meters above. The top was hidden from the ground by countless five-pointed, rich magenta leaves that turned pale pink before they fell each winter. Lasren had believed for most of his early years that it must touch the sky. The roots might reach all the way down to the center of the world. Heedless of the pull of the darkness, Lasren held tight to all he had ever tasted of eternity.

Glenn found Jent lying on his back on an elevated cot in a larger partition. A doctor stood over him, a Djinari female. Her gray smock was covered in sticky white fluid and grungy stains. Her hands, a deep shade of crimson splattered with Jent's white blood, worked with a skill Glenn immediately appreciated, gently cleaning the open wound to the boy's chest cavity.

A single metal pole stood beside the bed, with a sack of fluid suspended from a hook at the top. A clear line ran from the sack to Jent's arm, where a hasty puncture had been taped over. His respiration was weak. No other scanning devices were present to attest to his vitals. But the doctor's tentacles extended over her right shoulder and the tips gently touched Jent at several places on his head and neck. Glenn wondered silently what that touch was communicating to the doctor.

"I said I needed a donor!" the Djinari doctor shouted again as she glanced toward Glenn. Instantly she demanded, "Who are you?"

"I'm a doctor," Glenn said.

"From what colony? Ritella?"

"I come from the United Federation of Planets," Glenn said, stepping closer to the bed.

"Federation? What Federation?"

A white spurt of fluid shot up, and the doctor immediately returned her attention to Jent.

Glenn moved to the opposite side of the bed. At the doctor's left hand sat a tray of supplies. There was a stack of small, clean square cloth bandages beside a set of metal instruments. Glenn didn't want to think about the last time they might have been sterilized. Many used cloths littered the floor at the doctor's feet.

"Do you have extra gloves?" Glenn asked.

"We don't have extra anything here," the doctor replied, then added, "The sealant is behind you."

"Sealant?"

"For your hands. If you're here to help, make it quick or get out!" Turning her head toward the doorway, the doctor shouted again, "Donor! Djinari! Type 6G-alpha! Now!"

Glenn turned around and saw a cabinet stocked with more haphazardly arranged supplies. On top of it rested a low basin filled with a crimson fluid, reminiscent of but thicker than human blood. Glenn suddenly realized why the doctor's golden hands had appeared red when she first saw them. Gingerly, Glenn dipped her hands into the fluid and felt her skin tighten as a fine layer of film surrounded it.

"Are you sure you're a doctor?"

Turning back to the cot, Glenn lifted her hands, now coated by the liquid gloves. "I am," she said more confidently. "My name's Clarissa."

"I'm Kwer," the Djinari said. "Can you hold this? I can't see a thing in here," she said, handing Glenn a small tube. Glenn recognized its purpose immediately: suction.

Glenn worked carefully around Kwer's fingers, removing the fluid so Kwer could properly visualize the wound. As soon as one area was clear, another began to leak, pooling more fluid in the center of Jent's chest.

"Was the Source good enough to send me a doctor and a nurse today?" Kwer asked, nodding toward Velth, who had remained just outside the room.

Glenn motioned to Velth. "Dip your hands in that basin and get over here, Lieutenant," she ordered, reaching over Jent to grab a few of the cloths and applying pressure to one leak as she suctioned another.

Velth didn't look happy about it, but he did as he was told.

A stocky Leodt nurse entered, holding a scrawny young Djinari by the arm. "Your donor, Kwer."

Kwer glanced at him and said, "He'll do. Run the line."

The nurse guided the young man to the foot of the cot and sat him on a stool she pulled from beneath it. She then scuttled past Velth, who was lifting blood-red hands from the basin, and tossed several instruments aside until she found a coil of tubing terminating in a long, sharp needle.

The young man appeared accustomed to the procedures. He

was opening and closing his right hand and massaging his upper right arm. The nurse affixed one end of the tube to an opening on Jent's IV line and returned to the donor's side. After locating the vein she wanted, she punctured it with the needle. Once the flow of blood had been established, she nodded to Kwer and departed.

"Lieutenant," Glenn said, capturing Velth's attention and handing him a small cloth. "Hold this here—firm pressure, but not too hard," she ordered, placing the cloth over another leak.

"Aye, Doctor."

Counselor Hugh Cambridge was bored beyond belief. For any student of comparative mythology, a firsthand experience of an alien culture's religious observations should have been fascinating. The Confederacy's notions of the Source, however, were simply too new, too young, to touch the deeper mysteries of existence, let alone shed any light on them. These worshippers remained mired in the literal. They accepted without question the existence of the Source and, like Cambridge's ancient ancestors who believed the sun rose and set around them, saw themselves as the Source's chosen people.

Someday, he hoped, legions of skeptics would rise to challenge the authority, the very existence, of this *Source*. For a culture this technologically advanced to retreat from a scientific explanation for the existence of the streams was to willfully court ignorance. Inevitably, someone would be brave enough to question this acceptance, and at that point, assuming they survived the upheavals of religious adolescence, the true spiritual benefits of devotion might finally be open to them.

Faith was not a crime. Blind obedience should be. Too many years wasted in strict adherence to fabricated laws could damn a religion to oblivion. Only those that moved past such things, toward transcendental experiences of individual and communal awareness, had any hope of surviving or guiding their followers toward wisdom. Many humanoid cultures had flourished in the light of such practices. It didn't make them any more "true" than anyone else's. The path toward one's center was irrelevant. But it did bind communities together and, usually, by minimizing internal noise, had the added benefit of forcing people's attention outward toward the needs of their fellows.

Cambridge was momentarily distracted by movement over his right shoulder. A long line of pregnant women had assembled in the center aisle, and they were making their way slowly toward the stage on which the celebrant spoke.

"You have received the greatest gift the Source can bestow, the gift of new life growing inside you. Every life the Source has blessed us with is essential to its purpose. Every mother, a reflection of its perfection. Enter the ceremonial stream and allow its waters to renew you and the children you will bear."

One by one, the women descended into a small pool sunk into the stage. They emerged from a stairway at the water's far end and returned to their seats via the side aisles.

"The Source protects you. The Source gives you strength."

Does the Source also provide towels? Cambridge wondered, imagining how much more annoying this service would be if he were forced to endure it with soaked feet and pants.

Peering closer into the wound, Glenn saw small pieces of metal glistening against Jent's greenish flesh. The wound was not as deep as she had first suspected. The shrapnel was embedded in a layer of thick flesh just below his thoracic cage.

"What did this?" Glenn asked. "What sort of weapon was used?"

"A volvent," Kwer replied.

"It fires projectiles of some kind?"

"Projectiles?"

"It's not an energy-based weapon? It does not fire light?" Glenn asked.

"Source, no," Kwer said, shaking her head. "Do you have any idea what those cost? The kid with the thin skin and quick trigger finger who did this could never afford a disruptor."

Glancing toward the donor, Glenn noted his head beginning to weave a bit. "Help him," she ordered Velth, who seemed only too happy to remove his hands from Jent's chest and, after peeling off the sealant, placed them on the donor's shoulders to steady him.

"You don't have a ready supply of blood for your patients?" Glenn asked.

"Of course we do," Kwer said as she gently lifted a large piece of metal from the wound and dropped it in a small basin on the tray. "They usually start lining up in the middle of the night. It's the most honest day's bread most of them will ever earn."

"They are . . ." Glenn struggled to remember the word. "*Non . . .*" she began.

"*Nonszit*—nonproductive members of society," Kwer said.

"There's no work for them?"

"None that they are educated well enough to do."

"Aren't there schools?"

"Sure. If you can afford them. Poverty tends to run in families, though."

Glenn shook her head in disbelief.

"What does your Federation do with those who can't earn their keep?" Kwer asked.

It seemed cruel, with her hands buried in Jent's chest, to tell Kwer the truth: *In the Federation, there's no such thing.*

By the time the singing began, Lieutenant Lasren had been forced to close his mind to the congregation. Hundreds of voices around him were lifted in joyful praise of the Source. Beatific faces gazed in adoration at the central mural. The sounds reverberated around him, clear and strong.

Unable to breathe, Lasren excused himself and sought the cold air of the night.

Kwer had finally extracted all of the visible shrapnel and begun to close the wound. Glenn's fingers were unaccustomed to the task. No Federation surgeon in hundreds of years had closed a wound so crudely. But Glenn dutifully folded Jent's flesh together as Kwer's deft stitches followed her lead.

Three centimeters remained to close when Jent's body began to buck violently.

"What's happening?"

"What do you think?" Kwer said bitterly. "We're losing him. Release the donor," she said.

Glenn quickly pulled the line from Jent as Kwer interlocked her hands on top of one another and began compressions just above the wound.

Glenn then removed the needle from the donor's arm and ordered Velth to keep pressure on it. Turning back to Kwer, she saw beads of perspiration flowing freely from her forehead. Her tendrils had retracted and they stuck out stiffly behind her as she continued to try and restart Jent's heart.

Jent's golden skin had faded to an ashy white when Kwer finally relented. Stepping back, she struggled to catch her breath, running the back of her hand over her forehead.

"That's it," she said, her voice thick.

Though the muscles of her back and shoulders were now knit into very small, tight knots, Glenn lifted herself as best she could and said, "Time of death?"

"What difference does it make?" Kwer said, peeling off her sealant and stepping around Velth toward the doorway.

"You did everything you could, Doctor," Glenn said. "I can attest to that."

"No one will care," Kwer assured her.

Velth suddenly found his voice. "Why did this happen?"

"What?" Kwer asked.

"Why did this happen?" Velth asked again, his eyes glistening.

"He'd already lost too much blood by the time he got here," Glenn began.

"No, Commander," Velth said, staring hard at Kwer. "Why does a boy this age, living five blocks from a perfectly good, technologically advanced, incredibly well-supplied hospital, get shot by two other boys for no reason and die *here?*"

Kwer shrugged. "Maybe they were bored. Maybe Jent looked at them strangely. Maybe they just wanted to see what would happen. They're children who no one took the time to teach better." Stepping outside the partition, the weary doctor shouted, "Who's next?"

Janeway knew that there were worse ways to spend a few hours than quiet contemplation. She had used the time to separate in her mind the many conflicting impressions she had received thus far about the Confederacy and its people. Evidence mounted with each encounter suggesting Janeway should abandon any hope for a diplomatic alliance. The benefits were undeniable, but so were the differences between the Confederacy and the Federation. The admiral sought clarity, the quiet acceptance she had relearned over the last several months in her mother's garden. Sadly, it eluded her.

After thanking the presider for the invitation to the service, she, Decan, and Cambridge moved toward their security officers in preparation for the short walk to their waiting shuttle. She saw Psilakis standing beside Lasren. Psilakis was all but holding the young Betazoid up.

"Get him to the shuttle, now," Janeway ordered.

"Is there a problem?" the presider asked over Janeway's shoulder.

"No, Presider," Janeway assured her. "But it has been a long day and it's time we all got some rest."

"It is well earned," Cin said warmly. "I look forward to our next meeting."

"As do I," Janeway said.

Once inside the shuttle, Janeway moved to Cambridge's side. Lasren's unnaturally pale face was all she needed to order the shuttle to lift off immediately and make best possible speed back to the *Galen*. The counselor ran a medical tricorder over Lasren. Cambridge's expression assured her that, though obviously weak, the young man was in no immediate danger.

Turning to Psilakis, Janeway asked, "Did he say anything to you?"

Psilakis shook his head. "A little. By the time I got to him he just mumbled something about *nothing*."

"What did he say exactly?" Cambridge asked.

"He said, 'There's nothing there. Nothing there,'" Psilakis replied.

TWELFTH LAMONT

Lieutenant Harry Kim had learned a great deal in the two days he had spent aboard the *Twelfth Lamont*. He had learned that, outside of the subspace corridors, most CIF vessels could barely make warp five. He had begun to grasp the rank designations within the CIF. A "J" indicated a junior level, or the lowest of three possible iterations of privates, corporals, majors, or colonels. An "E" was the midlevel or executive designation. There were separate prefixes for generals, "Ranking" being the second highest.

He had learned that JC Eleoate didn't have many friends aboard but that many of the E-level officers had a regular *loks* tournament they played during their off hours. He had learned that Confederacy sidearms were so destructive that similar weapons had long since been banned within the Federation.

Most disturbing, he had learned that the protectors who had saved *Voyager* and *Demeter* from an alien armada and brought them safely to Confederacy space had not been lost due to the enemy fire they had absorbed, nor destroyed by the CIF. Only one possibility remained but it was difficult for Kim to understand, let alone accept.

"What are you afraid of, Lieutenant?" General Mattings asked as Lieutenant Kim paused before bringing the milky blue liquid to his lips.

Kim was afraid that the substance his nose suggested would taste like rotting eggs would come flying out of his mouth the moment he took a sip. Of course, he couldn't say that out loud.

"Nothing, sir," Kim said gamely. Inhaling briskly he steeled himself, but the worst never came. The *pianjay* juice had a bite to it, like most Confederacy dishes Harry had tasted, but the surprising cream that carried it down smoothed out the rough edges nicely. He had taken a second sip before he could help himself. "That's delicious."

The general's teeth jutted forward in a smile. "I told you."

"Why does it smell like that?" Kim asked.

"Like what?" Mattings asked innocently.

"Nothing, sir," Kim replied.

Mattings dropped his chin, clearly disappointed. He'd invited Kim to dinner and probed gently throughout the meal for the Starfleet officer's thoughts on his ship and crew.

"It smells like dead *lunfis*," Mattings corrected him. "My nose may not be as big as yours but it works just fine, Lieutenant Kim. The stench is part of the *pianjay*'s natural defenses. If their secretion smelled as good as it tastes, they'd never have survived this long."

"I'm sorry, General," Kim said. "I didn't want to give offense."

"The truth never offends me, son. Polite lies, on the other hand, bother me a great deal."

"Me too, sir," Kim said, surprised by the ease with which this truth slipped out.

Leaning forward over the table they shared in the general's private dining area, Mattings said, "I believe that your people and mine could learn from one another. Over the years, the Confederacy has admitted worlds to our union that shared almost nothing of our customs or values. They brought other resources, but little that made integration worth the pain and struggle. It's not for me to question the choices of our leaders."

"Of course, General," Kim said, nodding.

"But your people are different. You seem genuinely interested, not just in what we have, but in *who we are*. You are respectful, curious, intelligent, and incredibly accomplished. However, you don't brag about it. I know that many of your technological developments surpass ours. You wouldn't have made it from your home to the First Quadrant if they didn't. I'm certain that, for all our scans, we know next to nothing about your true capabilities. What I can't figure out is *why* you're hiding so much from us."

The tactical officer considered his words carefully before he responded. "If your fear is that we are attempting to lull you into complacency, we aren't," Kim said. "The Federation has learned the hard way, time and again, that the differences between cultures must be respected. That respect is the basis of our Prime Directive. As best I can tell, you possess technologies and resources that are beyond ours. But the Federation never wants our differences to become points of conflict. Above all, we work for peace, understanding, and, when possible, exchange of new ideas and technology."

"But that's all well above your pay grade, right?" the general asked.

Kim smiled. "We don't get paid."

The general's face fell. "Beg pardon?"

"When we interact with cultures that utilize currency for exchange of goods or services, we are issued whatever is appropriate to fulfill our missions. We receive no compensation for our duties beyond that. All of our day-to-day needs are met."

"By whom?"

"By the Federation as a whole," Kim replied. "Long ago, many of our member worlds had economic systems similar to yours. Some still retain vestiges of them. Everyone within the Federation has access to all the basic necessities, and anything beyond that they desire, there are ways to acquire."

"If you don't work to acquire life's necessities, why do you work?" the general asked.

"There are a lot of hours to fill in a day," Kim replied. "We do what interests us, what our skills make us fit to do. We serve our fellows and are served in return. We rise in rank, or status, not by what we have acquired but by the skills we have mastered and our personal accomplishments."

The general absorbed this quietly. Finally, he shook his head. "I can't imagine it. But if you have everything you need, and are free to spend your days doing whatever you wish, what are you doing here?"

"Exploring," Kim replied.

"To what end? You don't need us. You don't need our resources, our people, or our territory. Why risk your lives just to satisfy your curiosity?"

"What else is there?" Kim asked.

"Home, safety, security, good food, the companionship of wise men and willing women, and that's just off the top of my head," the general replied.

Kim smiled in spite of himself. "I have all that *and* I still get to spend each day learning new things."

The general nodded somberly. After another sip of *pianjay* he asked, "You've seen our engines, haven't you?"

"Yes, sir. EC Beeve walked me through the specs this morning."

"Just how far behind your Federation are we in terms of propulsion?"

Chakotay had already advised Kim that Mattings had seen their slipstream drive in use, so he knew to tread carefully.

"It's hard to say."

"Try. Best guess. I won't hold you to it."

"Twenty, maybe thirty years," Kim replied truthfully.

Mattings chuckled. "I would have guessed fifty."

Kim shrugged. "If you lost your ability to access the streams tomorrow, it might be ten. Civilizations tend to focus their efforts where they are needed most. Your engines do exactly what you need them to do, and will until you need them to do more."

"Does the same go for our weapons?"

Kim sighed. "I haven't seen the specs on those, General."

"You've seen the *Lamont* in battle, and as head of your ship's security, you memorized every word of those sensor reports as soon as you had them," Mattings countered.

"I did," Kim said.

"And?"

"I'll say this," Kim began. "The capacity of your energy weapons and the yields of your standard torpedoes surpass anything we would consider useful."

"You went up against the Borg and you can still say that with a straight face?" Mattings demanded.

"Force and size aren't everything," Kim replied. "Sometimes more is just more. That's not all you need to get the job done. With the Borg, we had to constantly redesign every aspect of our offensive and defensive capabilities. Their power came from the ability to adapt. We survived those encounters because we were always able to find new ways to get past them." As Mattings considered this, Kim said, "Mind if I ask you a question, General?"

"Please."

"All of your men carry sidearms, on and off duty."

"That's not a question."

"They don't have a stun setting."

"What's that?"

"My handheld phaser can disable someone without killing them. Yours can't. In fact, they destroy their targets by molecular disintegration: one of the slowest and most painful deaths possible for a life-form."

"We don't raise our weapons unless the target has already demonstrated that they are a threat. If we don't intend to kill, we don't fire. Civilians possess less lethal forms of self-defense, but the officers of the CIF don't have that luxury. In a battle, I don't want my people wondering whether or not they should use lethal force on their enemy. If we're in battle, that call has already been made."

"Have you ever fired on a target who turned out not to be an enemy?" Kim asked.

"No." After a moment, Mattings asked, "Did you get your questions answered about the ancient ones?"

Kim's stomach turned. "I think so."

"What were you looking for?"

"I spent a lot of time before we came here trying to understand the protectors." *And plenty more communicating with them,* Kim did not add. "It seemed odd to me that as soon as they reached this side of the Gateway, they were destroyed."

"We didn't destroy them," Mattings said. "We would never do that. They dispersed of their own accord."

"*You knew?*" Kim asked, surprised.

"Of course I knew."

"And that didn't bother you?"

"Why would it?"

"You allowed them to bring us here. You know that data on everything they contact is imprinted in their memory. You didn't want to know what they already knew about us?"

"The ancient ones have always been temperamental. I'd never seen one until your ships showed up. But it is accepted wisdom that we do not question their choices."

"Your ancestors did."

"How do you know that?"

Kim paused, wondering if he had already revealed more than he should have.

"They told us," he finally replied. "Or, rather, they showed us."

"Showed you what?" Mattings asked.

"Their past; history of their interactions with your ancestors," Kim said.

"And just how did you convince them to do that?" Mattings demanded.

"We asked," Kim said.

"How?"

"It's complicated."

"Lieutenant Kim, I'm a patient man, but even I have my limits," the general warned.

"The ancient ones are capable of more than data transmission into technology. They can also transmit data directly into your mind," Kim said. "We showed them a hull fragment from one of your ancient ships. They showed us how it came to be there."

The general sat back in his chair. Finally he said, "They still remember. They've lived with it for hundreds of years while we've allowed it to slip into the past. No wonder they destroyed themselves. *That's who they think we are*. We've always assumed that they brought so few here because they were still protecting us. They aren't. They ended their own existence to protect you *from us,* didn't they?"

"It is possible they thought you might enslave them again and force them to turn against us," Kim said.

Mattings shook his head in disgust. After a moment, he rose from the small table. "Forgive me, Lieutenant, but I've lost my appetite."

Kim rose as well. "You should know, General, that we don't hold you responsible for the actions of your ancestors. If you knew more of our history, you'd know we've made more than our fair share of poor choices. The important thing is to learn from them."

"That's the problem, son," the general said. "I don't know if we have."

Chapter Fourteen

Seven vaguely remembered Axum carrying her back to their quarters. At least, she thought she did. She had been conscious of his arms lifting her, cradling her against his chest. The slow and steady rise and fall of his breath had stilled her own. Screams had given way to whimpers and finally silence as the pain receded.

But she did not remember returning down the halls that had led her to the examination room, the alien woman, or the pain. The few times her eyes had opened, Axum had walked through an inky darkness, populated sparsely with distant stars.

Only when they had reached his quarters again did Seven's immediate surroundings make sense. Axum had placed her on the sofa and wrapped his arms around her. She had rested her head against his shoulder, for how long, she knew not.

When the pain had finally been banished to a corner of her mind reserved for things she intended to forget, she tried to retrace the steps that had brought her here.

Just before the pain, there had been an alien woman undergoing some sort of treatment. A hypo had been lifted to her neck. The individual injecting her had worn a biohazard suit, suggesting that the material he was using was deadly.

What was it? Seven wondered.

"Axum?" she said, lifting her head and turning to face him.

"Better now?" he asked.

"When they brought you here, they extracted some of your catoms, didn't they?"

"Yes."

"Did they only take yours?"

"As opposed to?"

"Mine? The ones the Doctor transfused into you?"

"I'm not sure their extraction methods are sophisticated enough to distinguish between the two," Axum said.

Seven pulled herself upright and free from Axum's embrace. "They can't," she said with finality.

"Does it really matter?" Axum asked. "They took yours too as soon as you arrived."

"Yes, but long before that, they had access to mine because they were part of you."

"So?" Axum asked.

"I saw what they're doing with them," Seven said.

"What did you see?"

"Someone—the Commander most likely—is injecting our catoms into others. He must be using them to try to cure the virus."

Axum shrugged. "I wish him luck. If that's his plan, the cure is going to be a long time coming."

Seven shook her head, forcing her mind back to the scene she had witnessed. She knew the answer was close but not yet fully formed. "But she wasn't sick," Seven realized.

"Who?"

"The patient," Seven replied. "The woman on the biobed: She showed no other signs of illness. That does not track with the symptoms of the plague. She should have been seriously ill."

"How do you know she wasn't?"

"She looked at me. She smiled."

"She could have been delirious."

"She *knew* me."

"Are you sure she even saw you?"

Seven rose from the couch and began to pace. Too many pieces of the puzzle were floating before her. Order must be imposed upon the chaos of her unruly mind. That determination felt strange but familiar, like a favorite dress she hadn't worn in a long time.

A new thought stopped her in her tracks. "You were being tortured before I came here."

"I wasn't. I told you," Axum began.

"Then what did I see?" Seven demanded.

"Annika . . ."

"*Don't*," Seven ordered. "Don't try to placate me. I saw the torture. I felt it. Our catoms connected us to one another once they were mingled. If it wasn't your pain, then whose was it?"

"I don't know," Axum said.

But he did. He had to. "If our catoms were injected into someone else, a connection between us and them could be established as well. That is the only possible explanation for the sensations of pain I have been experiencing. They are using my catoms. They are injecting them into others. Those experiments are incredibly painful for those who are receiving them. Their pain becomes ours."

"It becomes *yours,* Annika," Axum said.

Seven stared at him, searching his face.

"You're lying to me," she realized.

Axum rose and reached for her.

"You know I can't do that."

His face, his beautiful, strong, scarred face, was a mask of concern.

His eyes were not.

Seven did not think. She simply established a direct link between her thoughts and Axum's. In his mind, she saw the man on fire, and felt again the agony of the icy tank. In his mind, she saw the woman with lavender skin, her face, her hands, her entire body rippling as catomic particles flew at the speed of her beating heart through her bloodstream, transforming her tissues, *destroying them.*

Seven was thrown back several paces by the force of Axum's rejection. He retreated at the same time, stepping back almost onto the balcony.

"*No!*" he shouted.

Seven's breath came in great heaving gasps.

"Why?" she demanded. "Why didn't you tell me this had happened to you as well?"

"What difference does it make?" he demanded.

"What difference?" Seven was dumbstruck. "For days now I have suffered. You let me think that torment was mine alone."

"You will learn, as I did, to block those sensations when they begin. I didn't lie to you, Annika. I did not feel the pain they have inflicted on others through us. I *choose* not to. I have plenty of painful memories of my own to contend with. I won't accept theirs as well."

"But you've known all this time what they were doing and you didn't tell me," Seven said. "Why didn't you tell me?"

Axum shook his head slowly back and forth. She had never seen him so angry, so wounded, so devastated all at once.

"All the answers are here, Annika. They've always been here. I haven't hidden anything from you. I tried to show you. I asked you to enter my mind and my thoughts, but you refused. You took my body and my soul, but you wanted no part of my *truth*." A chill coursed over him, raising the hairs on the back of Seven's neck.

"Sometimes," he said softly, "I think you are no better than her."

"Who?"

The Borg queen in countless incarnations they had known reared her hideous face.

As if struck by the back of his hand, Seven reeled. A thousand new questions rose to the front of her mind. Axum turned and rushed out to the patio.

She didn't need to follow to find her answers. Seven had but to reach out and take them from his mind. But that horrible visage stayed her. She had just violated him, as surely as he had once taken her in what she had believed was a dream. To probe his mind again without his permission, now that she knew how simple it was, was unconscionable.

"Axum?" she called.

He was no longer visible in the darkness.

"Axum?" she said again, stepping forward gingerly.

A few more steps and she would find him. A few more steps and she would beg his forgiveness.

As Seven started toward him, a sound she had not heard since she arrived greeted her ears. She turned automatically as the door to their quarters slid open.

A figure stepped over the threshold. The face was one Seven knew well.

And one that could not possibly be here.

"Doctor Frazier?" Seven asked.

To Shaw's surprise, but not Tom Paris's, his mother had successfully cleared the latest hurdle placed before her. Less than twenty-four hours after she had learned that another grandchild was on the way and been ordered to prove that she could adequately care for both children, a Family Court investigator had visited her home and found a nursery already prepared. In addition, six individuals had all written statements confirming their intent to assist Mrs. Paris with the various duties involved in the care of two young children.

Two of those six were Tom's sisters.

Shaw had been disconcerted when the attorney provided this update. The matter now resolved, mediation would resume the following morning with the presentation of character witnesses for both parties.

Paris had known his mother well enough to anticipate her actions. The only thing more impressive than her organizational skills was her ruthless efficiency. He did not, however, know Shaw well enough to trust that the attorney had too much faith in his own abilities to flummox Julia Paris with the relatively minor inconvenience of adding another child's care to her list of responsibilities. Shaw had assured him from day one that he and B'Elanna would win. Paris always had his doubts. Now, it seemed, Shaw had begun to share them.

But there was nothing to be done about it today. Rather than sit alone and fester—or, worse, find a dark, quiet spot in which to drown his sorrows—Paris opted to do his duty. He had promised Doctor Sharak to contact Seven on a daily basis. First thing in the morning seemed as good a time as any.

Whoever was running this show made their first mistake when they chose to leave Paris waiting in the lobby of Starfleet Medical for more than two hours before anyone appeared to meet him.

Their second mistake was to send a shiny young ensign to deflect him.

When no one had appeared after fifteen minutes, Paris had understood that something unusual was going on. Sharak had already told him that communications from within the quarantined area where Seven was held were restricted, but it didn't take that long to find a secure data terminal and transmit a request for interface. When fifteen minutes had become thirty, Paris had grown annoyed. At the one-hour mark, Paris had pulled out his padd and reviewed the list of names the Doctor and Sharak had provided identifying the officers connected with the project. At that point, Paris would have been content to speak with any one of them. An hour later, Paris wanted answers from only one person.

The young man in a blue science uniform who finally approached made the Harry Kim Paris had first met in a bar on Deep Space 9 look worldly.

"Commander Paris?"

"Ensign," Paris greeted him tersely as he rose from the lobby bench.

"I have been asked to advise you that you will not be able to make direct contact with Seven today."

"Take me to Doctor Pauline Frist at once, Ensign."

"I'm not authorized to do that, sir."

"Do you know where Doctor Frist is right now?"

"Yes, sir."

"Then let's go."

"I . . . I can't . . . sir, I—" the ensign stammered.

"Ensign!" Paris barked, in a fair-to-good imitation of his

father. "You will take me to Doctor Frist, or five minutes from now, Doctor Frist will be ordered by *her* superior officer, the chief of Starfleet Medical, to receive me. He's also going to have a number of questions for Doctor Frist she probably doesn't have time to answer right now, starting with: Why are you refusing access to a decorated Starfleet officer who is a personal friend and, technically, responsible for an individual in your care who has volunteered to assist Doctor Frist with her current assignment?"

The ensign had no response to this.

"Should that fail to persuade Doctor Frist, the next call she receives will be from Admiral Kenneth Montgomery. In the event Admiral Montgomery is unable to communicate the urgency of this matter, the next person Doctor Frist hears from will be Admiral Leonard Akaar of Starfleet Command."

"I . . ." the ensign began.

"The only question you have to answer right now, Ensign, is: How much embarrassment do you intend to cause Doctor Frist before lunch?"

"This way, sir," the ensign said.

Three minutes later, Paris was ushered into Doctor Frist's office.

"I'm not sure what you thought you might accomplish by running roughshod over Ensign Pierce," Frist said by way of greeting. "He was told to advise you that Seven is unable to make direct contact with you right now. I don't have a different answer for you, Commander Paris."

"I assumed as much," Paris said.

"Then why are you wasting my time?"

"I don't intend to waste a lot of it," Paris said cordially.

Frist opened her hands before her. "So we're done here? You just needed to hear it from the horse's mouth?"

"Yes," Paris said. "Please take me to the horse."

Frist chuckled without amusement. "Surely you are aware that this is a classified project, Commander," Frist said.

"I'm not asking to check your work, Doctor," Paris said. "I

need to make contact with a civilian attached to the fleet I serve, a civilian I brought to you because you indicated that her expertise was required. Technically, Seven has not been reassigned while offering you that expertise. She's still under my authority. I know you're not going to tell me anything, so why don't you save us both a little time and take me to the officer who will."

"You're not cleared to enter our quarantined area."

"Then clear me."

"I can't do that."

"Contact the officer who can, and tell him or her that I am not leaving this area until I speak with Seven."

"Please don't force me to have security escort you from the building, Commander."

Paris smiled. "Go ahead."

Frist faltered.

"I don't know how much you know about Seven. I've known her since the day she was first severed from the Borg Collective. If she were aware that I wished to speak with her, she would contact me immediately. The fact that she hasn't done so means you haven't told her, or she is unable to do so. If the issue is the first, I'd suggest you apprise her of my request immediately. If the issue is the latter, I will know the reason why before the day is done."

Frist took a deep breath. "The work we are doing here is of a highly sensitive nature. Very few individuals in Starfleet or among the civilian authorities are aware of it. It was classified for good reason. Once Seven voluntarily entered the quarantine area, she understood that contact with the outside world would be limited. We have made an exception in the case of Doctor Sharak—also a member of your crew, I believe—because he was already aware of the nature of our work and has been willing to assist us."

"Doctor Sharak did not hear from her yesterday. He requested that I rectify that today. I came here at his request, but two hours later, my gut tells me something is wrong. *I'm* the one you need to satisfy now, which is bad news for you and whoever you work for. I've got five generations of Starfleet brass in my family tree and, unlike Doctor Sharak, I actually know how this game is played."

"Be that as it may, I cannot force Seven to contact you."

"Are you saying Seven refused to speak with me?"

"No."

"Good, because I know that would be a lie."

"Commander Paris, please . . ."

"I've actually lost track of the number of times Seven has been essential to a mission that resulted in the salvation of many lives, including mine, and probably yours. Were you here a couple of years back when she made contact with an alien weapon and turned it against an evolved Borg cube that was minutes away from destroying Earth?

"When the Borg Invasion began, the Federation president asked Seven to advise her throughout those dark days. Seven was in the Monet room when President Bacco watched the Caeliar transform the Borg. The president was holding Seven's hand when she returned to consciousness. I'm pretty sure Seven still calls her 'Nan.' I wonder if *Nan* would be interested to know that an individual who has done so much for the Federation is now being held incommunicado by Starfleet Medical. I don't know the president personally, but my sense of her is that, at the very least, she'd be curious as to why."

"The president's office is aware of our work and has offered us all the latitude we require to meet the threat we are facing. She will not question us or our methods," Frist said.

"Her office, maybe," Paris said. "*But her? Personally?*"

"You expect me to believe that you could contact the president of the Federation and demand she intercede on your behalf? You'd be cashiered out of Starfleet before the day's end for your insolence."

"If I'm wrong, maybe," Paris allowed. "But if my concerns prove well founded, that's another issue entirely. I do believe that if I were to bring President Bacco word that Seven might be in danger, she would start interceding immediately."

Frist stared at Paris for almost a full minute in silence. Finally she said, "A moment, Commander."

It took less than five minutes for Frist to return to her office. When she did, she rotated the display screen on her desk to face Paris and said, "The Commander will speak with you shortly."

"See, that wasn't so hard, was it?" Paris asked, as Frist left the room, shaking her head in frustration.

Moments later, the face of a younger man than Paris expected to see appeared before him. He was human, with fair white skin and a cleanly shaven scalp. A dark shadow visible above his ears and ending well before his forehead suggested that what hair had yet to recede was black, but he'd already accepted the inevitable. His nose was bulbous, his lips full, and his chin weak. They did little to convey a sense of authority. That task was left to his dark eyes, which held Paris's coldly as soon as they found them.

"Commander Paris, I am Commander Jefferson Briggs."

"A pleasure to speak with you," Paris said. "Where's Seven?"

Briggs wet his lips quickly before replying. *"I regret to inform you that yesterday, there was a security breach in the quarantine area. At that time, Seven was exposed, briefly, to a live and very deadly virus. It will take us several days to confirm infection, but our best hope of slowing its progress, should our worst fears prove correct, was to slow all of her body's systems as much as we dared. We have placed her in stasis, and she will remain there until we can pronounce her healthy or are able to find a cure for the virus."*

Paris believed him, but that didn't mean he trusted him.

"You will transmit confirmation of what you have just told me to this station and I will retain that record until Seven is released from quarantine," Paris said.

"That confirmation will be classified. You are not authorized to share it with anyone."

"I will share it with Doctor Sharak when he returns."

Briggs ran a hand over his scalp. *"That will be acceptable."*

"And as soon as Seven is able, I expect to hear from her personally," Paris said.

"Understood."

"In the meantime, I expect regular reports on her status."

"That shouldn't be a problem. In the future you may request those updates from Doctor Frist."

"You will return Seven to us in perfect health, Commander."

"We'll do our best," Briggs assured him.

"Paris out."

As the screen shifted to the insignia of Starfleet Medical, Paris sighed. It wasn't the answer he wanted. But at least the last few hours now made sense.

When Cadet Icheb emerged from the office of his academic advisor, he was amazed he was still attached to the Academy. Commander Treadon had wanted to believe Icheb's story about losing his way while attempting to trace a lost inventory requisition from the classified division. Had she suspected how thorough he had been in hiding any trace of his whereabouts from the facility's internal records she would have been forced to convene a disciplinary panel.

According to the computer, Icheb had been correctly located in an inventory room prior to a three-hour, eleven-minute contact loss, after which he had been located again in the classified area. That "contact loss" was blamed on sensor malfunction along the route Icheb claimed he had taken between the inventory room and the classified area. The viral algorithm Icheb had planted in that, and several other area sensors, had erased itself and any trace of its origin within seconds of its deployment. The discovery of several other affected sensors had, as Icheb intended, corroborated his story.

Most students who entered the Academy were proficient in the basic skills required to execute a mission such as the one Icheb had assigned himself. Some had the requisite nerve to carry it out. Few also possessed the sterling record of Icheb or the reputation for scrupulous honesty and social naiveté unique to the former Borg drone. Treadon had *wanted* to believe him. But his internship with Starfleet Medical had been terminated at their request, and Treadon had seen no reason to fight it. There were other positions available that would have been more challenging and better suited to one of her brightest cadets.

Naomi Wildman was not yet as tall as Icheb, but she had entered a somewhat gangly, awkward stage of her physical development that made her gait easy to pick out as she hurried through the morning crowd on the quad toward him.

"What happened?" she demanded as soon as she fell into step beside him.

"Nothing."

"Ambrose said you were escorted back to the grounds last night by security officers," Naomi insisted.

"It is not his or your concern," Icheb said.

"Are you in trouble?"

"No."

"Then why weren't you in morning PT?"

"I had a meeting with my advisor."

"Icheb," Naomi hissed, pinching his upper arm a little too hard as she grabbed it.

"Ow. Let go," he said, shaking her off.

"It has something to do with Seven, doesn't it?"

"Don't you have class right now?"

Naomi stopped, planting her feet firmly in front of him and crossing her arms at her chest. "I've sent more than twenty messages to Seven at Starfleet Medical since she arrived. She hasn't responded to one of them. That's not like her."

"She is working on a very important project and cannot be disturbed at this time."

"Maybe not by most people, but *us*?" Naomi demanded.

"Perhaps you overestimate her emotional attachment to us," Icheb said, and he knew he had erred as soon as the words left his mouth.

Tears sprang to Naomi's eyes and her cheeks flushed crimson. "You told me the doctor you met on *Voyager* was named Sharak. My mom left yesterday to take Doctor Sharak to Coridan, at his request. Coridan is one of those worlds that has been getting a lot of coverage lately in the news feeds. People are saying there's something going on there. A lot of people are sick. Seven is at Starfleet Medical. It doesn't take a big brain to connect the dots." Naomi's face contorted briefly as she said, "She's sick, isn't she?"

Icheb shook his head. "I don't know," he admitted. "I don't think so, but I don't know."

"Did you try to help her?"

"No."

"There's nothing *I* can do, but if I know *you're* trying, I'll feel better," Naomi said.

"There's nothing I can do either," Icheb admitted.

Naomi's hands clenched into fists. She looked ready to punch him. Sadly, it wouldn't be the first time Icheb had been assaulted during his time at the Academy.

"We have to try," Naomi insisted.

"*We* have to get to class," Icheb corrected her. His shoulder knocked hers as he brushed past her, overwhelmed by his failure and determined to do nothing to jeopardize Naomi's future in the same way he had just risked his own.

Chapter Fifteen

GALEN

The most comfortable, warm, and inviting space available on board the *Galen* was the Doctor's private office. The rich earth tones he had chosen for the wall colors and trim soothed the senses better than the stark grays and blues that adorned most sickbays. The unusual structure of the desk, a semicircle that ran from the middle of the rear wall, around the far one, and angled inward again to almost surround its occupant, was one of the most ergonomically pleasing and efficient Janeway had ever seen. Two soft chairs sat opposite it, but there was easily room for two more. Several cabinets ran above the rear of the desk and along the opposite wall. Personal photos of the Doctor's friends graced every horizontal surface that was not a workspace.

Janeway realized that she should have made time to see the Doctor and let him give her a personal tour of the sickbay he had designed. It was a remarkable accomplishment and she wanted him to hear that from her lips.

However, she hadn't come to admire his handiwork. She was checking on Lieutenant Lasren, who had undergone a full physical as soon as their shuttle had returned from the First World. Janeway had assumed that Commander Glenn would have done the honors, but when the shuttle docked, she was still on the First World. Glenn was several hours late but had continued to check in regularly. Janeway made a mental note to have a word with the young commander when she returned, about balancing the thrill of a first-contact mission with the requirements of her ship, one that was currently missing its CMO.

A newer version of the EMH, a Mark IX, had completed Lasren's evaluation, with Counselor Cambridge hovering nearby throughout. As soon as it was done and Lasren was released, Janeway had entered the Doctor's office to hear their report.

The pallor of Lasren's face was accentuated by his large, dark eyes, but otherwise he seemed much better. Cambridge insisted that the lieutenant sit before taking a position with his back resting against the wall next to the office's entrance, his arms crossed at his chest.

"What happened, Lieutenant?" Janeway asked as soon as everyone was settled.

Lasren took a moment to order his thoughts before beginning. "I waited until the service had begun to open myself empathically to those present. I thought that perhaps at a religious observation, where people gather to meditate and reflect, the intensity of the fear I usually sense from Confederacy citizens might have been more manageable."

"Was it?" Cambridge asked.

"No, sir. It was worse."

"How so?" Janeway asked.

"When I was young, my father used to take me to the pools of Warth. Pilgrims come there to meditate. Images of the Four Deities are everywhere, carved from fallen branches of the ancient *mect* trees that surround the pools. Every time I went, I couldn't help but open myself up to those around me. There was a powerful energy there, but it was calm and tranquil."

"It sounds beautiful," Janeway remarked.

"It was," Lasren said, nodding. "But there was something more—a tangible entity created by but also separate from the pilgrims."

"Are you saying that when people gather en masse to speak to those old gods, the gods show up?" Cambridge asked.

Lasren smiled as he shook his head. "I don't believe in the Four. I don't know if the meditation created that reality, or if what I sensed was the existence of something beyond that. I only know I sensed it multiple times."

"I'll be honest with you, Lieutenant," Cambridge said. "I've never felt disadvantaged as a counselor because I do not possess heightened, or really *normal*, empathy. But hearing you speak of this is enough to make me wish I had been born with your gifts."

"What did you sense tonight?" Janeway asked.

"The fear I get from the people of the First World is existential. I don't know if the scars of losing their homeworlds to the Borg never fully healed, or if the lives they lead are so fraught with uncertainty that there is no room for anything else. But they sincerely look to the 'Source' to ease that fear, to fill some great void inside them.

"The problem is there's nothing there. Whatever they are attempting to connect with when they gather in worship, it either isn't answering or doesn't exist. And the worst part is *I think they know it.* They're going through the motions, but the despair overwhelms them. They're doing something they feel they must. It is expected of them. But it brings them no peace, no solace, and no hope."

Janeway nodded somberly. Glancing at Cambridge, she found him gazing at some distant point, his face hard.

"Get some rest, Lieutenant," Janeway ordered. "Tomorrow we are scheduled to meet with the Market Consortium. I want you to attend, but only if you feel up to it."

"Understood, Admiral. Thank you," Lasren said as he rose and departed.

Once he'd left, Cambridge took his seat and crossed his long legs.

"Am I pushing him too hard?" Janeway asked.

"No," the counselor replied. "He's a remarkable young man. I don't know where his strength comes from, but there is a core in him of something solid. He takes risks I wouldn't. But I don't think he's trying to prove anything. I think he's really that curious. He *cares.* I wonder how long it will take for experiences like this one to force him to temper those instincts."

"You know what really scares me?" Janeway asked.

"Do tell, Admiral."

"I would never have guessed," she said. "I wasn't spiritually moved by the services in any way, but I thought the hall was magnificent, and the words, the readings, the songs, really lovely. And there were so many people there."

"See, that's the first tell," Cambridge said.

"Tell?"

"It's not a coincidence that most civilizations that unlock enough of science's mysteries to travel among the stars shift their devotion from whatever ancient gods that sustained them to a collective desire for secular progress. Sometimes that progress is defined as demonstrating their military or cultural superiority, but you don't find a lot of species out there spreading their own version of the 'good news.' The Confederacy is an exception. Everybody talks about the 'Source.' Membership in a church is required of every citizen—not by law, of course, but by custom. Everybody shows up, not to see their god, but to be seen."

"Bridge to Admiral Janeway," Benoit's voice came over the comm.

"Go ahead," Janeway said.

"Commander Glenn and Lieutenant Velth have returned."

"Thank you. Please ask Commander Glenn to report to sickbay immediately."

"Understood. Bridge out."

As Cambridge rose to go, Janeway said, "Any technology we might provide the Confederacy as part of an alliance is going to radically change their lives."

"That depends entirely on who receives that technology," Cambridge replied.

Janeway nodded. "Thank you, Counselor."

The admiral had only a few moments to reflect on Cambridge's words before Commander Glenn entered the office. Her uniform was torn at the shoulder and covered with stains that stood out, even on a black background. Her hair had fallen from its braid and her face was covered with grime. Her eyes glowed with a feverish intensity.

Janeway rose automatically at the sight of her. "Are you all right, Commander?"

"Yes, Admiral," Glenn replied.

"Where have you been?"

The admiral remained on her feet as Glenn made a complete report, including her initial impressions of the medical facility she had been sent to tour, the incident at the market, and her discovery of the clinic devoted to the care of the *nonszit*. Even after her failed attempt to save Jent's life, she had shadowed Doctor Kwer as she tended to another dozen patients before her shift had ended.

When Glenn had finished, Janeway ordered her to sit.

"Did you ask Doctor Kwer who pays for that clinic?"

"I did," Glenn said. "Private donors fund them. Their resources ebb and flow with the generosity of their patrons."

Taking the soft chair next to her, the admiral asked, "What impact do you think an alliance with the Federation would have on a place like Doctor Kwer's clinic?"

"I don't know," Glenn replied. "The Confederacy doesn't need our medical technology. They have their own versions of tricorders, biobeds, surgical arches, and well-stocked pharmacies. They can't replicate . . ." she began, then paused.

"Commander?"

"They need replicators," Glenn said.

Janeway sighed.

"The issue has to be scarcity. The advanced resources they possess are not easily replaced. If they could replicate what they need, that clinic wouldn't have to exist. Or even if it did, they'd have access to everything they required."

"What if the issue is not scarcity but will?" Janeway asked.

"*Will*? You honestly believe the Confederacy would allow their people to live and die in such desperate circumstances if they had another choice?"

"They wouldn't be the first," Janeway said, then asked,

"Knowing what you know now, do you believe it would be appropriate to form a strategic alliance with the Confederacy?"

"I believe it would be inhumane not to," Glenn replied. "They need us. They are on the brink of living as we do. We could hand them a few pieces of technology and change their lives for the better tomorrow."

"And you believe that all that is holding them back from living as we do is a lack of resources and technology?"

"What else would?" Glenn asked.

"Thank you, Commander," Janeway said, rising wearily. As Glenn followed suit, she said, "For the time being, I will not accept any further invitations for you to tour other facilities."

Stung, Glenn said, "If you feel I behaved inappropriately at the clinic, I will understand. But I did not assist Doctor Kwer until she requested I do so. At that point . . ."

"It would have been inhumane for you to do otherwise, Commander. I know," the admiral said. "Your instinct to investigate the situation with the wounded boy was sound. Your actions following that were commendable. But I won't put you in that position again."

"I'm happy to lend a hand where I'm needed most," Glenn said.

"You're needed here," Janeway said. "Lieutenant Lasren required attention tonight that you were unavailable to provide. In the absence of the Doctor, I want you nearby to attend to our people. But I do have another project for you."

"Name it, Admiral."

"Research," Janeway said simply. "Lieutenant Benoit can give you the details."

VITRUM

Lieutenant Commander Atlee Fife understood now what Commander O'Donnell had meant when he called Vitrum "another world." The fields of Femra had been beautiful things; row upon row, as far as the eye could see, of billowy silver *yint* bolls anchored in soil that was rich and dark. The fine, tall *hrass* bending with the breeze had been like a pale yellow ocean.

Overseer Bralt walked beside Fife on Vitrum's surface, each step kicking up dirt that rose in small storms at their feet. The sky above was a stubborn gray and the air was cold and dry. Producer Cemt, the land's owner, walked ahead of them, speaking quietly to Ensign Brill, who had not toured Femra. O'Donnell had insisted, however, that Brill see Vitrum. Brill's and Cemt's voices were pitched low, but their conversation had been continuous since the group had stepped outside the modest home where Cemt and his family lived. Theirs was the only productive land for a hundred clicks in any direction.

Fife wanted to know what Cemt was telling Brill, but it was impossible to make out over Bralt's constant cheery chatter. "It's true that Cemt can only cultivate one-twentieth of his land at present. But as you can see, the wide variety of vegetables he has chosen to plant this season are doing well."

Fife couldn't tell if that was so. The few sprouts he saw of orange and green leaves looked weak and wilted. Then again, he had no idea what they were supposed to look like.

"Why doesn't he use more land if he's got it?" Fife asked.

"Vitrum is in a rotation phase," Bralt said. "For several years, they were one of our primary producers of *leath*, a relatively easy crop to grow."

"Is *leath* food?"

"It's a fiber," Bralt replied, "used to create a particularly light-weight textile."

"If *leath* does well here, why isn't Cemt still producing it?"

"Demand has fallen off recently, as the desire for *yint* has replaced it. Cemt wisely anticipated that shift and began repurposing his soil before many others here on Vitrum followed suit. He also released most of his land workers to more profitable worlds, cutting his expenses. He purchased almost a hundred *geers* with the surplus from his last *leath* crops and has become one of the largest producers in the area of fertilizer and sells that to many other local farms. In time, his harvests will increase again and, eventually, he will likely be feeding hundreds of families, in addition to his own, with a wide variety of fruits and vegetables."

"How many families does he feed now with what he has?" Fife asked, certain Bralt was painting the rosiest picture possible of Cemt's circumstances.

"His own," Bralt said. "But I assure you—"

Fife raised a hand to still Bralt's discourse as Brill and Cemt turned and began striding toward them.

"Commander?" Brill asked, pulling Fife out of earshot of the two Leodts.

"Yes, Ensign?"

"We're done here," he said in a low voice.

"It's only been an hour," Fife said.

"There's nothing more to see."

Fife's brow furrowed. It had taken almost the whole day to scratch the surface of the agricultural marvels on Femra.

"The soil here is in dire need of nutrient enrichment, and Cemt is well on his way; but shifting from *leath,* which required comparatively light soil and little irrigation, to his current crops is going to take time. He's barely able to produce what he needs, and that's not going to change overnight."

"Are there quicker ways to restore his soil and increase his productivity?" Fife asked.

"For us? Yes. But Cemt doesn't need us. Bralt has thousands of cases of nutrient compound and seed stock in store on Femra."

"Why doesn't he forward them here?"

"Because Cemt can't afford them."

Fife shook his head.

Brill's hands rose to his hips as he struggled to suppress his obvious frustration. "Cemt is a tenth-generation farmer. He knows how this works. He knew what he was doing to his land by maximizing his production of *leath.* There are hundreds of other choices he could have made that would have maintained the soil better and kept it viable. Instead, he drained it dry, and now that no one needs *leath*, he's out of luck. *He knew better,*"

Brill insisted. "No one works land their entire life without understanding about reaping what you sow."

Cemt ambled toward them, his face somber. "You know, if you gentlemen really want to see what's what, you should head down the road a few hundred clicks to Izly's place."

"That won't be necessary," Bralt said. "You have been most generous to see us at all, Cemt. We are grateful for it."

"We've still got plenty of time," Fife said. "I would be most obliged, Overseer, if you would direct us to—Izly, was it?"

Cemt nodded.

Fife knew he was testing Bralt's courtesy, but he didn't care. Commander O'Donnell had wanted him to see this, and now that he had, he was beginning to understand why. "We should evaluate as much of the land as we can, shouldn't we, Brill?"

The ensign shook his head almost imperceptibly but said, "Absolutely, sir."

VOYAGER

"You wanted to see me, Doctor?" a bone-weary Commander B'Elanna Torres asked as she entered the science lab.

"Yes, Commander," the Doctor replied.

For several seconds, the Doctor merely stared at her, his arms crossed over his chest defensively.

"Was there a reason?" Torres finally asked, stifling a yawn. The Doctor's unusual call had awakened her only two hours after she had fallen asleep.

"Yes," the Doctor said.

When he seemed unwilling to provide any further information, Torres said, "Are you going to tell me the reason, or can I go back to bed? I'm sleeping for two now."

"It's complicated," the Doctor said, stepping away from the experimental station his body had been covering until this moment.

"What the . . ." Torres said as she immediately moved to examine the charred remains of what had once been a state-of-the-art molecular scanner, diagnostic station, and micromagnetic containment generator. Looking back at the Doctor, who appeared to be appropriately mortified, she asked, "What were you trying to do?"

"I really can't tell you," the Doctor said.

Torres raised a hand to the back of her neck to rub the muscles there already forming themselves into knots.

As she did so, the Doctor added, "I need to run this experiment again, preferably without destroying the science lab, or the ship."

"Do you have any reason to believe that's possible?"

The Doctor said nothing.

"Do you want me to help you revise whatever safety protocols you used here?"

"I want you to provide me with a few particles of antimatter," the Doctor said.

The laughter sprang from the center of Torres's belly without warning. It continued to build as the Doctor stared at her, stricken. When she had finally regained control of herself, she said, "I don't think so. I'll send some of Conlon's gamma-shift crew down here to clean this up. Good night, Doctor."

The Doctor crossed toward her so quickly she actually flinched and retreated a few steps. The intensity of his gaze was almost desperate.

"I must have it," he said.

The situation was no longer funny. A kick of adrenaline cleared Torres's mind completely. "Doctor, I understand that whatever you're trying to do here is important. I assume you can't tell me because it has something to do with the classified mission Seven just returned to the Alpha Quadrant to assist with."

"That's right."

"But we don't play with antimatter."

"I don't know what else to try."

Torres stepped forward again and placed her hands on the Doctor's arms. Meeting his eyes, she said, "Then let me help you."

"I can't," the Doctor said miserably.

"You can't tell me specifically what you are trying to accomplish," Torres said, "but *hypothetically*?"

The Doctor's expression shifted to wary consideration. "Hypothetically?"

"Yes."

The Doctor nodded slowly. "Okay."

"I'm guessing that you need to create a controlled explosion. *Hypothetically, of course*," Torres said.

"Of course."

"So, a few particles of antimatter could theoretically destroy, what?"

"An incredibly powerful and resilient subatomic particle. And I don't want to destroy it," the Doctor said.

"What are you trying to do?"

"Damage it."

"How badly?"

"Enough to limit its ability to bond with other particles but not enough to completely disable or annihilate it."

Torres looked away, attempting to visualize what the Doctor was describing. However, she could not imagine a subatomic particle that would be able to survive an antimatter explosion.

"Without understanding the nature of these particles, I don't know how to accurately estimate the appropriate antimatter yield," Torres said.

The Doctor's face fell. "If I tell you the nature of these particles, we won't be speaking in hypotheticals anymore."

"Then no antimatter," Torres said. "If you need to damage these particles, why not use a modulated phase pulse?" she asked.

The Doctor turned and gestured to the carnage that had once been the science station. "My attempts to modulate the pulse led to an overload of the phase emitter."

"Too high?"

"Too low, but sustained over too long a period," the Doctor said. "I'm trying to damage a single particle. More precisely, I'm attempting to re-create a hypothetical situation where these particles would have been exposed to an antimatter explosion—say, from a torpedo—but sustained limited damage due to the presence of variable modulation shielding."

"You can't re-create circumstances like that in this lab," Torres said. "How many of these particles would have been exposed in the scenario you are imagining?"

"Trillions, probably more," the Doctor replied.

Torres sighed. "Do you have a few million? With that, I could construct a controlled simulation."

"I have a few hundred left," the Doctor admitted.

"So you really need to do this with just one?"

The Doctor nodded.

Torres shrugged. "It's not going to work."

"It *has* to," the Doctor argued, his intensity ratcheting up again.

Shaking her head, Torres moved to the edge of the damaged station and perched gingerly on it. Despite the destruction to the central area, the edge still felt sturdy beneath her weight.

"I can't tell you how to do this," Torres said. "I can do it for you, but you have to let me see the particle and you have to let me run the phase modifications. You'll also need me to establish the shield resonance frequencies."

"Could you download the required information into my program?" he asked.

Torres shook her head. "This isn't about data. It's about experience. I promise you, a few hundred tries at this—which is all you have—won't be enough for you to get it right. And we don't have that many science labs on board."

The Doctor moved to sit beside her. "If I do this, I will be in breach of my ethical obligation to Starfleet Medical and the Federation."

"And if you don't?"

"Millions of people will die."

Torres considered the dilemma. "If you manage to save these millions, will your superiors suspect that you shared any classified information with me? Will they ever know you couldn't have done this experiment alone?"

"I don't know," the Doctor said. "If my work here saves millions of lives, they might not care. But that's not the point. *I'll* know I disobeyed a direct order."

"I understand," Torres said. "Living with that would be hard. You're the only one who can decide if it would be harder living with all of those preventable deaths on your conscience. Given the circumstances, the fact that you are tens of thousands of light-years away from the facilities and personnel you require to do this job, I imagine some latitude might be granted, particularly if you told me only what I need to know to help you complete this experiment. I promise you that if I am ever questioned about this, I will say that I refused to assist you without more information."

"I can't ask you to do that."

"You didn't. I offered."

The Doctor stared at her for a long time. Finally he said, "We're talking about programmable matter."

"Catoms," B'Elanna said.

"You know?"

"Not as much as you do, but enough. I've read every word that isn't classified about the Caeliar and the transformation. There's always a chance that Seven is going to need my help, and I can't do that if I'm not prepared."

"I never thought you and Seven were that close."

Torres smiled in spite of herself. "I didn't either. And then one day, I realized we were."

"When?"

"The day the two of you showed up on *Voyager* to tell us what you'd learned at the Federation Institute about the Curse of the Gods," Torres said. "It didn't surprise me at all when you walked into that room. I saw the way you looked at Miral the first time you placed her in my arms. *Of course* you came to help us.

"But Seven didn't have to. She'd moved on with her life by then. She had just begun to build something for herself separate from all of us and *Voyager*. You could have given us all the data. Seven didn't need to be there. But the way she looked at me when she walked into the briefing room, I just knew. She was willing to die for me and for my daughter. I don't know when she came to that conclusion. But that's when I realized what we were. *What we are.*"

"Family," the Doctor said.

"Yes." After a long pause, Torres asked, "You're doing this to help Seven, right?"

"Yes."

"Tell me."

The Doctor did.

All of his attempts to integrate catomic material into even the simplest virus had failed. The catoms immediately recognized the virus as something foreign to healthy blood tissue and rendered it inert. That was when the Doctor had begun to consider the real-world possibilities for how this mutated catomic virus could have come into existence. It was obvious the fully functioning catoms could not be fooled by a virus. But if catomic particles had been damaged, exposed to an antimatter explosion just after the transformation had occurred, they might have been unable to recognize a virus for what it was.

He had diminished his supply of Seven's catoms to almost nothing in multiple attempts to damage them before his last attempt had all but destroyed the science lab.

True to her word, when the Doctor showed her his data, Torres was immediately able to construct a contained and perfectly modulated phase pulse that could damage a single catomic particle. The experiment was repeated on a dozen other particles, varying the degree of damage.

At that point, the Doctor had thanked Torres for her work and ordered her to get some sleep.

Three hours later, back in sickbay and secured behind a level-ten forcefield, the Doctor had introduced a single damaged catom to the first virus he intended to test.

Three seconds later, he had successfully re-created the catomic plague.

He had destroyed it milliseconds after its birth. He had then repeated the experiment twelve more times and each time allowed the catomic virus to live long enough to introduce a single healthy catom to the tissue and analyze the results.

The experiment revealed a fundamental truth about the plague: The only option was to contain it, to limit its spread until it had run through every available host. In time, it could be eradicated. Unless the Caeliar returned and offered the Federation all the data required to reprogram catoms, it could never be cured.

Moreover, if the "best minds in the Federation" who were supposedly trying to cure this plague had not already reached this same conclusion, they were no such thing.

Tempting as it was to simply accept this as evidence of his brilliance and the obvious shortsightedness of Doctor Frist, a much more disturbing possibility quickly presented itself.

Tapping his combadge, the Doctor awoke Captain Chakotay and requested his immediate presence in sickbay.

Despite the lateness of the hour, Chakotay hadn't been disturbed by the Doctor's call. The journey to Lecahn was almost over and had progressed without incident. It might have been the boredom that set Chakotay's nerves on edge. But it was also the tangible sense of isolation. Even in only a few short months, he had become accustomed to thinking of *Voyager* as part of a fleet. The range of personnel and expertise available to him and the fleet commander had provided an unspoken sense of security.

Now all of the four ships remaining to the fleet were scattered, and the distances between them made them too vulnerable, at least in Chakotay's mind.

His general level of anxiety increased the moment he entered sickbay and found the Doctor pacing. He looked ready to climb the walls.

"You asked to see me?" Chakotay greeted him.

"I did. Thank you for coming."

"I wasn't sleeping anyway," Chakotay admitted. "What's the problem?"

"A little less than two hours ago, I successfully re-created the catomic plague," the Doctor said.

"So soon?" Chakotay asked, shocked.

The Doctor nodded. "I have now confirmed that catomic particles, when damaged, cease to recognize viral agents as hostile and merge with them, infusing these viruses with the ability to use their catomic properties to target any organ or tissue they find and destroy it with heretofore unseen efficiency."

"We need to get this information to Starfleet Medical right away," Chakotay said.

"I don't know if that's a good idea," the Doctor objected.

"Why not?"

"It only took me a few weeks to do this. There is no way that a year later, whoever is working on the plague at Starfleet Medical has not already reached the same conclusion I have."

"You believe they have also replicated it?" Chakotay asked.

"I'm sure of it."

"I'm sorry, Doctor, I don't see . . ."

"There's no way to cure this plague," the Doctor cut him off, his voice rising. "Once the virus has been compromised by the catoms, there is no means to reverse it. The only option is to limit its ability to infect others. It will cease to exist only when it no longer has access to a host and all existing carriers have been vaporized."

"The fact that they are still working on it suggests otherwise, doesn't it?" the captain asked. "What about Seven's and Axum's catoms? You said damaged catoms were susceptible to viral infection. Fully functioning ones might be able to reverse that."

The Doctor shook his head. "I already tried. When Seven's catoms were introduced to the virus, they only enhanced the speed with which the virus destroyed living cells. For reasons I do not yet understand, the damaged catoms overran the healthy ones."

"Why did they need Seven?" Chakotay asked. "Are they

attempting to modify healthy catoms to repair the damaged ones?"

"We are, at best, years away from reprogramming a single catom," the Doctor said.

"Maybe they intend to use them as a template to create new ones that can be designed . . ."

"Add a few years to that estimate for creating new catoms from scratch," the Doctor assured him.

Chakotay felt a chill creep up his spine. "What are you suggesting, Doctor?"

"They told us they needed Axum and Seven to help cure the plague. But there is no cure. And they must know that. They've already lied to us."

"Why would they do that?"

The Doctor paused, then said softly, "The Caeliar were responsible for ending the existence of the most hostile species the Federation has ever encountered. What does that make them?"

"Our friends, to whom we shall be eternally grateful?" Chakotay suggested.

"Or?" the Doctor asked.

"Or a new threat, even more powerful than the Borg," Chakotay said, horrified.

The Doctor nodded slowly. "The losses Starfleet suffered at the hands of the Borg during the invasion were massive. Thousands of ships, officers, entire planets were lost. Still, within a matter of months, Starfleet had equipped a fleet of nine ships with slipstream technology to explore former Borg space and confirm that the Caeliar have left the galaxy. For someone up there, this is a priority above and beyond reconstruction. Someone has decided that the next time we meet the Caeliar, we must have the ability to meet them with deadly force, should circumstances demand it."

"Are you suggesting that someone intentionally created this plague as some sort of weapon and it got out of hand?" Chakotay asked.

"I don't know how it was first created. There are many possible scenarios that could account for it occurring randomly. But there is only one that could explain the actions of Starfleet Medical since then."

"Even if you're right, Seven would never help them weaponize catoms."

"No," the Doctor said. "And I'm guessing *they* know that too, or they learned it in short order. Seven believed they were torturing Axum. She knew they might do the same to her, and she was willing to risk it if she thought a cure would come of it. I let her go, believing their intentions were pure, even if their actions might be misguided or their ignorance the cause of suffering. If Seven learns the truth, they'll never let her live to tell it."

"Seven is one of the most resourceful individuals I have ever known," Chakotay insisted. "If you are right, and this is some vast conspiracy, she will figure it out and act appropriately."

"We have to get word to her," the Doctor insisted. "Maybe we can use Pathfinder, but we must send a message only she can receive. We have to tell her what I know, and it can't wait until we are back in range of our communication buoys."

"That might not be possible, Doctor."

"Make it possible, Chakotay," the Doctor pleaded. "I don't know anyone else who can."

"As soon as we return to the First World, I'll contact Lieutenant Barclay and ask for his assistance."

"What am I supposed to do until then?" the Doctor asked.

Chakotay shrugged, knowing *he* would not be taking the advice he was about to give. "Try not to worry."

Chapter Sixteen

CORIDAN

Doctor Mik had been placed in charge of the capital city's quarantine facility one week after it had been constructed and one hour after the facility's first director, Doctor Chrims, had died from exposure to the catomic plague. He had not expected the facility to still be open a year later. Every day that it was meant that Coridan was one day closer to a catastrophe from which it would never recover.

"We transmit our reports to Starfleet Medical and the Federation Institute of Health daily, Doctor Sharak," Mik said impatiently. "They have all of our numbers. I don't understand why they've sent you to confirm data they've already received."

"I am not here to confirm," Sharak said. "I am here to re-evaluate."

"Reevaluate what? These are basic statistics," Mik said.

"The infection rates from the first three weeks of exposure were incredibly high," Sharak said.

"I know. We lost almost eight thousand in the first month," Mik said.

"Since then, the rates have dropped precipitously."

"Because the quarantine worked," Mik said. "Whatever causes this infection killed its victims too quickly to spread further."

"I agree," Sharak said. "What I don't understand is why it has continued to spread for the last six months."

"Six months?" Mik asked.

"Yes," Sharak said. "Every statistical analysis run of the cases you have reported indicates that six months after the quarantine was established, the infection should have been completely contained."

"But obviously it hasn't been," Mik said. "Analysis is one thing. This is real life. It's still out there. We get new patients almost every day. We have no idea how they are coming in contact with it, but their symptoms are consistent."

"It is crucial that we determine how the infection is continuing to spread. Were it still airborne, your rates should be more than a thousand times what they are at this point. If it has mutated to another state, which evolutionary biology tells us is highly unlikely, the rates should still be a hundred times higher, and we should have been able to discover several likely contaminated sources based upon the individual histories of the new victims," Sharak said.

"Nothing we have discovered thus far points to a single contaminated area," Mik said. "We usually can't question the patients by the time they get here. But we do complete histories with their next of kin and pay particular attention to their last known activities and locations before they were diagnosed."

"And there is no obvious pattern?" Sharak asked.

Mik shook his head. "Not yet."

Sharak nodded. "Are the histories you have compiled stored here?"

Mik shrugged. "Some. Most are still at the hospitals where the patients were admitted before they were placed in quarantine."

"Can you request copies from the hospitals?"

"I could," Mik replied.

"I would be most grateful if you would do so."

"I don't know what you think you're going to find, Doctor. But it's your time to waste," Mik said.

"Indeed," Sharak said.

GOLDENBIRD

It was well after midnight, local time, when Doctor Sharak returned to the ship. Lieutenant Samantha Wildman had spent most of the day getting caught up on her own reports and composing a lengthy letter to Naomi. She'd also received an urgent call from Gres, which had lasted over two hours. After replicating a Ktarian stew and salad for dinner, she'd settled into her bunk and had just dozed off when Sharak signaled he was ready for transport.

One look at his face told her he had not had a good day.

"Can I get you anything?" she asked as soon as he'd dropped his bag on the deck and sat down to remove his boots. "You must be hungry."

"No, thank you, Lieutenant," Sharak said. "I had a light meal several hours ago."

"Will we be returning to Earth now?"

Sharak shook his head. "I have only begun to evaluate the data I requested. This task will take several more days."

Wildman shook her head. "I was only given four days' leave for this trip. We don't have several days. Can you continue to study it back on Earth?"

Sharak shook his head. "When I return, this data will be ignored and I will be assigned other duties that will not bring me any closer to my goal."

"What goal is that?"

Sharak shook his head again.

"I'm sorry," Wildman said. "I know, you can't tell me what you're doing here. I just wish I could help."

Sharak thought for a moment. "Perhaps you could," he said.

"*Temba. His arms wide*," Wildman said, smiling.

A few hours later, Wildman was beginning to regret her offer. Sharak had told her that he was studying patient histories for a number of individuals who had been hospitalized on Coridan over the last year. As those records contained classified data, she could not review them for him. There was another data set, however, that the hospital had provided: visual records of hundreds of individual patients who had been treated at the hospital. These were actually footage from scanners installed in the hospital, and many covered several days in the lives of these patients as they had undergone treatment.

The audio from the scans had been muted. Even had it not been, there wasn't much to hear from patients who spent most of their time sleeping or watching whatever entertainment the hospital provided on their room monitors. After a while Wildman wished the audio was present, if only to catch the sound of news feeds playing in the background to break up the monotony.

The routine that played out before her eyes was mind-numbingly consistent. Patients slept, or ate, or watched monitors as a variety of doctors, nurses, and visitors entered and exited at regular intervals. Actually, after the first day, there were usually no visitors. Usually by the end of the second or third day, patients experienced some traumatic event, a radical decline in their condition that resulted in their transfer from the ward where they had been admitted to elsewhere.

She had accepted Sharak's need to be vague about what he was looking for. He had simply asked that she review the records and flag any that contained unusual events. Even speeding through the scans when patients slept did little to ease the tedium of the task.

To amuse herself, Wildman had begun to make up names for the many doctors, nurses, and medical technicians who attended the patients. Most were familiar after the first thirty records had been viewed.

"Good morning, Doctor Horse," Wildman said softly as an alien doctor with a long face and ears placed high on his head entered a patient's room. "Where's Pinky today?" "Pinky" was a short female with black hair and skin of a unique shade of pink who usually wore something like a nurse's uniform and often entered as Horse was completing his consult to adjust equipment and occasionally administer injections. She had caught Wildman's eye the first time she'd appeared, as the xenobiologist had been unable to identify Pinky's species. Many humans classified as Caucasian were called "pink skins," a mildly derogatory term, by other alien races. But Pinky was almost Thulian pink, a distinct shade of vivid rose that was unique to whatever her species was.

As if on cue, Pinky entered and checked the patient's vital signs on the monitor above the bed. She then removed a hypospray and injected it, checked vitals again, and left.

"Don't worry, breakfast is on the way," Wildman said to the patient, as she rubbed her eyes with one hand and increased the speed with the other. She was forced to pause and reverse the image when Pinky surprised her by entering again, this time with another nurse. "Ethel," Wildman called this one, given her unfortunate resemblance to one of the lieutenant's great-aunts. Ethel was clearly upset with Pinky. There was broad gesticulation as she spoke, several sharp points at the vitals monitor followed by Ethel actually taking Pinky by the upper arm and Pinky forcefully shaking her off. Ethel then ushered Pinky out of the room before her. A few moments later, a team of doctors, led by Horse, entered and circled the patient's biobed.

Wildman had to replay the scene several times to make sure she was seeing what she thought she was seeing.

After the third time, she froze the display and increased the magnification of Pinky's face. Her features were almost human, apart from the color of her skin. Her eyes were large and the irises were so pale as to be almost indistinguishable around the purple pupils. Her nose was a little flat and her lips wide but thin. Her chin protruded ever so slightly. At this magnification, Wildman also noted that her black hair was longer than she'd thought, pulled into a roll at the base of her neck and hidden by the collar of her uniform.

What transfixed Wildman was the color of Pinky's skin. It was no longer pink. As Ethel chastised Pinky for whatever she had done, her skin grew visibly darker, moving through lavender to a deeper purple before Ethel had finished with her. In addition, a dark black line—a centimeter wide that could have been mistaken for the shadow of a cheekbone but upon closer examination was actually appearing and growing darker the longer Ethel spoke—was visible on Pinky's right cheek.

Before waking Sharak, who was snoring softly in the back of the runabout, Wildman ran several cross-checks to confirm her hypothesis. It was no trouble to interface with the hospital's staff records, and to Wildman's surprise, Pinky was not among them. She then initiated a scan of volunteer personnel, common during times of crisis. Coridan had been one of several worlds that saw heavy fighting during the Borg Invasion, and many civilians had volunteered to assist with the large number of injuries.

She found Pinky among them. Her volunteer credentials had been issued within days of the invasion and were still valid. Her species was listed as Kyppr.

"Oh, I don't think so," Wildman said to herself as she moved to Sharak's bunk.

"Doctor," she said softly.

He jerked from sleep so abruptly, Wildman bumped her head on the low overhead as she moved to avoid a collision.

"Ow," she said, as he righted himself on the bunk.

"Is something wrong, Lieutenant?"

"Yes." Wildman nodded, still holding the back of her head.

Sharak rose. "You have injured yourself."

"I just need an ice pack," Wildman said. "You need to see something."

SAN FRANCISCO

Tom Paris had felt reasonably good after leaving Starfleet Medical. He was concerned about Seven, but he no longer felt he was being intentionally left in the dark. If her condition did not improve, Paris would send word to Admiral Janeway, and, if necessary, she'd send the Doctor back via Pathfinder to make sure Seven recovered.

That feeling evaporated as he entered the mediation chamber the next day. His mother sat stone faced, as usual, Clancy by her side. Shaw rose to greet him and shook his hand firmly.

Once they were settled, Ozimat entered.

"We seem to be no closer to resolving the differences between the parties. I am also ever mindful of Commander Paris's responsibilities to the *Starship Voyager*, and his need to return to his duties there as soon as possible. I have therefore asked both counselors to present testimony from character references for both Mrs. Paris and the commander. Mister Clancy?"

"Thank you, Your Honor," Clancy said.

The first witness to speak on his mother's behalf was Paris's older sister, Kathleen. He hadn't seen her in a few years, but, like their mother, she was trim, fit, and very forceful in her insistence that Julia was both more than capable of raising Paris's children and should be granted the right to do so.

The appearance of Paris's younger sister, Moira, was more of a surprise. She was almost eight years his junior, and they'd never been particularly close. He'd missed too many of her formative years. He remembered only a boisterous child. The moment Moira caught sight of anyone, she called, "Come play with me!" Now grown, she refused to meet his eyes as she echoed the sentiments of her older sister. At least Moira did him the courtesy of mouthing an apology to Paris before she left the room.

Paris assumed that their choice had more to do with their feelings for their mother than him. Both still lived on Earth. Julia was a constant in their lives. Tom was the brother they hardly knew, and he couldn't exactly blame them for siding with Julia. But if there were any future family gatherings, they were going to be incredibly awkward.

A parade of Starfleet officers followed, most of whom had been close to both his mother and father. Their praise of Julia was well deserved, if a bit heavy-handed. Paris didn't know if any of them knew the specifics of the case. None mentioned him. They painted a portrait of Julia as the most selfless, devoted, and loving woman on the planet.

After three hours, it was time for Paris to present his witnesses. Shaw began by saying, "It should come as no surprise to Your Honor that most of those who know Commander Paris the best, and have seen firsthand the love he bears for his wife and daughter, are too far from Earth at the present time to speak on his behalf."

"If the commander can provide no references, Lieutenant Shaw—" Ozimat began.

"No, Your Honor," Shaw interjected. "But, for instance, in the case of our first witness, he has come to speak in place of his wife, who is unavailable at the current time."

"Proceed," Ozimat said.

Paris turned to see a tall Ktarian enter the room, dressed in civilian attire. He barely remembered the man, but his cranial horns and smile were familiar; he shared them with his daughter, Naomi Wildman.

After introducing Greskrendtregk and thanking him for coming, Shaw said, "Can you please tell us how you know Commander Paris?"

"I don't," Gres replied. "But my wife, Lieutenant Samantha Wildman, and my daughter, Naomi, do. Sam was supposed to be here, but there was an urgent mission. We spoke for several hours last night and she told me what she would have said if she'd been able to come."

"Go ahead," Shaw encouraged him. Gres was clearly ill at ease and he spoke in a low, hesitant voice. "Sam spent seven years in the Delta Quadrant with Tom. They worked together frequently. She said at first, he was hard to get to know. He was funny, and a great pilot, but he kept everybody at a distance. She'd heard rumors about his past. But Sam isn't the type to let others make her mind up for her. She said where Tom started was not nearly as important as where he ended up. The crew was close. But Tom was the first guy you wanted by your side when things got tough. He didn't give in to the temptation to despair. He kept everybody else's spirits up, even when things were bad. And Sam said he and B'Elanna were made for each other. Nobody was more excited than Sam when B'Elanna found out she was pregnant. And Sam knew that child would be so lucky to have them as parents."

"Why is that?" Shaw prodded gently.

Gres considered this for a moment. "Sometimes love is a soft, safe place. Sometimes it's fierce. Sam said that nothing Tom and B'Elanna had done after Miral was born, including lying about their deaths, was a surprise to her. Their love was the fiercest thing she'd ever seen, and they care for Miral with the same passion. We should all be loved that way by our parents."

"Thank you," Shaw said.

Gres nodded to Paris as he rose from the table.

"Anyone else?" Ozimat asked.

"Oh, yes, Your Honor," Shaw said.

Paris couldn't believe his eyes when the next person to enter the room was Lieutenant Vorik.

Once he was introduced, Vorik said, "I had serious misgivings about appearing here today. But upon deep reflection, it occurred to me that whatever dispute has arisen here between Commander Paris and his mother, it is secondary to the needs of Commanders Paris's and Torres's daughter. It was difficult to learn that they had deceived their comrades and closest friends about B'Elanna's and Miral's deaths. It was an unnecessary burden to add to those so many of us have carried. But to think that way was to place my needs before theirs or their daughter's, and *my needs,* in this instance, are irrelevant. They are Miral's parents. The responsibility for raising her and keeping her safe is theirs. That they would go to such extraordinary lengths to do so says nothing about their regard for me. It speaks only to the seriousness with which they have assumed their responsibilities for Miral. I have come to see that their willingness to sacrifice the friendship and companionship of those who have been essential to their lives for so many years in order to keep Miral safe is the truest indicator of their fitness as her parents.

"I have known both of them to behave illogically. This choice was logical from their point of view, and one I doubt many humans would have the strength or courage to risk."

"Thanks, Vorik," Paris said softly.

"I have done nothing to earn your gratitude, Commander," Vorik said.

"You have it anyway," Paris said.

Vorik nodded sharply and departed without another word.

"Is there anyone else, Lieutenant Shaw?"

"There is."

"Who?" Paris whispered.

Before Shaw could answer Ozimat said, "It's been a long morning. We'll take a short break and resume the testimony in one hour."

Everyone rose as Ozimat departed.

"Who else has come?" Paris asked Shaw softly.

Shaw smiled faintly and passed a padd to him. The list of names appeared to go on forever. Tom scanned it quickly. People he hadn't seen in years or spoken to in longer than that were listed, among them Libby Fletcher, Dil Moore, Jenny Delaney, and dozens of other officers from *Voyager* who had served on her maiden journey but been reassigned once she returned home.

"I had no idea I had this many friends," Paris said.

"Neither did I," Shaw said. "But every person I asked gave me the names of two or three more who would be happy to speak for you, and *all* of them are here today."

"Do they know why?" Paris asked.

"Yes. They all said the same thing: 'If Tom Paris needs me for any reason, I'm there.'" Off Paris's shocked expression, Shaw said, "Make yourself comfortable. It's going to be a long afternoon."

Chapter Seventeen

The conference room of the Market Consortium was one of the most lavishly appointed spaces on the First World. The table was massive obsidian stone, inset with wide grooves through which liquid flowed in slowly shifting colors beneath a transparent surface. Thirteen chairs sat around it, constructed of metal and cushioned with a fabric that merged rather delightfully with one's body once seated. Though an odd sensation, Admiral Janeway had to admit that the confluence of comfort and support was extraordinary. It was the first technological accomplishment of the Confederacy the admiral seriously considered requesting should the alliance proceed.

Dreeg sat at the table's only head. From this one flat end, the rest of the table was shaped like a pendant. Janeway, Decan, and Cambridge sat to Dreeg's left. Among those assembled, she remembered Elvoy, Raniet, and Mistoff from the tour of the *Vesta*. Six other Djinari and Leodt she had met briefly at the Ceremony of Welcoming. She assumed Decan had made note of their names. Psilakis and Lasren stood along the wall on one side of the door. Two CIF officers mirrored them on the opposite side. Seated at two chairs behind the far end of the table were Yent, Dreeg's secretary, and Mister Grish. Running along a wall of windows that offered a stunning view of the capital city's skyline was a table set with a variety of finger-foods and beverages. Janeway hadn't brought an appetite, but she graciously accepted some *indacine*, a tealike beverage Dreeg suggested she might enjoy.

At 0800 hours precisely, Dreeg called the meeting to order. He wasted no time in addressing himself to the admiral.

"We have enjoyed the company of our distinguished guests from the United Federation of Planets for several days now. Counselor Cambridge, Commander O'Donnell, and several of their fellow officers began our diplomatic relations almost a full cycle ago, and with each passing day, we have grown more certain that an alliance between our peoples would offer great advantages to both parties."

"Thank you, First Consul," Janeway said. It was fair to say that she did not share Dreeg's optimism at this point, but she was obligated to hear him out.

"I have been authorized by Presider Cin to present you with a proposal. In order for our work to proceed, it is necessary for you to understand what our Confederacy is able to offer you in return for a pledge of mutual assistance and peaceful coexistence. Further, you must be apprised of those things we . . ."

"Excuse me, First Consul," Janeway interrupted. "Although I am aware that this august assembly is responsible for regulating and controlling the markets upon which the Confederacy's economy is based, it is common practice for our diplomats to enter into negotiations such as these with representatives of the government, usually including but not limited to representatives of an executive branch, monarch, or head of state, along with selected members of legislative committees responsible for regulating interstellar relations."

"I can assure you, Admiral, that I speak today on behalf of those who will have the final word in determining the status of our relationship with the Federation going forward and am duly vested by them with the authority to negotiate our terms."

"I see," Janeway said.

"Although the details will be left to others, in principle, the Confederacy is willing to offer your fleet ships use of a limited number of streams accessing vital resources within the Confederacy, as well as our spaceports orbiting the First World. As allies, you will enjoy unrestricted access to the goods and services available here, provided your accounts with us remain in good standing. Ships of the Confederacy Interstellar Fleet will be made available to you to assist with any exploratory mission you would care to undertake within our territory, with prior approval. Should you come under attack while within our space, the CIF will defend your vessels as they would their own. We understand that the ancient protectors have provided you with the harmonic resonance frequency required to access the Gateway. You will be free to use the Gateway to enter and depart, but you will also be granted access to several other streams less centrally located that still access our territory for the purposes of coming and going from our space as you desire. When you travel to worlds beyond our space, you will bear in mind that your actions will reflect not only on your Federation, but on your greatest ally as well, the Confederacy of the Worlds of the First Quadrant."

"That is most generous of you, First Consul," Janeway said.

"As you have no doubt surmised, Admiral, there are a number of items your fleet ships possess that we wish to acquire from you. I admit that when you first made contact with us, I did not nurse high expectations in terms of your technology. The fact that your ships were nearly destroyed at the Gateway suggested you could not be as advanced as the Confederacy. However, I have learned otherwise," Dreeg said, smiling as those around the table chuckled lightly.

"Each item will be appraised and assigned a designated value. Those values will be credited to your account with us, and a very generous exchange rate will be settled upon to ensure that you can always afford to purchase any Confederacy resources you require."

"And what items would those be?" Janeway asked.

At this, Dreeg gestured to Yent, who brought a small tablet and placed it before him. Dreeg reviewed it in silence for a few moments before he said, "Your holographic technology is unlike anything we have developed. We would place a high value on the firmware and software required to install such systems here for recreational purposes. Naturally, we would not expect you to part with your own. The schematics will suffice."

Janeway nodded for him to continue.

"Your propulsion systems are also very advanced. Intelligence from the CIF indicates that your vessels are capable of speeds that surpass the streams. In particular, your quantum slipstream technology would be of great interest to us."

Janeway kept her face neutral as she said, "Forgive me, First Consul, but I was not aware, nor did I authorize any of my officers to provide you with knowledge of the existence of that particular technology."

"It is possible that our scans of your vessels have been more thorough than you understood," Dreeg said.

"Clearly," Janeway said.

"In addition, there are several classes of ordnance we are interested in acquiring, as well as your multiphasic shielding, triaxilating forcefields, and regenerative circuitry. Raniet, here, is also intrigued by your bioneural systems—*gelpacks*, I believe they are called?"

"Those are essential to the functioning of our vessels. They cannot be replicated and we do not carry enough in reserve to consider trading them," Janeway said.

"Admiral, you have the ability to travel to and from the Federation where these devices are manufactured. Should you be reluctant to offer us the specifications for production, you could certainly return to the Federation and obtain enough to satisfy our needs."

"I—" Janeway began.

Dreeg immediately cut her off. "Finally, we would be most interested in learning more about the matter dematerialization and rematerialization systems you use for transportation."

Admiral Janeway did not waste precious time asking how Dreeg had acquired the intelligence he had just listed. He would never tell her, though Janeway suspected that the hapless Mister Grish had played a part. The more important fact was that in addition to violating the terms of their initial diplomatic agreement, which clearly limited the types of scans each party would use, he had completely misunderstood the interests of the Federation.

"I am curious, First Consul," Counselor Cambridge said before Janeway could respond. "Your interest in the items you have listed is understandable, but there are two notable absences, technologies you might have assumed the admiral was interested in sharing, as she has already demonstrated them for you: our universal translators and our replicators."

"Neither of those perform functions deemed necessary by the Consortium," Dreeg said.

Cambridge smiled. "Come now, First Consul. Your presider has already expressed an interest in our universal translator directly to the admiral. The only reason you could possibly be unwilling to trade for them is because you have already managed to acquire the technology by other means."

Janeway turned to Cambridge. "That's quite an accusation, Counselor," she said with feigned dismay. "Have you any proof?"

Cambridge nodded. "After Lieutenant Kim reported that Miss Ligah had damaged his combadge when she tried to steal it, I got curious. When Kim found that it no longer functioned, he recycled it and was issued a new one. I checked the recycling logs and determined that while Ligah did return the casing to Lieutenant Kim, she successfully removed the internal circuitry before she dropped it. Those components were not present to be recycled, according to our logs."

"I do hope she was well compensated for her efforts," Janeway said drily. "But you're not the only one who has been doing a little research, Counselor."

"Really?" he asked, intrigued.

"Did you spend much time yesterday in that beautiful library attached to the capital museum?"

"I did not," Cambridge replied.

"The presider was kind enough to offer our people access to all of the public records contained at that library. I asked Commander Glenn and her staff to begin working last night researching their material ownership decrees. Would it surprise you to learn, Counselor, that more than forty years ago, an industrious Leodt named Ugret was granted a decree for a new form of molecular conversion technology that is the most basic component of our replicators?"

"Not at all," Cambridge said, smiling. "Our friends among the Confederacy have demonstrated their industriousness time and again."

"Of course, that ownership decree was transferred to the Market Consortium immediately upon filing. Since then, no one has troubled themselves to pursue that technology's possible uses," Janeway noted.

"It would destabilize the markets considerably should Confederacy citizens be able to replicate their basic needs rather than purchase them," Cambridge said.

Turning to Dreeg, Janeway said, "While espionage on the level the Confederacy has displayed is not surprising, it is most disappointing. I'm much more concerned, however, by the fact that this Consortium would willfully ignore technological developments of their own people that might limit the stranglehold the Consortium currently enjoys on the Confederacy's markets."

"Admiral, I assure you that the values we will place on the items we have requested will be more than generous. You have but to name your price for us to move forward," Dreeg said.

"They have no price," Janeway said simply. "Honestly, I blame myself. In all our hours of discussion, I have clearly failed to help you understand what the Federation is and what we are seeking from those we ally ourselves with. The first and most important criterion is demonstrable trust."

"Admiral, please spare us your indignation," Dreeg said sharply. "Those in power are held to a different standard than common men. In time it is possible you would have agreed to share this technology with us. We could have forced you to do so against your will. Instead, we simply pursued the most efficient course before us. The Consortium was tasked with determining whether or not you possessed skills or technology of value to the

Confederacy. You do. Therefore, we will proceed with all due haste to secure that technology on terms you find acceptable."

"Or?" the admiral asked.

"Or our negotiations will end," Dreeg replied. "Your fleet ships will be recalled to the First World and escorted from Confederacy space and you will not return to it under pain of death."

Janeway nodded thoughtfully. "The Federation values the meaningful and peaceful exchange of knowledge, and sometimes technology, among sentient species. But before any such exchange can take place, we consider first how those technologies will affect the daily lives of the people who are to receive them. Were you interested in obtaining the items you have listed to better secure your people, or to gradually enhance their living standards, I would be open to further discussions. My fear is that this is not your intent. Your Consortium would acquire this technology in order to monopolize it. Your only intention is to further enrich yourselves, at the expense of your citizens and noncitizens."

"What higher intention is there?" Dreeg asked. "We would protect our people from that which they are not yet ready to integrate into their lives. When a need was perceived, we would begin production and facilitate the slow introduction of that technology into our society in the least disruptive manner. Change is good, but it must be pursued at a pace that will not destabilize the peace we currently enjoy."

"I will need time to consider your proposal, First Consul," Janeway said.

"Of course."

"I will contact your office when I am ready to proceed."

"Thank you, Admiral," Dreeg said.

Janeway and her team maintained a tense silence until they had boarded their shuttle to return to the *Galen* and the hatches were sealed. As they were lifting off, Cambridge said, "You're not seriously considering anything that man suggested, are you, Admiral?"

Janeway shook her head. "Don't be ridiculous. But the *Vesta*,

Demeter, and *Voyager* are still out there. I need to secure their safety before I officially shatter Dreeg's hopes."

"He doesn't expect you to agree, Admiral," Lieutenant Lasren said from behind her.

Turning, Janeway said, "I didn't think so, either."

"What does he expect?" Psilakis asked.

"I don't know," Lasren admitted. "He was withholding something, concerned you might detect it. He wasn't afraid, exactly. The people in that room aren't like the others here. They are the only individuals I have encountered so far who are actually happy."

LECAHN

Although rank had its privileges, the obligation Chakotay and many other Starfleet captains found most regrettable was the regulation stating that the captain of a vessel did not leave that vessel except under extraordinary circumstances. The heady days of leading away teams to make firsthand discoveries were behind those who accepted the center seat on a starship. The lack of a regular change of scenery, particularly on extended missions, was one every captain must learn to accept.

Of course, every captain also had the latitude to ignore that regulation when he saw fit. As soon as *Voyager* reached orbit over Lecahn, Chakotay handed the bridge to B'Elanna and ordered Lieutenant Patel to accompany him to the shuttlebay. His first officer had been incommunicado for two days, and Chakotay needed to know what Kim had learned before another day was spent touring the manufacturing center General Mattings had indicated was their first stop on the planet's surface.

Chakotay brought the shuttle to rest on a long circular docking platform placed in the center of parklike grounds that surrounded a collection of tall buildings. He and Patel exited the shuttle together to find Kim, Mattings, and two other officers from the *Lamont* waiting there.

Mattings extended his hand to Chakotay as he approached,

but there was a new sharpness to his eyes that the captain found disquieting.

"Captain, good to see you."

"And you, General."

"You remember JC Eleoate and JP Creak?"

"I do. Good morning," Chakotay greeted them.

"Your Lieutenant Kim is a good man, Captain," Mattings said.

"You'll get no argument from me there," Chakotay said, nodding to Kim.

"When we chose Lecahn for this visit, it was my intention to knock your socks off, Captain," Mattings said, gesturing to the complex of buildings constructed from a reflective surface that was blinding in the harsh morning light. "This facility, in particular, produces the most advanced tactical technology the CIF uses. Some of our best minds toil away daily in those buildings. And their chefs prepare food that you won't find in the best restaurants on the First World."

"It sounds like we have an interesting day ahead of us, General," Chakotay said.

The general handed Chakotay a small tablet containing coordinates for another location on the planet's surface. "We do, but not here. Twenty thousand clicks away, near the planet's southern pole, is another facility. I'd like you and your people to accompany us there."

"Why?" Chakotay asked.

"I have some questions. And I need the most honest answers you can provide."

The general's manner was disconcerting. Chakotay wondered if he might be courteously escorted into a trap. To refuse would hinder any alliance. Of that, Chakotay had no doubt. To accept might be more dangerous.

"I have a feeling I know where the general is taking us, Captain," Kim offered. "I think we should go."

"Mind if Harry accompanies me in our shuttle, just so I don't lose my way?" Chakotay asked.

"We'll regroup at the site, Captain," Mattings said, nodding.

"My men and I will transport there now using protectors and make sure the site's overseer is ready to meet with you. I hope you brought a jacket."

"We'll manage," Chakotay said.

As soon as he, Patel, and Kim were safely back on the shuttle and their course had been entered and confirmed, Chakotay said, "Where are we going, Harry?"

"One of the technologies Lecahn produces is the protectors, sir," Kim replied. "I had a discussion with Mattings last night about the ancient ones. He seemed surprised to learn that they communicated with us."

"I'm surprised you told him," Chakotay said.

"Your instincts about the general are right, Chakotay. He's doing his duty, protecting the Confederacy. He wants to learn from us."

"It sounds like he already has," Chakotay said.

"I did not provide any specific data on the means we developed to communicate with the protectors. But I did confirm my initial suspicion about the ones that brought us here."

"What was that?" Chakotay asked.

"They weren't too damaged to survive when they arrived here. Once we had been accepted, they destroyed themselves rather than risk capture by the Confederacy."

Chakotay sighed, shaking his head. "Do you believe they feared for themselves?"

"I think they didn't want to be forced to provide the data they had acquired about us to the Confederacy," Kim replied.

"That's awful," Patel noted sadly.

"I've got our landing area in sight," Chakotay advised them.

A few minutes later they had set down on an icy plain. After donning heavy-weather gear, they began to make their way carefully toward a small building standing in the middle of what appeared to be a vast, white wasteland. The single-story, square edifice was constructed of thick metal and surrounded by field emitters that likely provided additional shielding. As they approached the doors, Kim said, "Those look familiar."

"Where have you seen them before?" Patel asked.

"In the cavern below the surface of the Ark Planet where the proctor and the sentries were born," Kim replied.

A small sensor array was visible above the door. A soft blue light bathed the away team once they were within range. After a quick scan, the doors parted.

Chakotay found the general and his men already inside. Several Leodts clad in gray coats were busy monitoring the numerous science stations that lined all four walls of the room's interior. In the center, a transparent room had been raised a few meters above the floor on a round platform. Visible through the windows, a single Djinari male worked at a circular control station, not unlike the one in the center of a CIF vessel's bridge.

The general motioned for Chakotay and his team to follow him up the steps leading to the central office. Eleoate and Creak brought up the rear.

"Mister Hsu?" the general said as everyone filed in behind him. The Djinari looked up and nodded at his new guests. "These are the Federation representatives I told you about."

"Welcome," Hsu said briskly. "As I mentioned, General, we are on a tight production schedule. I can't spare much time."

"I think when you hear what Lieutenant Kim has to say, you'll find a few extra minutes." Turning to Kim, the general said, "Harry, tell Mister Hsu about the ancient ones."

Kim looked to Chakotay, who nodded for him to proceed.

"Several months ago, our ship discovered a vast area of space protected by a cloaking field generated by your ancient protectors. We had first encountered one of them almost forty thousand light-years away several years ago. It had transmitted a great deal of data to us, including the coordinates for that area. When we arrived, we transmitted that message back to the protectors and they disabled the cloaking matrix. We discovered what we called the Ark Planet—"

"You've seen the last *lemm*?" Hsu interrupted.

"We saw more than that," Kim said. "We discovered the cavern where the ancient wave forms were created. We subsequently learned how to decipher a number of data transmissions from the wave forms; essentially, we learned how to program and communicate with them."

Hsu looked to Mattings in wonder. Kim saw Eleote standing behind the general and staring at him for the first time with something resembling respect.

"What was the purpose of your communication?" Hsu asked.

"The planet was in pretty bad shape. A number of species brought there, saved by the protectors, were dying. We helped them reorganize many of the ecosystems and revitalize the atmosphere to enable most of the species still present to survive."

Hsu's mouth was now open, his jaw slack.

"When that work was done, we asked them to tell us about the Worlds of the First Quadrant. We had discovered a hull fragment from one of your vessels. They initiated telepathic contact and showed every person on our ship how your people first called them into being, used them, and how they were eventually freed."

"The ancient ones spoke to you?" Eleoate said reverently.

Kim nodded.

After a long pause, the general cleared his throat. "I was raised to honor the Source. I was taught that the Source carved the Great River to lead our people to the First World. The Source gave us the ancient protectors to sustain the streams and enable us to rebuild our civilization on that world. When that work was sufficient, the Source directed the ancient ones to cease their efforts and they were left in peace to protect the last *lemm*."

"How did your people learn to use the protectors to reinforce the streams?" Kim asked.

"By doing nothing," Hsu replied. "A fully formed protector will immediately seek out the nearest stream and take up residence there unless held and forced to do otherwise."

"And who decides how long they are allowed to function before they are replaced?" Chakotay asked.

"In a way, they do," Hsu said. "As soon as they demonstrate even slight resistance to new programming, they are dispersed and replaced. Those used to transport individuals have the shortest life span."

"Here's my question," the general said as his voice dropped to a low tone of warning. "Are the wave forms you create capable of evolving to the same point the ancient protectors achieved? Can they be taught to not just move living things from one place to another, but to cherish living things? Are the protectors we use so callously, in fact, sentient life-forms?"

Hsu shook his head. "They are not life-forms, General."

Mattings looked to Kim. "Is he lying to me?"

"No, sir," Kim replied.

"If I may," Patel interjected.

Mattings nodded. "Yes, Miss?"

"Lieutenant Devi Patel. I'm a xenobiologist. I assisted Lieutenant Kim with our efforts to program the protectors." Mattings nodded, and she continued. "The wave forms are technology. They do not possess many of the most important attributes of life. They have no metabolism and they cannot procreate. But they are also not the first technology we have encountered that is capable of advancing beyond its original design. It might be going too far to suggest that they are sentient."

"But it might not?" the general asked.

"I don't know," Hsu said.

"What would it take for you to answer that question?" the general asked.

"Disobeying my standing directives on the maintenance of the protectors," Hsu said. "I doubt the Consortium would agree to expend resources for even a single experiment."

"Why would the Consortium have the last word on this?" Chakotay asked.

"They own the technology used to create the protectors and regulate every aspect of its use and the distribution of protectors," Hsu replied.

"The protectors we use now are essential," the general said. "But it seems a waste not to explore their full potential. Imagine how much more they could do for us if we allowed them to reach the levels of functionality Lieutenant Kim has observed."

"It might displease the Source, General," Eleoate interjected.

"Our Confederacy has thrived by limiting the uses of the protectors. If the Source intended otherwise, surely it would provide us with a sign."

"I'm the last man anyone would call religious, but even I can see that the Source already has given us a sign," the general said, nodding toward Kim.

"General, a word?" Chakotay asked.

"Mister Hsu, kindly take Lieutenants Kim and Patel to the floor and show them how this facility works. See to their security," the general added to Eleoate and Creak.

When they were alone, Chakotay said, "I don't think Hsu is authorized to do what you're asking. Aren't there channels you could go through to request exploring the potential of the protectors?"

"If I didn't have any intention of living long enough to learn the answer," the general replied. "My people are great believers in the way things have always been."

"Is there anything wrong with the way things have always been?" Chakotay asked.

The general shrugged. "You tell me."

"I'm the wrong person to ask," Chakotay said. "My father, Kolopek, was also a great believer in the virtues of the past. He would have had me live there with him forever. But I was born a *contrary*. I wanted more. I fought him at every turn, demanding he allow me to go and find it."

"But you were born into a universe where there were ways to fulfill that need. The *more* my people acquire are only those things that can be measured and assigned a price."

"The day may come when they too want something different," Chakotay said. "One may grow complacent, but even in peace the spirit stirs."

"I didn't realize you were a man of faith."

"My people have a rich spiritual heritage," Chakotay said. "I spent many years refusing to appreciate it, but, like most truths, it found me eventually and held me."

"The Great River has carried me safely through my life, and

I am told that's because the Source ordered it so. If it did, I am grateful. But I wasn't made to spend my life on my knees thanking the Source repeatedly for its generosity. I was made to keep my people safe. That's getting harder to do." After a pause the general added, "I don't want to see the Confederacy fall into chaos because we refused to use every resource at our disposal to its fullest potential. Our ancient protectors gave their lives for you, in return for all you'd done for them. The day may come, sooner rather than later, when we need them to do the same for us, but we don't know how to earn that loyalty."

"Excuse me, General," JC Eleoate said, reentering the control center.

"What is it?"

"The *Lamont* has detected five ships on course to enter the system."

"Identity?"

"The Unmarked," Eleoate replied.

"Prepare for transport," the general said, nodding. Turning back to Chakotay he said, "You're welcome to stay here. This won't take long. The *Lamont* will take care of them in a matter of minutes. Just order *Voyager* out of orbit and tell them to retreat to the edge of the system until I give the all clear."

"I've seen your ship in battle. I know its power. Will it be enough?" Chakotay asked.

Mattings smiled grimly. "They sent five. We could handle fifty all by ourselves. I wouldn't mind showing your Lieutenant Kim how. He might have a few more helpful suggestions for us."

Chakotay nodded. "Lieutenant Kim may return to the *Lamont*. Patel and I will get back to *Voyager* and keep her out of harm's way."

"I'll see you on the other side, Captain," Mattings said.

VOYAGER

As soon as his shuttle entered the bay, Chakotay ordered Torres to set a course toward the edge of the system and hold position.

He ordered Patel to report to astrometrics to study the events that were about to unfold.

They were well on their way when the captain reached the bridge.

"Report," Chakotay ordered.

"We'll clear the fourth planet in fifteen minutes and reach the system's edge in under an hour," Torres said. "Five unidentified ships are approaching with shields raised and weapons hot. What's going on?"

"I don't know," Chakotay replied. "Stay close, acting first officer," he said, smiling.

Torres slid into the chair to Chakotay's left, asking softly, "Where's Harry?"

"Still observing. Waters, open an encrypted channel to the *Lamont*, audio only."

"Aye, sir. Channel open," the lieutenant indicated from ops.

"*Voyager* to General Mattings."

The voice of JC Eleoate responded. "*General Mattings is coordinating our defense of Lecahn, Captain Chakotay.*" Chakotay could hear the general barking orders in the background.

"Advise him that *Voyager* is out of harm's way. Is there anything I should know about these *Unmarked* attackers? If there's any chance we might become a target, I'd like to be prepared."

"*The Unmarked are a hostile faction comprised of individuals from several member worlds that are currently experiencing high levels of social unrest. They believe their elected representatives are not redressing their grievances adequately, and some are circulating petitions to leave the Confederacy. Their problems are of their own making. They must learn to work harder to improve their standard of living. Instead, they have recently begun to harass planets and outposts that are critical to the Confederacy in an effort to draw attention to their unfortunate circumstances.*"

"So this is a common occurrence for you?" Chakotay asked.

"*They have never attacked a planet as sensitive or well fortified as Lecahn. They must know their mission has no possible chance of success. Stand by, Voyager. We will make contact again when the threat is eliminated."*

"*Voyager* out," Chakotay said.

"A hostile faction made up of unhappy citizens of the Confederacy?" Torres asked.

Chakotay nodded. "I wonder what their grievances are."

"Want to open a channel and ask?" Torres suggested mischievously.

"Yes, but it's not our fight," Chakotay said softly.

TWELFTH LAMONT

Lieutenant Harry Kim stood along the wall behind the general's control panel along with six other security officers. From this vantage point he had the best possible view of the actions of every bridge officer, as well as the main viewscreen where the incoming vessels were represented in bright gold symbols.

"Two are breaking formation on course for the orbital array," Eleoate reported from his tactical station.

There must be planetary defenses on that array, Kim thought.

Within moments, the two ships had come under fire from several phase cannons mounted on the platform. Their evasive maneuvers were impressive, as were the sizes of the explosions that resulted from the impact of the torpedoes they released on their initial run.

"Orbital array six-beta disabled," Creak reported.

"Target the lead vessel and fire at will," Mattings ordered. "We'll deal with the others momentarily."

Kim watched as Eleoate unleashed the *Lamont*'s weapons in a steady stream. The helm matched the evasive maneuvers of the target and, within seconds, made contact.

"Direct hit to their shield generators. They're down," Creak confirmed.

"Finish them," Mattings ordered. The bridge rumbled under fire from the other two ships that had approached on the same course as the leader but were quickly moving beyond the *Lamont*'s range after firing a volley.

Eleoate launched a torpedo, and the lead ship vanished in a shock of white fire.

As Mattings selected the next target and Creak noted the destruction of another orbital array, Kim turned to the security officer standing to his right. "Why didn't the general make contact with the ships before opening fire?" he asked.

"The general knows why they're here. They lost their right to air their concerns the moment they entered this system with their weapons armed. The CIF does not negotiate with hostiles. We merely end any threat they pose."

"What if the threat could be ended without destroying them?" Kim asked.

"To discuss their demands would encourage others to launch similar attacks. We are following standard protocols."

Kim returned his attention to the main viewscreen. Another ship had been destroyed, and the *Lamont* was altering course to tend to one of the two vessels attacking the orbital arrays. He understood in theory that negotiating with terrorists came with inherent risks. But this wasn't much of a battle. It was slaughter. The *Lamont* hadn't so much as hailed them before opening fire.

Then again, the Unmarked ships hadn't requested a conversation either.

Kim shook his head. *Talking to each other might not get them anywhere, but wasn't it at least worth the effort?*

VOYAGER

"Captain Chakotay," Waters said, "one of the Unmarked vessels has altered course and is now in pursuit."

"That's ridiculous," Torres said. "They'll never catch us before the *Lamont* catches them."

"Onscreen," Chakotay ordered.

As the viewscreen shifted from the focus on the *Lamont*'s

battle to the single ship now approaching *Voyager*, the image of that ship distorted.

"Waters, realign your optical resolution," Torres ordered. "You're getting some sort of weird . . ." she began, but she trailed off as the ship almost vanished in a blur of speed no ship that size should have been able to achieve.

"Red alert," Chakotay called. "What just happened?" he demanded of Torres.

Torres was already on her feet and moving to the operations panel. Over Waters's shoulder she studied the display for a moment, then said, "This doesn't make sense. There's a subspace corridor there but they didn't enter it. They sort of skidded across the top of one section of it."

"Add that to the list of things I'd like to learn more about later," Chakotay said. "Helm, evasive maneuvers," he ordered, as the Unmarked ship reversed its course and orientation and began what was likely an attack run.

Likely turned to *certain* when the ship let loose a spray of fire from two small cannons mounted just above its thrusters. The shields rumbled, and Aubrey at tactical barely had time to say, "Shields holding," when a torpedo was released from the ship's belly as it passed directly overhead.

The ship rocked, and the sound of a thunderstorm breaking on the bridge rattled the deck.

"What was that?" the captain demanded.

"Ten isotons enhanced by a gravimetric warhead," Aubrey replied. "Forward shields took the brunt and are down to sixty-eight percent."

"Reinforce forward shield array," Torres ordered. "Gwyn, don't let another one of those things hit us," she added to the flight controller.

"I'm doing my best, Commander," she replied.

"How many life signs on that ship?" Chakotay asked.

"Four," Waters replied. "All humanoid."

Another round of fire struck the ship, but the effect was minimal.

"Return fire, sir?" Aubrey asked.

"Not yet," Chakotay said. The situation wasn't desperate. The *Lamont* had destroyed all but one of the ships they had engaged and would likely be available to do the same to this one momentarily. The Unmarked was clearly trying to draw *Voyager* into the battle. Chakotay could not allow that to happen, unless he was given no other choice.

"He's got one more torpedo loaded, Captain," Aubrey reported.

"Why hasn't he fired it?" Torres asked.

The ship had maneuvered itself around *Voyager* again, and Chakotay's gut turned as the vessel did, picking up speed on what looked like a suicide run. Depending on when that warhead exploded, and how much damage the impact did to the weakened forward shields, *Voyager* could be destroyed.

Options? Chakotay thought.

There weren't any good ones.

Chapter Eighteen

Doctor Riley Frazier, former Starfleet officer, former Borg drone, former instigator of a Borg Cooperative, and current "leader" of all that remained of that cooperative when most were taken by the Caeliar gestalt, wanted answers.

But first she wanted to fulfill a dream she'd been tending with great care for the last several weeks.

The first face she saw when she entered what looked like a large, comfortable living room was Seven's. The perfectly proportioned, graceful figure turned to face her, half lit and half shrouded in darkness.

"Doctor Frazier?" Seven said, clearly shocked. She remained still as Frazier closed the distance between them in long, purposeful strides.

Frazier had never faced such a compliant target. Focusing her rage into her right fist, she raised it with her last step and flung it forward, impacting painfully with Seven's jaw.

Completely unprepared for the assault, Seven's entire body turned to the right with the force of the blow. She was struggling to regain her balance when Frazier shook the numbness in her right hand out, then grabbed Seven with both hands and forced her down onto the floor.

At least Seven was now defending herself. She was much stronger than her lean frame suggested. She caught Frazier's next punch while reaching for her other hand and grasping it with inhuman strength. But on her back, she was working against gravity. Frazier reached for Seven's throat. Seven responded by bringing her left arm straight up to force Frazier's tentative grip to release. Seven then proceeded to try and wriggle free from her attacker, reaching for Frazier's throat with one hand and clawing at the left side of her face with the other.

"Riley!" Axum's voice seemed to come from some distant planet. In the next instant, a strong arm had wrapped around her waist and she was lifted from Seven, struggling in Axum's grasp but with little hope of doing anything more until he released her.

He carried her to the far side of the room. Her breath came in short gasps, but as soon as her feet hit the floor she was moving forward again. Seven had risen to a half-sitting position on the floor and was coming to her knees when Axum body-blocked Frazier and, taking her by both shoulders, pinned her against the wall.

"Seven did not know anything about this!" Axum shouted in her face. "I told you that! She had no idea your people had been targeted."

"She had to know," Frazier shouted. "Even if none of her people told her, she's one of us. *She knows.*"

Seven was now on her feet. Her breath was ragged and she held her jaw, already beginning to swell, in her hand.

Ignoring Axum, Frazier turned her fury on Seven. "You betrayed us. Why? We're no threat to you. All we wanted was to live in peace. Why pretend to give us that? Why take us to Arehaz if you had no intention of letting us stay?"

"Doctor Frazier," Seven said between gasps. "*Riley.* I have no idea what you are talking about."

The mingled shock and pain on Seven's face were too real for Frazier to doubt them.

"See?" Axum demanded. "I told you."

"When?" Seven asked of Axum.

"If I let you go, are you going to listen?" Axum asked of Frazier.

Her frustration spent and her curiosity aroused, Frazier nodded mutely. Axum released her shoulders a fraction, then more fully when he sensed no further forward momentum from her.

"When did you tell Riley whatever you told her?" Seven asked of Axum again. She had not moved toward the pair. Instead, she instinctively took cover behind the sofa that now stood between them.

"Doctor Frazier contacted me just before you arrived, Annika," Axum said.

"How?"

"How do you think?" Frazier asked. "It's not like I had time to enhance our communications array in the first few weeks we spent on Arehaz. We could barely contact *Voyager* again. Not that I'd ever want to."

Voyager had been responsible for saving Riley and her people on two separate desperate occasions. The most recent was only months earlier. The planet she and forty-six others had inhabited was taken by a hostile alien force, the Tarkons, and turned into a "relocation" settlement for travelers whose ships they had confiscated. Riley had hidden herself, thirteen children, their parents, and a few others beneath the planet's surface until she had been able to make contact with Seven through their catoms and begged for help. *Voyager* had executed a daring and costly rescue, at least for the Tarkons, and at Riley's request had resettled their group on a small but viable strip of land on what had been the planet of the Borg's birth, Arehaz.

"*Voyager's* crew has never done anything but assist you when you called for help," Seven said, stung. "Whatever happened to you, they had no part in."

"Well, someone told them where we were," Frazier countered.

"Starfleet Command was notified, as is procedure," Seven said. "You were once an officer. You understand regulations."

"Was once, and am again," Frazier said bitterly.

"I don't understand," Seven said, shaking her head in disbelief.

"A Starfleet vessel arrived in orbit over Arehaz a few weeks ago," Frazier said. "The *Viminal*. I was informed by their commanding officer that I have officially been reinstated by Starfleet. I was ordered to collect my people and bring them aboard for immediate transfer back to Earth. You can imagine, I'm sure, how I greeted that news."

Seven's face fell as the truth dawned on her. "They wanted samples of your catoms," she said softly.

"They did. And apparently, I was not going to be allowed to refuse that request. By agreeing to give them whatever they needed from me, and small samples from the other former Borg among us, I was able to secure their promise that once we arrived, I alone would be taken in for further study, while the rest were given temporary quarters. Once this plague is cured, we'll all be settled together on a permanent home, either here or on another Federation colony in the Alpha Quadrant. Apparently we're much too valuable to be allowed to simply live our lives in peace where we wished."

Seven stepped around the side of the couch and approached her. "I swear to you, Riley, I didn't know. Starfleet found Axum and, shortly thereafter, requested that I return here for study. I had no idea they would disturb you."

"Disturb me?" Frazier said, incredulous. "I'm fine. The children, on the other hand, have just suffered yet another massive trauma, and this time I can't tell them with a straight face that everything is going to be all right."

Seven turned to Axum. "Riley contacted you through your catoms?"

"Yes."

"Why didn't you contact me?" Seven asked of Frazier.

"I tried," Frazier said. "I couldn't find you. I could sense you, but there was something in the way."

"The neural inhibitor," Seven said softly.

"Instead, I found Axum. He told me you were coming here."

Seven was obviously angry now, but not with her.

"All those times I heard you whispering in your room? That wasn't a . . . what did you call it? A *lonely habit*."

"I was afraid if I told you what had happened to Doctor Frazier and the others that you would try to intervene on their behalf. But there is nothing you could have done, and the time you would have spent we needed for our work here, Annika."

"Our work?" Seven asked.

"Understanding our catomic natures."

Seven stared at Axum, then at Frazier, then back at Axum.

"Please, Annika," he begged. "You *know* me, better than anyone ever has. You know that you can trust me. I told Riley the truth, and I am telling you the truth now."

"Right now, I have no idea who to trust," Seven said.

GOLDENBIRD

The cold pack helped, but by the time Lieutenant Samantha Wildman seated Sharak at the navigational station and began the playback of the scene that had caused her to wake him, a dull throbbing was pounding through her skull; this was going to be one hell of a headache.

Sharak dutifully reviewed the short scene beginning with the arrival of Doctor Horse and concluding after the confrontation between Pinky and Ethel. He sighed when it was done and turned to Wildman, saying, "Forgive me, Lieutenant. Perhaps I was not clear when I asked that you review these visual logs."

"Look at that woman," Wildman instructed, pointing to Pinky. "Do you recognize her species?"

Sharak studied the image in silence for a moment, then shook his head. "No, but I am by no means an expert on all Federation species."

"Her name is Ria. She has been a volunteer at this hospital since shortly after the Borg Invasion. I'm a xenobiologist and *I am* an expert on all Federation species as well as many others, and before that nurse confronted her, I couldn't tell you where she came from either."

Sharak pulled up the record of Ria that Wildman had discovered among the volunteer database. "She is Kyppr," Sharak said.

"No, she isn't," Wildman insisted. "Kyppran skin varies from light to rich lavender, but it doesn't change. They've been members of the Federation for over a century. Their homeworld is in the Beta Quadrant. Apart from their Federation representatives, very few of them travel far from home. I'm not even sure if any are serving in Starfleet."

"I'm sorry, Lieutenant," Sharak said. "My mind is weary. I am not following."

"It would be almost unthinkable to find a Kyppran on Coridan for any reason, let alone volunteering at a hospital. They are unusually susceptible to alien infections. Starfleet Medical has worked for a long time to fix this, but it's a genetic issue."

"It is wrong for her to be there?"

"She's lying about her species," Wildman said, her voice rising. "I've watched her interact with I don't know how many patients, and every time I've been struck by the strange pink color of her skin. I just couldn't place it. Then Ethel upset her."

"Ethel?"

"The other nurse. Watch again what happened to Ria's skin."

Wildman reversed the scan and initiated playback at a dramatically reduced speed. Together they watched as Ria's flesh obviously shifted colors, from pink to deep purple. Wildman stopped the playback as soon as the dark black line was visible.

"See? See that?" she asked.

"What is that?" Sharak asked.

"A unique version of cellular degradation," Wildman replied. "The increased blood flow to her face brought on by emotional distress is causing toxic chemicals to be released. Those epidermal cells are dying."

"I've never heard of such a thing," Sharak admitted.

"It's a one-of-a-kind variation, unique to Planarians, but it is essential to their physiology. Planarians had amazing regenerative abilities, but in order for that regeneration to occur, their bodies had to be able to quickly destroy damaged cells. That dark line indicates necrotizing flesh. It will be replaced by new, healthy cells in a matter of minutes. She leaves the room before we get to see that happen."

"Planarians?" Sharak asked softly.

"Yes," Wildman said.

"I've heard that species referenced before, quite recently," Sharak said.

"Where?" Wildman asked.

"I don't recall," Sharak said.

"So what you're doing with Starfleet Medical has nothing to do with Planarians?" Wildman asked.

"It does not," Sharak replied.

Wildman shook her head. "I don't understand. I was so sure."

"If what you have just shown me was relevant to my mission, I would tell you," Sharak said.

"I just assumed," Wildman said. "According to every record I've ever seen, the Planarians died out thousands of years ago. Starfleet discovered their planet and fairly detailed records of their people prior to the cataclysm that made Planaria uninhabitable. Before we had warp drive, they were doing things with genetics that are still outlawed by the Federation. It was necessary for them. Their regenerative abilities were such that almost fifty percent of an individual's body mass could be lost and still recovered. There was a complicated system of designation built around determining when a Planarian could be considered a 'new' person, based on how much regeneration had occurred with that individual. I actually think," Wildman went on as she rubbed her forehead aggressively, "that someone reconstructed their complete genome not that long ago."

Sharak grew very still.

"Doctor?"

"You are right."

Sharak turned back to the control panel and opened a channel to the hospital. As soon as an administrator greeted him, he asked if a volunteer named Ria was currently on-site. After a few moments the administrator replied that she was due to return at 0800 hours.

"What are you going to do?" Wildman asked when Sharak had closed the channel.

"I am going to speak to Ria first thing in the morning," Sharak replied.

"I'm going with you," Wildman said.

"That is not necessary," Sharak said.

"Are you going to ask the hospital for security to accompany you when you speak with her?"

"Of course not."

Wildman smiled faintly. "Listen to the wise old fox, Doctor," she said. "This woman shouldn't exist. You won't know if she is lying to you. I will."

Sharak nodded. *"Kailash. The door opening."*

"Samantha and Sharak seeking the truth," Wildman said.

Sharak laughed aloud.

Chapter Nineteen

Overseer Bralt had begged off accompanying Fife and Brill to what Cemt had called "Izly's" place. Instead, the *Jroone*'s EC Hent and two of his security JPs had come along.

Hent had given Fife coordinates for his shuttle and Fife assumed he'd see a farmhouse or comparable structure when it came in range. Instead, he saw only several small fires, around which dozens of men, women, and children milled as the light of day began to fade. Crude tentlike structures and hovels made from packed mud dotted the area. Small animals milled restlessly about, along with a few large head of *geer*.

By the time Fife and Brill reached the outskirts of the encampment, Hent had located Izly, a wiry young humanoid with fair, freckled skin and long braids of reddish hair whose coat had seen better days and whose boots barely had a sole. A miser with his words, he had pointed Brill to a small field, and after half an hour, Brill confirmed what was obvious, even to Fife.

"I thought Cemt had been hard on his soil," Brill explained. "Mister Izly has leached his to a point I've never seen. It didn't help that he started using a particularly aggressive biocide a couple of years back that got into his groundwater. It's going to take years for this dirt to grow anything again."

"What about those?" Fife asked, gesturing to a few brown stems poking up.

"They're a wild root, but they're pretty much useless as a food source. I can't imagine what they taste like, but there's nothing nutritious in them," Brill replied.

They walked in silence back to the encampment, which had grown in size over the last hour. The faces that glanced at them were hardened, the eyes wary. Over several of the fires, large pots were filled with a bubbling murky liquid.

Izly approached them. "Seen what you came to see?"

"Yes," Fife replied. "Thank you for allowing us to visit your land."

"Is what it is," Izly murmured.

A Leodt boy whose shirt was thin and filthy approached them, carrying a small wooden bowl. He swallowed hard and lifted it to Fife. "For you, sir," he said softly.

Fife took a knee to look directly in the boy's eyes. "Is this your supper?" he asked.

The boy nodded.

"You should eat it," Fife said.

"We don't get guests much," the boy said. "But my mother says you are guests, so you eat first."

"My mother told me the same thing when I was your age," Fife said, nodding seriously. "But I've already had my supper. Don't let this go to waste."

The boy nodded, his relief painful to see.

Fife rose and took another moment to look over the crude camp. A few months earlier, he had wondered at Commander O'Donnell's insistence that the fleet do whatever they must to restore the Ark Planet. He had little doubt what his captain would say if he were here now.

"Mister Izly?" Fife said.

Izly's black eyes met his.

"How many families are there on Vitrum like this?"

"Most."

"How many of them will go to sleep hungry tonight?"

"All of 'em."

Fife nodded grimly.

"Don't," Izly said.

"I beg your pardon?"

"Don't pity me," Izly said. "I don't need it. Me and mine, the Source blessed us. Made us strong. Only the strongest can live in times like this. Men like you and those officers are blessed too, but not like me. The Source knows and chooses the best of his people to face trials. Those who can't aren't expected to. They need their full bellies and their weapons."

Izly's sudden generosity with words stunned Fife. The commander understood this man's need to make sense of his suffering.

"Who told you that?" Fife asked.

"Life," Izly replied.

Fife nodded, then turned. He walked away from the fires, Brill and their CIF detachment following at a distance, tapped his combadge, and opened a channel to *Demeter*.

"*On your way back so soon?*" O'Donnell asked.

"With your permission, sir, I'd like to stay a little longer."

"*Why, Atlee?*" There was unusual concern in O'Donnell's voice.

"There's a humanitarian crisis down here. If we ordered the crew to begin harvesting every consumable seed and foodstuff in our stocks, ran the replicators at maximum capacity, and tapped our emergency rations, I think we could make a difference down here. Brill will have more suggestions. The ground won't grow much right now, but I'd bet my life you could fix that in a matter of days."

Silence answered for what felt like a long time.

"*Atlee,*" O'Donnell finally said.

"Begging your pardon, sir," EC Hent interrupted, stepping closer to Fife and speaking in a low voice.

"What is it?"

"Under the Confederacy charter Vitrum signed, accepting assistance from unaligned or non-Confederate worlds is not permitted. We don't coddle our people. We encourage them to do better. Every resident on Vitrum has retained their citizenship during the last few years because every one of them continues to work daily to improve their lives. They're strong, just like Izly said."

"They're starving," Fife said.

"They are struggling to survive, just as our ancestors did when they fled their homeworlds. Their efforts resulted in the creation of the First World and the Confederacy. The people of Vitrum will overcome this just as they did. We do them no favors by demonstrating a lack of faith in their potential."

Fife listened to this in disbelief. He was glad when O'Donnell spoke again, because it gave him time to rethink the first words that came to mind at Hent's speech.

"*I understand your feelings, Atlee,*" the commander said. "*But you know our hands are tied. The Prime Directive applies.*"

O'Donnell had stretched the Prime Directive to its theoretical limits at the Ark Planet. This response stunned Fife.

"*The people of the Confederacy have a choice to make here. If they are willing to inflict . . . this on their own people in the name of personal growth, that's their right.*"

Fife bit out, "You knew what I would find down here, didn't you, sir?"

"*I had my suspicions.*"

Not good enough. "You *knew*, sir. And you sent me down here. I thought I understood you. But this doesn't make sense to me. How dare *you* put the face of a hungry child in front of me and order me not to feed him?"

"*Return to* Demeter, *Lieutenant Commander Fife. That's an order.*"

"Understood, sir," Fife said, slapping his combadge to close the connection.

Turning back to Brill, Hent, and his subordinates, Fife shook his head in disgust. Finally, one of the young JPs said softly, "EC Hent, I'd like to share my rations tonight with some of the people here."

Hent stared at him in disbelief.

"I would too," the second JP said.

Hent appeared shocked and uncertain. "That is not permitted."

The first JP shrugged. "I've never seen anything like this. If it's true that starvation will instill courage in these people to face their struggles, why does the Confederacy not ask the same of us?"

"Because starvation doesn't instill anything but desperation in a person," Brill said.

"Back to the transport," Hent ordered his men gruffly.

"Yes, sir," they replied in unison.

Fife and Brill exchanged a wide-eyed glance as Fife reminded himself again why he had first stopped doubting Liam O'Donnell's instincts. None of them could order the Confederacy to do the right thing here. But that hadn't stopped O'Donnell from trying to shame them into it. The reaction of Hent's junior officers suggested he might have achieved that aim.

"I think we just got them in trouble," Brill said softly as they turned toward their shuttle.

"They were already in trouble," Fife said. "They just didn't know it until now."

VESTA

"Welcome back, Admiral," Captain Farkas greeted Janeway as she entered her ready room.

"Report," Admiral Janeway ordered briskly as she moved to the replicator and ordered a fresh cup of black coffee.

Farkas paused. She'd never been on the receiving end of the admiral's ire, and she knew she'd done nothing to earn it. *What happened while we were away?* she wondered silently.

"When we first arrived at our recon point, nine ships were grouped at the Gateway," Farkas said. "Six more joined them before we departed. Most of them were a little bigger than *Voyager* and could hold *Galen* and *Demeter* in their cargo holds. They've all got impressive weapons arrays, phase pulse cannons, which according to Deonil are quite devastating, and bellies filled with torpedoes. They're ready for a fight, Admiral. I'd say another day or so at the most."

"Any that we recognized?"

"Two Vaadwaur, two Turei, one Devore, three Karlon, and one Skeen. She's a big 'un," Farkas replied. "The other two never identified themselves, but life signs indicated the presence of Turei, Vaadwaur, and Devore on both of them, among many other unidentified alien species. Between all of them, they're carrying crews totaling more than two thousand individuals."

"Did you learn anything specific about their attack plans or what they think they are going to accomplish once they've breached the Gateway?"

Farkas shook her head. "They did a few drills, close-quarters maneuvers, and attack patterns. Those were in preparation to welcome anyone the Confederacy might send out to meet them. There was some discussion of additional precautions in the event *Voyager* or the rest of the fleet joined the fight."

"You mean *Demeter* and the *Galen*?"

Farkas shook her head. "They had specifications on all nine of the original fleet vessels. They were particularly concerned that *Quirinal, Esquiline,* or *Achilles* might show up."

"What about the *Vesta*?"

"They didn't mention her," Farkas said, smiling grimly. "They've got detailed intel on *Voyager* and *Galen* that would make your blood run cold. If I didn't know better I'd think Eden had more than one spy aboard early on. They have accurate specs on all of our defensive systems and propulsion, including slipstream. I don't think they could build one of their own, but they know what our ships can do."

"But their intel is months out of date," Janeway realized.

"*Galen* was mentioned several times as a target that should be destroyed quickly, not because it posed a threat but because of its value to the rest of the fleet as a medical resource. They seemed to think *Hawking* and *Curie* would be easy to eliminate early in any battle."

"They don't know us quite as well as they think they do," Janeway said. "They must have learned about the fleet shortly after it first arrived in the Delta Quadrant. But they haven't been able to track its progress."

"That's what it looks like," Farkas agreed. "It also suggests that whatever the Voth were doing with our relays, their actions aren't connected to what's happening out here."

"Hmmmm."

"Admiral?"

"Our relays are forty thousand light-years away; that's half a quadrant. But apart from the fleet's missions to find the Children of the Storm and the Omega Continuum, most of the fleet has stayed well within range of those relays. I can't imagine how the Voth could have learned of our arrival. Their territory is just too far away. The Turei and Vaadwaur are close, and we know they were accessing their own subspace corridors long before we met them. Could they have somehow used them to reach out to the Voth?"

"Even if they did, would the Voth have listened?"

"Not in my experience," Janeway said, "but that experience was pretty limited."

"What about the Devore?"

"Their territory is vast and well protected. But they weren't conquerors. They were much more interested in keeping their space just the way they like it. I don't think they would take any preemptive action against us, even if they knew we returned. If we entered their territory again, that would be another matter. They'd attack us on sight." Janeway paused, placing one thumb at her temple and massaging her forehead. "The Voth are a separate issue. Somehow," the admiral continued, "the Turei, Vaadwaur, and Devore learned about the fleet's arrival months ago."

"Deonil said those species only started attacking the Gateway two months ago. Maybe *Voyager* led them here when they came to research the wave forms."

"Maybe," Janeway agreed. "One thing is for sure: Somebody must have some serious diplomatic chops to have brought them together for any purpose, let alone to join a greater alliance out here."

"So what are we missing?"

"I don't know yet," Janeway admitted.

"Is there any chance we're going to aid the Confederacy in the coming days as a Federation ally?" Farkas asked.

"No," Janeway replied coldly.

"Admiral?"

"The Market Consortium has given me a list of demands essential to any alliance, and it will not be possible for us to meet them."

"Their greed got the better of them?"

"They've clearly been using a lot more than passive scans to determine our capabilities. They knew about sensitive technology we've never shown them."

"That doesn't really surprise me, Admiral," Farkas noted.

"Me neither," Janeway agreed. "But it is disappointing. They think we need this alliance more than we do. And I'm willing to bet that when we decline their offer, they might attempt to take what they want from us by force."

"They can try," Farkas said gamely.

Janeway smiled mirthlessly. "*Demeter* is scheduled to return to the First World tomorrow morning. *Voyager* won't be back until tomorrow evening at the earliest. Until we have regrouped, we will do nothing to suggest that we are not giving the Confederacy's request due consideration.

"I want the *Vesta* to stand ready to engage our slipstream drive and make for our predetermined rendezvous coordinates in the event we come under attack and are unable to execute a synchronous departure."

"We're going to leave without saying good-bye?"

"I'm preparing a formal reply to the presider to be delivered after we have safely departed their territory."

"We need the folks on the other side of the Gateway to keep their powder dry for at least two more days."

Janeway shrugged. "Should they come under attack, I don't

think the Confederacy will ask for our assistance. They've never needed help before to deal with similar attempts to breach the Gateway. Any hostile action might actually provide a diversion we could use to cover our departure."

"There is one more thing, Admiral," Farkas said.

"What is it?"

Farkas took a deep breath. "This is just me talking."

"I don't understand."

"I didn't include it in my formal report, but it's been bothering me for the last few days."

"Go ahead."

"Listening to their comm chatter, I felt like they were being a little *too* generous with data."

Janeway's brow furrowed. "If they had no idea they were being monitored, why would they hesitate to speak openly over their own secure channels?"

"If they didn't know, this isn't going to be much of a fight. The *Hadden* practically has their entire battle plan as a result of our efforts. They spoke more often about the Federation fleet than there was cause to do, unless they suspected we were listening and wanted to send us a message."

"What message?"

"Stay out of this. We know you're here and we know your specs, so do everyone a favor and don't get involved."

"Do you think everything you saw could have been staged for your edification?"

Farkas nodded. "Deonil didn't suspect anything. But the Confederacy doesn't see these people as anything more than a nuisance. The intel confirmed that suspicion, which is exactly what I'd do if I wanted to catch a superior force off guard."

"Do you have any sense of what their true agenda might be?"

"None," Farkas replied. "There was no discussion of a target beyond the Gateway, which makes no sense. *Why are they here? What do they want?* Fifteen ships, no matter how well armed, can't take the First World, let alone the Confederacy."

"I agree," Janeway said.

Both women turned their heads automatically toward the door when a soft chime sounded.

"Come," Farkas ordered.

Janeway's Vulcan aide entered the room soundlessly and moved directly to the admiral.

"What is it, Decan?"

"Presider Cin wishes to speak with you, Admiral," Decan replied.

"I'll take it in my quarters," Janeway said, nodding to Farkas as she stepped toward the door.

"Not via subspace," Decan quickly corrected her assumption. "She is transporting directly here via a protector and will arrive momentarily."

"She's coming alone?" Janeway asked.

"And specifically requested that we not confirm her arrival with her office. She indicated that she had a personal matter to discuss," Decan said, adding, "in private."

Janeway turned back to Farkas. "Have security meet the presider when she arrives and escort her to my office. Tell them to wait outside the door until our discussions are concluded."

"Understood, Admiral," Farkas said.

"Thank you, Captain," Janeway said.

"Any time," Farkas assured her.

Chapter Twenty

As best Tom Paris could tell, the parade of character witnesses both he and his mother had provided had been a wash. Paris feared that Ozimat might give more weight to his sisters' testimony. However, there were dozens of statements provided by Paris and his wife's former friends and colleagues that balanced it out.

Once everyone had taken their seats, Ozimat opened the new day's proceedings. "After yesterday's testimony it is clear to me that both Mrs. Paris and Commander Paris share the ability to inspire loyalty in others. This is a good thing. It suggests that no matter how this issue is ultimately resolved, a number of people will be standing by to lend their support.

"It is still my belief that this matter would be best resolved between the two parties. I will render a judgment in the event that proves impossible. But I urge both of you to consider all that was said yesterday, not on your own accounts, but on each other's. Perhaps the wisdom of those closest to you will help you find a way through this current conflict."

The door Ozimat used to enter the chamber slid open, and an officer of the court emerged. He approached the mediator and whispered something softly to him. Ozimat nodded.

"Lieutenant Shaw, did you intend to call Mister John Torres to speak on Commander Paris's behalf?"

"No, Your Honor," Shaw replied. "Mister Paris advised me

that his wife would prefer that her father not be notified of these proceedings."

"As Miral's grandfather, he would have been included in all notifications from the Family Court," Ozimat said. He then sat back, clasping his hands together. After a long pause, he said, "Would either of you object to hearing from Mister Torres?"

"Mrs. Paris does not object," Clancy replied immediately, though the look on Julia's face suggested otherwise.

Shaw looked at Paris. He was torn. Part of him wanted very much to hear what the father-in-law he'd met only a few times had to say. The rest of him feared that if John Torres's testimony did anything to harm his position now, B'Elanna would never forgive either of them.

Finally, Paris said, "Mister Torres is Miral's and my future son's grandfather. My wife has not enjoyed a close relationship to him for most of her life. But that doesn't change the fact that he's part of our family. We should hear what he has to say."

"I agree," Ozimat concurred. He nodded to the officer, and a few minutes later, John Torres was ushered into the room.

He hadn't aged much since the last time Paris had seen him. His hair was more gray than brown, but his face retained the youthful vitality Paris remembered: a genetic gift B'Elanna had inherited from him. He extended a hand to Paris before sitting. Paris accepted it with an awkward smile. His mother stared at Torres with curious eyes.

"Thank you for joining us, Mister Torres," Ozimat said once he was settled. "You indicated that you wished to address the parties in this matter?"

"I do. Thank you," Torres said. He seemed nervous, and he had always been on the soft-spoken side. "The documents I received from the court indicate that Tom's mother is asking for custody of my granddaughter. I was a little shocked to hear that, as, last I heard, my granddaughter was dead."

"You didn't tell him?" Julia asked of Tom, aghast.

"B'Elanna and I have always agreed that it was up to her to

share whatever she felt appropriate with her father. As you know, we were assured of Miral's safety only a few months ago. I am sure B'Elanna intended to tell her father in her own time and in whatever manner she thought best," Paris replied.

Torres's eyes met Paris's. There was neither joy nor accusation in them. "The last time I saw my daughter and granddaughter, they were about to leave Earth on that shuttle she built. She told me that Miral was still in danger and that they were leaving to keep her safe. She promised she would never allow anything to happen to them. I thought she broke that promise when she died. I realize now that she didn't. You reported them dead in order to protect them, didn't you?" he asked of Paris.

"It was a little more complicated than that, but in a nutshell, yes," Paris replied.

Torres nodded. "I came here today to assure myself of that. Thank you."

"I would have . . ." Paris began.

"Suggested B'Elanna contact me eventually?" Torres asked warily.

"I'm sorry, John," Paris said.

"Don't be," Torres said. "Any amount of time my daughter sees fit to give me is more than I deserve. I know that."

Turning his attention to Julia, Torres asked, "Is that why you're here? Because they lied about Miral's death?"

"Not entirely," Julia said. "There have been a number of incidents that led me to conclude that Miral would be better off in the care of someone who does not suffer from my son's character defects."

"And my daughter's?" Torres asked evenly.

"I gave your daughter my unconditional love and respect. She repaid that time and again with lies," Julia said.

"I see," Torres said.

After a long pause, Ozimat said, "Is there anything else you wish to add, Mister Torres?"

"Yes," he replied. "My daughter is who she is because her mother and I made her that way. We were unable to create a home in which she could thrive. The differences between us only grew larger and louder the longer we were together. I decided B'Elanna would be better off not living in a war zone. It was painful to leave her. But I told myself it was in her best interest as well as my own.

"Looking back, I don't know if that was true. If B'Elanna has a hard time trusting people, even her family, it's because she learned, from me, that trust leads to disappointment. I know she's an adult now and is responsible for her own choices. But I also know that the wounds we inflict on our children are permanent. They may learn to live with them. They may overcome them. They may forgive them. But they can never be erased.

"Mrs. Paris," Torres said, meeting her eyes. "I have no doubt that you could provide a safe and stable home for Miral, just as my wife did for B'Elanna. But it will never be the home Miral could have with her parents. B'Elanna chose Tom to share her life with, and in my opinion, she couldn't have chosen better. Even when she told me they were separating, she assured me it was temporary and necessary. Apparently, they succeeded in keeping everyone safe until the threat to Miral's life was over. That they lied to me to do it doesn't make me think less of Tom. It makes me think more of him.

"Unless I've missed something, I don't think Miral should ever again be separated from her father or her mother. I've lived that life. I know what it did to my daughter. I really can't bear the thought of that history repeating itself with Miral. She needs her mother. She needs her father. Please reconsider what you're doing here."

Julia's eyes remained locked with his as she said, "I have considered it, Mister Torres. I can assure you that if I did not think it was in Miral's best interest, I would not be here."

Torres turned back to Paris. "The next time you see them, give B'Elanna and Miral my love."

"I will."

As Torres started to rise, Paris added, "You know, Miral's favorite bedtime story is *Timmy and the Targ*."

Torres smiled, incredulous. "Lana still has that?"

Paris nodded.

"Thank you, Tom."

"Thank you for coming, Mister Torres," Ozimat said. Once Torres had left, he continued: "Everything that you've said to each other since this mediation began has been in the presence of myself and your representatives. We're going to give you the room now, for as long as you need it. Nothing you say will be recorded or relayed to me. I want you two to talk to each other."

"Your Honor," Clancy began.

"It's fine," Julia said softly.

Paris looked to Shaw. The lieutenant nodded to Ozimat but whispered in Paris's ear as he rose: "You've got this. Don't screw it up."

"I thought we agreed that was my specialty," Paris said quietly.

Shaw laughed lightly, shaking his head as he gave Paris's shoulder a firm squeeze.

Finally, the room was theirs.

For a long time, neither of them spoke. Then both began to speak at the same moment.

"Tom, I . . ."

"Look, Mom . . ."

Julia smiled in spite of herself.

"Go ahead," Paris said.

Julia sighed wearily. "I don't expect you to understand this. You don't know yet what it's like to pour your entire life into a child, only to watch that child fail time and again to live up to your expectations. I don't know where I went wrong with you, Tom, but I did. Mister Torres was right about that much. I blame myself for what you have become, just he does for B'Elanna. But that doesn't change the fact that we are here now. Your children need safety and stability. Regardless of my other concerns, you and B'Elanna have chosen to give your lives to Starfleet. You know I honor that choice. But it is no life for your children. Give them to me. You know what they'll have here.

You know how I will cherish them. When you're home, you and B'Elanna will be welcome to see them. Someday they'll appreciate the sacrifice you were willing to make. Your father made the same one, and you understood eventually."

"No, I didn't," Paris said. "I accepted it because I had no choice, but even now I don't understand it."

"Your father loved you dearly. He set the example for you to follow. He held himself to the highest standards."

"Standards are important, Mom," Paris agreed. "But they don't fill the emptiness. That's what you're asking me to create in my children: a permanent empty space where the love I would give them should be."

"Tom—"

"No," Paris said. "I've listened. I've heard you. I get that nothing I can say is going to change your mind. So I'm just going to say this.

"I love you, Mom. I'm sorry I haven't been the son you wanted, or the son you thought you deserved. I'm sorry you can't see how much I hated hurting you the way I did. I'm sorry you don't understand that it had nothing to do with you. I'm sorry your only grandchildren aren't going to spend their holidays and their summer breaks with you in Montecito. I'm sorry that the choice you made to make this claim has probably irrevocably destroyed any chance you might have of regaining B'Elanna's trust. I'm sorry Dad died and left you alone.

"But I learned more than you know from Owen Paris. I learned that trying to live up to imagined expectations is a waste of energy. I learned that nothing can replace the time I spend with my daughter every day. I learned much too late that his way of loving me was just *his way*. I learned too late that he loved me at all. He chose his career over his children. He left us with you, and you are a great mom. But every day he wasn't there was another day I spent wondering what I had done wrong and why he didn't care enough to be with me.

"My children are never going to wonder that. I'm going to be there for every birthday, every school assembly, every science fair, every bad grade, every fight on the playground, every good-night kiss, every messy, hard, frustrating, perfect moment of it.

"I can't let them go, Mom. I won't."

Julia's face hardened. "You will, if the court orders it."

No, I really won't, Paris did not say aloud.

When Ozimat and the attorneys returned, the mediator confirmed that no settlement had been reached between them. He advised them that it would take several days for him to make a final determination and that they would be advised when his ruling had been filed.

Until then, there was nothing more to do but wait.

CORIDAN

Ria was disappointed when she received the order. The probability that it would eventually come was high. She was surprised it had taken this long. But in her ten months of service she had accomplished all that had been asked of her, and it was inappropriate to wish for more.

Terminate.

The word should have filled her with terror.

Instead, it filled her with purpose.

Her identification badge had been checked when she entered the hospital, as it was every morning. She considered completing her morning rounds before acting on her instructions, but as she had no idea why the order had been given, she opted to forgo checking in at her normal duty station.

Instead, she walked through the first-floor admissions area as she always had, nodding in greeting to several familiar faces. Upon entering the turbolift, she requested the subbasement. A quick turn to the right, once the door had slid open, brought her to another set of doors. Beyond them lay the main hub of the central environmental controls.

Shift change was under way, so few custodians anxious to end their night's work paid her any attention. The mechanism she had come to activate had been put in place nine months earlier and required only a quick visual check and the use of a duplicate command code to order the temperature increase that would activate the mechanism and automatically deploy its contents within the next few hours.

Once this task was complete, she again entered the turbolift and requested access to the fourteenth floor. The hallways here were very busy, as usual. The waiting areas were filled with both patients and individuals who had not been admitted but had been ordered to be tested in one of this level's high-resolution scanning devices.

Again, few paid her any attention. One notable exception was Doctor Beemz. The moment she caught his eye he stopped examining the padd he was holding and stared at her. He then whispered something to the nurse beside him, and she also stopped what she had been doing and made a quick call on the hospital's secure comm line.

This simple act filled Ria with urgency. Hurrying her steps, she made her way to the far end of the main hall and turned left.

"Stop where you are!" an unfamiliar voice sounded from behind as she turned the corner.

Ria did not stop, nor did she turn around. Instead she slipped into the nearest chamber that would suit her needs, the one holding the facility's largest scanner, and sealed the door to the outer safety chamber where the doctors or nurses running the scanner were protected from any unanticipated bleed from the device when it was in use.

She then activated the scanner. The moment it was fully operational, she set the level at maximum and ordered continuous operation, locking out any manual override.

She stepped through the safety hatch between the operation center and the scanner and sealed it from the inside. The room was already uncomfortably warm and there was a noticeable tingle in the air that made her ears ring and her head ache.

Turning, Ria saw several individuals arriving at the transparent aluminum viewing window separating the operation center from the scanner. Most were dressed in security uniforms. One was pounding on the window, obviously shouting her name. Another worked the panel, desperate to shut the scanner down. Perhaps they did not realize that she knew precisely what she was doing.

Two faces were new to her. Both wore blue Starfleet science uniforms. One was human, a slight, pale woman with blond hair. The other was an alien humanoid with a large cranium, flattened along the side lobes, an upturned nose, and dark brown mottled skin.

They did not seek to stop her. They merely stared at her, their eyes boring into hers.

The woman's eyes were the fiercest. They were the last she saw as the scanner finally overloaded and an explosion ended Ria's life on Coridan.

Chapter Twenty-One

The question Captain Chakotay had to answer was this: Would destroying the Unmarked ship now attempting to destroy *Voyager* be construed by the Confederacy as aiding them against their enemy or a lack of faith in their abilities? As important, would entering this fight on the side of the Confederacy make other representatives of the Unmarked more or less likely to target Federation ships in the future?

Chakotay was obligated to defend his ship, no matter what the exigent circumstances. Destruction of one's vessel was an option, but only as a last resort. Every other choice before him now was going to seriously complicate the Federation's relationship with the Confederacy, and quite possibly Chakotay's personal relationship with General Mattings.

Since there was no way to avoid this now, Chakotay opted for the course that would provide him with the most information in the shortest amount of time.

"Aubrey, target the ship's shield generators and disable them," Chakotay ordered. "Bridge to transporter room one, get a lock on all four life signs, and as soon as their shields are down, transport them directly to our brig."

Aubrey responded by firing *Voyager*'s phasers and surgically disabling its shields. A few moments later, the transporter officer reported, "*Transport successful.*"

"Aubrey, destroy that ship."

The tactical officer brought the Unmarked ship to a timely

end. The explosion was larger than it might have been had that second torpedo not been armed, but the ship's distance from *Voyager* minimized the effect.

"Waters?" Chakotay asked of his ops officer.

"The vessel has been destroyed, sir. The *Lamont* has finished off the last ship they had engaged and is now altering course to intercept us."

"Hold position," Chakotay ordered. "Don't accept any incoming transmissions until I tell you to," he added as he rose from his chair. "Aubrey, the bridge is yours. Your job is to buy me as much time as you can. B'Elanna, you're with me."

En route to the brig, Chakotay called to sickbay to ask the Doctor to join them in the event any of the prisoners were injured. He was advised by the nurse, who had just reported for duty when the ship was attacked, that the Doctor had sealed himself in his office and was refusing to answer repeated calls.

Chakotay was clearly frustrated by this, but he simply ordered the nurse to report in the Doctor's place.

Torres did not know what had prompted the Doctor to take such extreme actions, but she was willing to bet it had something to do with the assistance she had given him the previous evening. As soon as the crisis had passed, she would give Chakotay a full report and her recommendation that he go easy on the Doctor. Right now, she didn't think he would take that advice, but depending on how this situation developed, that could change.

Voyager's brig consisted of two holding cells. Each cell now contained two aliens, one female and three males. None were Leodt or Djinari. Torres could not even offer an educated guess at their species or homeworlds.

Chakotay wasted no time. Entering the brig behind her, he moved to the center of the security area and addressed himself to all four of his captives.

"I am Captain Chakotay of the Federation *Starship Voyager*. I've taken you prisoner because you attempted to destroy my ship. Were we in Federation space when that happened, you would all be taken from here to the nearest appropriate location to stand trial for this offense. But we're guests here, and as best I can tell, the Confederacy handles these things a little differently than we do.

"I'm not here to judge them for that. In fact, your choice to attack my ship has complicated my life. Therefore, you should take the fact that I am speaking to you as an indication of my reasonable nature, but please do not deceive yourselves by thinking that I'm going to waste my time playing games.

"I've been told that the Unmarked have some grievance against the Confederate government and that, rather than handle this grievance through proper channels, you have decided to unleash a terror campaign to force the government to accede to your terms. I have also been told that you are all well aware that your actions will be met by deadly force and came here knowing you would die shortly after entering the system. Is this true?"

"No, no, and no," one of the males replied, a short, stocky fellow with a thin, translucent second skin covering the entirety of his face, which was spotted in various shades of green. His face was wide and his features flat. His eyes gleamed with intensity, though not insolence.

"Were you that ship's captain?" Chakotay asked.

"I'm Yellna," he said, "and the *Frenibarg* was mine."

"You have one minute to help me understand how we all got here. If you lie to me, when the *Twelfth Lamont* arrives, I'm going to hand you over to them."

"You're going to hand us over anyway," Yellna corrected him.

A tight smile flickered across Chakotay's face. "I may. I may not. Fifty seconds."

"Don't tell him anything," the female, a ruddy-faced woman with short silver hair and exceptionally long earlobes, said.

"Forty-five seconds," Chakotay said. "Is this really how you want to spend the time you've been given?"

"We had no idea the *Lamont* would be here. We came to take out Lecahn's orbital defenses. Had we succeeded, the next wave would have attacked their initiation site."

"What's an 'initiation site'?" Torres asked.

"Lecahn is one of only three worlds in the Confederacy that produces protectors. For the last four cycles, the central government has ordered their protectors to destroy every vessel launched from our homeworld, Grysyen. Our world was hit by a massive ion storm eight cycles ago. Our cities were devastated. Our manufacturing centers were destroyed. Our agricultural production came to a screeching halt. Our lives changed overnight. We begged the central government to send help. They didn't."

"Why?" Chakotay asked.

"Our planet has a long history of welcoming great thinkers, philosophers, scientists, artists, anyone interested in finding new ways to attack old problems. Our economic interests are as diverse as our people. Most never wanted to join the Confederacy, but several critical streams of their supposed *Great River* intersect just outside our star system. The strategic significance of our location and our ability to hinder transit through those streams was too great for the central government to risk. We were ill prepared for armed conflict when the CIF first arrived and explained the benefits of membership. We were told we would be allowed to live our lives as we pleased. Four generations ago our leaders relented to the inevitable and attempted to make the alliance work to our benefit. But our ability to share our ideas with outsiders has been severely restricted, and when that ion storm hit, no one was happier than the central government. They've always wanted our planet but not our people.

"Once we accepted that help was not coming, our leaders petitioned for revocation of our charter so that we might be free to seek aid from other unaligned worlds. That petition was denied. Exile seemed our only hope for survival, but even that is now denied us. We are being slowly and systematically wiped out by the government that swore to protect us when we joined the Confederacy. If we cannot impact their ability to restrict our travel through the destruction of the protectors, we have no chance at all."

"If the protectors are being used as you say, how did your ships get by them?" Torres asked.

"I'm not going to answer that," Yellna said.

"You don't have to," Chakotay said softly. Turning, he met Torres's eyes, and ghosts of their shared past rose between them.

"Bridge to Captain Chakotay," Waters's voice called over the comm. Chakotay could hear the stress in it.

"Go ahead."

"The Lamont *is requesting an open channel. I've run through every excuse I can think of to deny it."*

"Thank you, Lieutenant," Chakotay said. "I'll speak to General Mattings from here."

"Understood. Bridge out."

"What are you going to tell him?" Torres asked softly. The captain had no time to answer before the general's voice crackled through his combadge.

"Are you there, Captain?"

"We are, General."

"I apologize for the fact that the Lamont *was unable to keep you out of harm's way. Our sensors confirmed that you destroyed the fifth and last Unmarked vessel. You have my gratitude and that of the Confederacy."*

You can keep your gratitude, Chakotay thought. The captain was experienced enough to know how bad relationships worked. Your gut told you from the beginning to stay out of it. You got drawn in anyway, telling yourself your eyes were open to the good and the bad. There was just enough good to keep you interested but not enough to allow you to commit. One day you woke up with nothing but regrets and wasted time.

Chakotay had no way of knowing whether or not Yellna was telling him the truth. But his version of the facts did not contradict what Eleoate had told him, nor did it seem out of character for the Confederacy. Sadly, it was all too easy to believe.

Worse, it did not change what he was now obligated to do. He had a duty to his prisoners, but first he must see to his own.

"General, I'll be happy to discuss what I'm about to tell you in greater detail when time permits. For now, I must advise you that Federation law and Starfleet protocols do not permit me to destroy another vessel and kill its crew unless every other avenue for a peaceful resolution has been explored. This was not our fight and we withdrew as you requested. It seems both of us were unaware of the Unmarked ship's capabilities. When the *Frenibarg* pursued and engaged us, we were prepared to defend ourselves. Their tactics forced us to destroy the ship. But prior to its destruction, we were able to rescue the four crew members who were aboard."

A long moment of silence followed, during which Yellna and his compatriots stared at Chakotay with unbridled rage.

"I have begun interrogating them," Chakotay continued.

"*Captain, I'm going to stop you right there,*" the general said, his voice cold. "*How were you able to rescue that crew?*"

Chakotay tapped his combadge to close the channel. To Torres he said, "Find out if their shields are down."

Torres requested the information directly from the bridge and confirmed that the *Lamont*'s shields were down, though her weapons were still hot.

Chakotay then ordered her to contact transporter room one and prepare to return Lieutenant Kim to *Voyager*. When all was ready, he reopened his channel to the *Lamont*.

"With your permission, General, I'll show you."

"*Show me what?*" Mattings asked.

"Chakotay to transporter room one. Initiate transport."

TWELFTH LAMONT

General Mattings could not pinpoint the exact moment when defeat had been snatched from the jaws of his most recent victory until Captain Chakotay spoke the words "Initiate transport."

Lieutenant Kim had given him ten plausible reasons why it had taken Chakotay so long to answer his initial hails once the battle was over. He liked Kim. He trusted him. He knew both Kim and Chakotay were under orders to withhold technological information from him, and he didn't expect that to change until the diplomats had finished their work. For his part, he had been completely honest with Captain Chakotay from the first moment they had met.

Mattings wasn't sure what he expected when Chakotay ordered "transport." In the back of his mind he'd wondered if *Voyager*'s relationship with the ancient protectors had gone even deeper than Kim had let on. The sight of Lieutenant Kim dematerializing before his very eyes hadn't even occurred to him as a possibility. He'd seen marvels in his day. None of them compared to this extraordinary technology.

The general maintained his composure as shocked intakes of breath registered all around him. Eleoate was the first to break the spell cast by the magic they had just witnessed. "All hands, command center orders threat level ten. Confirm."

"Belay that," Mattings barked.

"General," Eleoate began.

"Not another word," Mattings ordered. Eleoate's eyes widened, but his mouth closed.

"Captain Chakotay?"

"We're still here, General."

"Please tell me that Lieutenant Kim is now safe and sound aboard your ship."

"He is, General."

"So this transporter of yours is used only in emergencies?"

"Under normal circumstances, it is used on a routine basis."

"I see."

"I realize it was not your intention to negotiate with those who attacked Lecahn, but they tell an interesting story, one I think you should hear."

"Captain, my orders concerning the Unmarked are long-standing and explicit."

"You and I both know that sometimes the situation on the ground is more complicated than those who issue our orders understand. There are times it becomes necessary to uphold the spirit of them rather than the letter. Your superiors could not have anticipated our ability to rescue the crew. Presumably, you did not have the luxury

of even making the attempt. If you can assure me that these prisoners will be afforded legal protection, counsel, and the ability to air their grievances to the appropriate powers, I will release them to your custody. I know you to be a man of your word."

The general had spent the last several weeks imagining how his life and the life of his Confederacy might be improved by a relationship with the Federation and her people. They seemed soft to the untrained eye. Mattings saw past that. Two of their ships had taken on fourteen at the Gateway and survived. No one risked those odds unless they were confident or insane, and he knew Chakotay was not the latter. Mattings didn't know how the diplomats were proceeding, but he hoped it was carefully. The general was proud of his people, but despite their numbers, he had never believed they had the upper hand in this situation. Had the Federation arrived intent on conquest or advertising their superior technology, the general would have been content to see them fly away with their self-esteem checked. But they hadn't. They had kept their secrets close and asked only for the opportunity to get to know the people of the Confederacy. They had come to learn. And, even now, they were being honest to a fault.

The Federation was a worthy ally; this the general did not doubt. But he knew now that such an alliance would never be possible, and that grieved him more than he could say.

"I appreciate that, Captain," Mattings finally said. "I will not disrespect your position or your faith in me by telling you what you want to hear. You will turn over the prisoners to me now, and they will be executed immediately. They made their choice and, in doing so, determined mine. I am not permitted to question the orders I have been given."

"General, executing these people will not solve your problem or theirs. The Confederacy has taken a number of actions since its founding that are deeply troubling. You have already indicated that you hope to see your people move beyond that past into a better future. You risked a great deal in showing us what you did on Lecahn. I wish to repay that trust and will take full responsibility

for the rescue of the prisoners. What they have told me suggests that some who hold power are not utilizing that power in a manner that is consistent with your Confederacy's stated values of respect for its members and the rights of your citizens. At some point your people must face this. Allow me to take them back to the First World, and we will take this to your superiors together. Working together, we will find a way through this. Please allow me to help you."

The general bowed his head. After a few more moments of silent contemplation, he issued his orders.

VOYAGER

Lieutenant Harry Kim had been transported directly to the brig, so he had been privy to Chakotay's exchange with Mattings. He hoped that the general would accept Chakotay's offer. He didn't know the details, but he knew that his captain would not be taking this risk without good reason.

"Captain Chakotay," the general finally responded, breaking the tense silence following Chakotay's last request. *"I want you to know how much I appreciate your very kind offer. You serve your people with the same passion and dedication I have always felt for mine. As far as I am concerned, nothing that has happened here today changes the respect I have for you or the ideals of your people. You have given me a great deal to think about today."*

Chakotay nodded, looking to Kim, confident he had made his point.

Simultaneously, the ship quaked beneath Kim's feet in an all too familiar sensation. Seconds later, Kim felt the unmistakable charge of EM energy in the air. It passed near enough to crackle the air around him and sent sparks flying as it moved through the forcefields separating the cells from the secured area of the brig.

Chakotay immediately tapped his combadge. "Chakotay to the bridge. Report."

Waters replied, *"Four protectors have emerged from subspace and breached our shields."*

"Vent tetryon plasma," Chakotay ordered.

It was already too late.

The prisoners were lifted from the deck by an invisible force, their screams evident but silent as they were taken from the ship as easily as Harry had once been returned to the *Demeter* by the ancient ones.

"Harry, options?" Chakotay asked, grasping at straws.

Kim shook his head and shrugged. "There's nothing we can do until the protectors release them, Captain."

Chakotay looked ready to punch something but only ordered, "Waters, as soon as you can get a lock on those life signs, bring them back."

"I'm sorry, sir," Waters advised. *"The prisoners were taken into open space to the precise coordinates where their ship was destroyed and executed by the protectors. We could never establish a lock."*

Chakotay's face turned to stone.

His breath was heavy, forced through his nose as the adrenaline he was battling ran its course. Finally he said, "Gwyn, set course for the First World, maximum warp. Waters, advise the *Lamont* of our course and destination. Do not accept any further incoming transmission from the *Lamont*."

"Understood, Captain," Waters replied.

As Chakotay started toward the door, Kim asked, "What did you expect him to do, Captain?"

"Surprise me," Chakotay replied.

"He would likely have faced the CIF's version of a court-martial had he done that," Kim said.

"Probably," Chakotay agreed. "I understand his choice. That doesn't mean I have to like it. What I do know is that we're done here. There will be no alliance with these people."

"The admiral might disagree."

"She won't," Chakotay said simply. *"She wouldn't."*

Kim wondered if that was doubt or warning he heard in Chakotay's voice.

Chapter Twenty-Two

CORIDAN

"I'm sorry, Doctor Sharak, but you won't be able to access that room for the next twenty-four hours," Officer Crixell advised. The middle-aged civilian head of hospital security had met Sharak and Wildman when they arrived to question Ria and led them to her when she was detected on the fourteenth floor.

Shaka.

"There might be evidence we require," Sharak said. "Even a single cell from Ria's body could be essential."

"The radiation levels in that room are toxic. I've already requested a forensic team to investigate and they will be equipped with standard biohazard suits, but I can't even allow them to enter the room until we reduce the levels enough to ensure the safety of everyone else on this floor of the facility."

"It's all right, Doctor," Lieutenant Wildman attempted to comfort him. "The forensic team will find anything that might be left."

Shaka.

"I only wished to speak with her," Sharak said softly.

"This isn't your fault, Doctor," Wildman assured him. "We still don't know who that woman was, or why she was really here. The fact that she committed suicide rather than speak with you suggests she could not risk you learning her truth, whatever it was."

Shaka.

Sharak feared he already knew her truth. Once Lieutenant Wildman's efforts had pointed him to Ria, he had run a staffing search on every plague patient who had been sent to quarantine from Ria's hospital. Not every patient Ria had attended had fallen to the plague. But every patient who had fallen since the day Ria first volunteered her services had been attended to at least once by Ria.

A sense of controlled chaos reigned around them. As soon as the security team had witnessed Ria's abrupt suicide, they had begun to quickly and efficiently clear the area of all physicians and patients. The entire floor would be evacuated within the next few minutes.

Callimas at Bahar.

"I suppose we should try to speak with some of the doctors and nurses who worked with her on a regular basis. They might know something," Sharak suggested.

Turning to Crixell, Wildman asked, "Can you tell us who the volunteer supervisor was?"

"I think his name is Simnly," the harried man replied. "Doctor Beemz will know," he added, gesturing toward a man with a long face standing at the nurses' station.

"Doctor Horse," Wildman whispered softly as she pulled Sharak by the sleeve to get him moving toward the tall, thin man in a gray coat who was busy issuing orders to every nurse within range of his voice.

Ellanan. Her hands empty.

"Excuse me," Doctor Sharak interrupted. "Doctor?"

"Beemz," he replied. "Were you the visiting physician who wanted to speak with Ria?"

"Yes," Sharak replied.

"You're Starfleet," Beemz said. "This facility has observed every protocol Starfleet Medical and the Federation Institute of Health proscribed to the letter since the invasion. Why you would need to question one of our volunteers escapes me."

Kadir beneath MoMoteh.

"I am not here to question your methods, Doctor Beemz," Sharak said. "I have reviewed the work of the facility over the past year and can confirm that it has been exemplary under very trying circumstances."

"Ria was a devoted woman," Beemz said. "Her medical

training was limited, but she followed orders conscientiously and was always willing to work extra shifts when asked."

"Do you have any idea why she just killed herself?" Wildman asked.

Beemz looked away, clearly struggling to retain his composure. "None," he said.

Shaka.

"Were you the one who advised Ria that we needed to speak with her this morning?" Sharak asked.

"Of course not," Beemz replied. "Our volunteer coordinator, Mister Simnly, notified the staff this morning of your request and would have been the one to tell her. I saw Ria when she first came onto the floor."

"Was she normally assigned to this floor?" Wildman asked.

"No. I thought it was strange to see her here. I even asked the duty nurse, but by the time she checked for me, you people were running down the hall and shouting for Ria."

"We need to speak to Mister Simnly," Wildman advised Sharak.

Ellanan. Her hands . . .

A few minutes later, they were brought to the office of the elderly male Coridanite who assigned all volunteer staff at the hospital. He had already been advised of Ria's actions and was clearly shaken by this turn of events. The windowless office was small, tucked into a corner of the administrative wing. It barely held the three of them along with a desk cluttered with numerous padds.

Kira at Bashi.

"Mister Simnly," Sharak said in his most comforting tone of voice, "I realize this is a difficult time for you, but there is information we require about Ria."

"Of course, of course," Simnly said. "Anything I can do to help Starfleet. Was Ria in some sort of trouble?" he asked, then answered himself: "Obviously she was. She must have been. She wouldn't have . . . but she was so kind and so dedicated to her work. I don't know where she would have found the time to do anything inappropriate. She was here every day. She worked more shifts than any other volunteer, even after the initial crisis had passed. I think she always wanted to be a nurse, but her circumstances did not allow her . . ." he trailed off.

"When you told Ria that we wished to speak with her today, was she disconcerted?" Wildman asked gently.

Simnly raised a blank face to Wildman. "I didn't tell her," he replied. "I hadn't seen her yet this morning. I intended to call her to my office as soon as she arrived, but I was speaking with Doctor Mettiger when the alert sounded on my companel. I didn't interrupt the doctor. I never do, you know. They work so hard for our people."

Kadir . . .

"I'm sorry, sir," Sharak interrupted, "but if you did not tell Ria we wished to speak with her, why did she attempt to elude the security staff?"

"I don't know," Simnly said.

Sharak and Wildman exchanged a puzzled glance. Wildman found her voice first. "Can you tell us where Ria went this morning before we found her on the fourteenth floor? Someone else might have mentioned our request to her, and we should speak with them too."

Simnly nodded and accessed his data panel. "Her access card was checked in at ten minutes to eight. She arrived early for her shift," Simnly said with a faint smile. "So dedicated." His face clouded over as he continued to read. "It appears that she entered the central environmental control area just after she arrived. Why would she do that? Perhaps she wanted to speak with one of the custodians. A special patient request, no doubt. She was always so good with our patients and their families. No concern was beneath her attention."

Temba . . .

"After she left there, where did she go?" Sharak asked.

"The secondary lift brought her directly to the fourteenth floor," Simnly replied.

Klemar. When it rises.

Sharak looked again to Wildman. "Perhaps we should . . ."

"Environmental control," Wildman finished for him, nodding.

Simnly personally escorted them to the subbasement and introduced them to the custodian in charge, Mister Alwen. A heavyset native of Coridan, Alwen did not report seeing Ria. She had entered the area just before his shift had begun. He offered to ask around to see if anyone had seen or spoken to Ria, and as he did so, Wildman asked to enter the area Ria had accessed.

Sharak followed. Force of habit caused Wildman to activate her tricorder the moment they had entered the bowels of the facility's environmental control system. Every wall was lined with data interfaces and large display panels. Beyond them a lattice of conduit and piping was visible.

Sokath. In darkness.

"What are you looking for?" Sharak asked.

"Cellular residue," Wildman replied. "If she touched anything, we might find a few random cells she left behind."

His eyes uncovered.

Sharak nodded. After a few moments Wildman said, "Only three panels in this room have been touched in the last hour. Mister Alwen?" she called.

When Alwen joined them, Wildman asked, "What does this station control?"

"Thermal regulation," he replied.

"Has it been malfunctioning?" Wildman asked. "It's a little hot in here, isn't it?"

Alwen shrugged. "I haven't received any complaints yet. But it is warmer than . . ." he began as he studied the thermal regulation logs displayed before him.

When he paused, Wildman said, "What is it?"

"Someone intentionally increased the temperature here at shift change. There were no orders and I can't find their command code. No one has access to this system that isn't on staff."

Shaka.

"So it couldn't have been Ria?" Sharak asked.

"No," Alwen said.

Wildman keyed a new command into her tricorder and began scanning the room. When she angled it toward the nearest conduit, it registered a faint alarm. Moving past the custodian onto a small catwalk that accessed the innards of the environmental systems, she continued to scan. Finally she dropped the tricorder and stared hard at a small metal box affixed to a pipe.

"What's that?" she asked.

Alwen joined her on the catwalk and scratched his head. "I don't know. I've never seen it before. I don't think it's supposed to be there."

"I'm reading traces of organic material inside it," Wildman said. "There is also some sort of membrane around the organic component that is destabilizing as we speak."

Shaka. When the walls fell.

"Evacuate the hospital at once," Sharak said.

"I beg your pardon," Alwen said, clearly shocked by the suggestion.

"*Shaka. When the walls fell.* Evacuate the hospital. Get Officer Crixell down here now. Tell him to wear his biohazard suit, bring emergency forcefield generators. Do it now," Sharak said. Taking Wildman by the arm, he said, "You must leave, Lieutenant. Return to your *Goldenbird* and wait for my next instructions."

"I'm not leaving you down here alone."

Kiazi's children. Their faces wet.

"Yes, Lieutenant. That's an order," Sharak corrected her.

STARFLEET MEDICAL

Seven retreated into Axum's lab, desperate to bring order to the chaos that was now her mind.

I need to speak to the Commander.

The Commander who had requested her assistance, brought her from the Delta Quadrant to Earth, forced her to undergo a humiliating battery of tests, and still not troubled himself to actually utilize her abilities to help him cure the catomic plague?

The Commander is using my catoms, Axum's, and soon Riley's to attempt to cure the plague. He must have discovered how to alter their programming. His methods are unsafe. He is experimenting on healthy individuals as well as those already infected. He does not want me to know what he is doing because he knows I would not permit my catoms to be used in that manner.

Seven had no idea how to make contact with the Commander. Axum had said *he* would reach out to her in his own time. Seven was all but certain that time would never come.

He now has access to all known catomic particles in this galaxy. Should the Full Circle Fleet discover any other former Borg who remained outside the gestalt, he would likely imprison them, just as he has us.

Was this prison? It hadn't felt like one until now.

But what else should she call it?

"Annika?"

Axum had known all along what the Commander was doing, but he had allowed Seven to suffer until she had learned the truth on her own. He had known Riley's fate long before she arrived. He had intentionally denied Seven information, but why? To prolong their time together here? Did he think she would forget why she had come?

But I did forget, didn't I?

She had allowed her personal concerns to blind her to the greater threat before her. Her fears for Axum had soon given way to the reality of physical intimacy augmented by catomic connection. She had wasted too much time exploring that pleasure until the overwhelming pain of the Commander's experiments had forced her to remember her priorities.

"Annika?"

It was critical now that she maintain her focus.

"Go away," Seven said firmly. Turning her attention to the last series of programming algorithms she had created, she examined the disappointing results.

"I love you, Annika."

"Love is irrelevant," she said.

"You don't mean that."

"People are dying, Axum. Riley and those who trusted her to keep them safe were just taken from their home and brought here to become test subjects. You and I are forced to experience the suffering of those being subjected to brutal and possibly fruitless experiments. We are *complicit* in their suffering because we provided the means by which they are being tortured.

"This must end. Your feelings for me, whatever you choose to call them, are not going to change these facts, nor are they going to help us put an end to all of this."

"Yes, they are," Axum said softly.

"How?"

"I know that you love me too."

"Go away," Seven said again.

"Tell me that you do. Say the words. Tell me that you will not forget what we have shared when . . ."

"When what?"

Axum shook his head. "It doesn't matter."

Seven stepped back instinctively as he approached her.

"You're going about this the wrong way," he said simply, gesturing toward her data panel.

"Just because I have not yet found the answer I am seeking . . ." Seven began.

"You don't have to look for the answer. It is already yours."

Seven shook her head in frustration.

"These are *your* catoms, Annika. If you wish to see their programming, you have but to ask."

"I don't understand."

"*Because you don't want to.* You're afraid of them. You think you have accepted them. You think you can limit your access to them. You think you can control them, but until you acknowledge that you and they are one and the same now, you will never understand."

"Fine," Seven said. "I accept them. They are mine."

"Order them to reveal the code you wish to study."

"This is ridiculous," Seven said.

"You won't even try?"

"I don't know what you are asking me to do," Seven shouted.

Axum sighed. With his left hand, he touched the screen that displayed the molecular representation of a single catom and then brought his hand in front of him in a sweeping gesture. Suddenly the molecule floated in three dimensions at eye level between them.

Seven knew what she was seeing. *How* she was seeing it made no sense, but she could not deny the reality now hanging suspended before her eyes.

"Order them to reveal their programming code," Axum said again.

For a split second, the image before her shifted. Insight flashed through her mind like a leaf being carried on a strong wind. As soon as it brushed her fingertips, it fled.

"I can't," she said again.

"Promise me you will remember what we had this time. Promise me you will not let it fade as you did after Unimatrix Zero. All I have done was for you, Annika. For you, I sacrificed perfection and paradise. Twice."

Sensing his urgency without truly understanding it, Seven nodded.

He stole into her mind with shocking ease and force. Somehow she knew he had always been capable of this but had tempered his advances until now, lulling her into submission. She expected to hear his thoughts, instructions perhaps. Instead, she *saw* . . .

Joined as they were now, their bodies were merely shells with faint, permeable boundaries merging into one form, seeking complete oneness. Cells, molecules, and atoms that were intrinsic to them as individuals appeared as a gray haze. Scattered throughout it were pinpoints of blinding starlight. Each star burned with endless energy, sending and receiving signals that shot through the darkness, flaring and subsiding in milliseconds.

Her focus shifted to a single star. Looking past its brilliance, she grasped in an instant its individual components. The lines that divided it from the haze were absolute. The clumsy tag that identified it was a mere distraction. Seeing it like this, it was impossible to mistake it for anything other than the beautiful, perfect, and immensely powerful construct it actually was.

Seven had known on an intellectual level what she had become when the Caeliar had transformed her implants into catoms. To see the truth of it, as Axum saw it, was to grasp the utter magnificence of the Caeliar.

Finally, Seven understood.

Somewhere in the distant real world, delight released itself in laughter.

Seven followed that laughter, allowing it to lead her from the inner space Axum had shown her back to the lab.

The catom floating between them was no longer a molecule. It was now an endless stream of programming code Seven could read as easily as her native language.

"Good afternoon, Naria."

"Hello, Jefferson."

The Commander removed the hypospray from its case. His hands betrayed him and it fell to the floor. Bending gingerly to retrieve it, he glimpsed her bare feet. They were light lavender today.

For a split second he was back in his first lab, the secluded research outpost on Deneva, his first station after graduating from the Academy. How many times had he watched those feet develop from simple buds to differentiated structures? He could not recall now. *Too many to count.*

He retrieved the hypo and stood, steadying himself by holding firm to the side of the biobed.

"Will it hurt?" she asked.

Yes.

"Not for long."

Willing his hand to stillness, the Commander lifted it to Naria's neck.

Seven was still staring in wonder at the section of programming code controlling a single catom currently located in her parietal lobe and capable of previously unimagined enhancements to her visual perception, when a bloodcurdling scream registered in her mind well before it reached her ears.

Riley.

Chapter Twenty-Three

Presider Cin entered Admiral Janeway's quarters and stood for a moment just inside the door. She wore an exquisitely tailored white suit under a long, shimmering silver jacket and carried herself regally. As soon as her gaze settled on the admiral, standing before her desk, Janeway clearly read the uncertainty in her eyes.

"Welcome, Presider Cin," Janeway greeted her.

"Admiral."

"May I offer you something to drink? Some tea, perhaps?"

Cin shook her head, the tendrils extending from the base of her neck snapping taut briefly before settling themselves again.

Janeway stepped toward her slowly. "I'm sure you are aware that I met with First Consul Dreeg a few hours ago. I'm still considering his proposal."

"That meeting did not go well," Cin said simply. "I was not surprised."

"Would you care to sit down?" Janeway asked, gesturing toward one of two chairs set on either side of a small table the admiral used when dining privately.

Cin shook her head again as she looked toward the long port that ran along the far wall, currently offering an unobstructed view of the First World. "May I?" she asked.

"Of course," Janeway replied, following the presider as she moved to stand directly in front of the window.

"Everything seems simpler from up here, doesn't it?" Cin asked.

"Sometimes," Janeway agreed.

"But not today?" Cin tore her gaze from her homeworld and turned to stare down into the admiral's eyes.

"No," Janeway said.

"I did not authorize Dreeg to utilize illegal means to gather intelligence about your ships," Cin said apologetically. "When I signed the documents initiating our diplomatic relations, I intended to follow both the letter and spirit of our agreement."

"Your first consul obviously thought he knew better," Janeway said.

"He has disappointed both of us," Cin said. "I suspected when he brought Grish aboard your ship that he must intend to test my patience, but I had no idea how far."

"Is Grish some sort of telepath?" Janeway asked.

"He is Aurothazian," Cin replied, "one of the translators I told you about when we first met. Their ability to remember what they see and hear is astonishing and essential to their skill in grasping new languages. From a few words, Grish can usually begin a conversation in a tongue he has never spoken. A glance at exposed circuitry is more than enough for him to render a precise schematic. Any data displayed on an interface can be reproduced with complete accuracy. And yes, information contained in the minds of susceptible species can be read with varying degrees of accuracy."

"Remarkable," Janeway noted.

"Between Grish's tour and several sensor sweeps, Dreeg was able to compile his wish list. I asked that he wait before presenting it to you. I honestly wanted to know what data and technology you intended to share with us before making any demands. I would have been content with your friendship."

"As would I," Janeway said.

"Is that still possible?" Cin asked.

"Of course," the admiral replied. "Our friendship will always be yours and the Confederacy's. The other terms Dreeg presented will require more thought."

"Dreeg is a fool."

"No, he isn't," Janeway corrected her gently. "He occupies a place of great power here and intends to secure an agreement favorable to him and his interests. I can't fault him for that."

"Dreeg believes you were awed by our civilization and the ways in which an alliance would enhance the Federation's prestige."

"Your civilization has many attributes that recommend it. What you have built here is worthy of admiration."

"I have always believed that to be true. But this Federation of yours . . ." She paused, searching for the right words. "There is no hunger, no want. Even without these basic motivations you continually push yourselves. It almost seems unwise to me," she admitted.

"I have always found the risks to be worth the rewards," Janeway said.

"Had Dreeg demonstrated the patience I counseled, would you have any other reservations about the prospects of an alliance with the Confederacy?" Cin asked.

Janeway paused, inhaling deeply.

"That many?" Cin asked, smiling faintly.

"There are cultural differences between us that would require further discussion," Janeway admitted.

"Such as?"

"Your society is structured in what we call a 'caste system.' Certain individuals enjoy all rights of citizenship, while the rights of others are limited."

"Only by their willingness to strive to better themselves."

"So you say, and you clearly, honestly believe it." Janeway took a deep breath, carefully measuring her words. "The Federation mandates that all who live under our laws are treated equally, regardless of their circumstances. Full participation in our representative system and protection of our laws is not a boon to be granted or withheld on the whims of fate. They are rights conveyed at birth. Even Federation members who still use forms of currency for trade do not oppress members of their society or limit their ability to advance."

"But you live in a society where resources are plentiful and can be created from thin air," Cin said.

"Replicators are not magic. They require energy to perform their functions. And there have been many times in the Federation's history when disasters or natural calamities have seriously limited available resources.

"Where we differ is in our approach to those circumstances. You see privation as motivation. We see it as something to be immediately corrected, and those who can sacrifice whatever they must so that others can live without fear for their survival."

"Our system of trade has vastly improved the lives of many who have joined our Confederacy," Cin argued.

"But that system is controlled by individuals who are personally enriched by the regulations *they* impose," Janeway countered. "Are you aware, Presider, that the Market Consortium has held a material ownership decree for technology that is very similar to our replicators for forty years without developing that technology?"

Cin's eyes narrowed. "It doesn't surprise me. Dreeg made haste to point out the many ways in which the introduction of replicators to the Confederacy would destabilize our entire system of trade when I first proposed that we negotiate for an exchange including their specifications."

"The only thing replicators would destabilize is the power of the Market Consortium," Janeway said. "Your first consul sees your people as limited in their abilities and therefore in need of a strong guiding hand."

"Like children," Cin said softly.

The admiral nodded. "There was certainly a time in the history of your people when such strong centralized authority was required. But your civilization has evolved. Its structure and capabilities are limited only by the restrictions you choose to impose upon yourselves."

"Are there other restrictions you find troubling?" Cin asked.

Janeway paused, choosing her words carefully. "Those placed upon the women of the Confederacy," she finally said.

"I don't understand," Cin said. "There are no limits to what a woman of the Confederacy may achieve. Surely I am proof enough of that."

"Only after she is no longer fertile. And those incapable of bearing children are not as fortunate," Janeway said.

"If a woman chooses to place her own desires above the needs of her people, she has no one but herself to blame for her circumstances," Cin countered.

"There are several cultures within the Federation that from time to time had faced reproductive crises, not unlike the one your people were enduring when they discovered the First World. Societal pressure may encourage members of those cultures to shift their priorities toward ensuring the continuation of their species, but reproduction is not regulated or imposed upon any individual capable of bearing children, be they male, female, or one of many hybrid life-forms."

"You believe that the women of the Confederacy are unfairly disadvantaged by our society's expectations?"

"How many women have led this Confederacy in the last five hundred years?"

"I am the third."

"And how many have served as first consul or head of the Market Consortium?"

Cin sighed. "None, though many have risen to other positions of authority within the Consortium."

"Is there any history in the Confederacy of women protesting this situation?"

"Never on the First World," Cin replied. "Some of our member worlds struggled initially with this regulation, but soon enough they came to understand that the survival of our people depends upon our ability to secure each successive generation. We were billions before the Borg found us. Tens of thousands had to rebuild what was lost. The women of the Confederacy consider their contribution to our society an obligation, not a burden."

"The women of the Federation would never accept the notion that they be required to produce children prior to doing anything else they wished with their lives."

"They should count themselves fortunate that they do not know what we know—how fragile our civilizations truly are."

"I assure you, Presider, they do," Janeway said. "But we work diligently to ensure that the challenges we have faced, including potential extinction, do not allow us to abandon our values, including every individual's right to absolute self-determination."

"Here we must agree to disagree," Cin said. "Is there anything else?"

"You've said that your people abandoned the *lemms* because the Source intended you to do so once you had secured sufficient resources," Janeway said.

"When the protectors became resistant."

"Didn't it trouble you to destroy those planets and the life-forms inhabiting them?"

"Why would it? Do you mean to tell me that the Federation does not extract resources from the worlds they find and colonize?"

"We do," Janeway acknowledged. "But every effort is made to conserve nonsentient life and to determine if any unusual sentient life-forms may exist on a planet before we extract anything from it. We prefer to take resources from uninhabited planets whenever possible.

"We have learned in our travels that all of space can be thought of as one vast ecosystem. It is in constant motion and subject to changes. We proceed into the unknown, conscious of the fact that any action we take may have unintended, harmful consequences. Where our technology has been found to damage space or worlds, we abandon it and make every effort to repair it."

"As we abandoned the *lemms*."

"Should you learn tomorrow that the Source no longer deemed it necessary to restrict your actions, would you use the protectors to destroy entire planets to obtain their resources?"

"If the Source willed it."

"Even though the ancient protectors have already demonstrated to you that they do not wish to be used in that manner?"

"The ancient ones are a special case. No protector would be used long enough to develop similar reluctance. I am assured it is a simple matter of programming and elimination once their ability to imprint data has been compromised."

"I see."

Silence reigned between them for some time before Cin said, "When you said that there was much to admire about the Confederacy, you did not mean it, did you?"

"I did," Janeway insisted. "There are matters of principle that divide us because the circumstances that led to the development of the Federation differed from those that gave rise to the Confederacy. We do not value the same things in equal measure."

"But your way is better?"

"Our way is our way. It is subject to revision as new ideas, developments, and influences are encountered. We are always open to the incorporation of new ways of thinking and working."

"Finally, common ground," Cin said.

"Presider?"

"Our contact with you and the Federation has given me much to consider. I do not believe your way of life to be superior to ours, but I cannot deny that there are capabilities you possess that could improve the lives of my people. I came to you today because I have an alternative proposal I would like to present."

"Please."

"The Market Consortium is technically a civilian authority. They have always held considerable influence over the government, and thus far, the government has never entered into any trade agreements without the Consortium's approval. I am considering breaking with that tradition."

Janeway kept her face neutral as she asked, "How?"

"The government might purchase items directly from the Federation and distribute them as they see fit, without including the Consortium. I can guarantee you that your compensation in such an agreement would be less lucrative than any offer you would receive from the Consortium, but you could rest assured that my priorities in introducing those items into our society would not be the same as the Consortium's."

"You would be risking a great deal, wouldn't you?"

"Perhaps. But I find the possibilities of such an arrangement strangely liberating."

Janeway smiled.

"The items you speak of would not include weapons or defensive technology," the admiral warned.

"Source, no," Cin replied. "On that front I believe we are more than adequately advanced. I only hope that, in the coming days, I'm not proven wrong about that."

"You are referring to those outside the Gateway?" Janeway asked.

"They keep coming, more and more. Such contacts were once rare. They have become all too common of late, and I don't understand it. They have seen others who attempted to breach the Gateway destroyed by our interstellar fleet. They must know they have no chance of success."

"Have you attempted to make contact and simply asked what they are seeking?"

Cin shook her head. "The Confederacy does not make diplomatic overtures to species that have proven themselves untrustworthy by their actions. My people would see it as operating from a place of weakness."

"The Federation would see such a gesture as operating from a place of strength. Force of arms may be the only potential resolution to some conflicts, but only after every other possibility has been exhausted."

Cin considered Janeway's words. Finally, she said, "Would the Federation be willing to assist me in opening that dialogue?"

"What did you have in mind?"

"Your universal translators would make it possible for me to address the aliens at the Gateway directly. You could accompany me there. We are not yet allies. Your people could be considered a neutral party in any dispute between the Confederacy and these aggressors. You could provide us with an unbiased viewpoint of their demands."

"Sadly, the Federation has already encountered some of the species that are now massing against you. I am not certain they would consider us *neutral*."

"You are challenging me to break with generations of tradition and explore a new possibility for my people. Are you unwilling to risk confronting your own past? Are you certain that a new understanding between the Federation and these other species might not come of such an attempt on your part?"

"It is actually one of our stated mission parameters for the fleet I now command," Janeway replied. "The first time the Federation came to the Delta Quadrant, our circumstances were quite different. We attempted to make peaceful first contact wherever possible, but when our survival was at stake, that took precedence over achieving more permanent understandings.

"Now I will offer any species we previously encountered the option of renewing our acquaintance in hopes that we might move beyond the past. But you must understand, were we to assume the role of neutral party in your discussions, we would not be able to come to your aid in the event hostilities broke out."

"I understand, and I am willing to accept that," Cin said. "The CIF is more than capable of securing our safety. Your fleet would not be called upon to enter into any action. Should our negotiations fail, and our forces engage these aliens, I would expect you to retreat."

Janeway nodded. "When would you propose making the overture?"

"First light, tomorrow," Cin said.

The admiral felt her eyebrows rise in surprise.

"This is another initiative I intend to take without consulting my first consul. He would not approve."

"Perhaps you should reconsider."

"I don't think so," Cin said, smiling. "Dreeg's concern is the prosperity of those whose influence he protects. My concern is the safety of all of my people.

"I understand that your reluctance to accept Dreeg's proposal had as much to do with the means he used to gain the information as the deeper differences between our cultures. But for all those differences, there is much we share in common, most importantly our desire to live in peace among other spacefaring peoples. If I could show Dreeg that by embracing some of the Federation's methods we were able to successfully end the threat posed by these aliens, it would be much more difficult for him to resist future collaborations on your terms. Help me, and I assure you that whether you decide to pursue an alliance or not, the Federation will always be counted as friends of the Confederacy of the Worlds of the First Quadrant."

Janeway extended her right hand. It took Cin a moment to remember the gesture from their first meeting, but when she did, she took the admiral's hand and shook it lightly.

"Give us a few hours' notice. When you're ready, signal and we will follow you through the Gateway. Let's see if those assembled out there have any interest in diplomacy," Janeway said.

"Thank you, Admiral. I have no doubt that this will be the first of many productive initiatives between my people and yours."

"I certainly hope so, Presider."

DEMETER

Fife and Brill reported to the bridge immediately upon their return from Vitrum.

Commander O'Donnell rose from the center seat, ordering, "My ready room, Commander Fife."

With a nod, Fife complied, following the captain to the small office just off *Demeter*'s bridge. Before O'Donnell could speak, Fife said, "You don't have to explain, sir. I understand what you did down there."

"Did it work?" O'Donnell asked.

Fife shrugged. "Hent was horrified by the thought of offering aid to the people we found there. I have a feeling that the circumstances of the people of Vitrum aren't widely known among the Confederacy. Hent's men were pretty upset by what they saw and wanted to help."

"They won't be allowed to. But it's a start," O'Donnell said, smiling mischievously.

"Due respect, sir, was there a class I missed at the Academy about inciting mutinies?" Fife asked. "Because you're awfully good at it."

O'Donnell's smile gave way to laughter. "Watch and learn, Atlee."

"Captain O'Donnell to the bridge."

"We're on our way, Vincent," O'Donnell replied.

When he crossed the threshold, the captain was surprised to see the face of Overseer Bralt on the main viewscreen.

"Commander O'Donnell."

"How can I help you, Overseer Bralt?" O'Donnell asked congenially.

"Our tour of Vitrum has concluded and we are ready to escort you back to the First World."

"Very good," O'Donnell said. "If you'll transmit our course to Ensign Vincent, we'll be under way."

"Before we go, I have a question for you," Bralt said uncertainly.

"Ask away."

"In the absence of a formal alliance between our people, I understand that your options in terms of offering aid to Vitrum are limited," Bralt began.

"They are nonexistent," O'Donnell corrected him.

"The people of Vitrum are considering severing their relationship with the Confederacy."

All traces of levity fled from O'Donnell's face. Such a revelation from the overseer was unexpected, to say the least.

"Not on our account?" O'Donnell asked.

Bralt did not answer his question. *"Should their severance be approved, would your vessel be willing or able to provide the relief these people require, including supplies and your expertise in helping them to restore their land to productivity?"*

"With Admiral Janeway's approval," O'Donnell replied. "But

that would not be forthcoming unless she was assured by your diplomats that rendering such aid would not be considered an affront to the Confederacy."

Bralt's teeth protruded ever so slightly.

"So that's a 'yes'?"

"A qualified one," O'Donnell replied.

The viewscreen shifted abruptly to its previous view of Vitrum hanging below them.

"What happened?" Fife demanded of Vincent at ops before O'Donnell had the chance.

"They closed the channel, sir," Vincent replied.

O'Donnell turned to Fife. Both were equal parts puzzled and concerned. It was Fife who acted first on that concern.

"Take us to yellow alert," Fife ordered.

"You don't think . . ." O'Donnell began.

Before he could finish that statement, however, *Demeter* rocked subtly beneath their feet and eyes darted all around the bridge as four armed CIF officers appeared to move through the bulkheads and settle on the small bridge, their weapons raised.

Had O'Donnell not already witnessed a version of this while in orbit of the Ark Planet, he might have been mystified. As it was, he was merely disappointed.

EC Hent, who had led the team, said in a cold, clear voice, "Do not move from your stations. The Confederacy Interstellar Fleet hereby seizes this vessel for suborning treason on a Confederacy world."

Turning to Fife, O'Donnell said, "Atlee, the bridge is yours."

"Thank you, Commander," Fife said. "Will you be retiring to your quarters for the duration?"

"Oh, I think I'd like to see this," O'Donnell replied.

"Very good, sir," Fife said. Turning to his security chief, Lieutenant Url, Fife said, "Lieutenant, relieve our guests of their weapons."

"If you move, we will be forced to fire," Hent said.

"Lieutenant Url?"

With a nod, Url stepped away from his tactical console. As soon as he did, the nearest CIF officer trained his weapon on Url and depressed his trigger.

A low click was the weapon's only response.

Surprised, the officer tried to fire again. Each of his companions did the same, to no effect.

"Your weapons were disabled the moment you entered our bridge," Fife advised Hent. "I assure you, they are quite useless."

"A dampening field?" O'Donnell asked.

"Installed just after we entered Confederacy space," Fife replied, "and set only to affect Confederacy weapons."

"Excellent choice."

Fife shrugged.

"Hand to hand," Hent ordered.

He barely moved forward half a pace toward Fife, before the commander removed his type-1 phaser from his pocket and fired, stunning Hent and dropping him to the deck. Vincent, Url, and flight controller Falto quickly disabled the other CIF officers with their own phasers. Although sidearms were not always carried on the bridge, this was another precaution Fife had ordered while in Confederacy space.

"Stunned, Atlee?" O'Donnell asked.

"Yes. We could reconfigure one of our labs as a temporary brig, or . . ."

"Let's send them home." O'Donnell sighed. "But," he added, "I think it's time Overseer Bralt and I spoke face-to-face again."

"Ensign Vincent, transport these men back to the *Fourth Jroone* and simultaneously bring Overseer Bralt to the bridge. Open a channel to the *Jroone* as soon as that's done."

"Aye, Commander," Vincent acknowledged.

Moments later, the CIF officers had vanished and Bralt appeared before them. His shock at having been unexpectedly relocated from his ship soon gave way to fear for his person. He looked about *Demeter*'s bridge in alarm while randomly feeling his arms and upper torso as if to assure himself he had arrived all in one piece. "How?" he asked, shocked.

"The Federation has their own version of transporter technology. Welcome back to the *Demeter*, Overseer," O'Donnell welcomed him warmly.

"Commander O'Donnell, what is the meaning of this?" EC Irste demanded from the main viewscreen.

"Well, as best I can tell, Bralt here decided to try and concoct a flimsy excuse for taking my ship from me, and we found that unacceptable. We prevented your men from harming us or our ship and returned them to you uninjured. Now I need to speak with Mister Bralt, but just so there's no further confusion, I'd like you to listen to our conversation."

"EC Irste," Bralt said abruptly, "have a protector bring me back to the *Jroone*."

"Lieutenant Url?" Fife said.

"Venting tetryon plasma," Url replied. After a moment, he added, "All local protectors have been returned to subspace."

"We could keep playing these games all day, Overseer, but they're a waste of valuable time," O'Donnell said. "My XO, Commander Fife, has spent many hours pondering and preparing countermeasures for any attack your ship could execute against us. It's what he does," he offered apologetically. "I don't honestly believe that at this point you could justify opening fire on us, but should you decide to head down that road, we're ready for that too. You know and I know that if you do, any hope for an alliance between our peoples ends here and now. While I don't think that would bother either of you, I'm guessing a decision like that is above your pay grades.

"I'd like to offer you a suggestion and really hope you'll hear me out."

Bralt's gaze could have leveled O'Donnell on the spot, but he said, "We do not appear to have a choice."

"I've spent a few weeks among your people. I've seen and learned a great deal. As best I can tell, the Confederacy has no need of an alliance with the Federation, at least as far as your agricultural production is concerned. You have all of the capabilities you require to correct your current deficiencies. In some cases, you lack the political will to do so, but in others, you simply aren't utilizing what you have to its maximum potential."

"You are incorrect," Bralt insisted.

"That's never true," O'Donnell said, "but I'm not surprised to hear you say it. Why don't you let me show you what I'm talking about."

"By all means," Bralt said a little too sarcastically.

"Excellent," O'Donnell said, ignoring Bralt's tone. "Commander Fife, bring the slipstream drive online and set course for system Delta M 198. Let's avoid the Gateway and access it through our initial course of discovery and initiate long-range scans as soon as possible to make sure we won't be interrupted by any of our old friends." Turning to the viewscreen, O'Donnell continued: "Mister Irste, I'd love to take you with us, but, sadly, the *Jroone* won't be able to keep pace. We will return to these coordinates, with Overseer Bralt, in twelve hours."

"Where are we going?" Bralt demanded.

"I believe you call it the last *lemm,*" O'Donnell replied.

"I am your prisoner?" Bralt asked.

"Absolutely not. You're our honored guest. If you'd prefer to continue to live in ignorance, I will return you to your ship immediately."

Bralt turned to look at EC Irste.

"*The last* lemm*?*" Irste said reverently. "Is that even possible without utilizing the Gateway?"

"Yes," O'Donnell assured him.

"You will await my return, EC," Bralt ordered.

"*Understood, Overseer,*" Irste said. "Fourth Jroone *signing off.*"

As the viewscreen shifted back to a view of Vitrum, O'Donnell said, "With your permission, Overseer Bralt, Commander Fife will show you to your temporary quarters. I'm sure they won't be up to your considerable standards, but I promise you, you're going to love our food."

VESTA

"Thoughts?" Admiral Janeway asked. "Speak freely," she added.

Captain Farkas and Counselor Cambridge locked eyes briefly over the conference room table. Decan, who stood behind the admiral's chair, was busy making notes on the padd he held in his hand.

Farkas was the first to speak. "Have you considered the possibility that the presider was not entirely forthcoming with you?"

"Yes," Janeway replied. "But whether she intends to seek a diplomatic solution with the aliens at the Gateway, or simply means to use this overture as cover for an attack, the results will be the same. The entire fleet has our emergency rendezvous coordinates. *Voyager* and *Demeter* are scheduled to return to the First World today. Should our mission not go well, we will all regroup in a safe location and put this unfortunate episode behind us."

"Regardless of the presider's intentions, she's shooting herself in the foot by bringing us with her," Cambridge said. "Even if the armada out there is interested in negotiating with her, *Voyager*'s past interactions with them aren't going to aid her cause."

"I told her as much," Janeway said. "But the fact remains that those ships are aware of the Federation's presence here and are already prepared to attack us."

"Then why are we giving them the chance?" Farkas asked.

"If they can come to terms with the Confederacy, and we can help them do that, they might consider reevaluating our relationship with them as well," Janeway replied.

"In the best of all possible worlds," Cambridge said, "but this is the Delta Quadrant."

"The presider knows we can't enter this fight on her side. If hostilities break out, we engage our slipstream drive and depart."

"Leaving the rest of our fleet in Confederacy space?" Farkas asked.

"I trust Captain Chakotay and Commanders O'Donnell and Glenn to see to the safety of their ships," Janeway said. "They'll know where we are, and should they fail to arrive in a timely manner, we do whatever we have to do to find them."

"Or," Cambridge suggested, "you could tell the presider to wait one more day and see the rest of the fleet safely clear of Confederacy space before we attempt this fool's errand."

"Unless, of course, you've changed your mind after speaking with the presider and now believe that an alliance is possible," Farkas added.

"It's not," Janeway said. "The Confederacy will never be an appropriate safe harbor for our fleet. I wouldn't trust anything Dreeg agreed to. But I'd just as soon not have them as an enemy either. If we make this attempt, and it fails, no one on either side can claim that we didn't do everything in our power to establish a positive working relationship. If we depart now, and the Confederacy comes under attack and suffers considerable losses, we abandoned them in their moment of need."

"Do you honestly care?" Cambridge asked.

"I do, but it's more than that," Janeway said. "The Turei, the Vaadwaur, and the Devore could prove to be powerful adversaries and make our next few years here incredibly unpleasant. If a series of previously undetected subspace corridors runs throughout the Delta Quadrant, sufficient for them to have discovered both our presence here and the Confederacy, they could attack us at any time. Our past differences aren't going away. We have to face them at some point. We are not their enemy, and they need to know that."

"I think I'd feel better about this if we had any idea what they're really doing here," Farkas said.

"As would I," Janeway agreed, "and right now, this might be the best way for us to find out."

"We're using the Confederacy for our own ends, just as they think they are using us?" Cambridge asked. "Is that the diplomatic definition of a 'win-win' scenario?"

"Sometimes," Janeway allowed.

"Don't you think there's enough of the Delta Quadrant left to explore without risking this?" Cambridge asked. "We've been traveling through the Alpha and Beta quadrants for centuries now and still haven't seen all of them."

"The admiral is right," Farkas said. "*Voyager* encountered a number of interesting species and cultures out here on her maiden trek, but these three—the Turei, the Vaadwaur, and the Devore—were on a short list where no accord could be reached. Worst-case scenario, they make peace with the Confederacy as well, and all four of them decide the Federation cannot be allowed to maintain a presence here. Never mind the Voth," she added.

"The only place we have detected the Voth was near our communications relays. It is likely that they are completely unaware of our actions here," Janeway reminded her.

"Yes, but they don't like us much either, so that's potentially five heavy hitters out there gunning for us," Farkas noted.

"Maybe they'll contact the Tarkons and things will really get interesting," Cambridge said with a smirk.

"Let's hope not," Janeway said. "Unless there are any other concerns, I think we're done here."

"I think we're just getting started," Cambridge observed.

"Stand ready to move out when the presider signals she's ready."

"Aye, Admiral," Farkas said.

VOYAGER

Once he was assured that *Voyager* was on course for the First World, Captain Chakotay wasted no time in reporting to sickbay. He suspected the Doctor's odd behavior was related to their conversation of the previous evening, but his concerns for Seven did not relieve him of his present duties to *Voyager*. Chakotay hadn't been able to take the Doctor to task during the battle over Lecahn, but now he had time, and a spleen that needed venting.

He found the Doctor, just as the nurse had reported, seated at his old office desk staring at his data screen. Using his command overrides, he entered the office. The Doctor did not turn or speak a word in greeting. The screen displayed a photograph of Seven standing with the Doctor during some sort of celebration in *Voyager*'s old mess hall. Chakotay had never imagined he would think of anything from that time as the "good old days," but the image captured both of them in a moment of unrestrained happiness, and, truth be told, he hadn't seen either of them smile so freely in a long time.

"Doctor," Chakotay said, clearly startling the hologram.

He turned to face Chakotay, tears streaming down his face.

The anger Chakotay had carried with him to sickbay was forgotten.

"She's dead, you know?" the Doctor said.

"What are you talking about?" Chakotay demanded.

"I was going to save her. I was going to cure the—" The Doctor ceased speaking abruptly. "Forgive me, Captain, but you are not cleared to receive that data." After another pause, the Doctor asked, "Are you?"

Chakotay immediately moved to sit opposite the Doctor, saying, "Slow down. What data?"

"It's classified," the Doctor said. "They wanted to keep it a secret because they knew she would never approve. But she must know by now. They would have had to kill her."

"Doctor, we already discussed this last night," Chakotay said, alarmed. "We're en route now back to the First World. I'll speak to Barclay as soon as I can."

"I'm sorry," the Doctor said. "I know how much you loved her."

Fear settled itself firmly in Chakotay's gut. "Doctor, we've been over this. Seven and I ended our romantic relationship years ago."

"That's right," the Doctor said. "You did. Did I?"

"Did you what?"

"Love Seven?"

Chakotay shook his head. "You and Seven are very close friends, Doctor. But neither of you—"

"I did," the Doctor insisted. "And now she's dead."

"Doctor, I think your program might have been damaged," Chakotay said, rising. "We'll be rejoining the *Galen* shortly. I'm going to deactivate your program until then, and as soon as I can get Reg Barclay over here, he'll figure out what's happened to you and fix it."

"Reg? But he's still at Jupiter Station, isn't he?"

"Computer, deactivate Emergency Medical Hologram," Chakotay ordered. "Command authorization override Gamma Pi Six Nine Delta."

The Doctor vanished.

For a few seconds, Chakotay toyed with the idea of bringing the slipstream drive online so that *Voyager* could regroup with the *Galen* in a matter of minutes rather than hours. But he'd already revealed more than he should have to General Mattings, and the *Twelfth Lamont* was surely monitoring their course. Any unexpected deviation from the plan he had submitted before departing Lecahn would surely be greeted with suspicion, if not worse.

The Doctor's existence might depend on it. Then again, it might not. Surely no further harm could come to his program as long as it was deactivated.

Twenty-four hours, Chakotay told himself. *Reg will fix this.*

He hoped.

Chapter Twenty-Four

CORIDAN

Doctor Frist had remained silent throughout the entirety of Sharak's report. He had told her of his suspicions about the infection rates that had driven him to Coridan, his discovery of Ria, her suicide, and the results Doctor Mik had just confirmed. Apparently, several months earlier, Ria had attached a device to the hospital's main environmental controls intended to disperse throughout the entire hospital an airborne virus similar to one Mik had discovered in several of his quarantine patients. Had it not been discovered, every person in the facility would have succumbed within a few days. Further analysis of Ria's contacts with the patients at the hospital over the past year indicated that she had personally attended every single plague victim that had been sent to quarantine. No likely accomplices had been identified thus far.

"I grant you, this is remarkable information, Doctor," Frist finally said, *"but you were not authorized to perform this investigation, and you are hereby ordered to return to Earth immediately and suspend any further work on this matter."*

"Why?" Sharak asked.

"Our team needs to review your findings. Once that's done, we will proceed as we see fit. Your services are no longer required. You may remain at your temporary quarters until Seven has been released from our secured area."

"I wish to speak with Seven immediately," Sharak said.

"That will not be possible."

Uzan. His army. With fist closed.

"That is unacceptable, Doctor Frist," Sharak said simply. "For more than a year, your staff, despite expending considerable energy attempting to contain and eradicate this plague, has failed to learn that it was not being spread by natural forms of transmission. An individual unknown to you has been able to access infectious materials and transmit them to patients, artificially inflating your casualty rates.

"I came to Coridan seeking answers to questions you have failed to ask, and I found those answers. I was brought here by a fellow Starfleet officer, Lieutenant Samantha Wildman, who has not been advised of the details of my work, given its classification. Before I spoke with you, I contacted her superior officer and advised him of the seriousness of our situation and the need for timely action. He has agreed to release her from her current duties in order to continue to assist me.

"As soon as our contact is terminated, I will brief Lieutenant Samantha Wildman on every aspect of the catomic plague with which I am familiar. We will then proceed to Ardana, to determine whether or not Ria was acting alone here or had accomplices on the other worlds where this plague has arisen."

"You are not authorized to do that," Frist said.

"I'm not asking for your authorization, Doctor. According to Lieutenant Wildman, there is a very good chance that Ria was a member of an extinct species, the Planarians. Unless you agree to allow me to continue my investigations, I will immediately contact the head of Starfleet Medical to advise him that a Planarian might be involved in this crisis. I am sure he will remember sooner than I did that Commander Jefferson Briggs came to enjoy his current reputation by first extrapolating the Planarian genome.

"The implications of this potential connection are most disturbing. If we are able to find any accomplices on Ardana or Aldebaran, and confirm that they are not Planarians, we might conclude that Ria's species was identified in error. As we were unable to collect any samples of her DNA following her self-annihilation, we cannot confirm or deny our theory. I am certain that Commander Briggs would prefer that we verify our suspicions before taking them to a higher authority."

Frist stared silently at him for almost a full minute. Finally she said, *"I will speak to the Commander and advise you as soon as possible."*

"I will set course immediately for Ardana. I will report any significant discoveries I make there to you. Sharak out."

Once the connection was terminated, Sharak rose from the comm station and contacted the runabout, requesting transport. His fears for Miss Seven troubled him deeply. But he was certain that his best chance of securing her safe return lay in completing what he had begun on Coridan. Should any harm come to her as a result of his efforts, he would grieve. But he could not allow thousands more to suffer and die needlessly in the name of protecting a single individual.

As soon as he materialized on the runabout's transporter pad, he nodded to Wildman, saying simply, *"Mirab. His sails unfurled."*

SAN FRANCISCO

For the first time since the mediation had begun, Commander Tom Paris had taken his seat beside Shaw before his mother arrived. When Julia finally entered, Paris immediately understood what had delayed her. She normally wore her gray hair in a roll at the base of her neck. It was convenient and efficient, without being severe. Today she had obviously taken some extra time with her appearance. Her hair was loose, resting in soft curls on her shoulders. It framed her face and softened it. It also made her look younger.

Ozimat had advised both counsels that he had made his decision the previous evening, too late to convene a session. Paris wondered if Julia was worried her age might bias Ozimat against her and now, too late, was seeking to remedy that.

Despite all that had passed between them in the last few weeks, Paris was touched by his mother's appearance. It was easier to see her today as the young woman he remembered, the one he had yet to disappoint.

Ozimat entered the room just after Julia had taken her seat, and once the pleasantries had been observed, he addressed himself directly to Paris.

"Commander, I'm not certain, even now, that you fully appreciate the damage you have done by the choices you and your wife have made over the past few years. I do understand that your circumstances were uniquely grave and that, when desperate, people often do unwise things. It surprises me that you seem intent on defending those choices, rather than acknowledging many of the valid points your mother has raised."

Paris's heart rate had increased as soon as the mediator's eyes had locked with his. His opening remarks had done nothing to calm it.

"It is also clear to me that you possess a propensity for bending the truth to suit your present needs. I agree with your mother that it would be most unfortunate for this character flaw to be passed by example to your daughter and son."

Finally, Ozimat turned to Julia. "Having said that, I have concluded that no cause sufficient to warrant awarding custody of the offspring of Commanders Paris and Torres to Mrs. Paris has been demonstrated by the claimant."

A deep breath Paris was unaware he had been holding flew from his gut as he dropped his head into both his hands, relief flooding through him.

Ozimat continued: "You painted a damning picture of your son and daughter-in-law to me. On numerous occasions their behavior toward you has bordered on heartless. And while I do find many of their choices irresponsible and somewhat reckless, I give more weight to their motivations than you have. Their primary responsibility toward Miral is to keep her safe. They've done that. You have provided no evidence that their daughter has suffered in any way by the choices they made. In fact, to a person, every witness presented who has seen Miral in the last few years has spoken of her as a happy and well-adjusted child. They have also spoken of the care both Commander Paris and his wife display for her.

"What has become clear to me is that their relationship with their daughter is everything it should be. Their relationship with you, however, leaves a great deal to be desired. I am not attempting to assign the blame for this to either party. I would suggest to you, Mrs. Paris, that when you consider the number of times your son has misled you, you ask yourself if there is anything you have done to warrant this. You speak of your love for him. I do not doubt it is genuine. But, clearly, neither Commander Paris nor his wife feel they can confide in you as you would wish. In part, this has been the result of extreme circumstances; but not entirely. I believe we teach others how they should behave and that, unintentionally, you have taught both of them to trust you only to a point."

Turning again to Paris, he went on: "Which is not to say that you are blameless in creating grievous faults in this relationship. Commander, you strike me as a singularly selfish individual, in every respect but one: where your daughter is concerned. Going forward, should you desire to avoid further damaging your relationship with your mother, you are going to have to proceed with greater caution. It is inappropriate for you to expect her to trust and understand your choices when you have given her little cause to do so.

"It is my fear that the decision reached here might bring an end to your relationship. It is my hope that it will not. The commander and his family will not be stationed in the Delta Quadrant forever. When they return, it would be advisable for all of you to consider spending more time together. Clearly, all of you desire the same thing: that your children and grandchildren know how deeply they are loved. Don't allow the mistakes of the past to deny them that knowledge.

"The matter brought before the Federation Family Court by Julia Paris regarding the custody of Miral Paris is now concluded."

Ozimat rose from his chair and left the chamber swiftly. Paris had watched Julia's face as he had pronounced his judgment and seen only shock. Once Ozimat had gone, she remained frozen. Clancy whispered something softly in her ear. She did not appear to hear his words and did not respond to them.

Shaw pressed a hand on Paris's shoulder and nodded, clearly pleased. Paris had expected to feel relief and gratitude should the matter be concluded in his favor. He did, to a degree. But beneath them, his stomach churned.

His mother stared past him, confronting a future he could not bear to imagine. He wondered if she had used this case to postpone facing that future, the one that had begun the moment Owen Paris had been killed in action. Paris had seen her several times after the invasion was over. He'd been preoccupied watching Harry recover from serious injuries sustained at the Azure Nebula and beginning the work of assembling the Full Circle Fleet in Chakotay's absence, but he had thought his mother was doing well, beginning to come to terms with her grief.

Now he wasn't so sure.

"Mom?" he said softly.

Without meeting his eyes, Julia Paris rose from the seat opposite him and walked from the chamber with her head held high.

She had always known how to make an exit.

Paris's heart began to burn in his chest. His duty was clear. This matter resolved, he should make all possible haste to collect Doctor Sharak and Seven and get back to the fleet. Last he'd heard, Seven's condition had not changed, but Sharak and Sam should be back soon. It might be possible to transfer Seven to the Delta Quadrant in stasis. What Commander Briggs could not cure, the Doctor would surely handle with characteristic skill and speed.

But Paris knew now he could not leave his mother like this. She needed something from him, something he wasn't sure he could give her, but for the love he felt, he must try.

"Congratulations, Tom," Shaw said, pulling him from his thoughts.

"Thanks for saving me from myself," Paris said.

"It wasn't as hard as I thought it might be. You should get back to your fleet as soon as possible. Your wife shouldn't wait any longer to hear the good news."

Paris nodded. "I know."

B'Elanna and Miral and his unborn son needed him. Soon enough they would have his undivided attention.

Right now his mother needed him. He wasn't going to fail her again.

Chapter Twenty-Five

Presider Cin had chosen to attempt to open negotiations with the aliens arrayed near the Gateway from one of the Confederacy's most imposing vessels, the *Fifth Shudka*. Though not as large as the *Vesta*, it was a magnificent ship. Three large rear thruster arrays were spaced evenly along the stern of the multilevel hull configured roughly like an isosceles triangle, though its prow was gently curved. It boasted the Confederacy's most advanced tactical systems, including a 360-degree weapons array and multiple phase cannons. Eight torpedo tubes were mounted just beneath the bow.

The *Shudka* would be a formidable adversary for anyone foolish enough to engage her.

"We are nearing the end of the Gateway," Commander Roach, Farkas's XO, advised.

Silence had reigned on the bridge during their transit of the stream. Farkas appeared relaxed, her legs crossed and arms resting easy. The admiral suspected that inside she was coiled tight as a spring, but she respected that Farkas's manner did not betray this to her crew.

Janeway sat at her right hand, Roach at her left. In addition to the *Vesta*'s regular alpha shift officers, Counselor Cambridge and Lieutenant Lasren held open stations near the tactical post, one normally reserved for a science specialist and the other for supplemental engineers. Their seats were turned to face the main viewscreen, away from their consoles.

The moment they emerged into open space, a channel was established between the *Vesta* and the *Shudka*. Simultaneously, the *Vesta* began sending out standard friendship greetings on behalf of the Confederacy and the Federation to all nearby vessels, as well as hailing the largest Skeen ship. No one knew which vessel was technically leading this group, but, when in doubt, that honor usually went with size, so the admiral had opted to start there.

Janeway had expected hostilities to erupt the minute the *Vesta* was visible. She was pleased when the Skeen vessel identified itself as the *Lightcarrier*. A few moments later, the face of its commander, Rigger Meeml, a tall, fleshy humanoid with jet-black skin hanging in loose folds and small silver eyes barely visible beneath an intricately carved copper helmet, appeared on the viewscreen.

The *Vesta* was facilitating this exchange, but Janeway had already agreed that Cin alone would address the aliens should they answer *Vesta*'s hails.

"Rigger Meeml, I am Isorla Cin, presider of the Confederacy of the Worlds of the First Quadrant. I have come in hopes of opening a dialogue with you and the others who have assembled here. Losses have been suffered on both sides of this conflict. The Confederacy does not know, however, what cause you have to make war on us. Please explain your presence here and help me to understand if there is anything you require of us that we might be able to grant you. It is our intention to end hostilities between our people."

"Presider Cin," Meeml began in a deep bass, *"for many years now, my people, the Skeen, have traveled through space, enjoying the unrestricted use of thousands of subspace links."*

"We call them the streams of the Great River," Cin interjected.

"There are many links present in the territory you claim as your own, but you are the only civilization we have encountered that refuses to allow others the opportunity to access them. That position is unacceptable. Beyond your space, valuable resources exist that are accessible only by passing through your territory. We have been assured by our Kinara, other species we have joined with, that you

will never allow outsiders to utilize your 'streams.' Should you continue to hold fast to that position, we will force you to yield."

"What you are asking of us is something we rarely grant to those who are not members of our Confederacy," Cin said. "Fifty-three worlds all connected by the streams fall under our protection, and we would be a weak Confederacy indeed if we could not assure our members of their ongoing security.

"That said, if you would be willing to present to us data on the streams that would be most useful to you, I would be willing to consider offering you safe passage, either through them, or through other local streams that would not carry you close to our member worlds. There would, of course, be restrictions you would have to observe, and any deviation from proscribed courses would be met with deadly force. But if it is possible for us to end this senseless violence between us, we are willing to explore it."

"I must speak with my Kinara," Meeml said.

"Of course," Cin agreed. "As you can see, we are accompanied here today by the Federation Starship Vesta, under the leadership of Vice-Admiral Kathryn Janeway. They are facilitating our conversation through their translation technology. Their home is thousands of light-years away, in the Fourth Quadrant, and they are not official allies of the Confederacy. If you and your Kinara are amenable, I would suggest that you select a diplomatic assembly to meet with me aboard the Vesta. They have been designated a neutral party in these negotiations."

"Patience, please, Presider Cin," Meeml requested.

The connection with the *Lightcarrier* was terminated, but Janeway could still speak with Cin.

"Congratulations, Presider," Janeway said warmly, once the third channel was closed. "You handled that very well."

"That remains to be seen," Cin said. "But it is a good sign that they were willing to speak with us at all, isn't it?"

"In my experience," Janeway agreed.

"Captain Farkas?" Lieutenant Kar called from tactical.

"Report," Farkas ordered.

"The other fourteen vessels present are altering their configuration, forming into attack groups."

"Acknowledged," Farkas said, turning to Janeway. "A precaution?" she asked.

"A warning, perhaps," Janeway suggested. "I assume *our* precautions are in place?"

"Yes, Admiral."

Janeway did not know how many CIF vessels were standing ready on the other side of the Gateway to come to the *Shudka*'s aid, should an attack commence. Cin had assured her that she had seen to her own safety, and she reiterated that if hostilities ensued, the *Vesta* should retreat. The admiral had not advised her that the *Vesta*'s plan was to retreat thousands of light-years away. She sincerely hoped that the congenial tone already adopted by Meeml was not an aberration.

"We are being hailed, Captain," Jepel reported from ops.

"By the *Lightcarrier*?"

"No, Captain. The largest Devore vessel, the *Manticle,* has maneuvered itself closer to the *Lightcarrier* and is requesting to speak with the presider."

"Are you ready to make another friend?" Janeway asked of Cin.

"*Absolutely,*" Cin said.

The channel was opened, and a face Admiral Janeway would never forget appeared on the main viewscreen beside the image of Cin.

From the corner of the viewscreen, Janeway was cognizant of movement near the presider, but her attention was focused on the face of Inspector Kashyk. He was handsome as ever, his black hair trimmed shorter than she remembered. The slight cranial protrusions that replaced his eyebrows, centering a small bony ridge that ran vertically from the center of his forehead almost to the bridge of his nose, were the only significant differences between his rugged face and any human male's. His cheeks dimpled broadly when he smiled, as he did now, presumably in greeting. But his eyes, soft brown orbs in which the admiral had once found both respect and considerable passion, now held only unrestrained contempt.

Looking back to Cin, Janeway started to speak but stopped. First Consul Dreeg was now visible on the screen, standing directly behind the presider.

VOYAGER

Sensors had confirmed to Captain Chakotay that the *Galen* was in orbit of the First World, exactly where she was supposed to be. *Demeter* had not yet arrived.

Hoping Commander Glenn might know something about *Demeter*'s absence, Chakotay ordered Waters to open a channel as soon as they were in range.

"*Good morning, Captain Chakotay,*" Glenn greeted him. "*You're back a little earlier than expected.*"

"As soon as we are in range, I need you to transport Lieutenant Barclay to *Voyager*," Chakotay said briskly.

"*We can dispatch a shuttle now, sir,*" Glenn suggested.

"That won't be necessary. The Confederacy has seen our transporters in action."

"*Understood, sir,*" Glenn said, clearly curious as to how this had come to pass. "*Is there a specific problem?*" she began.

"Our EMH is not functioning properly," Chakotay said, choosing his words carefully. "I am certain Lieutenant Barclay will be able to rectify that."

Glenn's eyes widened in alarm. "*Several hours ago, we received new orders from the* Vesta. *Admiral Janeway departed less than an hour ago to join an exploratory group, including high-level representatives of the Confederacy, seeking to address the alien ships assembled beyond the Gateway. We were told to await your arrival here, as well as* Demeter*'s, and the* Vesta*'s return before taking further action.*"

Chakotay exhaled slowly, reading between the lines. The admiral had gone with the presider to confront the aliens at the Gateway. It had to be a diplomatic overture. There was no way Kathryn had decided to join the Confederacy's fight, in the absence of the establishment of a formal alliance. There was also no way she had agreed to an alliance without hearing his and

O'Donnell's reports. It was also likely that the presider was not advising her own people about her intentions.

Presumably the admiral had provided Glenn with an expected return time, and if she failed to arrive as scheduled, or worse, Glenn was to take the *Galen* to their predetermined rendezvous point along with *Voyager* and *Demeter*.

"Has *Demeter* reported in?"

"*No, sir. She is due back shortly.*"

"*Demeter will not arrive in orbit of the First World any time soon, Captain Chakotay,*" the voice of General Mattings said as he broke into the comm channel *Voyager* was using to speak with the *Galen*. "*Forgive the interruption, Captain, but I needed to speak with you urgently, and your operations officer hasn't been receiving our hails—or was, perhaps, ordered not to respond to them?*"

"Waters, put the general on the viewscreen," Chakotay ordered. "Commander Glenn, maintain your open channel."

"*Yes, Captain,*" Glenn said.

"General Mattings," Chakotay said evenly, "until I am able to provide a full report of our last mission to Admiral Janeway, you and I have nothing to discuss."

"*Yes, we do,*" Mattings said. His face had lost much of the confidence and congeniality it had held the first time he had spoken face-to-face with Chakotay. The captain sensed that some, but not all, of that was due to the events that had transpired at Lecahn.

"*As I am sure you are aware, this channel is being monitored by the CIF.*"

Someone is listening, and he can't speak freely now either, Chakotay realized. Otherwise this reminder was pointless.

"*I received word several hours ago that your Commander O'Donnell illegally transported Overseer Bralt to the* Demeter. *He then departed Confederacy space with the overseer using something he called his 'slipstream drive' and advised the* Fourth Jroone *not to expect their return for twelve hours. The commander insisted that Bralt was not his prisoner, but I'm not sure what else to call him.*"

"Where were they going?" Chakotay asked.

"*The last* lemm," Mattings replied.

The Ark Planet? What would have led O'Donnell to take this action was impossible for Chakotay to imagine, though he was certain the commander would have fifty good reasons the next time they spoke. None of them would change the fact that even the appearance of abducting a Confederacy official was a grievous offense. More important, the space around the Ark Planet was no longer secure. *Voyager* and *Demeter* had been chased from it at high warp several weeks earlier by five alien ships that had joined those attacking the Gateway. O'Donnell was intelligent and resourceful. This choice seemed neither to Chakotay, but there was nothing he could do about it now.

Worst of all, Admiral Janeway clearly intended her fleet to rendezvous outside of the Confederacy, possibly in very short order, and *Demeter* was now too far out of range to receive her orders. Their last known destination, Vitrum, was hours outside comm range, and depending on when they had left, they could not be expected back at Vitrum for a minimum of six to eight hours, assuming their mission went exactly as planned.

"*I have been ordered to maintain position in orbit of the First World until* Demeter *makes contact and we can confirm the safety of our overseer.* Voyager *and* Galen *are to remain here, secured by my officers, until that time,*" Mattings advised.

Chakotay didn't like the sound of that, but as long as he could get Barclay on board, *Voyager* and the *Galen* would stand ready to depart with or without the general's blessing. Once clear of the Confederacy, *Voyager* could regroup with *Demeter* at the Ark Planet. If they timed it wrong, however, *Demeter* could be trapped in Confederacy space when they returned, unless O'Donnell simply set course for the rendezvous coordinates when he discovered that the rest of the fleet was gone. Should rescue of *Demeter* be required, the situation would be more complicated, but Chakotay would cross that bridge when he had to.

"*The problem, Captain, is that I'm a ranking general, and right now forty ships normally under my command are assembling on our side of the Gateway, awaiting orders to enter and engage. That's a fight I have no intention of missing, and my rank permits me a certain amount of discretion in situations like this."*

"If you're asking for my word that *Voyager* and the *Galen* will remain here . . ." Chakotay began.

"No, Captain," Mattings said. *"I'm asking you to join us. I think* Galen *is safer here, and* Demeter *will need all the friends she can get when she returns."*

"General, you know I can't take sides in this," Chakotay said.

"I do. I don't need your tactical expertise. It occurs to me that your interests on the other side of the Gateway would be best served by your presence there. We both know how to take care of our own, don't we?"

At last, Chakotay understood. *Demeter* wasn't the only fleet vessel in harm's way right now. The general clearly suspected that *Vesta* was as well, though he wasn't free to say more on a monitored channel.

"Give me a few minutes to bring a specialist from *Galen* to *Voyager* and we'll follow you through the Gateway, General."

"Don't take too long," Mattings advised.

"We won't. *Voyager* out."

As soon as Waters had confirmed that the general's signal was gone and transporter room one advised that Barclay had arrived, Chakotay addressed himself again to Glenn. "Wait here as long as you can. *Demeter* needs to know what has developed here. But tend to your own first. Understood?"

"Yes, Captain. Galen out."

Turning to Lieutenant Kim, who sat at his left hand, Chakotay said, "Impressions?"

"What was O'Donnell thinking?" Kim demanded.

"We'll know soon enough," Chakotay replied. "But why is the general helping us?"

"He might not be," Kim said. "Or he might feel bad about Lecahn and is looking for a way to make amends. I think he still wants this alliance. Maybe he thinks this is the only way to secure it."

"Either way," Chakotay said.

Kim nodded, tapping his combadge. "This is Lieutenant Kim to all hands. Red alert."

VESTA

"Greetings, Presider Cin. I am Inspector Kashyk. My people, the Devore, control a vast imperium many light-years from here that, like your Confederacy, has brought peace and stability to all of the territory we control."

All that was missing for Admiral Janeway was a little Mahler playing in the background. Perhaps Kashyk had outgrown his infatuation with Earth's classical composers. Otherwise he seemed cheerful enough, though the steel behind his words was impossible to miss.

"Several years ago, I encountered the Federation Starship Voyager. They claimed to be explorers far from home and sought safe passage through our space. We were quite moved by their predicament and most willing to allow this, as long as their leader, then Captain Kathryn Janeway, agreed to abide by our laws while traversing our territory.

"Had I known then as much as I do now about the people of the Federation, particularly their penchant for duplicity, I would never have asked my superiors to consider their request. Like you, I fear, I was misled by the assurances they gave of their peaceful intentions, as well as their stated willingness to abide by our customs.

"I don't know if their technological advances have given them the mistaken impression that they are superior to other spacefaring people, or if they simply make a habit of placing their needs and desires above anyone else's. What I do know is that in the seven years the Voyager traveled through the First Quadrant, they left a swath of destruction and devastation in their wake. They demonstrated time and again that, while they will say otherwise, they have no respect for other cultures, their laws, or their territories."

"Inspector Kashyk," Cin said. "While I appreciate your intentions in warning me about your history with the Federation, there are certainly two sides to every story, and before I accept yours as *truth, I must hear the other. Representatives from the Federation have been our guests for several weeks now, and they have shown us nothing but respect and courtesy."*

Cin paused as Dreeg stepped forward and whispered something in her ear. Confusion furrowed her brow before she waved him away impatiently. Janeway could not understand all of what Dreeg said, but she clearly heard the word "Vitrum" fall from his lips.

"That is easy to believe, Presider, as it was my initial experience as well. Sadly, I learned much too late that every word spoken by Kathryn Janeway was a lie."

Janeway knew Kashyk too well to take offense at these words. The complicated dance they had done for several weeks included absolute deception on both their parts, personal as well as professional. Her only regret was that when the music had stopped, part of her had truly hoped she was wrong not to trust Kashyk. Apart from his surface charms, he was a fascinating, complicated man, something she had found too rarely in her life and almost never in the days she had spent leading *Voyager* home through the Delta Quadrant. Ultimately he had told her that she had made a most tempting offer. Vanity, perhaps, had allowed her to believe that he'd meant it. It stung, but only for a moment, to realize that even that had obviously been a lie. The admiral's primary focus now was to find a way to diffuse this situation.

"Our newest allies—or Kinara, as Rigger Meeml calls us—including the Turei and the Vaadwaur have similar frustrating tales of their encounters with Voyager *and Captain Janeway when she entered their territory. Those events ended in higher casualty rates than my people suffered. I grieve with them. It would be easy to lay all of this at the feet of the desperate circumstances in which* Voyager *found itself when she first arrived in our quadrant. A single ship so far from home is certainly within its rights to defend itself from aggressors. They did what they must in order to survive, Janeway will most certainly opine.*

"However, recent reports from a First Quadrant species known

as the Tarkons suggest that the Federation's pattern of reckless behavior has continued, despite the fact that they have returned to our quadrant with significant resources, more powerful ships, and are no longer under threat of becoming stranded here, given their vastly improved propulsion systems. I had hoped our experience with Captain Janeway was an isolated incident. Now I can say with absolute confidence and authority that the Federation's intentions toward any civilized society are hostile, and their actual goals will likely bear no resemblance to those they have discussed with you.

"I have also learned since how miserly Janeway can be with significant intelligence. She has likely told you much about the grand history of her Federation, but details that would be of great use to you, or us, are withheld in the interest of preserving their tactical advantages.

"Given your location," Kashyk continued, *"you may be unaware of several recent changes to the landscape of the First Quadrant. Large areas once considered too dangerous to explore are now open to any spacefaring race with the ability and the nerve to hazard them. As a result, numerous species, including our own, have discovered and begun to map the subspace corridors you call 'the streams' and utilize them to further their exploratory goals.*

"We have also received intelligence indicating that the Federation was responsible, less than a year ago, for annihilating the Borg completely. Did the admiral happen to share any of this with you or your people during your brief acquaintance?"

Janeway's stomach fell simultaneously with Presider Cin's face. There was much the presider was likely willing to take with a grain of salt, but given her people's history with the Borg, this lie of omission was going to feel like a betrayal.

"Is this true?" Cin demanded of Janeway.

"It is a long story, Presider," Janeway said, "one that I have not yet been at liberty to share with you."

Kashyk smiled. *"Not at liberty, Admiral? No citizen of this quadrant would greet such news with anything but joy and unrestrained gratitude toward those who brought it to pass. Yet you have chosen to withhold it, perhaps because your Federation has now* returned to occupy the territory once held by those you have vanquished?"

"No," Janeway said simply.

"The bottom line, Presider, is this," Kashyk said. "Every species assembled here is more than willing to accept your suggestion of peaceful negotiation for passage through the Confederacy's streams; on one condition.

"The Confederacy of the Worlds of the First Quadrant must disavow Admiral Janeway and end any discussion of alliance with the Federation she represents. You will release Admiral Janeway into our custody so that she may stand trial for her crimes against numerous First Quadrant species. Once that is done, our work, the work of truly like-minded and peace-loving people, can begin."

After a long pause, Cin again addressed herself to Janeway: "It is not my place and may not be within my power to meet the Inspector's terms, but before I even consider them, I require an explanation from you."

"As you indicated earlier, Presider, there are two sides to every story. I will gladly share mine with you. I believe our conduct while we have been guests in your territory has demonstrated our true character and purpose here. I can assure you that I have not lied to you about anything. There is intelligence I possess that it has not been appropriate for me to divulge at this stage in our relationship, but as it progressed, I would have been able to be more forthcoming. Our version of the encounters Inspector Kashyk speaks of differs greatly from his, as you might well imagine. I suggest we return to your territory to discuss these matters before you continue in your negotiations."

"Be advised, Presider," Kashyk interjected, "that no matter what she tells you or where you ultimately decide to place your faith, our terms will not change. The price for peace includes the transfer of Kathryn Janeway to our custody, and it is not negotiable."

Chapter Twenty-Six

Doctor Riley Frazier lay on the long sofa. Axum knelt at her side, one hand gently resting on her forehead, the other holding her left hand in his.

Her pain had passed relatively quickly. No doubt the Commander's most recent patient had been reduced to dust shortly after the injection of Frazier's catoms into his body. Seven assumed the Commander must be growing more desperate now. How long could he have had access to Frazier's catoms before attempting a new therapy? She had only just arrived.

Hadn't she?

"Axum," Seven said softly, "one of us must leave and attempt to speak with the Commander directly. Now that we are aware of his actions, he must know that we will not permit him to continue doing this."

Axum turned to stare up at her. His eyes held longing as well as disappointment.

"Can you teach Riley to ignore the pain as you do?" Seven asked.

"Of course."

"But what of the others?" Seven asked. "Do you know where he would be holding them?"

"The others?"

"The rest of Riley's people?"

At this, Frazier's eyes fluttered open. How long she had been listening, Seven could not tell, but she was obviously conscious.

"The captain of the *Viminal* told me they would be housed outside this facility," Frazier said.

"Their location may not matter," Seven insisted. "If the Commander has taken samples of their catoms, like ours, soon enough they will experience what we have, but they may not understand it."

Axum helped Frazier sit up. Her face was wan and her movements listless, but her eyes were clear and focused. She closed them for a moment, inhaling deeply and exhaling slowly. After a few more breaths, her eyes opened again.

"I can't sense them," she said.

"Have you been able to communicate with them using your catoms since the transformation?" Seven asked.

Frazier smiled bitterly. "We had an understanding," she said. "Once our cooperative was no more, once the Caeliar restored our individuality to us, very few were interested in willingly returning to a joined state of being. The conflict that had driven us apart in years past no longer existed. There were so few of us left, and we all shared the same purpose. It took time for us to understand at all that any connection remained between us.

"I was the first to find it. I was the first to experiment with it. I sensed you and Chakotay. And then I found you. Once you told us what our catoms were, and we had seen some of their potential, we debated quite strenuously initiating further experiments. We agreed not to. Some were frightened. Most were beginning to acclimate to their individuality and were loath to part with it."

"Whatever their choice may be, the potential still exists for the Commander's experiments to affect them. They must be warned," Seven said.

"They will know, soon enough," Axum said.

Both Seven and Frazier turned to stare at him in confusion.

Axum smiled faintly, his eyes staring at some distant point beyond them. "Shilea, Nocks, Jillant, Lezlin, Kilpora . . ."

"How can you possibly know them?" Frazier demanded.

"How can you possibly not know?" Axum asked. "Their

desires are irrelevant. Had they mastered their catoms they might well be able to shut us out. As it is, they are open vessels, vulnerable to our will as surely as the Commander's work."

Frazier rose unsteadily and reached for Seven's hand.

"We are one," Axum said. "Our catoms will not allow it to be otherwise. This is our new gestalt."

Frazier turned to Seven with fearful eyes.

Seven closed hers and, with great tenderness, reached out to the men and women she had met briefly on *Voyager* what felt like a lifetime ago. Just as Axum had said, they were present, but oblivious of the connection that now bound them to one another. It was almost as if they were sleeping and Seven dared not wake them.

Sleeping.

Unconscious.

Seven turned back to Frazier. "How long have you been here?"

Frazier's brow furrowed. "We arrived this morning. At least, I think it was . . . I have been with you all day. I haven't slept yet."

"I have been here . . . I don't know how many days," Seven said, "and *I have never slept.*"

The truth had been hers for the taking since she arrived, but only now did Seven reach for it.

"How long have you known?" she asked of Axum.

"I knew the moment I arrived here," Axum said. "This is not a Starfleet facility, Seven. This is all I remember of Mysstren before I was assimilated. My catoms created this world for me, for *us.* They work constantly, sometimes at my bidding, other times of their own accord, to make this condition as comforting as possible."

"Just as our collective nanoprobes once created Unimatrix Zero?" Seven asked.

Axum nodded. "Here, as there, every individual brings something of themselves." Axum gestured to a low table beside the sofa. To Seven's amazement, a small rucksack she had never seen before rested there. Frazier followed her gaze and inhaled in surprise.

"That's mine," she said. "Those were my tools on Arehaz. I don't remember bringing them with me."

"What did I bring, Axum?" Seven asked.

He turned his head toward the patio.

Seven stepped past him and searched the familiar landscape, the exterior of buildings she had assumed were conjoined with this space. Slowly, she lifted her eyes to the balcony she had tried to access. A light still burned.

"You said you sacrificed perfection and paradise for me twice," Seven said.

Axum bowed his head, unwilling to meet her eyes.

"I thought you meant Unimatrix Zero and the Caeliar gestalt, but you didn't, did you?"

"Unimatrix Zero was hardly paradise," Axum said. "We knew what we were. We knew what we would do once our regeneration cycles ended: that we would assimilate others, destroy their homes; that our lives as Borg were our only reality. Unimatrix Zero granted us temporary relief, nothing more."

"You believe *this* is paradise?" Seven asked.

"It could be," Axum pleaded. "At least this place will always be ours now. That makes it real."

Seven looked again at the light.

"No," she said softly. "It doesn't."

"I don't understand," Frazier interjected, placing herself between Seven and Axum.

"You will," Seven assured her. "Axum will explain." Stepping past Frazier, Seven stared directly into Axum's eyes. "You could have ended this long ago."

"I love you," Axum said.

"This is not love," Seven said. "Never again attempt to deceive me while calling it love. Love is not meant to be so used."

Seven turned abruptly and moved to the wall connected to the balcony. She needed a way up. The moment the thought entered her mind, a sturdy ladder appeared before her. Seven began to climb, throwing her legs over the side of the balcony as soon as she came level with it.

There was no door separating the exterior from the light burning within. Nothing could tempt her to turn back now. Squaring her shoulders, Seven stepped forward.

The next thing Seven knew, she was lying prone inside a confined space. Her eyes took a moment to forget the blinding brilliance she had just entered and adjust to the dimness now visible through a transparent window directly in front of her.

Seven reached up. The lid of the chamber . . . *a stasis chamber* . . . was locked. Instantly terrified, she began to pound on it from the inside.

The Commander was working late, as was his wont. Thirty-four new sets of catomic data were now his to master, and he intended to take full advantage of them. Initially, Riley's catoms had revealed an entirely new set of permeable sites. He had rushed to take advantage of them, but, obviously, in his enthusiasm, he had been too hasty. He would not make the same mistake again. He was now in the process of running several complicated cross-analyses of the entire data set with Axum's and Seven's catoms. He had expected to find immediate differences.

No useful ones were apparent thus far.

A faint alarm sounded from his console. Entering his access codes, he searched for the source and shot to his feet the moment he found it.

"*Breathe,*" a calm voice suggested from the front of Seven's mind. Her primitive brain had other ideas, but, as none of them had proved effective, she forced the panic it was generating to stillness and inhaled deeply.

Had she still been unconscious, living in Axum's shared gestalt, she could have released the pod's locks with a thought.

But this was the real world.

Finally.

A new thought occurred to her. The chamber's locking mechanism normally had a manual override. Running her fingers along both sides, she finally discovered a metallic bar. Grasping it firmly, she felt along it until she found the cross beams securing it. Just past them, embedded in the casing, was the manual release.

The chamber opened with a loud hiss. Seven clambered outside of it immediately. Once freed, she studied her surroundings. She stood in a cavernous room, larger than most cargo bays. A single door was embedded into the far, smooth wall. Between Seven and that wall were five rows of stasis chambers. Each row but the last contained ten chambers.

Just behind Seven, Axum rested peacefully in stasis. His face was far more disfigured than she had previously seen. His scalp was bald but for a few tufts of white hair.

Seven did not need to examine the other chambers to know what they contained, though she did pause over those housing the children of Arehaz, some still less than a year old. After assuring herself that the children's vital signs were normal, she started toward the door.

She still had several meters to go when it slid open and a figure shrouded in shadow entered, allowing the door to shut behind him.

"Hello, Seven of Nine," a male voice said.

Seven risked an educated guess. "Commander."

Chapter Twenty-Seven

The eyes of Isorla Cin were filled with misgivings. The eyes of her first consul, Lant Dreeg, were filled with amused resolve.

Janeway did not need to consult Lieutenant Lasren to know that this was Dreeg's work. He had presented his opening offer but, like any good gambler, hedged his bets. For all she knew, he had made contact with Meeml or Kashyk, without Cin's knowledge, well before she attempted to negotiate with him. Dreeg believed, foolishly, that Janeway, the fleet's commander, was the only thing standing between him and the technology he intended to acquire. She must be removed or repositioned to enhance his hand. Whether or not the suggestion to take her prisoner had been Kashyk's idea or Dreeg's didn't matter. Dreeg assumed those she commanded would part with anything to secure her safe return, and everything Dreeg had asked for would now be included in the price for the Confederacy's aid in freeing the admiral, should she be captured by Kashyk and his *Kinara*. No matter what happened here, Dreeg won.

The admiral could not allow that to happen.

Was it possible, however, that there was any truth in Kashyk's words? There was a first time for everything. Had Kashyk been instrumental in forming the alliance now arrayed against the Confederacy for his own ends? Had they come, as he and Meeml had said, seeking only access to the Confederacy's streams? Were they willing to negotiate a peaceful settlement in order to guarantee that access?

Had she, simply by her presence here, scuttled any hope the Confederacy might have of ending these attacks on the Gateway?

"Admiral," Captain Farkas said softly.

Janeway turned to her.

"Jepel, cut the audio on the channel," Farkas ordered.

Once the ops officer had complied, Farkas said, "I'm not sure what you're thinking, but my feeling is that we have now officially worn out our welcome here."

"I agree," Cambridge said from his position just above them.

"They say they want peace. Let them work it out," Farkas suggested. "We don't have to be a part of this."

"We are a part of this, like it or not," Janeway said.

"No, we really aren't," Cambridge countered. "The Confederacy is not bound by agreement to defend us. No alliance exists here. They have proven themselves capable of routing these attacks on numerous occasions. Whatever they decide to do here is no concern of ours or yours."

"Rigger Meeml spoke of resources they intend to access beyond Confederacy space. If that's all they want . . ." Farkas began.

"Aren't you even a little worried about what resources could be so valuable to them that they are willing to sustain such heavy losses to acquire them?" Janeway asked. "You were the one who pointed out how inconvenient it could be for our fleet to count all of these species as enemies while we are here, and how much more challenging will it be if they become allies of the Confederacy?"

"We've been through worse," Farkas said. "Let's deal with that reality if and when it becomes necessary."

"You can't give Kashyk what he wants, Admiral," Cambridge said. "You can't turn yourself over to him and hope for a fair trial."

"Is that too high a price to pay to ensure the safety of our fleet in addition to billions of Confederacy citizens?" Janeway asked.

"Yes," Farkas and Cambridge replied simultaneously.

"Have you ever known Kashyk to be on a first-name basis with the truth, Admiral?" Farkas asked.

"There will be no trial," Cambridge added. "I'd say a quick execution is the most you could hope for."

"I do not believe we are responsible for bringing this threat to the Confederacy," Janeway said. "If Meeml spoke the truth, it was coming, whether we were here or not. But we can't be responsible now for allowing this to disintegrate into all-out war if we can stop it."

Cambridge shook his head. "It's not our war, Admiral."

"I don't think the Devore, the Turei, or the Vaadwaur are going to appreciate the distinction," Janeway said. "And if we leave now without answering the presider's questions, she will be predisposed to believe Kashyk's version of events."

"Run and we look guilty?" Farkas asked.

"I can live with that," Cambridge said.

"Your concerns are noted," Janeway said, "and appreciated," she added more gently. "Restore the open channel to the presider only."

Farkas nodded to ops as Janeway rose from her chair and approached the main viewscreen. "Presider Cin," she said.

"Your translation system is malfunctioning, Admiral," Cin said. *"We have been forced to rely on Mister Grish for the last few minutes."*

"I apologize, Presider," Janeway said. "I needed a moment to confer with my crew. My offer still stands. Let us both retreat to your territory and I will provide you with the entire story of the Federation's interactions with the species assembled here."

"First, I must know," Cin said. *"Did the Federation destroy the Borg?"*

"Not exactly," Janeway said. "The Borg invaded the Federation. Billions died during their attacks."

"Then you have come seeking reparations for what they took from you?"

"There are no reparations to be had, Presider," Janeway said. "We have come to explore former Borg space, not to annex it. We did not destroy them. Even with our advanced technology, we couldn't. The species that unknowingly gave rise to the Borg thousands of years ago returned. The Borg were transformed, accepted back into what they called their gestalt, and have departed our galaxy for parts unknown. Our mandate in returning here is to confirm this data. Thus far, it appears to be true."

"Why didn't you tell us?" Cin demanded.

"The fate of the Borg had nothing to do with our discussions, Presider," Janeway insisted. "Given the comparative states of our technological advancement, sharing that intelligence might have been seen by you as an attempt to assert superiority over you. I would not have you accept us as an ally under threat of force. Had you seen us as the conqueror of your ancient enemy, would you not have feared meeting the same fate were you disinclined to pursue our negotiations?"

"We have been completely honest and forthcoming with you and your people since you arrived, Admiral," Cin said.

Janeway shook her head. "You, perhaps, but your first consul?" she asked. "These are complicated situations, Presider. Every choice may be seen in hindsight as a misstep. But you must believe that, from day one, I have done everything in my power to protect the possibility of an alliance. I was sincere in my hopes and willing to set aside many significant cultural differences in the name of peaceful coexistence and mutual support. It was your first consul who presented terms he knew I would be unable to accept. But I was even willing to overlook his impatience to assist you in managing this crisis."

"Are you still willing to do so?" Cin asked.

"How?"

"I want to believe you, Admiral. I want to believe that Inspector Kashyk is determined to divide us because he understands, as I do, how powerful our alliance would be."

"That is certainly a possibility," Janeway agreed.

"A protector is being dispatched now to cloak your vessel. Move your ship to the coordinates we provide and wait there," Cin said. *"Our forces will eliminate the current threat. When that is done, you and I will have much to discuss."*

"Very well," Janeway said. To Farkas, she added, "Take us to red alert."

"Aye, Admiral," Farkas said.

Inspector Kashyk again appeared on the viewscreen. *"Have you reached a decision, Presider Cin?"* he asked.

"*I have, Inspector,*" Cin replied. "*Although your claims are troubling, I cannot allow you to muddy the issue by making any agreement between us contingent upon your past disagreements with the Federation. My offer still stands to select an appropriate neutral location where we may continue our discussions. But I will not purchase my own safety at the cost of another's freedom.*"

"*You might have chosen peace, Presider. Instead you have chosen your own destruction for a most unworthy ally.*"

"*So be it,*" Cin said.

The Devore vessel immediately closed the channel. Once it had, Cin said, "*Our reinforcements will arrive momentarily. This won't take long, Admiral.*"

Admiral Janeway started to wish her luck when a burst of static spiked over the comm channel.

"What's that?" Janeway asked.

"Out protector has arrived," Farkas replied. "We are now invisible to the *Kinara*, but our comm system will remain inoperable until we are released."

"Are we on course for the coordinates Cin provided?"

"Yes."

"Can we break free of this protector should the need arise?"

"Yes, Admiral," Farkas assured her. "But until we do, we can't use our warp or slipstream drive."

Janeway nodded as she resumed her seat beside Farkas.

FIFTH SHUDKA

Before the *Manticle* had fired the first shot, the *Shudka*'s viewer shifted to reveal a ring of six ships now positioned around the entrance to the Gateway. A subtle lurch beneath her feet alerted the presider to her flagship's motion. A faint rattle suggested her ship had taken fire, but it sustained no serious damage. Its speed seemed to increase by the second.

"Where are we going?" Cin asked.

"We will observe our enemy's destruction from a safe distance, Presider. We dare not risk your safety, though your courage in confronting these aliens was most impressive," Dreeg replied. "A protector has been summoned to reinforce our shields and cloak us."

"You assured me that the *Shudka* could destroy these vessels alone," Cin retorted.

"It can, Presider. But in this instance, we will leave that task to . . . ah, there they are now."

Cin's heart stilled in her chest at the sight of a steady stream of CIF battleships emerging from the Gateway. She lost count at twelve. She was distracted by their maneuvers as they were immediately fired upon as they exited the Gateway. Each moved clear, targeted one of the enemy vessels, and engaged them.

Still, more came.

Behind her, from a seemingly great distance, the voice of the *Shudka*'s acting general could be heard coordinating his ship's maneuvers. The Skeen vessel that was commanded by Rigger Meeml was pursuing them blindly.

Her attention was focused on her other ships, those that had come to defend her. Angry flares of energy burst from the alien ships, and each one that met the hull of a CIF vessel seemed to simultaneously strike Cin. Her tendrils stiffened behind her and remained taut, tasting the tension around her. The officers appeared confident, but their fear rolled through her in disquieting waves.

"What's he doing here?" Dreeg asked softly.

"Who?" Cin asked.

"The *Twelfth Lamont* was ordered to remain in orbit of the First World to secure the remaining Federation ships," Dreeg replied. "It appears Ranking General Mattings took issue with those orders."

The presider would have been hard pressed to pick out the *Lamont* from the more than fifty ships now maneuvering around one another at close quarters. Forty of them were hers. The aliens had already lost three. A chill crept up Cin's tendrils.

"Why would you have ordered the Federation ships secured?" she demanded of Dreeg. "You had no idea until we arrived here that there was any cause to doubt our Federation friends."

"The *Jroone*'s report troubled me deeply."

"Bralt is not their prisoner. Irste confirmed that, didn't he?"

"He was clearly misled, Presider. Forgive me, but I engage in battles daily on your behalf. Until the truth is known, nothing is beyond the realm of possibility, and it pays to be prepared for the worst to come to pass."

"Thus far, Admiral Janeway has kept her word to us."

"She obviously did not extend the same courtesy to the Devore," Dreeg noted.

"We will have the truth of that from her lips soon enough," Cin said. "Until then, no harm is to come to any Federation vessel currently located in Confederacy space."

"Our space begins at the entrance to the Gateway, Presider."

"For the purposes of this engagement, I am claiming this area of engagement for the Confederacy," Cin said sternly. "No harm is to come to the *Vesta* here either."

"We must see to our own first, Presider."

Cin looked again at the battle raging before her. Three more alien ships were gone. "It won't matter," she said, relieved. "They have already lost almost half of their complement. This battle is all but over."

"May the Source will it," Dreeg said.

VESTA

Captain Regina Farkas watched the unfolding slaughter with a heavy heart. She had little sympathy for those who had challenged the Confederacy, or the CIF, for that matter. But the destruction of any starship was a shocking thing to witness. Resilient and ferocious as they might appear, she was keenly conscious of the fragile life-forms protected by the hulls and armaments. Those weren't just ships exploding before her eyes. They were sentient beings, each of whom had families, friends, hopes, dreams, *lives*, until they met with unassailable force and ceased to exist in a brilliant flash of light.

"It appears the inspector overestimated his *Kinara*'s abilities," Cambridge said softly over her shoulder.

Why Farkas doubted this, she couldn't say. She wasn't witnessing a battle so much as a complete rout. Outgunned more than three to one, it seemed insane for the nine vessels remaining, including the *Manticle* and the *Lightcarrier,* to continue to hold their ground. Yet they fought on, aware, surely, but apparently insensate of the futility of their efforts.

"Captain Farkas, *Voyager* has just emerged from the Gateway," Jepel reported.

"Onscreen," Farkas ordered.

As soon as she emerged, *Voyager* executed a sharp dive that took her clear of an incoming Turei vessel. Another CIF vessel quickly made a hole for her and she began to maneuver at full impulse, obviously attempting to move away from the battlefield without engaging the enemies of the Confederacy.

Janeway looked to Farkas. "We can't contact them?"

"Not unless you want to dispatch our protector and join that battle."

The *Vesta* suddenly lurched hard to port.

"Ensign Hoch?" Farkas demanded of her flight controller.

"Sensors have just picked up an incoming vessel," Hoch replied.

"Time to intercept?"

"None," Hoch replied, as one of the largest vessels Farkas had ever seen came into view from beneath the *Vesta*, on course directly toward the battle.

A huge torpedo-shaped body containing as many as twenty levels was surrounded like a shawl by an additional construct that began several hundred meters from the prow, flared out, and terminated in an incredibly complicated propulsion array. The hull was made of a greenish-blue metal, softer in appearance and more fluid than many starships.

The admiral came to her feet the moment the vessel appeared on the viewscreen.

"Where did she come from?" Farkas demanded.

"The vessel emerged from a previously undetected transwarp conduit bearing 33 mark 190, Captain," Kar advised from tactical. "Our database cannot confirm a precise match, but several attributes register as—"

"The Voth," Janeway finished for her.

"Is that a city-ship?" Farkas asked.

"No, it's much too small," Janeway replied. "But its configuration is similar."

"It's three times the size of the *Vesta*," Kar noted, "and will be within range of *Voyager* in two minutes. The remaining CIF forces are adjusting formation to attack. Half their fleet is now moving to engage them."

"*Voyager* is adjusting course as well, Captain," Roach reported.

"She's trying to give them a wide berth," Farkas said.

Suddenly, *Voyager* vanished before Farkas's eyes.

VOYAGER

"The battle has already begun, Captain Chakotay."

Chakotay nodded grimly at General Mattings. Both *Voyager* and the *Twelfth Lamont* were inside the subspace corridor known as the Gateway and would emerge into a maelstrom in less than two minutes.

"I trust these hostiles will enjoy the same fate as their unfortunate predecessors?" Chakotay asked.

"If I have anything to say about it," Mattings said, his teeth protruding in the Leodt version of a smirk. *"I'll know more once we reach the other side. Preliminary reports indicate fifteen vessels against my forty. Set course away from the battle. Your* Vesta *should be doing the same. Find her and keep yourselves safe. I'll be in touch. Lamont out."*

"Assuming the *Vesta* is not engaged, follow the general's orders," Chakotay said. To his flight controller, he added, "Gwyn, choose your course wisely. I don't want to get dragged into this."

"Aye, Captain," Gwyn said.

"Waters," Kim advised, "your sensors are about to be overloaded.

Prioritize reception of any Federation signals. We need to find the *Vesta* quickly, and that's going to be hard to do with fifty-five other ships out there and all hell breaking loose."

"Aubrey," Chakotay ordered his current tactical officer, "if we have no choice but to open fire to clear a path, I'll understand, but do not return fire unless I give you leave."

"Aye, Captain," the young lieutenant replied.

As battles went, this one should be easy. It wasn't *Voyager*'s fight. All she had to do was stay in one piece until the massively outnumbered alien hostiles learned the hard way why one did not pick fights with the CIF. But the general's actions gave him pause. What did he know right now that Chakotay didn't? Why did he assume that the *Vesta* was in danger?

"We're about to clear the Gateway, sir," Waters reported.

"Just stay focused on your respective responsibilities. This is going to be over before we know it," Chakotay said.

Seconds later, the swirling orange tunnel that had carried them ten thousand light-years from the First World dispersed, and the main viewscreen displayed absolute chaos. Gwyn adjusted course with practiced ease, avoiding an incoming CIF vessel that was attacking a small Turei ship. Weapons fire skimmed their shields, a soft roar of thunder.

"No damage to shields," Waters reported.

"Where's the *Vesta*?" Chakotay asked.

Waters remained silent.

Gwyn executed a sharp dive, rolling the ship between three other CIF vessels forming up for an attack run. Chakotay held fast to his armrests as his stomach momentarily revolted. The good news was that they were moving steadily away from the area of heaviest engagement.

"Aubrey, report," Chakotay ordered.

"Five hostile vessels have been destroyed. Make that six, sir," he added. "Three CIF ships have broken off, damaged but still intact. The others are continuing their attacks."

"The aliens have lost one third of their force in a matter of minutes," Kim said softly. "They have to retreat soon."

"Any sign of the *Vesta* yet?" Chakotay asked again.

"None, sir," Waters reported. "They're not engaged, but they're nowhere nearby either."

Chakotay turned to Kim. "Where are they?" he asked.

"Commander Glenn indicated that if things did not go well, the admiral intended to take the *Vesta* to our prearranged rendezvous coordinates. From the looks of it, things did not go well. Maybe they're already gone."

"Any trace of gravimetric distortions suggesting the activation of their slipstream drive?" Chakotay asked.

"None, sir," Waters replied. "But this area is lousy with highly charged particles right now that could be masking the distortions."

Chakotay's jaw clenched.

"Captain, we have incoming," Aubrey advised.

Turning his attention back to the main viewscreen, Chakotay watched as a familiar shape shot from a subspace aperture. Altering course at once, the vessel moved directly into *Voyager*'s path.

"Is that . . . ?" Kim began.

"The Voth," Chakotay confirmed.

"What are they doing here?" Kim asked.

"Doesn't matter," Chakotay said. "Helm, evasive maneuvers."

"Aye, sir," Gwyn said.

"Sir, the *Lamont* has transmitted a message: Per General Mattings, '*Help is on the way.*'"

"Confirmed," Aubrey reported. "CIF vessels altering course to engage the Voth ship. A protector . . ." he began.

But he didn't need to finish that sentence. A gentle hum settled over the bridge, alerting Chakotay to the arrival of a protector, likely intended to fortify his ship's defenses.

"Mattings is serious about keeping us safe," Kim noted.

"Do we still have helm control?" Chakotay asked.

"Yes, sir," Gwyn reported. "Helm responding."

The Voth ship continued on its previous course, ignoring *Voyager*.

"Maintain course and speed, but show me the battle," Chakotay ordered.

"Why are the Voth just ignoring us?" Kim asked.

"Would you prefer they didn't?" Chakotay asked.

"Not at all," Kim said. "I just . . ."

"The harmonics of this protector are unique, sir," Waters reported. "More like the old sentries."

"They've cloaked us," Kim realized.

"I'm less worried about us right now," Chakotay said. "Look."

The Voth ship had opened fire. In addition to its powerful weapons, which seemed capable of disabling some of the smaller CIF vessels' shields with a single shot, dozens of recessed phaser cannons had emerged all over the ship's massive hull and were targeting multiple CIF vessels simultaneously. As Chakotay watched, what had been forty ships became thirty-two in less than two minutes.

"Captain," Gwyn said, "I've lost the helm."

"The protector?" Chakotay asked.

"We're slowing," Gwyn advised. "Coming to all stop."

Why? Chakotay wondered.

His question was answered a few moments later when Waters said, "Sir, the *Vesta* is hailing us."

Chakotay had rarely been so relieved to give an order. "Onscreen," he said.

VESTA

Admiral Janeway's relief at seeing Captain Chakotay's face was mitigated by the constant reports now streaming in indicating that the tide of battle had definitively turned.

"Good to see you, Vesta,*"* Chakotay said. *"Why are our comm systems suddenly working?"*

"The two protectors surrounding us have merged, making our contact possible," Farkas said. "It's a standard tactic employed by the CIF during recon missions."

"Okay," Chakotay said, nodding. *"Did you have any idea the Voth were coming?"* he asked.

"No," Janeway replied. "We assumed until now that their attacks on our subspace relays were an isolated act of aggression."

"Well, unlikely alliances appear to be all the rage in the Delta Quadrant these days, don't they?" Chakotay asked.

"There's more to it than that," Janeway said. "Presider Cin spoke with the forces here. They call themselves *Kinara*, a Skeen word for 'allies.' They indicated that they were willing to forgo further hostilities if an agreement could be reached allowing them passage through Confederacy space utilizing some of their streams. Apparently there are resources beyond the Confederacy that these aliens have some interest in."

"What resources?" Chakotay asked.

"They didn't say," Janeway replied.

"Four additional CIF vessels have been destroyed, Captain," Roach reported.

"How many do they have left now?" Farkas asked.

"Nineteen," Roach replied, "against the *Kinara's* ten."

"I think we have to count that Voth ship as at least three or four," Farkas suggested.

"Make that twenty CIF vessels, Captain," Roach corrected himself. "The *Fifth Shudka* has shed its protector and is moving to engage."

"The presider is on that ship," Janeway said softly, struck by both the courage and the likely futility of the choice Cin had just made.

"If the CIF falls here, what happens?" Chakotay asked.

"Presumably they have more ships waiting on the other side of the Gateway, should the *Kinara* breach it," Janeway said.

"I don't think so, Admiral," Farkas said. "Ten of the CIF vessels have broken off and are now headed toward the Gateway."

"Retreating?" Janeway asked. "Are they moving to cover the *Shudka*?"

"There's a back door to the Confederacy not far from here," Farkas said. "It's a much longer trip to the First World. That's how the

Hadden and the *Vesta* were able to recon the area without using the Gateway. If they were trying to protect the *Shudka,* they'd just send her home that way. I think they need the *Shudka*'s firepower."

"Why?"

"General Deonil said that should it appear enemy forces were about to breach the Gateway, the CIF would destroy it."

"If they do that, every CIF ship out here will be lost," Janeway said.

"I would think so," Farkas said. "But the CIF wouldn't want to run the risk of leading these guys into their territory through the other nearest streams, which are a few light-years away. The *Kinara* don't seem to know about them yet."

"*Admiral?*" Chakotay asked, clearly sensing her thoughts.

"Presider Cin came out here at my suggestion," she said simply. "She might have been able to reach a bloodless settlement had it not been for our presence here."

"*What does that mean?*" Chakotay asked.

"Two additional CIF ships destroyed," Roach reported. "The *Kinara* are adjusting their formations to protect the Gateway. The *Shudka* has taken fire from the Voth ship."

"Damage?" Janeway asked.

"Minimal, so far," Roach replied.

"It means we're going to help them," Janeway finally said. "Captains, vent tetryon plasma and disperse our protectors. Concentrate your attacks on the Voth ship. Every technology at our disposal is fair game. If we live through this, there will be no more secrets between us and the Confederacy."

"Aye, Admiral," Farkas said.

"*Admiral,*" Chakotay said, "*the* Galen *has your rendezvous coordinates and will be able to utilize them. But* Demeter *has not returned from Vitrum. If* Voyager *and the* Vesta *are lost, when* Demeter *does return . . .*"

"In that instance, Commander O'Donnell already has standing orders."

Chakotay nodded, then said, "*One more thing: I'm short a CMO right now.*"

"What happened to the Doctor?" Janeway asked.

"I don't know. Reg is working on it as we speak."

Janeway turned to Farkas. "Can you spare . . ." she began.

"Farkas to sickbay. El'nor?"

"Yes, Captain?" Doctor Sal replied.

"Grab a couple of medics and get yourselves to the nearest transporter room. *Voyager's* sickbay is shorthanded and we're about to join the battle."

"Damn it, Regina," Sal said.

"I'll note your protest in my logs, El'nor. Now, go."

Farkas closed the channel before Sal could *protest* more colorfully.

VOYAGER

As soon as Chakotay had confirmed the arrival of his temporary medical staff and the restoration of *Voyager's* shields, he asked, "Ensign Gwyn, has helm control been restored?"

"Yes, Captain."

"Set course, full impulse for the Voth ship. Aubrey, let's see if we can draw a little fire and take some of the heat off of the CIF."

"Understood, sir," Aubrey said.

"Harry?" Chakotay prompted.

"Waters, reroute additional power to the shield emitters, sufficient to support multiphasic alignment. Aubrey, as soon as you can, shift to multiphasic shields. The last time we met the Voth, their phasers and torpedoes weren't that much stronger than ours, but they were able to transport us directly inside their vessel."

"The modulated shield frequencies should disperse any transporter beam," Aubrey said.

"That's the theory," Kim said.

"Any other suggestions, sir?" Aubrey asked.

"Keep the torpedoes tightly focused," Kim said. "It will probably take several shots just to weaken their shields."

The *Vesta* came within range before *Voyager* and opened fire on the Voth ship's port flank. Six cannons immediately realigned to return fire but only grazed *Vesta*'s shields as she skimmed closer to the vessel on an unlikely course to avoid them.

Pull up, Chakotay thought. *Vesta*'s helmsman did so, just in the nick of time to avoid impact.

Gwyn followed the same attack course and brought them in range to follow Aubrey's initial phaser fire with the release of two torpedoes. Only one breached the shields, but its impact was followed by a burst of greenish fire from the Voth ship's hull. Not to be outdone, Gwyn took *Voyager* up in a roll, avoiding the responding cannon fire by a hair.

"Well done," Chakotay said. "More of the same, please."

VESTA

While maneuvering to reengage the Voth ship, Lieutenant Kar managed to fire a sustained phaser burst at one of the remaining Vaadwaur vessels that sheared off a sizable chunk of its aft propulsion array, sending it into a spiral. A CIF vessel moved in to finish the job as Kar selected her next target on the Voth ship.

A direct hit, aft, jostled everyone on the bridge, but Jepel quickly reported only slight damage to their shields.

"Who was that?" Farkas asked.

"The *Manticle,*" Jepel replied.

"Figures," Farkas said. "Kar, I'd like to see a few less cannons firing at us after this next pass."

"As would I, Captain," Kar agreed.

Four quick bursts of phaser fire succeeded in taking out only one of the Voth's cannons, but it was a start.

"Jepel, how are the other CIF ships faring?"

"They've destroyed one more Karlon ship, and the Skeen vessel has taken significant damage, but it's still engaged."

"And the Gateway?" Farkas asked.

"The CIF is not making any visible progress against that blockade."

A loud detonation from the *Vesta*'s belly jolted the captain upward. "Report," Farkas ordered.

"Direct hit," Kar said through gritted teeth.

"Shields holding at eighty-nine percent," Jepel added.

Farkas turned to the admiral. "Do you want to try to end this with one shot?" she asked.

"With what?" Janeway asked.

"A transphasic torpedo."

"Last I heard those were still on the drawing board," Janeway said.

"They were put on the fast track shortly after you died. Their use was restricted during the Borg Invasion to the *Enterprise*, much to the frustration of the rest of us," she added. "But I was able to convince Montgomery to give us a few in the unlikely event the Caeliar didn't do as thorough a job as we'd hoped."

"What are the risks?" Janeway asked.

"They were specifically designed to penetrate the Borg's shields. They're untried against the Voth. And it's not something I'd ever like to see used against us."

Janeway turned back to the main viewscreen. The remaining CIF forces had clearly been rejuvenated by the entrance of the Federation ships onto the battlefield. But many had sustained heavy damage. *Voyager* and the *Vesta* were distracting the Voth ship for the moment but not exactly making significant headway.

Suddenly, a volley of torpedoes flew from a forward bay aboard the Voth ship, headed directly for *Voyager*. The flight controller immediately compensated, but the torpedoes adjusted course with her and, seconds later, directly impacted the deflector array.

"Damage report," Janeway ordered.

"*Voyager*'s shields are down, Admiral," Jepel said. "She's lost her main deflector."

"Another direct hit will finish her, and she can't go to warp now, much less slipstream," Janeway said.

"Captain," Jepel called from ops. "The *Shudka* is sending out a message to all ships to cease hostilities. They wish to discuss terms."

Janeway looked back at Farkas. "Just say the word, Admiral," the captain said.

Janeway paused.

"Stand down," she finally ordered. "Order *Voyager* to do the same."

"Admiral," Cambridge piped up from behind her, "the *Kinara* only made one nonnegotiable demand for peace."

"I know, Counselor," Janeway said.

"We just came to the Confederacy's aid," the counselor continued, "and they're about to betray you."

"It looks that way," Janeway agreed.

"Chakotay would not hesitate to purchase your safety with his own," Cambridge said.

"I know that too," Janeway said. "Open a channel to the *Shudka*," she ordered.

As she had expected, the face of First Consul Dreeg appeared before her. Presider Cin was nowhere to be seen. Dreeg said, "*Admiral Janeway, while it grieves me to ask, I must request that you agree to Inspector Kashyk's demands. You know, I presume, that I could force you to do so.*"

"Let him try," Farkas suggested under her breath.

"That won't be necessary, First Consul," Janeway said. "Where is Presider Cin?" she asked.

"She was fatigued, Admiral," Dreeg said. "I thought it best she retire to her quarters for some much-needed rest."

Although Janeway could not confirm whether or not Cin had approved Dreeg's choice, the result would be the same. "I will surrender myself to the *Manticle*, First Consul, but only under my own nonnegotiable terms."

"*May I bring the inspector into our conversation?*"

"Please do," Janeway said.

Chapter Twenty-Eight

"I'm sorry, she what?" Chakotay asked in disbelief.

The bridge was not in what Chakotay had come to accept as its customary state of disarray following battle, although the destruction of *Voyager*'s deflector had caused systemwide overloads. Only the engineering and sensor panels had caught fire, and a few overhead plates had fallen, exposing conduits belching sparks and fumes. Emergency teams led by Torres had already begun repairs. Weapons were still operational, but Lieutenant Conlon had warned him that shields would not be restored for several hours.

It was disquieting to hold station virtually defenseless, surrounded by so many enemy ships, but ever since the *Shudka* had called for a cease-fire, both sides seemed to be honoring it.

Controlled chaos ran rampant all around him, but as soon as Kim had presented the first report from the *Vesta*, Chakotay's focus had narrowed to the face of his acting first officer.

"Admiral Janeway is preparing to turn herself over to the alien fleet," Kim repeated.

This made absolutely no sense.

And it must not, under any circumstances, happen.

"The bridge is yours, Lieutenant Kim," Chakotay said, stepping briskly over the debris that littered the path between his chair and his ready room.

As soon as he'd reached his desk, he opened a channel to the *Vesta*. Captain Farkas's tense face greeted him.

"I need to speak to Kath . . . to Admiral Janeway immediately," Chakotay said.

"She's a little busy at the moment, preparing for her departure," Farkas said. *"You're on my main viewscreen, and all of our communications are being monitored, Captain."*

"Can you tell me why this is happening?" Chakotay asked.

"Counselor Cambridge will be returning to Voyager, *as soon as the admiral is safely on her way, with a full report."*

Dozens of possibilities occurred simultaneously to Chakotay. They included transporting to the *Vesta* himself at once; immediately opening fire on every ship now in range, both CIF and otherwise affiliated; and begging Farkas to patch his comm channel through to wherever Kathryn currently was.

Farkas's face told him that none of these measures would prove fruitful or helpful.

Finally, Chakotay settled for, "Thank you, Captain."

A half-meter-sized chunk of overhead had fallen from its place and now rested on the floor near the door to his ready room. Chakotay picked it up and threw it with all his might behind his desk. It impacted a small sculpture that had belonged to Captain Eden of a cat, balancing on its forepaws atop a metal ball, toppling it from the credenza.

Momentarily relieved of a little adrenaline, but by no means calmed, Chakotay returned to his bridge.

VESTA

"My place is by your side, Admiral," Lieutenant Decan said.

The admiral was rifling through the drawers of her desk, searching for something she obviously considered significant. She had agreed to transport, via shuttle, to the *Manticle* and needed to be under way in the next eight minutes for the ceasefire to continue to be honored.

"I understand why you feel that way," she said as she continued her search. "But you can't come with me, Decan. You're a telepath, and the Devore cannot abide telepaths. Kashyk would take it as an insult, and while that wouldn't trouble me on a personal level, it's the wrong way to begin this process."

"I don't believe the inspector's personal prejudices should be relevant here," Decan argued.

"Lieutenants Psilakis and Cheng will see to my safety in the short run."

Decan paused, unsure. It was an incredibly unusual sensation for the Vulcan. Finally he said, "Admiral, I did not wish to accompany you, only to assure myself personally of your well-being. I sensed something during Inspector Kashyk's initial communications. I believe I can best confirm it in his physical presence."

"Here it is," Janeway said, finally withdrawing a padd from a lower drawer and immediately handing it to Decan. "This needs to go to Reg Barclay as soon as possible. He'll know what it is. Tell him I have ordered him to review it." This task done, she moved toward her bedroom, removing her uniform jacket in the process. Clearly she intended to don a new one prior to transporting to her new home for the foreseeable future.

"What did you sense?" she asked before disappearing from Decan's sight.

Her absence made it easier for him to explain.

"The distance between our ships made it difficult to establish a solid telepathic connection, but I was able to receive a number of impressions while the inspector was speaking," Decan began.

The admiral's head popped around the side of the doorway separating the main area from her bedroom. "How was that possible?"

"I'm an extremely adept telepath, even by Vulcan standards," Decan said.

Janeway stared past him, as if attempting to bring a far-distant object into focus.

"I know that," Janeway said. "No one has ever been able to guess my needs as well as you have. It was downright eerie to have you at hand almost as soon as I'd called you, sometimes before, until I figured out how you were doing it. But the Devore's fear of telepaths provoked them to institute special training regimens for all of their officers. They are supposed to be able to deflect any attempt at telepathic intrusion into their minds."

"It is possible that the inspector has not applied himself with sufficient diligence to perfecting that skill," Decan said, "but that would not explain what I sensed."

Janeway stepped into the doorway, her new uniform jacket hanging from her fingertips.

"What?" she asked again.

"The inspector is an incredibly angry person. The rage within him goes beyond anything you might have done to him years ago. The source of it is deep and very old. It is almost as if he has many lifetimes of injustices to redress."

"He's not that old," Janeway said.

"He is also at war with himself."

"How so?" Janeway asked.

"I believe he is acting on someone else's orders in suggesting this trial. He would just as soon kill you now. There is, however, a small part of him that is resisting. There is a small part of him that wants to see you safe."

"I have a hard time believing that to be true," Janeway said.

"I can't explain it better," Decan said. "I need to get closer to him to confirm what I sensed. I don't believe he is simply fighting a battle within himself over tactics. There are almost two distinct minds at work, and there is no accord between them."

Janeway's gaze again shifted past Decan. She moved like a sleepwalker toward the sofa that ran beneath the port in her office and sat down as if in shock.

"We must get you to your shuttle, Admiral," Decan said. "Allow me to accompany you during transit."

A faint smile crossed Janeway's lips. She shook her head slowly as if in disbelief.

When she rose to her feet, she squared her shoulders and said, "That won't be necessary. Ask Lieutenant Lasren to report to the shuttlebay with us. He can pilot the shuttle and return it, and he will also be able to confirm your suspicions, now that I know exactly what to tell him to look for."

As she threaded her arms through the sleeves of her jacket, she added, "I also need to speak to Counselor Cambridge before he returns to *Voyager.*"

VOYAGER

Every bridge officer and technician paused in their work when Waters reported that the admiral's shuttle had departed the *Vesta.* Silence reigned as the small ship maneuvered its way through the wreckage, debris, and remaining ships that had been battling one another to the death half an hour earlier.

Chakotay watched its progress with equal amounts of fear and anger. Self-sacrifice was hard-wired into Kathryn Janeway. It was her greatest strength and most inconvenient weakness. It was also one they shared. But this choice went beyond anything he considered rational, and in the absence of fuller understanding, it infuriated him. He wanted to trust her instincts. He wanted to believe that whatever had led her to step into that shuttle was warranted.

But he couldn't.

"Captain Chakotay, General Mattings is hailing us," Waters reported.

Chakotay didn't want to put it on the main viewscreen. He watched until the shuttle had reached the *Manticle* before saying, "I'll take it in my ready room."

As sitting would have necessitated clearing the mess he'd created a few minutes earlier, Chakotay turned his screen toward the desk's front and remained standing as he opened the channel to the *Twelfth Lamont.*

The bridge of the *Lamont* had seen better days. The lighting was malfunctioning, but, even in the faint flickers, Chakotay could see a wide gash running down the side of the general's face, caked with a sticky white fluid.

"*Captain.*"

"General."

"*You came to our aid. You didn't have to. You fought with us.*"

Your choice to risk death saved the lives of those I command. I know you don't want my friendship right now, but you have it nonetheless."

"*Voyager* entered the battle because our commanding officer, Admiral Kathryn Janeway, ordered us to do so. It was a call made in the heat of battle and in ignorance of all I have learned about the Confederacy in the last few days."

"She has our gratitude as well."

"Turning her over to your enemies to secure your own safety is a funny way of expressing that gratitude, General."

"As you can see, Captain, things are a mess over here right now. But I want you to know that I am aware of all that transpired here, and as soon as I am able, I intend to brief you fully. Your people on Voyager, Vesta, Galen, *and* Demeter *have earned more than my respect. They have earned my trust and my protection. I intend to see that those protecting the Confederacy's interests remember that. I have your back, Captain. No matter what the diplomats decide, I consider your people my ally, and for me, that is a sacred trust. You don't have to believe me. But in the days to come, you will see just how much those words mean to me. Lamont out."*

The hiss of the door opening behind him broke the silence that followed the end of the general's transmission.

"Captain?" Counselor Cambridge's voice asked.

"Counselor," Chakotay said, turning. "Please tell me the admiral had a very good reason for doing what she just did."

"I argued against it until the last possible moment," Cambridge said. "Even now I'm not convinced it was the best choice. But . . ."

"But?"

"Based on intelligence the admiral received just before she departed, and which she intends to confirm in the next few minutes, I think at the very least she might just have saved all of us from dying ignorant of the magnitude of our miscalculations."

"What the hell does that mean?" Chakotay demanded.

MANTICLE

Lieutenant Lasren remained at the shuttle's helm as the admiral and her security detachment disembarked. His ability to confirm the admiral's suspicions depended on the presence of Inspector Kashyk in the shuttlebay.

Lasren had sensed nothing unusual while watching events unfold from the *Vesta*'s bridge. He had not attempted to read the feelings of those the admiral spoke with before or during the battle. He did not believe it possible for him to collect meaningful impressions from such a distance. Other Betazoids who practiced their skills more regularly might have managed it, but Kenth's abilities were not so finely honed.

Almost as soon as the shuttle's hatch had opened, however, a flood of confusing sensations washed over him. Through the shuttle's forward port he could see the small group arrayed to greet the admiral. They included Inspector Kashyk; a Saurian female of advanced age wearing a long, finely embroidered robe and a heavy gold chain of large, diamond-shaped links; a Turei officer; and a Vaadwaur officer—the latter two in uniform. Twelve other security personnel of varying species stood in formation near the doors of the shuttlebay, all armed with large rifles.

From this vantage point, it was difficult for Lasren to isolate the sensations he was seeking. He had been prepared to target the inspector at the admiral's request. Decan had suggested the presence of two distinct minds at work. Although only four officers stood near the admiral, at this distance he sensed seven discreet entities—*not* including the admiral or her two security officers.

Lasren stole softly to the shuttle hatch, remaining hidden from view, and reached out with his mind, beginning with the Turei and Vaadwaur officers.

Four, he realized, two in each.

The Saurian female whom he believed to be Voth was more of a mystery. There was a single consciousness present within her, but she was somehow intangible. Had he not been able to see her with his own eyes, or sense the mind at work within her empathically, he would not have known she was there.

Lasren hurriedly turned his attention completely on the inspector just as the admiral reached for him. Although she had advised him of her intention to attempt to confirm Decan's impressions personally, in the event Kenth was unable to do so, it was still shocking to witness. It clearly stunned everyone else in the room momentarily.

In full view of all assembled, and after saying only a few words of greeting, Admiral Janeway wrapped her arms around Inspector Kashyk's neck and kissed him firmly on the mouth.

For a moment, the inspector seemed to appreciate the gesture. As his lips met hers, the weaker of the two minds within him surged in intensity. Rage quickly won out, however, banishing all other emotions, as the inspector grabbed Janeway firmly by her upper arms and pushed her back, roughly.

Kashyk then raised a hand over his shoulder, clearly ready to strike the admiral with the back of his hand for her insolence. In less than a second, the phasers carried by Psilakis and Lieutenant Cheng were lifted and aimed directly at the inspector's midsection. When the second had fully elapsed, a dozen rifles had been lifted by the hands of the *Kinara* security detachment and aimed at the admiral and her officers.

"Stand down," the Saurian female ordered in a voice that brooked no argument.

Lasren did not know what intelligence Admiral Janeway might have gained from that kiss, but he could now confirm that what Decan had said was true.

The admiral glanced back toward the open hatch of the shuttle. Lasren stepped into full view and stood at rest, awaiting her orders. Her eyes met his. Ever so slightly, he nodded.

Admiral Janeway nodded in return and said, "Return to *Voyager* at once, Lieutenant. Advise Captain Chakotay to await further instructions. Tell Lieutenant Barclay that I kept my promise."

"Aye, Admiral," Lasren said. Returning to the shuttle's

control panel, he sealed the hatch and awaited clearance from the *Manticle*'s operations officer to depart.

As soon as his shuttle was clear and his course was set, Lasren hailed *Voyager*.

VOYAGER

It had taken Counselor Cambridge only a few minutes to provide his captain with a full report of the last few days' events, including the demands of the Market Consortium, the intriguing visit from Presider Cin, the opening of negotiations with the *Kinara*, the unexpected appearance of Inspector Kashyk, and all he had said to sow discord between the presider and the admiral.

"The admiral can't honestly believe that she somehow deserves to be tried for the actions she took during our voyage in the Delta Quadrant," Chakotay said when Cambridge described the change of heart Janeway displayed once Kashyk had relayed his demands to Presider Cin.

"It's more complicated than that," Cambridge chided him. "She has come a great distance in a short time and is well on her way to laying all of her past demons to rest. I think part of her reluctance to abandon the Confederacy came from a fear that, by doing so, she would be falling back into a bad habit."

"*A bad habit?* Is that what we're calling acting to preserve the safety of our crews?" Chakotay asked.

"The habit I was referencing was making a decision that could have cataclysmic consequences in the absence of complete understanding," Cambridge corrected him.

"What is there to understand?" Chakotay demanded. "We cannot create an alliance with the Confederacy, but by doing what she did, she's made it impossible for us to avoid one, at least in the short term."

"By doing what she did, she has denied the *Kinara* the ability to enter into an accord with the Confederacy that might bring them closer and add a powerful enemy of the Federation to a list that's already much too long," Cambridge said. "She has also placed herself in a position to observe the *Kinara* at close quarters and acquire critical intelligence."

"We already know most of them," Chakotay said. "The Turei, the Vaadwaur, the Devore, and the Voth all managed to make bad first impressions. I don't think that's going to change by getting to know them better."

"The Turei, the Vaadwaur, the Devore, and the Voth," Cambridge repeated. "It's been staring us in the face for weeks, and I'd guess that on some level, their inconceivable alliance drove the admiral to acquiesce to their demands as much as your helmsman's inability to avoid those torpedoes. Had *Voyager* not been moments away from destruction should the battle continue, the admiral might yet have ordered retreat and learned to live with the consequences later."

"The admiral accepted that risk when she ordered us into battle," Chakotay said.

"Yes, but there's acceptance, and then there's *acceptance*."

Chakotay sighed, nodding. After a moment, he seemed to really hear what Cambridge had said. "*Their inconceivable alliance*. What does she think brought them together?"

"Not what. *Whom.*"

Chakotay considered the question for a moment, then shook his head in frustration.

"*Captain Chakotay,*" Waters called from the bridge. "*Lieutenant Lasren is hailing and wishes to speak with you. He is en route to* Voyager *now.*"

"Put him through," Chakotay ordered.

"*Captain Chakotay, I can confirm the admiral's safe arrival on board the* Manticle. *She advises that new orders will be forthcoming shortly. In the meantime, she wants Lieutenant Barclay to know that she kept her promise.*"

"Thank you, Lieutenant," Chakotay said. "Report to the bridge as soon as you arrive."

"*Aye, Captain.*"

Once the channel was closed, Chakotay said, "What did she promise Barclay?"

"I can't say for sure, but I'd guess it was something to the effect that she would solve the problem he has worked tirelessly to address since our encounter with the Indign."

Suddenly, the light dawned.

Cambridge continued: "The admiral's aide, Lieutenant Decan, reported sensing two minds at work within Inspector Kashyk. I believe the admiral has just confirmed that we are not only battling the Turei, the Vaadwaur, the Devore, and the Voth."

"No, we're not," Chakotay realized. "How did that never occur to me?"

"Don't feel bad," Cambridge said. "I missed it too until the admiral drew me a very detailed picture."

Chakotay shook his head. "She was alone in territory she didn't know. Any intelligence she possessed was thousands of years out of date. She used our data to compile a list of the most powerful species we encountered who were also predisposed to mistrust the Federation. And then she guaranteed their support by giving the bodies of high-level officials to her companions just as she took our hologram."

"The Turei, the Vaadwaur, the Devore, and the Voth," Cambridge said again. "Including her, that's five. There were eight. What did she do with the others?"

"I don't know, but that has just become item one on the very long list of problems now before us that require a solution," Chakotay said. "Have Harry assemble senior staff in the briefing room in one hour. We have a lot of work to do."

"Aye, sir."

Epilogue

"*I know it's not home, gentlemen, but try and make yourselves comfortable. We're all going to need our rest.*"

"*Yes, Admiral,*" *her two subordinates replied.*

"Yes, Admiral," the voice of Inspector Kashyk mimicked.

He had retreated to his private quarters with his beloved. She stood before the large data screen embedded in the wall behind his workstation. She had watched every move the admiral made since Janeway had arrived in the quarters arranged for her and her officers until the trial could commence.

"Turn it off," he demanded. "I've had my fill of that woman for one day."

She turned to him. The eyes of this form were small golden orbs recessed beneath prominent cranial ridges that began at the tip of her nose and divided her head, branching outward in dual bony crests, one just above her eye sockets and the other a few centimeters above it. Her hard, dark brown flesh was deeply lined. Her hands terminated in three large digits from which sharp claws extended.

"Why did you kiss her?" she asked.

"She kissed me," he insisted. "It was disgusting. You should add criminal presumption to the list of charges you plan to bring against her."

She moved toward him, placing her hands on his chest and clumsily caressing him. "You did not enjoy it?"

"I will enjoy watching her execution. I cannot believe the

Federation assigned her to this fleet, given her past history in this region of space."

"I can't believe she's alive. *Voyager*'s logs indicated she was deceased."

"I wonder how many other errors those logs contained that might be beneficial to us."

"Don't underestimate her or any of them," she insisted. "Their choice to seek an alliance with the Confederacy could have been motivated by some warning they received about our intentions."

"There is no one to warn them," he said. "They have no idea who they are really dealing with." As she brought her monstrous face closer to his, he said, "Why do you retain that abomination of a form now that it is no longer necessary?"

She smiled and, in a shimmer, transformed into a slight female human with dark hair, a heart-shaped face, and large, lambent eyes.

"You prefer the form of this 'Meegan'?" she asked.

Wrapping his arms around her tiny waist, he replied, "I prefer the form of your eternal glory. But for now, this will suffice."

The Adventure Will Continue in
Star Trek: Voyager—Atonement

ACKNOWLEDGMENTS

From my family, I have received acceptance, even in the absence of understanding.

From my friends, I have received companionship, even when mine was not the best company.

From my fellow authors, I have received inspiration and the knowledge that I am not alone, even in lonely pursuits.

From the professionals who guide me in this work, I have received faith, even when mine has gone absent without leave.

From my readers, I have received praise I have difficulty accepting, and criticism that immediately makes itself right at home, even though I try to weigh both the same.

From my godson, Jack, I have received many happy hours of abandon and unconditional devotion, even though I see him much too rarely.

From my daughter, Anorah, I have received the truth that no pain is so large it cannot be extinguished by a single hug, even a quick one.

From my husband, David, I have received the support essential to all acts of creation and the willingness to sacrifice countless hours together, even though we will never get them back.

Thank you all. Without you in my life, this work would not be possible.

ABOUT THE AUTHOR

Kirsten Beyer is the author of seven *Star Trek: Voyager* novels released by Pocket Books. Between the first and second, she wrote an *Alias* novel and the last novel ever written for *Buffy the Vampire Slayer*. She has also written a few short stories and articles, most about *Star Trek*, and a few original screenplays, not about *Trek*.

She does not have a website, a blog, a Facebook page, nor does she Tweet. Those wishing to find her online should check out the literature section on the TrekBBS. She looks forward to establishing a more robust presence on the Internet—just as soon as she figures out how to write faster or discovers more than twenty-four hours in each day.

Kirsten received undergraduate degrees in English literature and theater arts. She also received a master's degree from UCLA. She never intended to use her education to pursue a career as a novelist. But, apparently, somebody up there had different plans.

Right now, she's writing the next *Voyager* novel, which will complete this particular story arc. When she's not writing . . . she tries to extract every last drop of happiness she can from her life as a wife, a mother, a daughter, and a friend.

For now, she has no complaints.